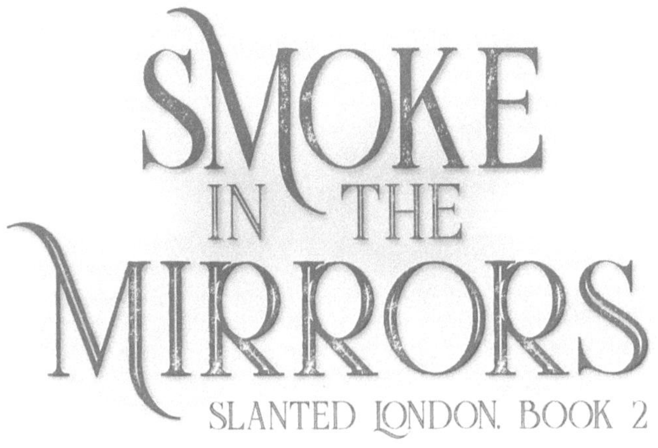

SMOKE IN THE MIRRORS

SLANTED LONDON. BOOK 2

JESSICA SCARLETT

Smoke In the Mirrors Copyright 2026 © Jessica Scarlett

Cover art by Draženka Kimpel and Creativedust.com

Published by Oliver-Heber Books

0 9 8 7 6 5 4 3 2 1

For anyone who's ever complained that the angst died too soon.
I see you.

1

London, England, 1889
The Samaritan

Returning the victims was futile.

The Samaritan stared at the drugged woman—they were always drugged—curled up in the corner, features softened by sleep. The cracked window above her let in starlight and wafts of fish from the emptied river markets, masking the decaying scent of the abandoned warehouse.

Carefully, he lifted her onto his back, slipped out onto the riverwalk, and wound through the city. She weighed practically nothing, which was what she'd come from, based on her matted hair, patched dress, and the address he'd looked up. To the sound of wood creaking in the warm wind, he dodged the light streaming from worn taverns—not only to conceal his gray mask, but because once the woman roused, the screaming would start.

Returning her was futile.

But the Samaritan did it anyway, because it was wrong to do anything else.

Quietly, he stepped over a gutter teeming with sewage and passed through a gaping hole in the side of a building which masqueraded as a window. After hefting the woman, he laid her gently on her straw mattress. Again, he stared at her angular face, wishing he could do more. No one knew why innocent people were being stolen—but he did, and there was only one way to put a stop to it.

The scrape of a match striking filtered under the door.

The Samaritan swept out the hole and hid in the shadows of the alleyway, watching.

Candlelight flooded into the tiny room as the door squeaked opened. "Sarah!" an older woman sobbed, throwing herself beside the bed while her hands shook her limp daughter. Behind her, a little boy rubbed his bleary eyes and smiled, making the Samaritan's heart lurch.

Edmond.

He took a deep breath, reminding himself that Edmond was long dead, and that in a few hours, this boy would no longer be smiling.

He swallowed, then turned away before his thoughts ventured to dangerous places.

The woman's kidnapping—and return—wouldn't make the morning *Post*; only washerwomen and costermongers would hear her deranged screams once she awoke and found her memories missing. But each kidnapping, highborn and low, sent a ripple through the city; drops of fear that eventually exploded into a single, pensive whisper:

Who will be next?

The Rook, the Samaritan vowed, jaw clenching as he ducked into the shadows and wove toward Westminster, hatred hardening his chest.

The Rook will be next.

2

Dorothy

I delved into my mind, tunneling through firing synapses. Deep in my mind's eye pulsed a blue ball of magic, and when I finally found it, I gave it a small tug. *Grow.* I wound back through a different offshoot, calling the magic to follow as I wove through the maze, creating a blueprint.

As I worked, I had no sense of time beyond my phrenic muscles starting to tremble. I angled toward an uncharted section, but too late I saw it glimmered darker. The walls vibrated with warning. Out of the shadows, a face swam into view. Green eyes glowed back at me, and the magic shuddered and jerked away.

The wobbly image snapped.

I gasped and opened my eyes, immediately accosted by the bright light of the printing shop's back room. The boot falls of Lightfoot agents loudened then receded behind the closed door. Nicholas Hart, arms folded, leaned against the wall by the unlatched window, a breeze tousling his rich, sweeping hair, like a ripple in a cup of hot cocoa. The shade of his eyes was similar to mine, though grayer—and intensely guarded and absorbent. A camouflaged sponge.

I watched them for disapproval, but it never came.

"Good." Nicholas nodded. "You're getting better."

"Not quickly enough," I said, swiping curly brown hair out of my eyes. Expanding my slant—my magical ability unique to me—was different from any other work I'd done. It was like knowing the layout of your house, then augmenting the surrounding streets—the angles of the roofs, the weeds cracking the sidewalk, the width of the gates. Then meticulously extending to the neighborhood, the district, the city.

Except, what you were mapping was your *mind*, and it was entirely vaster.

My head pounded from the lingering magic pulsing there. Since my slant took up to six hours to recharge, my daily practice was limited, but the effort still left the space behind my eyes sore.

Nicholas looked me up and down, then cracked the window wider. Clattering from the busy London street drifted inside, carried on a gust that kissed my damp skin. He turned back. "No one expects you to have caught the Rook in the three weeks you've been training."

I bit my tongue to keep from saying that *I* had. My father was alive—mind evidently intact, according to Emme—which filled me with relief. But given the timing, Nicholas strongly suspected the Rook had kidnapped Father for his research, and there was only so much time before he'd be forced to recreate the formula. It was anyone's guess what the science was needed for.

Ironic, that I could generate the same findings as my father, but because the Rook hadn't known, he hadn't taken *me*. Even though he'd been so close—

I inhaled a quick, deep breath, throat knotting.

Nicholas noticed me tense. "Time for a break." He opened the door and spoke to someone in the hallway, then returned.

For the thousandth time, I shoved the past away. It was too painful to dwell on. "I can keep going—"

"You need *food*, Dorothy." Clasping my arm, he guided me to the table and chairs in the corner and gently forced me to sit. "And sleep, just as soon as you've had a bite." Over the past three weeks, he'd been like this; perceptive and thoughtful. I stared at his strong hands, the masculine veins and ridges, wondering at the ease with which they'd touched me. He didn't seem to notice.

A coffee-stained newspaper lay open on the table after an agent's break, crumbs strewn across the bold headline.

SIR GEOFFREY ST. JAMES REPORTED MISSING COULD HE BE THE LONDON PHANTOM'S LATEST VICTIM?

I wasn't sure who had leaked the news—it hadn't been me or Emme, and it certainly wouldn't have been Uncle Benedick. Where *he* was concerned, I felt a pang of satisfaction—small though it was—that the rabid whispers would hamper his social climbing, being my father's brother-in-law.

My heart twisted. I missed my books, now languishing under Uncle's nose. I missed being surrounded by familiar floral walls and stepping on familiar checkered tile. I missed drawing the smallest measure of comfort from having Father's journals, instruments, and clothes within reach.

Nicholas caught what I was looking at and turned the newspaper over as he slid into the chair opposite mine.

"Do you really think he'll give him up?" I muttered.

A primary motivation for joining the Lightfoot Agency had been finding my father—but that required capturing the Rook and making him talk. All the failures—the lack of progress—were getting to me, because my thread of hope frayed with every passing day.

I needed to *do* something, or it was going to snap.

Clasping his hands together, Nicholas said confidently, "He'll be made to. Do not trouble yourself over it." He cleared his throat. "I've been meaning to tell you...Her Majesty wishes you to attend her birthday celebrations, as the daughter of one of England's greatest chemists. An invitation is to be delivered to your flat shortly."

I pulled my curly brown hair to the side and weaved it into a braid that fell nearly to my waist, using a scrap of ribbon to tie it off. "A pity invitation to apologize for my missing father, after he served the Crown faithfully for so many years? No, thank you." The second the cynical words fell from my lips, I wanted to pull them back. The bitterness was still a stranger, one that seized control of me too often.

Nicholas answered with a sorry smile. "It's an honor, none-theless."

Reclaiming my senses, I sighed and nodded. It *was* an honor. Even if I was too distraught and distracted to appreciate it. A minute later, an agent set a platter of sliced ham, roasted chestnuts, and miniature Chelsea buns on the table. I studied the man, recognizing his face but unable to summon a name—although I did remember he could turn small objects to glass. Some Lightfoot agents had been recruited because of their slant, as I had, but most—like Nicholas—didn't possess any magic. The glass agent and I were lucky; we'd been considered too useful for the gallows, unlike everyone else caught using their slant.

The man disappeared.

Nicholas cocked an eyebrow and gestured to the spread.

My stomach soured at the scent of the hot food, and I

turned my head away. How could I eat when my father was trapped somewhere? Shackled, or...suffering?

"You can't catch a phantom if you're in a casket." Genuine worry shone in his gray eyes, rendering his handsome face even more striking.

I took stock of the loose gray skin stretching my knuckles, before shoveling a Chelsea bun into my mouth. It tasted like ashes, but Nicholas was right; I needed to keep up my strength. "Maybe I deserve a casket," I murmured after swallowing.

"Don't misunderstand. Your...*incalculable* loss is our gain, and I'm selfishly grateful to have you as an agent." He paused, seeming to choose his next words with delicacy. "But if you're not careful, this revenge will drive you to distraction. Blind you to the real truth."

Chills swarmed the nape of my neck, because hadn't I just made the same realization? The simmering hatred that fueled me was mighty, but insensible—like my mocking answer to the Queen's invitation.

After an uncomfortable silence, I shook off the feeling and laughed mirthlessly, but it was soft. Pitying, because it was *before* that I'd been blind; not now. I tore off a piece of ham. "Truth only reaps sorrows. I'd prefer a few less."

I will always tell you the truth.

I tackled the memory and methodically ripped it to shreds.

Nicholas reached across the table and skimmed his fingers over my clenched hands, leaving a trail of tingles. It was such a fragile touch, but intentional. As if testing my reaction. I stared at his hand again, heart skipping a beat.

"We can weather it all together, Dorothy," he said, low but firm.

My eyes swept up to lock onto his. His gaze was weighty and steady; the feeling of stone pillars shoring me up after freefalling for too long. Yet there was something leashed there, as well—something to do with his experimental brush against my skin.

Before I could respond, a hasty knock sounded on the door, followed by an agent marching in and passing Nicholas a slip of paper. Nicholas retreated and my hand felt cold.

A neat crease formed between his brows as he read the note, before announcing, "He's been sighted on Commercial Road, headed west."

Blood drained from my extremities, all sensations going numb. He didn't have to specify who *he* was.

Nicholas glanced at me urgently. "Do you have enough magic to try?"

Even though I wasn't sure, I nodded. Since the day I became a Lightfoot agent, the Rook had all but disappeared, kidnapping no one and keeping out of sight—until now. We were close enough to Commercial Road that theoretically we could arrive in a matter of minutes; any further into my future than that, and I wouldn't be able to see it.

Now was my chance, and I wouldn't waste it.

I summoned the dregs of my magic to my eyes and squeezed them shut, trying to see a future. A million threads plaited the rope of my timeline, and I tugged at the brightest one—the one most likely. An image sparked to life, sputtering in and out as my mind struggled to hold it steady. I was still weak at controlling the futuristic leg of my slant.

An old man led a donkey cart down the lane, and behind it, a dark blur caught my eye. I glimpsed wavy black hair before my strength gave out and the vision disappeared. Even in the future, my heart had stopped, because there was no mistaking him. I knew the lines of those shoulders. The easy, nimble stride of one walking among his possessions.

"He'll be at Whitechapel," I said, shoving my future reaction down where I wouldn't have to think about it. "Near the donkey stalls."

"Perfect." Nicholas stormed out into the printing shop, ordering which agents to position on which streets, and what signals to watch for, while reminding them to be vigilant in detecting magical activity. *Anything* could be the Rook's illusion. Lightfoot agents scrambled for their slant guns, pistols, and various disguises. "And I need him alive. Unfortunately."

3

Dorothy

Whitechapel Market echoed with the haggling of buttoned headmistresses and street urchins alike, driving prices down by precious pennies. Sacks of broccoli and rhubarb piled the cobblestones. A melon-like smell was the result of produce mixing with frying white fish, oily steam wafting from a corner stall. Baskets of summer flowers hung from hooks while piles of oysters, brushes, soap, and ironware lined the broad street.

A seamless blanket of clouds hung over the market, muting its colors to shades of gray, but sweat still trickled between my shoulder blades as I walked. I stopped, clutching my skirts. "Here," I said, recognizing the surroundings in my vision. "This is where I saw him."

Nicholas halted too. "Before now, or after?"

My eyes brushed over every shadow. "It's hard to say."

Nicholas signaled something to his agents, and the majority of them branched off as he wrapped his arm around and pulled me under a candle stall. His touch lingered on my waist.

"Thank you for your help. I think it's best that you return to the agency, in case there's any crossfire."

Along with helping me control my slant, Nicholas had trained me how to shadow someone, shake someone off my tail, and operate a pistol. I'd even viewed a few magic-riddled hands through a slant gun, with neon blue particles dusting their fingers and palms. Three weeks wasn't much time to practice those skills, but I wasn't wholly bad. Protests formed on my tongue.

"Hart, I see him!" a brawny, mustached agent whispered to Nicholas. Balling my skirts in my fists, my head whipped around. All I saw was a pressing crowd.

Nicholas squeezed my waist, making my stomach flutter. "I'll rejoin you at the agency." Then he and the rest of the agents dove into the streets.

I sighed, frustrated, even as some tension unknotted at the base of my neck. Refusing to examine why, I turned back, ducking under slim candles that hung from connected wicks and smelled faintly of honey.

"...aren't workin' anymore," muttered a heavyset woman shelling nuts into a bowl a few paces away. Her graying hair twisted into a tight bun, her pinching lips forming wrinkles around her mouth. "And haven't been, since the explosion."

I grabbed a candle, ears perking up.

"'Magine he's displeased," said a hunching, sinewy man as he hefted a crate of walnuts to the ground.

"All the Acherons are."

I nearly dropped my candle, then gripped it so tightly I indented the wax. *Acheron.* As in, the family who ruled the Necropolis, London's undercity.

Their voices leveled to whispers, preventing me from hearing more. I edged around a table and dropped to my knees, crawling through a maze of crates and empty walnut shells until I heard their voices once again.

"Without the portals, how are any of us s'posed to scrap a livin'?"

I tugged an earring off and gently set it on the cobblestones, then peeped out from behind a tower of baskets.

The lean man grunted. "Some portals still work. The ones at the carnival, Stepney, and Jacob's Island are down, while Notting Hill is runnin'."

The woman tossed more shells into an overflowing crate at her feet. "Not for much longer, mind. Even the functioning ones are dicky. The Acherons will be findin' a new home, and we'll be out of cushion tin."

The explosion—the one we'd created to escape the Necropolis. Was that what they were talking about? Had it caused some of the portals to stop working?

But even if they all went down, the Necropolis was originally the Variance, the place magic was first discovered—which meant there had to be a non-magical way to reach it through the miner's tunnel. A back door somewhere. Why wouldn't the Acherons just use that?

Perhaps its location was somewhere they couldn't control, like they could the portals.

A passerby sauntered near, making the pair cut off and cast furtive glances, both of which caught on me and the hourglass cut of silk that I was sullying. I smiled and scooped up my earring, gesturing to it in explanation. Then I stood, brushing off my skirts as I spun away and moved into the crowd. Allegedly, anyone who wandered into the Necropolis was trapped there forever, but there were apparently exceptions. Which made sense. Lark Acheron had to have suppliers up top; people he trusted.

Apparently, the streets knew everything, if you were in the right place to hear it.

More beads joined the sweat pooling on my back. I didn't recognize any agents among the sea of faces, and though I worried something had gone afoul, Nicholas had told me to steer clear of the action. A flush crept over my face as I remembered the feeling of his hand covering mine at the agency. Then touching me on the waist.

I knew the careful way he stared at me when he thought I wasn't looking, like there was something he couldn't quite bring himself to ask. Maybe it had to do with the months of stolen glances across a society dinner table, back when I was still a naïve girl trapped in her house. My tender hopes from that time seemed so distant. Buried, but when I dug deep enough, still there.

And maybe I could excavate that hope; let it breathe, just a little, to soothe the ache that threatened to overwhelm my senses when I thought about—

A figure emerged from behind a cart, and my heart stopped, all thoughts of Nicholas vanishing.

There he was.

Because of the blistered storm it left in its wake, I hadn't been able to even think his name since the night I'd found the black feather inside my grandfather's statue, where a magical bracelet should've been. He'd remained fixed in my mind as *The Rook,* and it was better that way because it drew a line in the sand—one he was on the other side of, so my foolish heart could never doubt that he was the enemy. *My* enemy.

And yet, to my horror, the sight of him filled every corner of my eyes, dark and hypnotic in the lithe way he moved; his smell filled my nostrils, warmed cardamom and smoke; and my pulse thudded with the doom and heartbreak that was his name.

Ashley.

Ashley.

"Ashley," I breathed, and though barely audible, longing threaded my voice. I swallowed it down, disgusted at myself.

Then came the flare of agony, pulsing in the cavity that used to house my hopes, until he'd shattered them. Torn them like wings off a butterfly. Swift and brutal, and *so easily* just as he did everything else.

And then—the anger. And the relief that came with feeling it. If not for the anger, I'd be nothing. Nowhere. A driftless soul screaming questions into the void—

Why did you steal my family's bracelet?

Why did you kidnap my father?

Was any of it not a lie?

Why don't I dare think your name?

What am I afraid of?

I reminded myself to breathe, then turned the cyclone of emotions to stone.

Ashley didn't hurry, didn't glance over his shoulder, and somehow I knew—Nicholas's insistence that I stay behind had led to this future. The agents had chased Ashley in the opposite direction, but he'd circled back and easily evaded them.

I couldn't capture him alone. Even stalling him long enough for the other agents to arrive... Could I bring myself to speak to my father's kidnapper?

No.

I gasped for breath. I wasn't ready.

A weight in my dress poked for my attention: the slant gun all agents were required to carry. If Ashley had evaded the Lightfoots using his illusions, knowing that might help us form a better plan for next time. On impulse, I raised the glorified magnifying glass, aimed, and pulled the trigger, activating the cartridge into releasing its store of lumagenic acid. White smoke filled the glass and dissipated, allowing me a clear view for a few moments before Ashley disappeared through the crowd.

I froze.

Everyone I'd ever viewed through a slant gun had a fine misting of magic on their hands, a few drops that, though small, were unmistakable because of their neon blue color.

Ashley's hands didn't have a few drops. In fact, I couldn't see his hands at all. A vibrant, painful green glowed where his hands *should've* been—the same unusual color as his eyes. The same color I'd seen beneath shards of glass, the last day I'd experimented with Father.

And Ashley's hands weren't just coated with mutated magic.

They were *dripping*.

4
Dorothy

I strode for the slender wooden staircase squeezed against the back wall of the Lightfoots' main headquarters. I'd only been here once before—to sign a contract with Mr. Brass, the head of the Lightfoot Agency for the Crown, which swore me to secrecy and certified me as a Lightfoot agent. The fact that Nicholas had summoned me here meant he'd gone up the chain of command in hopes of solving our dilemma with the Rook, and I didn't know how I felt about that.

Guilty, that I hadn't done something when I'd had the chance.

Nervous, because I wasn't sure I could, if given another one.

Angry, because of both those things.

I took a deep breath and shoved everything down, welcoming the familiar numbness. It was better than the pain. I stopped halfway up the stairs when I sighted the woman on the landing above, her graceful figure poised even when relaxing against the polished railing.

Polina Mikhailova puffed a cigarette, then blew a stream of

smoke through her carmine lips. The ballerina's grin accentuated her sharp, striking features. "You are lost, *zaychik?*"

I bristled. Though I knew little Russian, the mocking endearment was one she'd called me before, and I'd later looked up. *Bunny.* I'd almost forgotten she too was an agent—and that our drinking game on the train had given Nicholas the needed information to recruit me. Fleetingly, I wondered where she'd been recently, that I hadn't encountered her before now.

"I'm looking for Mr. Hart," I replied calmly.

"Ah." She tapped her cigarette, unconcerned with the hot ash tumbling to the cerulean carpet. "He is handsome, no?"

My insides squirmed uncomfortably. I frowned. "How is your husband, Polina?"

Her eyes slitted, sharpening into daggers. "He is dead. *Tem luchshe.*"

Good riddance.

A shiver coursed down my spine, not wanting to believe she'd killed him, but unable to discard the thought either. But there was one more thing I wanted to say.

"You knew, didn't you?" And when she waited, not understanding, I added, "About Ashley." Being so close to him while undercover as a Lightfoot agent, it was impossible for her to have never suspected he was the Rook.

A little smile curled her lips, an amused burst of air passing between them. "Does it matter so much?"

Yes, I wanted to say. *Yes, it does matter.* "If you like Mr. Hart as you claim, why did you never tell him the Rook's identity?"

"I like Ashley Gardner better." She took another drag, smoke curling around her knowing lips. "So, I think, do you."

My teeth clamped together. "If we are going to be working together, it's in our best interests to put our differences aside and call a truce. We're on the same team now."

"Are we?" While Polina's acrid exhale hit my sternum, she analyzed me slowly. "So much. So much you still do not know, *zaychik*." She pushed past me and down the stairs, leaving me to stew in her words.

When I reached the third level, Mr. Brass's door was slightly ajar, Nicholas's heated voice filtering through. I entered just as Nicholas ran a hand through his hair in frustration.

"He's *toying* with us! It's the fourth time this week we've gotten a tip and blundered it up."

Sullivan Brass sat behind his desk, quietly listening to Nicholas rant. With a thumb and forefinger, he rubbed his eyes, narrowly missing the scar that dripped from one eye like a teardrop. Only a matter of weeks ago, after I'd seen him arguing with my father aboard a steam yacht the night my father was kidnapped, I'd suspected he was the Rook—and then the Samaritan. My suspicions had even prompted me to scope the button factory he owned. It was still hard to believe my father had secretly worked for him—a man who reported to Queen Victoria herself.

Settling against the window displaying rolling green hills and pockets of trees, I crossed my arms.

"I wouldn't be surprised if he's catalogued half our agents by now," Brass finally cut in, bouncing the end of a pen on his desk. Somehow the move made him seem younger than his forty-two years. "One glimpse of the wrong face is enough to turn him to smoke. But the Rook is not all knowing."

"Bloody feels like it." Nicholas sank into a chair, eyes tired. "I appreciate your optimism, Brass, but you've not been tracking him for a *year*. Every time I believe we finally have the upper hand—like yesterday, with Dorothy's vision—he slips through our fingers."

Guilt curdled in my stomach. I'd had a chance to go after him, and cowardice had gotten the better of me. Again. But this time was different, because it wasn't the danger that had frightened me.

I uncrossed my arms. "We'll keep trying."

Nicholas turned, only now noting my presence, and when our eyes locked, his expression softened.

"My father's prototype gun can track his magic," I went on. "That, coupled with my visions—"

"Won't be enough." Brass smoothed a hand down the side of his head, and the few gray hairs peppering his temples and short beard seemed to multiply. He unlocked a drawer, pulled out a folded piece of paper, and slid it across the desk. "I received these this morning. Orders from Her Majesty that we are not to take the Rook into custody until we have in our possession the magical bracelets he stole."

I scanned the paper, noting the official stamp at the bottom. "But why?"

Brass and Nicholas shared a look.

"She's afraid he won't give them up," Nicholas murmured, forehead furrowing. "Even with torture."

Bile inched up my throat. I swallowed it down. "The Rook is after the bracelets, and so is Queen Victoria... Why are they so important? What exactly do they do?"

Brass and Nicholas shared another look, this one weightier. At Brass's slight nod, Nicholas turned and poked his head out to scan the hallway before closing the door again and locking it.

Brass coughed mildly into his fist. "Few know of the bracelets' abilities, my dear, and the Crown would like to keep it that way."

I blinked at the grave turn in the conversation and waited.

Nicholas settled against Brass's desk, hands in his pockets. "Each bracelet lets the wearer temporarily steal another person's slant. With your father's research allowing us to detect magic, one rogue actor with a bracelet would greatly complicate our job. We might follow a magical trail and *think* we nabbed the right man, only to discover his slant was stolen for a few hours to commit the crime. The Rook currently has six of the seven bracelets, making their recovery a top priority."

I absorbed the information, remembering a night long ago where I'd played with my grandmother's jewelry. That must've been what had happened—I'd accidentally stolen my grandmother's slant by touching her while wearing the bracelet. Both my grandparents had flinched away in fear; to me, though, the bracelet's power didn't necessarily sound dangerous.

Maybe they hadn't fully understood it.

Maybe *I* didn't.

My mind raced, trying to complete the whole picture before realizing that if Ashley had six of the seven—

I glanced up. "What do they do all together?"

Behind his desk, Brass's dark eyebrows ticked up, cheek twitching. "Very good, Miss St. James. Nicholas did not exaggerate your intelligence while convincing me to recruit you."

My face warmed at the high—and unwarranted—praise. Back then, we'd barely exchanged more than a few sentences, and those had been spaced out over several months. Nicholas must've seen something in me from a distance.

He must've watched me very, very closely.

Politely disregarding my blush, Brass clasped his hands atop the shiny wooden desk before him. "Together, the bracelets..." He grimaced, seeming reluctant to impart the information.

"They take away someone's magic," Nicholas cut in. He turned to me, mouth grim. "Permanently."

The word landed in the room like an anvil smacking the floor. My insides shriveled as if my slant was recoiling in terror; it didn't want to be bonded to anyone else.

Fifty years ago, King William IV's assassination opened the

floodgates among the poverty class for rebellion against the high-ranking slanted. In turn, the slanted had retaliated, and the streets of London had descended into magical warfare. *The Gloaming*, it was called in the history books. Victoria's ascension had been bloody, and so she'd instituted the iron law: No one could use their slant, or they'd face the gallows. But a life without magic would be cold and barren, and I couldn't imagine any other slanted feeling otherwise.

Not being able to use magic was better than not having it at all.

"It's a *legend*," Brass said, once the silence had underscored Nicholas's point. "But one we can't ignore, for national security reasons. One lost bracelet is an inconvenience. Six, a nightmare. But *all* of them... All of them would be catastrophic."

"Why? Are you afraid the Rook will go on a city-wide rampage, stripping the slanted of their magic?"

Nicholas gave a weighty shrug. "It would make him the most powerful person in the world. Untouchable."

Based on all the kidnappings and the madness they came back with, I couldn't deny the possibility. Who knew Ashley's mind? His secrets, his ambitions, his heart? My teeth softly gritted together.

Not me.

"And what of my father? If the Rook won't even reveal the bracelets' location, why would he reveal his victims'?"

Nicholas's mouth pinched, like the news was equally devastating to him.

Brass nodded. "An excellent point. We have agents looking for Geoffrey St. James as we speak, but our resources are stretched thin; they'll be thinner still, after the directive from the Queen. Help us conclude this business, Miss St. James. Then, once the Rook is captured and the bracelets in our rightful custody, we'll be able to shift our priority to your father's rescue."

I released a slow exhale. I was frustrated by all the impediments, but I also knew it was the quickest way forward. So, we had to find the six magical bracelets, capture a kidnapper, and *then* the whole agency could scour London for Father's whereabouts.

Should be simple enough.

Nicholas pushed off the desk and paced the far wall. "The Rook won't go anywhere near wherever he's storing them. Not now that he knows we're watching him."

"Which is why," Brass enunciated while finally getting to his feet, "we need someone undercover who can earn his trust and discover their location." After a meaningful pause, both men's gazes settled heavily on me. My breath tightened in my chest. I'd hoped to help catch the Rook behind the scenes, not literally be the one to bring him down. Not because I feared *him*, but because I feared *myself*. My weaknesses.

Remembering the sight of mutated magic dripping from Ashley's fingers, I shuddered.

The agent selected to go undercover needed to be new to the Lightfoots, to ensure Ashley wouldn't recognize them. Yet, that night on the steam yacht, he'd acted so strangely. So guarded. Like I'd betrayed him somehow, rather than the other way around. He hadn't sought me out since. No sudden appearances at my father's house, no chance meeting in the streets, not even a suspicious shadow on my way home from work.

Not once.

Maybe I would have to build the trust between us from scratch, but our history together—and seeing him work up close —gave me a clear advantage no one else possessed. It made sense.

It made my organs quiver.

"I'll do it," I said quietly before they could hesitantly ask.

Nicholas sauntered near, his gray eyes catching mine with a hint of granite in them, before he said in a low voice, "He kidnapped your father, but I know you were close to him too. Will you be all right with this?"

My cheeks warmed. Nicholas had a way of making a moment feel intimate even in front of other people. I yearned for that easy intimacy, even as I stood trembling on an escarpment, terrified to take that leap again. To trust someone.

Maybe he could sense that. Maybe that was why he was always holding back. I sucked in a breath and nodded.

"Excellent." Brass sat on the corner of his desk. "Now all we need is a way to throw you together, optimally where we can ensure your safety."

Still looking at me, Nicholas said, "The Queen's birthday celebrations take place next week. Buckingham Palace is a black hole for magic, which would hinder his ability to slip away. *If* we can retrieve the bracelets before the end of the fortnight-long festivities."

I swallowed. Two weeks to earn Ashley's trust. Even with all the time in the world, I wasn't certain it could be done.

"But"—Nicholas turned and shrugged—"I don't know how we'd entice him there in the first place."

Brass stood and opened a safe built into the wall behind his desk, and behind it lay another, more intricate safe that took him a full minute to unlock. When he finally rotated back, he held a silver band, inset with a sapphire being devoured by inverted lion heads.

The sight of the magical bracelet, identical to my grandfather's, made my spine snap up. The seventh and final one.

"With this," Brass announced.

Nicholas shook his head. "If we offered the last bracelet as bait, he'd be long gone with it before we had a chance to find the others."

"He needs a puzzle to solve," I mused aloud. Snippets from past conversations drifted through my ears. Ashley lived for the game—and that could be his weakness. Keep him lost in a riddle long enough, and he would never notice the dagger at his back.

Brass pointed at me in agreement, catching my train of thought. "We need to stall him without him suspecting he's being stalled."

Nicholas shook his head again. "We can't fabricate it. He'll see through anything we contrive."

"What if we didn't have to?" The question slipped out before my thoughts had fully formed, and both men swiveled to me expectantly. I remembered what I'd overheard in the market. Things in the Necropolis were volatile, and that meant its rulers would be desperate. Desperate enough to make a deal.

The beginnings of a plan formed in my mind. "It carries great risk, but..." I glanced up. "I have an idea."

5

Emmeline

I breathed in coils of steam as I sipped the complimentary tea, wondering why it had to be peppermint. But while the unpleasant concoction scalded my soft palate, it was free, and the porcelain cup was pretty, so I kept drinking.

Women dressed like maids glided across the green motif carpet with trays of jellies, custards, and crispy biscuits, serving customers at round tables nestled under domed windows. A violinist played Bach in the corner, and the napkin on my plate was folded to resemble a peacock.

In short, the tea shop in which Dorothy had asked to meet me was fancy enough to make me surreptitiously snap open my purse and count coins.

I wasn't penniless...yet.

Since my father had disowned me, I'd been forced to dip into my gambling earnings to rent a hotel room, chipping at my soul one shilling at a time. My dreams of travelling Europe were silly to some, but it was the first time I'd wanted something for myself that I hadn't been *told* to want, and though I'd encountered multiple setbacks, I couldn't shake the dream alto-gether. It gave me direction and put hope in my step.

But first things were first. I had to help my family; repay my debt to them. Then, once Uncle was found, I'd pad my purse past bursting, buy a one-way ticket, bid Dorothy a tear-filled farewell, and finally see the world.

Although...

My luck as an urchin at the tables had been dismal lately, another reason my current spending rate was unsustainable. Becoming a Lightfoot agent would certainly be lucrative, but apparently one needed a highly exclusive invitation first, one which they seemed disinclined to extend.

Perhaps I could become a governess. I chuckled to myself at the thought, because who in their right mind would trust me with their children? The laughter soured and drifted off, because destitution really wasn't funny.

Glancing up, I sipped my tea again—gah, it was still ghastly —before noticing Dorothy approaching my table, dressed in a striped, rose gold dress that accentuated her figure to perfection.

Was that new? It had to be new. I would have borrowed it by now if it wasn't.

Oh pooh, it was going to be an age before I could afford a new gown.

"Sorry I'm late." Dorothy tucked a stray brown curl into her low bun as she sat.

"Enjoying time with your new beau a little too much?" I raised my eyebrows.

She frowned. "What beau?"

"Please." I smiled. "Nicholas Hart is a fine agent, but as I'm sure you've noticed, he is *fine* in *many* other areas."

She sighed. "Emme."

"Sorry, too soon after Ashley?" The man whose perfect face I wanted to claw off.

"Can we please not talk about Ashley right now?" Her gaze darted down, and her voice was strained, a deviation from the teary, vengeful way she'd told me of his betrayal. Something was wrong.

"What's going on?"

Dorothy glanced to the side, then waited for a server to pass before saying quietly, "They want me to spy on him."

I blinked at her, too stunned to turn it into a joke. How could the Lightfoots think of letting her anywhere *near* that— "You mean from afar?"

"I mean, they want me to earn his trust and find the bracelets. And I said yes."

My eyes narrowed. "Earning his trust... That entails what, exactly?"

Her gaze met mine, determination crackling. "Whatever it takes."

Ah. I sat back. And she still had feelings for him.

She wouldn't admit it, of course. How could she? He'd kidnapped her father, but that didn't mean the emotion building between them had dissipated—merely changed dynamics. Into anger. Acute, embittered longing. The kinds of feelings that stupid decisions were born from.

I knew all about stupid decisions.

I reached for my most nonchalant tone. "Do you think that wise?"

A serving girl, ever gifted with reading the mood, decided now was the best time to stop at our table with her pudgy nose and beaming smile. "Are you two ready to order now?"

"I'm not hung—" Dorothy hesitated, then consulted the handwritten menu on the table. "I'll have a slice of lemon pie, thank you."

The girl nodded and turned to me.

I held up my peppermint tea. "This is enough for me."

The girl gave me a tight smile, eyed me, sniffed, then left. Well, excuse me for not wanting to be impoverished *a la* pastry.

Dorothy rolled her lips together and leaned forward. "Enough about me. Do you have any news?"

I grimaced, head ducking. Before being arrested three weeks ago, I had run to Lincoln Square to investigate a tip Dorothy had gotten about her father. It had been dark, but when a carriage encountered a traffic jam under a gas lamp, I saw Uncle Geoffrey within, spectacles perched on his nose. I'd scrambled forward, calling to the driver who was cursing in Italian—but not fast enough. The congestion cleared and the carriage flew over the cobblestones, disappearing into the night.

We'd formed a joint plan: Dorothy would work with the Lightfoots to catch Ashley, and I would pursue any leads related to that sighting.

The problem was...I hadn't found any. I'd approached almost every hackney cab service in the city, but no one recognized the license plate or my description of the driver. I had a few more establishments to try, but my hope was dismal.

"Still nothing," I said quietly.

Dorothy's shoulders sank. But after a moment she rallied and murmured, "It will be all right. We'll find him."

My heart broke a little more.

Reappearing, the pudgy-nosed server set Dorothy's lemon pie on the table and flashed her a smile—one that vanished when she glanced at me.

"Actually," I said, rising and eyeing her right back, "I should be going. I wanted to find a new apartment today."

The server curtsied and left, her mission of shooing away the rabble completed.

Dorothy frowned. "Are you still at the hotel? Oh Emme, I

wish your father didn't own the mortgage. Then the house would be mine, and neither of us would have to dwell in-between." She sighed, and I wholeheartedly agreed. My father was a dirty rotten, scum-sucking, soulless blight upon human-ity, and I wouldn't be praying for his downfall quite so fervently if not for Mother and Clarence.

"As it is," Dorothy went on, "I'm sorry I've been so caught up in everything, but there's plenty of room in my new flat. You can come live with me."

No, I couldn't.

As a Lightfoot agent, Dorothy had a clean apartment and impressive wage, but asking for money from her—or a place to live—was out of the question.

A month ago, I'd craved adventure. Finding Uncle Geof-frey kidnapped, getting arrested, and being minutes away from swinging by my neck—before being miraculously rescued by Dorothy's deal with the Lightfoots—hadn't *exactly* been the adventure I'd had in mind. She'd already sacrificed so much for me, it felt narcissistic to ask for more.

Foolish Emmeline. Impulsive, childish little Emme. Needs looking after. Needs help. Dorothy would never think those thoughts because she was too *good*, but a lesser cousin would have no compunction. I wouldn't blame her. Now Dorothy was a working woman, and the stubborn part of me wished to prove my self-sufficiency too.

Perhaps that only proved how foolish I was.

Tapping nervous fingers against my thigh, I resolved to look for employment while I was footing the streets. My needlepoint wasn't half bad, or I could try the tables again... I pasted on a too bright smile that I was sure didn't reach my eyes. "I wanted to find an apartment closer to my investigation, anyway." Which wasn't actually a lie.

Dorothy blinked, then nodded. "I suppose that makes sense. Take care of yourself, Emme."

I nodded back. Because I *could*; I was independent. I'd called the streets home long before Dorothy had dared brave them. How hard could it be to make my own way?

6

Dorothy

As the last gleam of sunset dissolved on the Thames, I darted across the bridge spanning the filled-in moat of the Tower of London.

According to the gossip I'd overheard, the portals to the Necropolis were finicky at best, and I didn't fancy being tossed in a cell like last time, so I'd found a workaround. Locating a map and triangulating the center of the seven Necropolis portals around town had led me here. To the Tower.

Passing a pair of Beefeaters in their red-trimmed uniforms and Tudor bonnets, I pulled my silver hood lower, then ducked into the white tower, where the stale air of the council chamber greeted me. The location of the Necropolis's back door explained why the Acherons weren't utilizing it more, despite their malfunctioning portals; the Tower was both an armory and barracks for the Queen.

Venturing out this way would be suicide.

Nicholas had pulled some strings for the tower guards to look the other way, but my mouth still dried, because dealing with Lark Acheron was another matter.

Though I'd never met the king of the Undercity, escaping the Necropolis last time had required a miracle, one that had involved taking down a litany of guards while destroying his bridge. He wasn't known for his mercy.

Or, if Lark traced the deal I offered back to the Lightfoots, his loathing for the government might make him refuse out of spite, and the entire plan hinged on his involvement. So, though it had made Nicholas frown and glance me over with worried eyes, he'd agreed with Brass that it was best I go alone.

I took the stairs down to a musty cellar lined with greasy kegs. Tiny feet scurried across the floor. Dim light spilled from the stairs as I felt along the wall, searching for a small opening. After circling the room unsuccessfully, I retraced my steps more slowly, peering behind the barrel.

In the back corner, under a filled-in arch, a fissure in the stone was just visible above a massive keg. After some awkward maneuvering that left me panting, I scraped the barrel a few inches, enough to see a hole big enough to crawl through. Exhilaration surged in my chest. Several minutes later, I'd worked it away from the wall. A fetid odor of ammonia seeped through the opening. My nose wrinkled.

Summoning my magic, I checked my future, hoping the back entrance to the Necropolis was somewhere else on the grounds. Even with my expanded abilities, I couldn't check farther than maybe ten minutes into the future. This time when I looked, I saw bobbing lights and the flash of a maroon hood—the uniform of the Talons, Lark's guards—before the vision shuttered.

This was the entrance.

I eyed the pitch-dark hole again. All the preparation of discovering and triangulating the portals, and I hadn't thought to bring a lantern. Sucking in a deep breath through my mouth, I dropped to my knees and crawled into the blackness.

Rat droppings squished under my palms, and I imagined the sludgy grime staining my skirts. At least I'd had the forethought to change into my simplest cotton dress. I didn't know how long I travelled the downward slope, trying not to breathe the rancid fumes too deeply, before the tunnel widened and allowed me to stand. Far below in the distance, a faint glow of light burned. I sagged with relief. I'd never been afraid of the dark, but the journey was starting to feel like eternity.

I nearly stumbled when the slope morphed into stairs. Quietly, I descended them. Faint light burned up ahead. Like before, a filled-in arch bore an opening large enough to crawl through, and I clambered to my feet, shaking my skirts while my eyes adjusted. This place, too, seemed to be some kind of storage room, packed to the ceiling with wheels of cheese, sacks of potatoes and apples, and curing meat. Torchlight flickered through its entrance, illuminating a stationed guard.

Here goes nothing. I approached and tapped the man on the shoulder.

The Talon startled, then whipped out a pistol and aimed it at me with his tattooed arm. "Who are you?"

Anxiety spiked in my stomach, but I straightened my spine and stepped farther out of the shadows, holding up my filthy hands in a signal of peace. "My name is Dorothy St. James. I have an offer for Lark Acheron."

MY ARMS and legs strained uselessly against the coarse ropes tying me to the chair. My head was the only thing I could move, but it was covered with a cloth that let in little light and smelled faintly of starch.

When the guard had marched me across a bridge and into an enormous, hollowed stalactite, I'd managed to glimpse the night's revelries. Seven stories shaped like rings stacked the cacophonous cavern below, with packed arcades and hallways that branched off into the earth. Couples locked in embraces draped over balconies. A pack of foaming dogs sprinted across the plaza. Someone screeched, followed by unhinged laughter. From the largest stalactite dangled a cage, with a bedraggled, bellowing man inside.

It was enough to reignite the flame of fear in my belly, as I remembered what it had been like to be *in* the action. A stranger's fingers up my skirt. His tongue on my neck. Ashley ruthlessly slicing his hand off, saving me.

No.

My nostrils flared.

Everything between us was now tainted. He hadn't cared about me, he'd used me. It had all been lies, lies, *lies*.

Boots scuffled by every few minutes. The guard behind me wheezed an exhale every five seconds, on average. A drop of sweat trickled down the crook of my knee. And I waited. And waited until the air under the cloth grew so humid I was going to suffocate.

An entourage of what I guessed to be a dozen men entered the room.

The sack ripped off my head, and I was immediately blinded by stick-straight ash-blond hair and a cunning smile staring down at me. His breath—cold and cloyingly sweet—hit my face before his words did. "So. This is the girl who demolished my bridge and has been snooping around my portals. Aren't you missing a few co-conspirators?"

He—Lark—didn't wait for a response before fisting my curls and yanking my head back. My eyes watered from the unnatural light scintillating in the fixture above.

"Hm," he said, the syllable sounding pleased as he took in my face. "Only the best for Ashley Gardner, it would seem."

I gritted my teeth. "I am not affiliated with him."

He shoved my head and turned away. "In that case, I'll not waste my time." He stuffed his hands in his pockets. "Kill her," he said lightly, like he was ordering something from a menu.

I shot up—but the ropes over my arms jerked me back. "Wait!" I balled my hands, calming my voice. "I've come to offer you a deal. It wasn't—" A gag covered my mouth, and a steel barrel pressed into my temple. My heart bounded out of my chest. *No, no!*

Lark turned back, sighing. "Fate has delivered the girl who wrecked my kingdom into my hands; no reward you can offer me would be greater than your death. I merely wanted to see your face first. And the knowledge of our secret entrance will die with you." He sauntered toward the door.

In my periphery, the fingers holding the gun to my head shifted toward the trigger—

I thrashed against the ropes, dodged the gun, spit out the gag, and managed to scream, "The map!" before something blunt rammed into my temple. I coughed, forehead pulsing. The room spun. Blood trickled down my cheek. Every inch of my skin was chilled with fear.

But Lark held up a hand and everyone froze. He pivoted back, eyes sparking with interest as he enunciated, "What... map?"

"You need it," I breathed. Not knowing how long his benevolence would last, I spat the words out in quick succession. "This Necropolis is where miners struck a magical vein. In the aftermath, this place came fully formed; not made by man, but born—constructed—from the magic. That's why the lights aren't gas, why everything is so symmetrical. It was the magic's doing.

"My father told me tales of a rumored second Variance, whose entrance was locked and hidden by the first mages.

They feared unleashing so much power might upset the natural world. Now that magic has been diluted, however—"

"Yes, *thank you* for the history lesson—"

"They created a map to it and gave it to England's monarch for when the time came. Ever since Ashley blew up your bridge —cracked the foundation of the magic—your portals keep shutting down. Soon it'll be permanent. You need a new kingdom, and for that, you need the map. I'm the only one who can find it."

"Really?" Lark's grin was mocking. "You? A debutante?" Low laughter echoed among the Talons. He canted his head, obviously deciding to humor me, at least for now. "I have all my men searching for it. What makes you different from them?"

"I found out how to get down here, didn't I?"

Lark's brow cocked, appraising me more intently.

"If the map has been passed down through England's rulers, it must be hiding somewhere in Queen Victoria's palace. As a member of the *ton*, I can secure an invitation and move about with ease; be granted access to places your men can't. Now untie me."

Lark breathed a chuckle—probably at my boldness—but knocked his chin at the Talon who'd been about to blow out my skull, and the ropes fell away.

I stood, legs shaking, but I hid it well.

"And you're offering to find the map to the second Variance —what? Out of the goodness of your heart?"

After the last three weeks, I didn't think my heart would ever have room for goodness again. But I didn't say that. Instead, I mustered my bravery, knowing that once I said the name, there would be no turning back.

I evened my breathing and steeled my voice. "I'll do it in exchange for Ashley Gardner."

Lark snorted, and I blinked at its immediacy. "Believe me,

deb, I'd love nothing better, but it's as likely as a widow in white. He saved my sister's life, so I'm bound by the code not to lift a finger against him down here. And up top... Tracking him is a witch hunt; not just difficult—*impossible.* The man's a literal shadow."

I knew from firsthand experience how true that was. "I don't need you to capture him. All I want from you is to play your part. I'll do the rest."

"Even still." He shook his head. "He's not going to come poking his nose around here again."

"Then lure him to you up top."

"With what?"

Mouth setting in a firm line, I seized the bracelet from the hidden pocket in my dress. Lark—everyone—straightened at the rare sapphires sparkling in my palm, entrusted to me by Brass. It was surprisingly light for so valuable a thing. "This is what he wants. The *only* thing he wants." The bitter truth stung the back of my throat. I swallowed it down. "He'll do anything to get it."

Even lie to you for weeks.

Even kidnap your father.

Even kiss you in the dark and make you believe he loves you back.

Greed flashed in Lark's eyes, but I tossed the bracelet to him before he could order one of his men to rip it away. It clinked when he caught it with a surprised hand.

Now came the risky part—the part that ensured this was all or nothing.

"It's yours," I said. "Think of it as a show of good faith. Collateral. You won't cheat me; I won't cheat you. Ashley and I find the map, we deliver it to you once you've returned the bracelet, and Ashley Gardner goes down. Win, win, win."

Head tilted, Lark appraised me for a long moment, before

finally emitting another low chuckle through his red lips. "I can see why, you know. Why Ashley picked you." He glanced pointedly at my filthy dress. "Current state aside, obviously."

The suggestion hit me between the ribs, squeezing the breath from my lungs. *He didn't pick me,* I wanted to say. *He picked himself, again and again and again.* I didn't know why I couldn't form the words.

"What's your skin in this game? I thought you and Gardner were chums." Lark squinted, discerning far too much under my now-warming face. "Ah." Amusement pulled at his cheek. "Not anymore then. He jilt you?"

"Something like that," I muttered through gritted teeth. My corset felt looser when he finally turned away.

Rubbing the bracelet in his hands, Lark turned in a slow circle, casting his gaze over every Talon in the room before finally landing back on me. Sharp, ruthless lines cut his pale face, and my belly sank. I'd gambled with the bracelet and it hadn't paid off.

It was too far-fetched for him to entrust the map-finding to me.

He was going to say no.

He'd rather kill me and cut his losses.

Instead, Lark grinned. "All right, deb. Luckily for you, I do love to win."

7

Ashley

The first—and most important—item on my agenda today was rummaging around in a dead man's ashes, and I exhaled deeply in gratitude. Because although investigating the urn required breaking into a house replete with maids and butlers and dogs that might tattle on me, this score also marked the end of an era.

Besides. It was nothing I couldn't manage.

Mid-morning sun warmed my back as I scaled the drainpipe of the Galverstone manor. Though it rested on the outskirts of the city, it couldn't escape the clatter of horse hooves and rustling of newspapers travelling up its long driveway.

My muscles worked from memory, but my collarbone burned white fire as I climbed, a reminder that my knife wound still hadn't fully healed. I swung over the ledge of a balcony and slipped through the French doors, trying to forget the night I'd been given the injury—when I'd stolen into someone *else's* bedroom. I panted, pressing the heel of my palm into the scar.

To my left, Lord Umbridge's curly blond hair peeked out

from lumpy, tangled sheets, the occasional snore making them wiggle. His love of hosting flamboyant parties was surpassed only by his love of wine, and I repressed a grin, remembering how easy it had been to slip the sleeping drug into his cup a few hours earlier. From inside the wardrobe, I withdrew the servant's clothes I'd also stashed, casting another cursory glance at the lord.

"In another life," I muttered, unbuttoning my collar, "I would've ended up like you. Rich. Titled. Carefree and sloshed." I shrugged out of my tweed coat and squinted at his lolling tongue dripping saliva onto the sheets. "Though marginally more dignified, one can only hope."

Three tentative raps sounded on the door, making me reflexively reach for my slant. I threw on an illusion to make me invisible—but the magic in my blood came slowly, and the illusion flickered like it had forgotten how to do what it'd done a thousand times before. I blew a curse through my teeth, then dropped it.

Every day my magic became harder to control. For a long time, it only affected my ability to see memories, but just in the last few days, it'd begun leaking into my illusions too. I couldn't risk it doing something faulty and exposing me. My collarbone still burned; I could hang from the ledge until the intruder retreated, but I'd pay for it later.

And today of all days, I needed my strength.

Quickly, I mussed my hair until wavy black strands hung over my eyes, then snagged an abandoned ascot from the floor, slinging it around my neck. I undid the top four buttons of my undershirt and splashed liquor onto my clothes using an open bottle on the dresser. With a bushed expression and an elbow propped on the frame, I cracked the door open.

Atop a glinting silver tray sat a bowl of tapioca pudding swimming in a sweet-smelling purple syrup, with sides of berries and honey. "Your breakfast is ready, my..." The young maid's words died the second she locked onto my face. Then came the look—the one full of rapture and flooding desire that none of them ever knew what to do with.

"Excellent," I said groggily, ignoring my wayward magic and plopping one of the raspberries in my mouth. The tart juice awakened my hunger, making me realize I hadn't eaten since yesterday morning.

Her eyes darted appreciatively over my arm poised above her, then glued to the skin exposed by my open shirt. Pink dusted her cheeks. "Is..." She shook her head, raising her gaze with some effort. "Is his lordship in?"

"Oh, yes. But I daresay he has no need for this, at present. Fitful night, what with—" I straightened and took the tray from her, scooping up a bite of pudding and restraining a moan of pleasure. Yes, this was much more enjoyable than hanging over a ledge. I gestured to the plate with the fork. "What with the drinking and throwing darts at his stepmother's portrait until her face was pocked beyond recognition." I plopped some berries over the pudding and took another bite.

The maid watched me eat in fascination, until I'd nearly devoured the whole bowl. "I thought his stepmother's portrait was in storage?" Her words came slowly, her attention clearly not in them.

I hated using the *pull* to my advantage, but sometimes I had little choice.

"It was indeed, until I helped him dig it out and lug it up the stairs. Twenty-nine rounds of darts knackered him."

The maid's fingers ventured past my open shirt and brushed over my chest. A shockingly audacious move for a servant, but it wasn't really her doing it.

I caught her hand and gently forced it away. "What his

lordship needs is a good morning tonic. Some soot warmed in milk. That should rouse his spirits."

"His...lordship?" Her lips formed a dazed O.

To give her an extra push, I lifted my eyebrows haughtily. *Now*, I was sure my expression said, just like a man of privilege.

That broke the spell. She blinked and straightened, head ducking as she scurried away. Exhaling a short breath of relief, I shut the door, shoved one more bite of tapioca into my mouth, and threw the servant clothes on before stepping out of Lord Umbridge's bedroom and into a hall lined with a blood-red runner, combing my hair with my fingers.

Portraits taller and wider than his lordship hung on the walls I passed, some ancestral, but most were of him posing with dogs or thrones, and even one in front of his bathtub. I kept my steps casual as I descended the stairs, hands behind my back like a deferential servant. No one spared me a glance, not even when I slipped into the study half a minute later.

Another portrait the size of a carriage bore the likeness of Lord Umbridge's great-great-great-grandfather, England's first prime minister. Beneath his giant likeness, atop the mantle, sat a stony urn carved with murals of grapes, pineapples, ferns, and one central figure holding a scale in one hand and magic in the other. Horror-stricken faces were etched into the urn's handles, and I covered their gaping mouths as I hefted it from the mantle, nearly dropping it under the weight.

"Blasted heavy ashes—" I set the urn on the carpet, narrowly missing my toes. Like his descendant, England's first prime minister must've been a *very* large man. After waiting for the dust inside to settle, I carefully lifted the urn's lid, grimacing at the gray powder within. No matter that I'd done it before, this part never got easier.

Averting my eyes, I reached an arm in and dug through the dust, working my way down as I groped for the bracelet.

The last one.

The one that, combined with the other six in my possession, would strip me of my magic forever. Before my slants destroyed me, or worse—

Destroyed everything else.

The powder coating my fingers turned to clay as it absorbed my sweat, but I dug deeper. It had to be here. I'd been searching for weeks for this last one, before finally getting yesterday's tip about it being buried with the prime minister. His choice of burial—and its location—wasn't common knowledge and had taken me a full eight hours to find even with my entire network on the case. Then I'd infiltrated Lord Umbridge's party, slipped him the sleeping draught in the early hours, and here I was. No one else could've staged a heist sooner.

My fingernails scraped the stony bottom and I gritted my teeth, but then...no, there was something. Not a bracelet, but something dry and thin. I grabbed it and lifted my arm out, motes of the late prime minister drifting down to speckle the carpet.

The message on the dusty paper was written in maroon ink.

Elizabeth says eleven.

Underneath that, crudely drawn, pointed a downward arrow encased in a circle, the fletching replaced by bird wings. The Acheron family insignia.

I scowled at the arrow fist. Marvelous.

Lark had the last bracelet.

I crumpled the paper in my fist. Bloody plaguing *marvelous.*

THE NOTE—ALONG with being a taunt—was an invitation to meet. I didn't know what Lark would ask in exchange for the bracelet, but his choice to meet in Big Ben, not the Necropolis where he knew he couldn't touch me, made me wary. It was undoubtedly a trap.

One I couldn't afford not to walk into.

Men with top hats and canes bustled in and out of the House of Lords, too stiff-lipped to appear bothered by the dirty smell wafting off the Thames. As I briskly approached the sheer, gold architecture of the Elizabeth Tower, I tested my slant again, subtly creating birds and fire between my finger-tips. It appeared to be working fine, now. My shoulders relaxed.

I hid behind an abandoned carriage, covered myself with an invisibility illusion, then crossed the crowded square, dodging a pair of bluedusters before plunging into the tower. I stole up the several hundred stairs to the clock room, the clatter of giant cogs grinding louder with each step.

Vast opaque circles striped with steel boxed me in, forming the clock faces. On one end of the room stood a figure with ash-blond hair, hands stuffed in his pockets. Here above, he looked even paler. Less sharp. Less likely to cut your throat.

I knew better than to trust appearances.

The walls shook with deep chimes, vibrating my bones eleven times before finally falling silent. Lark turned from the clockface and glanced around, perhaps sensing my presence. When I dropped my invisibility, he flinched back, mouth parting upon finding my glower and the illusion of smoke curling at my heels.

Then his lips crooked into a wicked grin. "I knew you'd find my note."

I said nothing, trying to read him before I revealed my cards too quickly. Or how desperate I was.

"I want to offer you a trade."

I languidly wandered the room, feigning disinterest, but searching for Talons hiding behind the steel while plotting an exit strategy. "Doesn't sound as though I'll like it."

He chuckled, and it grated on me. "This one you will."

My eyes snapped to him, but I otherwise didn't move, waiting. Eventually he rewarded me.

"My Necropolis is crumbling, thanks to you. I want the map to the second Variance, and as much as it pains me to admit, you're my best chance at finding it." Reclining against the glass clock face, Lark dredged up some toffees from his pocket and unwrapped one of the wax papers before tossing the caramel in his mouth. Cheeks sucking, he held a candy out to me. "Want one?"

I said nothing, mind racing. Maybe this wasn't a trap after all; he needed me as much as I needed him. The second Variance—it was a myth. The map to it even more so. All I knew was that the three mages were rumored to have given it to the monarch centuries ago, who in turn hid it where it couldn't be found. To unearth the map was an impossible task.

And despite myself, excitement pulsed in my blood.

Lark grinned wider, pale eyes sparking. "I knew you'd like it."

Ignoring his gloating, I said, "When would you need it?"

"A fortnight." Now it was his turn to feign disinterest, but I could see the fear curdling behind his smile. The Necropolis wouldn't last much longer than that. We made an interesting pair—two powerful enemies, both teetering on the edge of powerlessness.

"Then you'll give me the bracelet?"

Lark shrugged, snapping another hard caramel between his teeth. "Then I'll give you the bracelet."

"How do I know you have it?"

"I have it."

"Do your little blood promise thing."

Lark's expression darkened, and his chewing slowed. For several moments he glared at me, before unsheathing a knife from his sleeve and pricking the tip of his thumb. With a trickle of blood coating his fingertip, he stamped it inside the circular Acheron tattoo on his neck—the one he shared with each of his family members. "I, Lark Acheron, vow to give Ashley Gardner the magical bracelet in my possession once he brings me the map to the second Variance."

My upper lip curled. "And let him walk away unharmed."

Lark rolled his eyes. "And let him walk away unharmed." He dropped his thumb, holding his hands out. "Satisfied?"

I sized him up, pretending to deliberate for a long minute, before— "Done. I'll find it for you."

Lark cocked his head and squinted like there was something more he was holding back. My skin prickled, senses heightening, searching for the ambush, and then...

From behind the gears and cogs, the brush of skirts swished, and I didn't know why I could hear them or why my breath seemed tied to their every rustle. Maybe I could sense it even then: her absence that had ripped a seam in the universe, the gash of emptiness that followed me like a vortex, sucking, sucking at my soul, was suddenly just...gone. Stitched together, making my heart pound slower. Heavier.

My muscles seized when she stepped around the corner and into a spoke of sunlight that pinwheeled the tower. My eyes traveled up the full royal blue skirts, the cinched-vest bodice, her delicate creamy neck and brown side braid, and...

never quite found Dorothy's face, because of the raw cowardice knotting in my throat.

My gaze flicked to Lark, eyelids spasming in mounting fury. Panic. "What is she doing here?" The words tumbled from my tongue, scraping gravel.

"She," Lark said, pushing off the wall, "is going to help you."

A million emotions pulled in my chest, but I kept my expression neutral, fighting the impulse to look at her. *Drink her.* Sparks of magic raced under my skin, seeming to say, *Her. It's her.* Lark sauntered closer, tossing the last caramel toffee into his mouth.

My eyes narrowed. How did they know each other? Was Lark threatening her? Or was he using her to get to me?

If so, it was working.

I pushed down the anger, the dread, to say in a blasé tone, "I don't need her help."

"The map is inside Buckingham, and as the daughter of the esteemed chemist, Sir Geoffrey St. James, Miss St. James has received an invitation to the queen's 70th birthday celebrations. You, as I understand, have *not*."

"I can get one."

"By tomorrow?" Lark chuckled. "Maybe someone like you could manage it, but there's no need for that. We've already secured your invitation—as Miss St. James's fiancé."

Now I couldn't stop my eyes from whipping to Dorothy, but I wasn't ready. Not for her round lips and large gray eyes, nor for the way they did...nothing. Betrayed no reaction.

"Fiancé?" I asked her, disbelief that bordered on a whisper.

She glanced down.

I swung back to Lark. "No one will believe it."

Lark sighed like I was dim. "We spin the story to our advantage. You're in the silk trade are you not? Wealthy silk tycoon meets baronet's daughter. A match made in heaven. And *this* way"—Lark blinked innocently—"no one will cry scandal if you two happen to be caught alone." His smirk lobbed between us, perhaps detecting the heightened tension. "Looking for the *map*, that is."

I clenched my jaw but didn't outwardly react. "You still haven't answered why I need her help."

"She's your ticket in, but also, there's no using magic at Buckingham. It's a black hole not even my cuffs can bypass. That means you'll be crippled of your usual resources." Then to my surprise, he gestured to Dorothy. "Both of you."

My gut rammed into my feet. I tried to mask my shock, but knew I wasn't wholly successful. She was slanted. She was *slanted* and she'd never told me. I'd never told her I was, either, but her features stayed cool, collected. Practiced, in the way they remained looking at Lark and never at me. Like she'd always known.

Could it be she hadn't given Wren over to the bluedusters? I'd seen it for myself, when I'd tapped into Wren's memories— how Dorothy noticed when she spilled some soup and used magic to create a hole—but... Would the timid Dorothy from before risk turning Wren in, if she were slanted herself? I swallowed, itching to *do* something, though I didn't know what.

Shoving the confusion and betrayal aside, I stepped toward Dorothy, forcing her to finally look at me. "And you're fine with this? Your name being tied to mine, even if it's only for two weeks?"

"I am up to the task." She worked her jaw, spine stiffening. "Are you?"

I frowned. There was something different in that question, a goading challenge that didn't fit her. Something about her face, too, was changed, but I couldn't put my finger on it—

Her words brought me back to the carnival when we'd been throwing knives.

Are you even sure what game you're playing?

Are you?

I forced myself to smile lazily. "Never found one I'm *not* up to."

She inhaled a deep breath, chin tipping up. Her next words came so nonchalantly, I almost missed the dagger in them. "And was it entertaining? Gliding into my life, dangling a few promises, kissing me, and then gliding back out?"

Lark gave a low whistle.

Claws scraped my insides, my arms tensing with the impulse to clout Lark and tell him to leave. When had she learned to do that? Be so...?

I made my muscles relax, slipping a grinning façade into place. "Wildly."

Her nostrils flared.

I stepped closer, tilting my head and lowering my voice. "I told you from the start it was a game, Miss St. James. No one likes a sore loser."

Her expression remained blank, immediately tossing back, "Or a sore winner."

My smile wilted.

Lark whistled again.

"Feel free to shut up anytime now," I shot at him, but my attention stayed on Dorothy, trying to work out the puzzle of her appearance. And then the pieces clicked into place.

The innocence. That was why she looked different. Spoke differently. It was gone.

Ignoring the twisting in my gut, I inched forward again, stopping close enough to touch her, but holding back a hairsbreadth. "If it is a fiancé you want..." I let the air between us heat with questions. With answers. "I'll give you one."

She watched me from under her lashes, an emotion stirring in her eyes that almost resembled...fear.

My brows twitched down.

"I'll leave you to work out the particulars," she breathed, before skirting around me and down the stairs.

I watched her go, every muscle screaming at me to follow, to beg her to tell me what that look in her eyes had meant. To ask what had happened with Wren, if she was a spy, or if I'd made a grave error in not trusting her. Demand to know why the world's axis had tilted and fractured open a chasm between us.

I stayed perfectly still. Because even with all the new questions, nothing, really, had changed. The job was the same as last time: To stay emotionally detached. To charm her enough so she didn't suspect anything was amiss, but not so well that I lost my wits.

Sweet fire, I was going to lose my wits.

In the silence, my wrath toward the white worm across from me built, and I rotated back. How dare he drag her into this game, after everything I'd sacrificed to keep her out of it.

"If anything happens to Dorothy, I will hold you responsible." Even I was surprised at the icy calm chilling my voice, and I didn't care that it made me vulnerable. That now, Lark knew where to strike to cut me deepest. He needed to know that when it came to her, I wouldn't hold back.

Lark cocked a brow. "You're the one about to spend two weeks in her presence. What's the matter, Ashley? Afraid of what you'll do to her?"

My jaw clenched. *Yes.* When I died—a day that loomed ever closer, with my mutating magic—I would take everyone around me down with me, and I wouldn't let her be one of them. Her *or* Miles. I just had to find this map quickly and keep her at arm's length until I did. Instead, I said, "I'm afraid you've brokered a deal you'll come to regret."

"I doubt that. My only regret is not killing you when I had the chance."

"That implies you had one."

Lark lurched forward, fists balled, then halted. His eyes tracked the space between us, as if measuring the distance between his hands and my neck. "While we may have an agreement, don't think I have forgotten that it was *you* who blew up my bridge. Who destroyed my home."

I smiled. "Pity you made it so easy."

"One day," he said through his teeth. "One day I'll have the honor of cutting out that tongue of yours."

"Looking forward to it. The thing's more trouble than it's worth." There was one last thing I needed to know. In exchange for the map, Lark would give me the bracelet, but— "What is she getting out of this?"

Lark stayed silent for a long moment, glancing to one side, and when he finally looked back, he shrugged. Too carelessly. Like he was inventing something on the spot. "I promised to tell her who kidnapped her father."

I stilled. Breathed in, and out, and in again slowly. Then in a soft voice, "If you care about your life at all...you won't." I illusioned to smoke and fled Big Ben, just as the tower struck noon.

8

Miles

My leather glove blasted my opponent's jaw. Blood spilt from his mouth and speckled the taut canvas floor. He stumbled toward the rubber rings. From the other side, a raucous crowd shouted and whistled with cupped hands. Wads of cash passed between threadbare pockets in the dim light, the air sour with liquor and cussing.

My opponent, a Spaniard, judging from his golden skin and dark curly hair, stood four inches taller than me and a good fifty pounds heavier. He swayed against the rubber, trying to prop his legs beneath him even as his eyes slowly swelled shut. One well-placed blow and he'd be out.

Feet still light, I stalked across the ring to a rising tide of cheers. The Spaniard raised his head as I wound my arm back, and we locked eyes. Something in the set of his lips reminded me of *him*, and just for a moment, I hesitated. The cacophony faded to a muted roar and a bitter taste slid down my tongue.

A glove cuffed my temple, jarring me back to the fight at hand. I spun back and swiped sweat-drenched brown locks from my eyes with my forearm, regaining my bearings while the Spaniard lumbered to his feet.

That was his first good blow of the night. I shook my arms loose, refocusing and raising my fists. It would be his last too.

My hands tightened inside my gloves.

The Spaniard swung and I dodged, sensing my opening.

I pummeled him. Left—right. He grunted, and so did I. Left—right. Again and again until it felt like my fists were saying all the words I never got to.

Why.

I punched harder.

Why did you have to ruin it.

"Kel-ly! Kel-ly!"

Like you ruin everything.

Something primal rumbled in my throat. I threw my body into an uppercut, making the Spaniard spin, teeter, and collapse, earning more shrieks from the crowd. A bell signaled the end of the match and I left the ring, shaking out my limbs which were taut with dissatisfaction. Usually, boxing was a blissful distraction from the chaos simmering inside me, but some days—like today—it made my shame unfurl its sails and catch an ireful wind.

In an anteroom, I unwound the bandages protecting my fists and slid into a collared linen shirt, followed by my brown trench coat. My muscles pulled in exhaustion as I trudged to the counter nestled between brick walls at the back of the now-empty arena.

A man counted bills on the other side, his greasy blond hair brushing his shoulders. "Winnings for Miles Kelly," his scratchy voice said, sliding a paper stack across the counter.

With each successive win, my fights had been drawing in thicker crowds, and it showed in the bills. I counted them. Five dollars short of my goal. Not as thick as last week, then.

One more fight—win or lose—and I could buy the boat off Barnam and sail away. I'd have to tell Nevin I hadn't made as much money as anticipated and still needed the flat until then. Knowing him, the chiseller had already lined up another tenant to replace me, even though my rent was paid up for a few more days.

I banded the bills, then using my magic, stuffed the wad in my coat pocket where it disappeared, adding to my invisible arsenal. To everyone else, my pocket was empty, but I could store up to five objects—large, heavy, or like the money, anything I didn't want stolen. The arsenal could technically reside inside another coat, or a pair of trousers if I was in a bind, but I couldn't split the items up. Any pocket, but only one.

I pulled my brown trench coat tighter, even though I was already sweating from the evening heat. Keeping the arsenal in the same place was worth the temporary nuisance of summer, because then I always had access to it, and simultaneously never forgot where it was. Besides, the worn leather so comfortably contoured to my frame that I didn't want the hassle of breaking in something new.

Not to mention that I needed every sixpence I could get my hands on.

"Kelly!"

I turned to find the Spaniard marching toward me, his face still cut but less swollen than it had been half an hour ago. He must have a slanted healer on his team.

He stopped a foot in front of me, dark eyes sparking. "Let me see your gloves."

I said nothing.

"No rookie fights that clean and wins."

"If you have a problem, take it up with the manager." I sidestepped, but he stepped with me.

"What trick did you play?" A fleck of spittle hit my chin.

I stared at him coolly. "The fight was fair."

"You lie. You're *cheating!*" He grabbed my collar and shook me. I let him.

Then I cut his hold and slammed him into the wall. His head cracked against the brick. I held him there, his limbs trembling. "And what about now?"

His jaw snapped open and shut, eyes glossing in pain. I let go and he slumped to the floor.

I strode out of the dank room. A sunset cast jagged shadows as I wound away from the urban architecture, mentally replaying the interaction. Maybe I should've softened my force, but my patience these days was thinner than watered rum.

The Spaniard had been right about one thing though: The fight wasn't fair. Not because I'd cheated, but because I wasn't a rookie. For fourteen years, Bram had trained us, honed us into weapons that could take down the Order, and the world was our practice arena.

Boxing was just the quickest way to earn cash.

I passed a barrel of turning fish and the brine whisked me into a memory.

Salty air whistled in my ears as I struggled with the correct footing. My arm burned with each swing of my wooden sword. We'd been at it for over an hour, and Ashley's blows rumbled through the wood, still full of strength.

Back, back, back he drove me. Too quickly. The crack of my sword split the air, and I slipped in the puddle at my feet. I fell against some barrels near the stern, scraping my elbow on the iron hoop and drawing blood. I hissed at the sting.

A shadow passed over me, a tall figure with short black hair, sharp cheekbones, and deep-set eyes that swirled with a haunted past. "Again, Ashley." Bram turned his back to me, unsheathing his own practice sword and tipping it toward his godson. "Again."

I swiveled down an alley strung with drying sheets. Rancid puddles splashed my boots, and like my rancid memories, I forged through them.

Mindless drills on a ship out at sea. Shirts off under scorching heat. Enacting blueprint missions at various ports: New York, Hamburg, Shanghai, Copenhagen. The pride that gleamed in Bram's eyes when he looked at Ashley, a gleam that morphed into expectation when his gaze inevitably shifted to me. *Take care of him*, the look said. Payment for raising me out of poverty and giving me a future.

Ashley was nobility, but also someone I'd sacrifice anything for. A brother. I never minded the imbalance.

Until now.

Ashley had undertaken the same training, but I knew—as Bram did—that his skill wasn't in fighting. It was in *winning*.

And because of that, I could practice longer, I could push myself harder, I could learn new techniques while docked in foreign ports, I could fight better, faster, deal more blows, have him pinned to the ground with a sword against his neck, and even then, I never managed to *win*. There was always something I'd overlooked; some way he'd outsmarted me.

And maybe that was the whole point of Bram's training. To go against Ashley, to play his games, was to lose. So I'd done the only thing I could and taken myself out of the equation, Bram's expectations be hanged.

I was *tired* of losing.

Guilt stalked me through the streets, the ever-present reminder that I'd assisted in his crimes. How many people had gone mad? How many lives had I unknowingly destroyed? The magic had stolen my friend, bit by bit, leading him to a place too dark for me to follow. And yet, sometimes, in the dead of night when I could sense that somewhere in the city he moved, I worried. Not just for his victims.

For him.

Ahead, a row of buildings caved in like old, haggard men that nodded deeper into sleep with each passing year. I crossed a tiny bridge and plunged into the second one down, passing a whiskered man smoking a pipe while a baby wailed nearby.

Running a hand through my hair, I ascended the squeaking, uneven stairs, entered my room, and shut the door, ready to fall into bed. When I turned back, a head peeked above the open lid of a large trunk. I jumped. The woman caught sight of the blood dried to my head and screamed. I froze in my skin.

"You— What are you doing in my...!" Emmeline Morgan fell silent, eyes narrowing. Her jaw dropped open. She slowly stood. "Mr. Kelly?"

I fell back against the door. *Black fog.* The light flickered too low to see her features clearly, but I didn't need to. I knew those brown-black eyes. The delicate freckles bridging her nose. The pillowy pink lips that had once been inches from my own and had since haunted my nightmares.

You're a moron, Miles. Only morons use words like pillowy.

Why did she keep cropping up in my life? Why was it always *her?*

The open trunk at her feet vomited skirts and layers of white petticoats. A yellow flower popped out of a porcelain vase on the sill. Even the air smelled disturbingly feminine, like she'd spent the last hour spritzing rosewater in a room smaller than a royal horse stall. It was almost like she thought she lived...here.

Nevin.

My hand tightened on the doorknob until I was sure I had bent metal, then I uttered a string of curses.

Miss Morgan crossed her arms, grinning. "So you *can* speak."

I booted the door behind me open. Splinters flew from where I'd broken the jamb, but I didn't care. Nevin would fix it —right after he fixed this blasted blunder he'd made. Distantly registering Miss Morgan calling my name, I marched down the stairs and toward the back of the lobby, into a room crowded by a desk and yellow-stained, peeling wallpaper.

"Kelly," Nevin said behind the desk, a sleazy smile spreading under his ulcerous nose. "What can I do for you?"

"You can kindly remove the woman I found in my room."

His brow furrowed. "What woman?"

My hands curled into fists. "The one turning everything into a frilly circus act."

"The only circus here is this one." Miss Morgan poked her head into the cramped room, and the rest of her body followed. I inched away from her radiating heat. "Nevin sold the room to me yesterday."

"I don't care," I said to Nevin, ignoring her completely. "I want her out."

"Shift it, Kelly, you're complaining about *that*?" Nevin's gaze raked her over, and he smiled in a way that made my muscles wind tighter. "If you ain't takin' her, she can kip with me."

A surge of protectiveness nearly bowled me over, making my blood spike hot. Like the *devil*—

"I beg your pardon!" She stepped forward before I could, eyes wide with indignation. "There will be no more indecent speak, sir! I've already paid for the room. Everything moderately affordable within ten miles is booked—my blistered feet will prove it to you. Now, I want to know why Mr. Kelly believes he has a right to stay."

"Mr. Kelly informed me he no longer needed the room after tonight."

I hit his desk. "*After* tonight—"

Nevin shrugged. "So she moved in a day early."

"I've paid through the month. The room is mine. Come the eighteenth, she can have it."

"*She* doesn't like that option," Miss Morgan said, folding her arms. "*She* can't very well live on the streets until then."

I ground my teeth. "Give her back her money. Now."

"'Fraid I can't do that." Nevin held his hands out, palms up. "It's been spent."

The room settled into fuming silence.

"On what?" I demanded quietly.

"Repairs."

More silence, but this one was louder and reeked of stubbornness.

Nevin inhaled slowly through his crooked teeth, gaze darting between his two upset patrons. "You could... You could *share*...the room."

Miss Morgan uncrossed her arms. I glowered at Nevin, willing him to combust.

"It is, after all, only fourteen days."

Fourteen days.

An eternity.

"True, that isn't long," Miss Morgan chirped.

It sounded strained, and she looked pale, but still I felt my eyes bug. She hadn't required nearly enough convincing.

Steepling his fingers and then tapping them, Nevin reclined. "As yer landlord, I cain't be seen approvin' of mixed relations, but since some fault lies with me, I shall be the soul of discretion this once."

Some fault. As if his greediness for an extra half month's payment hadn't caused this entire calamity.

If availability of rooms was as bad as Miss Morgan claimed, shelling out the cash for her to go somewhere else would set me back several weeks, and I was scheduled to meet Barnam on the twenty-first about my barquentine. My dream ship that I was only one boxing match short of having the funds for.

Of course, back at the old flat... Tucked under the mattress was a bill of sale for a two-masted schooner; smaller than a barquentine but still ocean worthy. Barnam had offered the schooner for a reduced price, and I had the money—all that was left to do was front the brass and sign the document. I'd been tempted more times than I could count, but I'd held out.

I wanted a vessel powerful enough to outrun the memories.

Miss Morgan sighed. "I suppose we'll just make the best of it."

I sweated faster than bilge water through a rotten plank as I remembered unwittingly touching her chest in an alleyway, and feeling her body beneath mine, strawberry blonde curls tumbling around her face. I thought about how much time we'd be spending together. The proximity. Whole nights. Her curious, dark eyes the first thing I noticed when I woke up.

The *only* thing I'd notice for two weeks.

I fought the waves of nausea long enough to curse one more time, then stormed upstairs.

9

Emmeline

Mr. Kelly's figure disappeared up the stairwell. I'd never shared a room with a boy before, except the nursery with Clarence when we were young. But Mr. Kelly was not a boy.

No, no.

His chiseled jaw and broad shoulders made that crystal clear.

I steeled myself as I ascended the stairs, hands twitching. I didn't think the man would try anything, but at the bottom of my trunk was a pistol that Dorothy had given me, and if I needed to, I'd use it.

Somehow. How hard could operating a pistol be?

Funnily enough, I still found this situation preferable to asking Dorothy for help. Maybe because I already trusted Mr. Kelly wouldn't harm me—more than I'd trusted my own father, whom I'd lived with for seventeen years.

When I reentered the flat, Mr. Kelly was nowhere to be seen. A cat poked its nose from under the bed, meowed, and arched against my skirts, leaving a trail of black hairs. It was the

same animal I'd encountered in Mr. Kelly's other apartment—
Alice, I had named her. I crouched. "Where has your owner
gone, hm?" I scratched behind her ears, and she purred. "Care
to help me finish unpacking?" The cat blinked and settled
against my trunk.

I strategically arranged my gowns on the coat rack, working
out the wrinkles. On my last dress, Mr. Kelly materialized in
the doorway.

I sucked in a breath, but he didn't acknowledge me as he set
a plate of chicken bones in a corner and poured milk into a
bowl. Alice leapt for her dinner. Mr. Kelly petted her a few
times, then stood and slipped out of his jacket.

He moved to hang it on the coat rack, but stopped upon
finding it covered in my things. Frowning, he shook his head,
wadded the article, and tossed it into the corner.

I dragged my eyes away from the muscles pulling against
his undershirt and cleared my throat. "I'm glad you brought
some food for Alice. She was getting hungry."

Mr. Kelly faltered, then glanced at me.

"Oh yes, I named her that time I broke into your apartment.
Right before you tackled me to the floor."

Color rose to his cheeks.

It was somewhat refreshing, talking with someone who
wouldn't defend themselves. Maybe I needed to present his
argument for him, since he was unable.

Pretending the grubby window was my audience as I
approached it, I said in a comically low voice, "But Miss
Morgan, you broke into *my* apartment. And, might I add, I had
no idea you were a girl!" I raised my pitch. "That would've
stopped you, would it?" Lowered. "Definitely. Your hideous,
girlish features put me in such a stupor, I cannot bring myself to
speak for fear I will vomit."

The floorboards shifted behind me as Mr. Kelly strode to the small wash basin, apparently unbothered by my dramatics.

"But Alice is a girl, and you don't seem to mind *her* features!" I said in a high, petulant tone, then deepened my voice again. "That's because Alice is quiet, like me, and also because she is a cat."

"He."

I latched onto the syllable and spun.

We locked eyes, and they were the only soft thing about him. Warm and kind, even while the rest of him—jaw, neck, shoulders, hands—was cut like a piece of machinery. Even one of his cheekbones sported an abrasion. The lips were borderline; masculine, but still shapely and not too thin, though maybe that was because of the purple bruise blooming on one of the corners.

Stop noticing him.

I raised my eyebrows. "What was that? Did you...*say*... something, Mr. Kelly?"

He swallowed and turned away.

I smirked. So the cat was a boy. Well, how fortunate that *Alice* still captured his essence, because it was much too late to change the name.

Mr. Kelly scooped water from the basin and rubbed his face, taking special care where blood had dried to his temple.

I resumed my "Mr. Kelly" voice. "No, I prefer to ignore women who sometimes masquerade as street urchins."

The water *shush-shushed* as he continued to work.

"And where'd you get that? Did the urchin you accosted *today* decide to fight back?" He kept scooping, but his nostrils flared. He remembered that morning too, when he'd thrown me against a warehouse wall because he thought I was a boy, stupidly gambling. When in fact I was a *girl,* stupidly gambling. I grinned wider. "Good for her."

With a towel, Mr. Kelly patted his face and approached, lips slashed downward. Water droplets clung to the rich brown hair kissing his forehead. He opened his mouth like he wanted to say something. He grimaced and hesitated. Then stepped forward again, until I had to crane my neck to look up at his looming height.

My heartbeat spurred into a gallop, but my hands fisted at my sides. "You are big and strong," I muttered, "but I am not afraid of you, Mr. Kelly." *Most of the time.* I summoned my bravado, and maybe it was foolish, but I decided to speak it anyway. "And unlike all of London, I'm not afraid of *the Rook*, either."

His face was stone, but his blinking doubled.

"Yes, I know who he is. And since he's your *friend*," I fairly spat the word, "I imagine you're about to defend him to me."

His breathing froze, and though he wasn't a man of words, this silence seemed intentional. Like even if he could bring himself to speak, he wouldn't. Interesting.

"Then, will you denounce him?"

His jaw tightened, a conflicted emotion trapped in his eyes. When he turned away, again, it felt like silence *was* his answer.

Again, interesting.

After crossing the tiny room, he laid on the floor next to Alice, back turned to me, using his wadded coat as a pillow.

I put my hands on my hips, unable to filter the anger now. "What *have* you got to say about Ashley Gardner and the way he betrayed my cousin?"

More silence. I waited for an answer so long, the light drifted into shadows and my feet were screaming at me to get off them. But what did I expect? That he would suddenly find his tongue?

The mattress squeaked when I finally settled onto it, too tired to find a private corner somewhere to change into my nightgown. Laying on my back, I stared at the mold speckling the ceiling, wondering what kind of criminal would save an urchin from a beating and save a young woman from the streets without expecting anything in return. Someone who laid on the floor facing away, to give me privacy.

What kind of man still saw some good in the Rook?

Mr. Kelly's breathing evened. The room darkened to a charcoal gray. And my eyes were just about to close when I heard the whisper from the corner, so soft and deep I almost convinced myself I imagined it:

"He betrayed me too."

10

Emmeline

Sometime near sunrise I must've finally drifted off because when I awoke, Mr. Kelly's form in the corner had disappeared, and Alice was licking up the last drops of a bowl of fresh cream. It smelled like the breakfast table at our home in the countryside.

A needle pricked my heart at the thought of Mother and my younger brother, Clarence. In the weeks since I'd been disinherited, I'd wracked my brain for a way to extricate them from Father's tight fist, but until I had a mountain of cash to support them—and a larger flat—it was hopeless.

Before the Rook had taken Uncle Geoffrey, his debts had mounted and his research—once lucrative—could no longer sustain him. On the brink of ruin, Uncle Geoffrey had transferred the ownership of his mortgage to my father, who had since made the payments. It was Father's house in every way that mattered.

But as my mother's brother, there was still much Uncle Geoffrey could do to protect her. For now, the fastest way to help my family was to bring him back.

I looked around for signs of Mr. Kelly readying for the day, but besides a shaving knife, a spare set of clothes tucked under the bed, cufflinks, a compass, and a coin collection, there were no signs he existed at all.

Ribs aching, I unlaced my corset and changed into a simpler tea gown, a creamy yellow dress that was far more comfortable. Then I washed my face, re-pinned my hair, and prepared for this to be the day I found some answers.

After tearing paper into thin strips, I scrawled all the bits of information I knew about the case and tacked them to the wall. They mentioned things like the taxi driver's description, hackney routes, where I'd spotted Uncle Geoffrey, a list of carriage services to make inquiries into—all but one crossed off —and any other nugget I might find useful.

I only dared do it because, one, I needed a fresh perspective if I were ever going to make headway, and two, I expected Mr. Kelly would be gone until dusk, as he had been yesterday.

Wrong.

An hour later, I returned from the water closet to find Mr. Kelly, hands in pockets, wordlessly studying the jumble. His hair parted on the side, looking incredibly soft. My face burned with the impulse to tear all the paper down, but it was too late; he'd already seen it. And it wasn't as if Mr. Kelly didn't already *know* my uncle had been kidnapped. In fact, he'd likely aided in it.

I tucked myself between him and the wall, hands on hips. *"This,"* I said, not bothering to disguise my haughty tone, "is all to discover where your *friend* has taken my Uncle Geoffrey. Have you anything to add?"

His expression tilted in a way that was...melancholy? Yes, perhaps. But as usual, he turned away without saying anything.

I'd expected the non-answer, but it still fanned my anger— until I heard the crinkling of a handbill right before he set something on a plate and scooted it over to Alice. The cat attacked the fish and watching him wolf it down made my mouth water. When had I last eaten?

Ah yes, the peppermint tea with Dorothy. But that watery disaster could hardly be called a meal. I felt the weight of Mr. Kelly's study, but when I turned toward him, his gaze darted away, a bit of color smudging his cheeks. So this was how it was to be between us. Awkward glances.

I returned to my papers, trying to ignore the sudden hunger pangs stabbing my middle. A few minutes later, something nudged my elbow. The paper crinkled but didn't completely block the buttery aroma of a pastry wafting from its opening.

Mr. Kelly squinted out the window like he was extremely uncomfortable. He glanced at the food in his hand and nudged me with it again. I took it mutely, too stunned to thank him. He turned and walked out the door.

Inside the wrapping sat a steaming roll and two hard-boiled eggs. My stomach grumbled at the sight. I devoured the roll, frowning at the doorway he'd disappeared through as I chewed, an annoying trickle of guilt worming its way into my heart.

I didn't want to like Mr. Kelly. But that was rather hard not to do when he resorted to underhanded methods like feeding me. I hardly knew what to make of all his contradictions. Good and bad were so black and white, and my gut told me Mr. Kelly fell somewhere in the gray area.

Not dark enough to hate, but not light enough to trust, either. Even if the roll *was* delicious.

Halfway through the eggs, much to my surprise, he materialized again—stalked in like it had taken all his courage to do so —and held out a piece of paper. Blinking, I took it and read the hasty scratches that bordered illegible.

Mr. Florian Joule

My confusion volleyed between the note and the man before me for a full ten seconds before understanding dawned. He wanted to *help*, and stone me if it wasn't a bit rich.

"Ho!" I mock-laughed. "And how do I know that you and Mr. Gardner aren't laying some perverted trap to throw me off your scent? Why should I believe *anything* you say?"

Mr. Kelly continued to watch me in that way of his, where our eyes never met directly—like he didn't want to believe I was flesh and bones. But his brows arched slightly—an aristocratic move if I'd ever seen one—as if to say, *Did I say anything?*

"Point taken," I muttered, and fisted the paper. Guilt needled my conscience, because although I still didn't trust the man, he had just brought me my first meal in two days and had clearly struggled to find the courage to approach me. Was he Mr. Gardner's friend, or wasn't he? Did he have ulterior motives for helping me, or was it genuine? I softened my tone when I added, "I shall consider it."

And by *consider it* I meant that, as I had not the slightest inkling of another plan, I would definitely be going. But he didn't need to know that.

11

Dorothy

"I can't believe she sewed these in only a few days." I fingered the line of gorgeous dresses hanging from the rolling cart in the back room of the dress shop—sapphire taffeta, burgundy crepe, light yellow cotton, lavender *mousseline de soie*. The boutique smelled of wool, and something musty, but it was tidy and fashionable, and the dresses twinkled even brighter than its windows.

"Let's just say the French seamstress was highly incentivized," Nicholas said, ruffling the hair on the back of his head and sitting on a worn wooden worktable littered with bolts of fabric, scissors, and lengths of ribbon. "There are a few more things I'd like to review before she returns."

Nicholas had insisted on meeting in the back to avoid us being seen together, since we didn't know where the Rook had eyes, and our association, for now, was best left a secret. Said seamstress was sewing in an adjacent room while we inspected our order, and when a sneaking suspicion made me reach for the present leg of my slant, I felt a cold rush of magic swim under my skin.

I was right. That explained why the dresses were so beautiful.

Before I'd understood the science, I used to think I had three slants—but then I'd discovered they were merely different *abilities* that fell under the same magical slant. Seeing visions of the future, sensing magic in the present, or seeing into the past —they all had to do with time. Up until Nicholas began working with me, I couldn't control my magic that dealt with the present or the future.

Now I could choose when to use it—without fear of a blue-duster clamping me in irons—and that power was still foreign. But it also had its pitfalls. Where before I would've automatically sensed a stranger slanting nearby, now, unless I was shrewd enough to reach for my magic like I had with the seamstress, I would never be the wiser.

I nodded for Nicholas to continue.

"Guests of your rank would normally be placed in the grace-and-favor apartments within the palace complex, or a nearby townhouse. However, Mr. Brass arranged for your quarters in the North Wing, while the Rook will be in the East Wing. We wanted him inside the palace where we can watch him, but not so close in proximity as to put you in danger."

"And the queen agreed to this? Does she know the Rook's identity?"

Nicholas hesitated, a sheepish expression telling me I'd caught him unprepared and he was calculating how much to disclose. "Her Majesty knows that the Lightfoot Agency is currently conducting an operation to do with the bracelets' retrieval. Nothing more. Mr. Brass went directly to the Lord Chamberlain about the room reassignments, to avoid over-worrying the queen. If we ever suspect her life is in danger, we will of course apprise her of the necessary details."

I blinked, trying to work out my feelings on the situation.

Nicholas decoded them before I did, because he went on, almost defensively. "This is exactly why we exist, Dorothy—why *she* created the Lightfoot Agency—to quietly handle matters she knows nothing about."

"You're right." I sighed. "I suppose holding more secrets just makes me nervous I'll slip up."

"I understand, but you won't be alone. Agents will be watching his every move, and during the events you attend together, we'll use that reconnaissance to find the bracelets. Meanwhile, work on getting him to reveal their location to you. In your spare time, it wouldn't hurt if you searched for them too.

"I'll, uh..." He approached me slowly, eyes downcast, head canted, fingers brushing so lightly over my skirts that I barely registered it. My heart did a pleasant little flip. "I'll be busy, but I'll try to visit you as often as I can. If you ever need me, tie a handkerchief around your doorknob."

He glanced up and we locked eyes. Heat flooded my face at the knowledge that he'd be watching my bedroom door. And I couldn't help but notice his choice of words. Not, *need to talk to me*, or *need to relay important information*.

If you ever need me.

Was I imagining this? Were those butterflies flurrying in my stomach? And were they hatched from real attachment, or were they just a desperate pivot from heartache I wasn't strong enough to carry?

I turned away from his touch to examine the dresses' beautiful lines so I didn't have to analyze my emotions. "You've already paid for seven new wardrobe pieces from when the agency took me on. I'm not sure I understand why we need even more for the queen's birthday celebrations."

Nicholas hooked a thumb in his pocket and casually backed

away, taking my cue. "You'll be spending two weeks with the toast of London. We need you to dazzle like the rest of them."

Still... I traced a hand down a chiffon gown, noting its layer of *point d'esprit*, a pretty lace with an elegant, dotted pattern. It was stunning. They all were. So ridiculously luxurious that I wasn't sure someone like me wearing them could do them justice. The fashions were much better suited to Emme.

The thought of my cousin made me smile. I hoped she was well. At tea the other morning, I'd noticed her furtively counting coins, but what really tipped me off was her declining the opportunity for a pastry—something I didn't think her capable of.

She was broke.

But she was also stubborn, and I understood. It wasn't about being too proud to accept help so much as needing to prove something to oneself. Unless her straits became too dire, I wanted to respect those wishes.

I eyed the dresses closer. But that didn't mean I couldn't send her a gift to cheer her up.

The seamstress swept into the room, her graying dark curls piled and pinned on the crown of her head. "Ah! So you have found them. I used the measurements you sent me, so they are correct." A French lilt infused her voice and her wrists twirled in elegant arcs, fingers quickening and slowing but never quite resting from their smooth dance.

Nicholas ambled to the other side of the rack, smiling at me above the dresses. "Do you like them?"

I chuckled. "Like them? I—" Words died in my throat when I saw a sparkling onyx fabric. I pulled the dress out from the others, breath catching. It was black, with short, off-shoulder bell sleeves, and a skirt that glittered like a winter's night sky.

"Strange," Nicholas said, eyeing it. He turned to the seamstress, who beamed. "I don't remember commissioning a dress from that fabric. She won't be in mourning."

"But it suits her, no? I could not resist."

Almost in a trance, I swept the dress over to the full-length mirror. Something about the sight—the black fabric draped against me—surfaced the memory of Ashley inside Big Ben's clock tower. *I told you from the start it was a game, Miss St. James. No one likes a sore loser.* The words had made my blood boil, and I was lucky he hadn't noticed my balled fist behind me.

The night I'd stitched him up...of course it hadn't meant anything to him. It was my first kiss, but he'd probably had dozens like it. He'd been the one stabbed, but I'd been the one bleeding out, heart in my hand, so certain he'd actually cared.

I wouldn't let him anywhere near that heart again.

The seamstress joined me, smiling wider as she dissected my reflection over my shoulder. "Look at how it reddens your lips—sharpens your angles. You will be as a seductive night, gliding over constellations, irresistible to every man. This dress is not for a girl. This dress, *ma chérie*, is for a woman." She was right that it would cause quite a stir in any ballroom.

But I'll never wear it, I mutely replied. It was too bold, too dark...

Too much like the bitterness festering inside me.

Nicholas tugged the black garment from my grasp and handed it to the seamstress, who shuffled off to re-hang it. "I prefer you in something like this." Using his forearm, he pinned the top of a soft blue silk to my sternum, angling around to stand flush against my back. "Much more like you." His voice vibrated against the back of my head, his warmth seeping into my spine.

I forgot how to breathe.

"It would go beautifully with a string of pearls, don't you think?" he murmured into my ear, a smile in his voice.

Sparks crawled over that side of my neck. Swallowing, I nodded, admitting, "I've always wanted pearls."

"Do you not have any? We'll need to rectify that immediately." Nicholas lingered for another few moments, and through our reflections, I watched him stare at me, his eyes tracing the curves of my cheek, ear, and neck. My skin prickled with a giddy awareness. Slowly, his smile softened and ultimately disappeared, then he stepped away with the dress.

That moment, I had not imagined.

"We'll need them all packaged up directly," he said to the seamstress. "Miss St. James will be taking a crucial carriage ride to the palace in a few hours."

12

Dorothy

I tried not to look at him as I entered the carriage, but it was difficult; his darkness lapped up all the air in the small contraption. Settling into the plush green velvet of the opposite corner, I released a careful breath—not too slowly, not too quickly—aware that he studied me. And that he would detect any deficiency.

As the traffic thickened, we moved at a snail's pace through the city, and not for the first time I cursed this plan, wishing we didn't have to arrive together. The tense silence between us clawed at my ears, making them bleed. When I could no longer stand it, I turned to Ashley with a mild expression.

My heart skipped a beat. It still wasn't used to his perfect face.

Wavy black hair kissed his earlobes and temples, obviously uncombed but still neat in a chaotic way. It was longer than I remembered. He reclined against his seat, head angled slightly forward so the collar of his black coat framed his jaw. His green eyes watched me from under long lashes, making my stomach curl.

"Beautiful weather we are having," I said lightly.

His answering tone was bored. "Is it? I hardly noticed."

"Odd." I sat forward in challenge. "For *you* to not notice something."

"One might think I have something distracting me." He squinted, gaze quickly flashing over me. "Like a beautiful woman."

I lifted my brows in feigned ignorance. "Hm. Do I know her?"

A hint of a smile touched his lips as he appraised me more slowly. "Not well enough, I think."

My feet dug into the carriage floor. I immediately relaxed them. If I was to earn his trust, I needed to push my anger aside long enough to be charming—which meant easy sparring, like we used to do. "I'm inclined to believe that neither do you."

"Or maybe," he sat forward too, completely ignoring my remark, "I'm distracted by the fact that you're talking about the weather, when you really wish to talk of something else."

"I don't wish to talk at *all*."

He cocked his head. "I'm not the one who started."

We settled back into the silence for several minutes, the muffled clatter of the streets seeping through the curtained windows.

"Actually," I began, and it took a mountain of effort to sieve the accusation from my tone, "I was wondering what you've been so occupied with. You disappeared for three weeks without a word, and given the nature of our reunion, you had every intention of keeping things that way."

He blinked. "Did you not receive my telegram?"

I blinked back at him. "What telegram?"

Ashley analyzed me for a painfully long moment, debating whether to say more. At last, cautiously, "Never mind. You obviously did not."

And I hated the curiosity burning in my sternum, eager to know— *What had it said?*

He sat back, sighing. "I told you. The game was up. You had nothing more to offer me."

"And that isn't exactly answering my question, is it? Where were you for three weeks?"

He grinned. "Did you miss me, Dolly?"

The nickname rankled and my jaw tensed. "I missed the part where you answered my question."

"And that's what I like about you—you're a person who remains ever undeterred. Unfortunately for you, so do I." And I read in the set of his lips what he was really saying, the only thing he'd told me from the very beginning:

Give up.

I inhaled a quiet, steadying breath. I'd forgotten how frustratingly deflective he could be. If I wanted him to reveal his secrets, I'd have to tread more delicately, because giving up was not, and never had been, an option. "Well then, Mr. Gardner, it looks as if we are to be at odds once again."

"On the contrary, I am very much looking forward to working together." His eyebrows ticked up. "Once you reveal what your slant is."

I scoffed. "Why is that important?"

"Planning out how to acquire the map would go a lot smoother if I knew all of our assets."

My thumbnail bit into the side of my forefinger. "And who decided *you* get to do the planning?"

"Frankly, it's already done. But I'd like to know if I need to make adjustments."

Of course he'd already found something; I shouldn't have expected anything less. Worry that he'd unwittingly outmaneuver me before I could discover the bracelets flashed through me. I forced myself to say in an unconcerned tone, "No adjustments will be necessary."

His eyes narrowed, just for a beat. I refused to whet his curiosity, and it was starting to fascinate him. "So, it's not a useful slant."

"Perhaps not to you," I lied, aiming for indifference.

"You think me so unresourceful?"

"I think you *too* resourceful. Which is why you'd do well to take your guesses elsewhere."

His smile widened. "But perhaps there's a deeper reason why you're so skilled at chemistry. Do you infuse your concoctions with magic?"

"Mm, pity no one will drink them."

"Or perhaps your power lies in conjuring the blackest dark."

"*Nothing* can match your soul, I'm afraid."

He snorted. "Or, it would seem, your wit." He cocked his head again. "Have you used your slant against me?"

"Define *against*."

"Ah, so you have. When?"

"That is valuable information. A secret like that requires a secret in return." If he caught the way I'd twisted his own words against him, he didn't show it.

Instead, he was silent for a painful moment before saying slowly, "You play the game differently now. You are changed."

I straightened. "For the better, I'd hope."

"I think not." His response was immediate but too quiet and buried under his next words. "Very well. Tell me what your slant is, and I'll tell you where I was for three weeks."

I stilled, and I could practically read it in his eyes: *A token for a token.* My lips pressed together before I finally said, "I know better than to make a deal with a devil twice."

"But not to make one in the first place."

We stared at each other, so long. So long I felt my insides crack, and then splinter when a slow smile crawled across his lips, cunning and wicked and intimate enough to make my blood burn.

"You know I'll find out anyway."

Dread eked into my stomach. Not because it mattered whether he uncovered my slant—it didn't, and it was silly to be so stubborn about holding it back, but a part of me relished in finally being the mysterious one. The one with the upper hand.

No, it was because that smile was a reminder that Ashley Gardner was not someone who failed. Ever. And all it would take was one little misstep and every secret of mine would unravel.

I cleared my throat. "I know you'll try."

From his breast pocket, Ashley withdrew a gray newspaper clipping and set it on my lap. I resisted looking at it for all of three seconds.

***The Banns of Marriage between Ashley Gardner**, of **St. John's Parish**, and **Dorothy St. James**, of the same parish, will be published for the third and final time at **St. George's Church** on Sunday, June 2, 1889. If any person knows of any lawful impediment why these two persons should not be married, they are to declare it.*

Reading both our names strung together in the same sentence as the word *marriage* gave me peculiar flutters in my stomach. My slant couldn't see years ahead, but flashes of a future flitted through my eyes as if it did—kisses in the dark, a hand catching me about the waist, laughter in the grass, dark curls on little heads—

"Very good," I pushed out before the thought took hold, not

knowing what more Ashley wanted me to say. I handed the paper back to him.

But maybe it wasn't my words he desired, because he tracked every twitch in my expression like he was deciphering clues in a mystery novel. "We'll need a story."

Right—how we became engaged. "It should be as close to the truth as possible. Anything built on lies falls apart." The last half came out sharper than I intended, and Ashley frowned, noting it.

Careful.

Ashley didn't know I knew about the statue, the feather, my father, and I needed to cling to that advantage.

"I couldn't agree more," he muttered.

I strangled the anger coiling my chest. *Earn his trust. Earn his trust.* I sat forward, hating the sense that I was losing this conversation. "For propriety's sake, we'll say we've known each other for months, but your attentions grew more pronounced the last few weeks. It culminated one night in"—I swallowed, remembering the floral wallpaper in my room—"in a garden, where you kissed me and declared yourself."

Ashley's lurid green eyes fixed on me, but they seemed to pulse, and I grew hot. His next words came soft and low. "In a *French* garden. Full of roses. And lavender."

I'd told him I loved lavender in my father's lab; its smell reminded my father of my mother. Was it coincidence, him bringing it up now? I flushed. "I hardly think the flora matters."

"It doesn't hurt to iron out as many details as we can. And when I kissed you..." He sat forward too, but it was slowly—so slowly that it felt like he was pulling *me* toward *him*. He didn't stop until our noses were almost touching, his warm breath and gaze grazing my lips. "Did you like the taste of it?"

He was toying with me, only this was a game of a different kind.

Just as before, I was the bug, he was the boot.

But shoes came in a pair, and now I could stomp back.

I schooled my features and dove headlong into his emerald eyes, turning my mouth up in a smile I didn't feel. "*Wildly.*"

Ashley's jaw ticked, nostrils flaring just slightly.

"Though I hardly think it appropriate to go around sharing."

"Appropriate, no. Convincing? Yes." His gaze fell to my throat where my pulse beat erratically. A little tug on his lips. "Perhaps we should offer them a demonstration."

All of my nerve endings sparked to life. Every inch of me tensed up, and my belly warmed. Warmed with so many emotions, but the anger was winning—

Ashley retreated far enough that I could breathe again.

But before I could sort out the confusing tornado of emotions that sentence had produced, I felt it: a silent force subtly tugging my insides toward him. Shivers coursed my arms the second I realized what it was, remembering viewing the green magic on his hands through the slant gun.

His mutating magic.

Ashley stilled, like he felt it too, then his eyes shot to mine, a spark of alarm passing through them. Hand flexing, he leaned back into the window, glancing away and not acknowledging the moment. The colors in the carriage swelled with soft edges, like a dream.

The magical urge inside me built, pulling and pulling...

Ashley's jaw tightened.

Heat burrowed under my skin and melted my core. I contemplated scooting down so our knees would brush, cheeks warming at the idea but not seeing another reprieve from the building tension inside, the headiness swirling behind my eyes that was making me burn—

The urge dissipated, leaving me empty and disoriented. I

squinted out the window to see the carriage had ricketed onto the palace grounds. Though no one knew how, Buckingham—along with all other royal residences—had been warded off, preventing anyone from using magic in the palace, even someone as powerful as Ashley. It was mainly to protect the reigning monarch, but I wouldn't complain about it protecting me too.

I released a slow sigh. I could've been mistaken, but I thought I heard Ashley do the same.

Why?

As the carriage rolled to a halt, I tried to settle the terrified pounding of my heart. I'd never felt a loss of will like that before. Even more alarming, if I hadn't known what it was and resisted, I might never have noticed it at all.

Sensing magic within my radius always gave me a cold rush —except with Ashley. His magic felt warm, and I was almost positive it had to do with its sentience. It was chemically different from other magic, after all; why wouldn't it feel different too? But that begged the question—

Was this mutation able to control me now because it was growing in power, or had it been secretly influencing me this whole time, pulling me toward him, and I was only just waking up to it?

How many more lies were twisting between us?

Knowing seduction was part of his magic only reinforced my determination to stay emotionally apart. *He kidnapped Father,* I reminded myself. *He took everything from me.*

Ashley disembarked. When my turn came, out of habit I extended a hand for the gentleman's assistance down. And even though our eyes met briefly, Ashley backed away and trained his gaze on the horizon, refusing to take my glove.

HALF AN HOUR LATER, I strode down a long blue carpet through a gilded hall lined with pompous stares. Hushed whispers met my ears as we passed, making it difficult for me to hold my head high.

"But that's Mr. Gardner—!"

"Engaged?"

"...matched to her favor..."

Heat rushed to my face. Because I couldn't control my magic before, I'd never had my Season—a formal introduction into London's society. I wasn't accustomed to being noticed, and I wouldn't have been if not for the man whose arm linked mine.

Ashley held it without any of the aversion he'd exhibited earlier, flashing a winsome smile to the one hundred and twelve guests cushioning the walls. Apparently, we were one of the last to arrive. The connection seared through my dress; it was the first time I'd touched him since knowing the full truth. I took deep, calming breaths.

Finally, we came to our designated spot on the sidelines— closer to the throne than I'd imagined. The weight of everyone's stolen glances bore down on me, making me wish for a fan to distract myself with.

"...wearing to the garden party tonight?" a high female voice said, somewhere behind us.

Another girlish voice answered. "Something sheer and flowery. I heard Her Majesty has a game planned—to do with the hedge maze."

"The hedge maze?" They quieted to a disbelieving whisper. "But isn't it enchanted?"

"Just the half that's off Buckingham grounds. Though it apparently hasn't been pruned since the day it was planted. Hasn't needed it."

"Still. To venture into the maze, a place that's been blocked off since the start of the queen's reign, carries great risk. The deeper you venture, the thicker the enchantment—"

"I think it a romantic notion," a third female voice cut in. "Through the centuries, it's been a favorite spot for lovers, somewhere star-riddled and full of magic. A *lot* of kissing those hedges have seen."

"Then do you think I can chase down Mr. Gardner in the maze?"

"For shame!" the first voice hissed, while the other two giggled. "He is engaged, and he will hear you if you don't quiet!"

Too late, I thought, when his lips quirked in...not amusement. Perhaps bitterness. And I remembered what I'd once thought of him in the Necropolis—that he was someone who wished to disappear but couldn't help but be seen.

I didn't want to see him.

I didn't want to notice the bitterness on his lips.

I glanced away.

A resplendent duchess approached, silencing all chitter-chatter. Ashley slipped a piece of paper into my gloved hand. "Someone who might have an idea of where the map is," he whispered.

My brows slightly lifted. Straight to business, then. Furtively, I unfolded the paper, reading the name. *Jacintha Brook.* That he'd written the name down instead of whispering it meant he didn't want anyone overhearing it. But why was it so covert? And why hadn't he mentioned it in the carriage? *Perhaps because we were too busy dueling.* "Is she in the palace?"

Ashley inclined his head at the passing duchess, then said, "Word has it she hasn't left the archives since Victoria began her rule."

My lips parted. For fear of my slant being discovered, I'd

sequestered myself in my home for two years—but that was nothing compared to a half-century imprisonment. But why? What secret was she trying to hide?

"She manages the palace archives," Ashley went on, bending so close his breath tickled my neck. "We should try to meet with her before the garden party tonight. Say five o'clock?"

Trumpets blared, announcing the queen's arrival. There was surprisingly little ceremony as the regal woman glided in wearing an acre of lace, her features possessing a falling quality despite the roundness of her face. She nodded to half of the guests before sitting on a chaise at the end of the hall, a puppy at her heels. An announcer then informed us we'd be shown to our quarters, where we would find our itineraries for the week.

The moment Ashley stepped away, the tightness in my chest loosened.

I was relieved that my room was nowhere near Ashley's, however inconvenient. Even if Buckingham was a black hole for magic, I didn't fully trust old feelings not to flare up again— or his mutated magic to not strangely addle my senses—and welcomed the distance.

Inside my rooms, mint green paper lined the walls and met the plush floral rug. Draping white flowers spouted from a vase on a stand in the corner, next to a window with gauzy curtains and a washbasin. I sat on the fluffy white bed, just as a knock vibrated the door. "Come in."

Nicholas entered, and my spirits immediately lifted. I tucked the thought of *why* away, to be analyzed later.

He closed the door behind him, a little quickly. "I apologize for brazenly visiting your quarters—risking someone linking us together and compromising our plan—but it was much faster than sending a note." He lifted his brows to form that intensely earnest look I'd come to know so well. "I trust you are finding everything suitable."

I smiled and patted the soft mattress beneath me. "Very much."

"Good." He settled next to me on the bed, and maybe I imagined it, but his placement seemed intentional—just next to me, but not too close. "How did your conversation with the Rook go? Does he suspect anything?"

The inquiry carried a strange undercurrent, and suddenly I knew the real reason Nicholas had hazarded a meeting. He was worried for me; he knew the toll such a conversation would take.

It was incredibly sweet of him.

"It's hard to tell, with Ashley," I admitted, "but I don't think so."

"Did you learn anything of the bracelets?"

I shook my head. "No. But about the map—he already has a lead."

Nicholas frowned, pulling the little freckle above his lip closer to his mouth. "We'll need the full two weeks to root out the bracelets. If he appears to be solving the puzzle of the map too quickly, you'll need to stall him."

"Stall...how?" I tried not to let them, but my eyes widened a little.

"I know you'll find a way." The pad of his thumb swept my cheek, light and quick. His body leaned an inch toward mine, and again, I felt as if he was stopping himself from saying something.

Abruptly, Nicholas stood and stepped away. "I'll let you rest. Watch for a note from me with details of when we'll next meet." Then he left.

I sighed, the sound short and hopeless. Arms out, I

collapsed on the bed, trying not to think about the carriage ride here but failing utterly. My stomach squirmed.

If that conversation was indicative of how my mission would go, I was going to lose. Ashley was still cleverer; he discerned too much. I groaned and rubbed my temples, knowing I should change for the garden party, but lacking the energy.

Then I thought of something else Ashley had uttered in the carriage—about kissing me in a garden of lavender—and drifted into a memory.

"Dig a little more here," Father said, his smooth hands pointing to the dark splotch of soil next to Mother's headstone.

Fingers pink from cold, I gripped the trowel tighter and plunged it into the earth, scooping around the hole to widen it. The damp grass beneath me soaked into the stockings I'd gotten for my fifth birthday, and Father's trousers, too, were wet at the knees. Papa worked to loosen the pot of lavender that he'd grown in his lab—to plant by Mama, he'd said. He said it didn't like so much rain, but he was determined to come back every year to plant more, because it was her special flower.

After removing the base of the plant and transferring it into my hands, Papa went on. "You have to be gentle, Dory. The lavender is leaving the only home it's ever known. Don't loosen the roots or they won't take." He helped me place it in the earth and delicately fill the gaps with loose soil, guiding me to pat it down firmly.

He loved growing things.

But he also loved dead things, because he loved Mama.

We'd taken a long train ride and ended up somewhere with a big house and lots of woods, the stony cross of her grave dividing the two. Papa said Mama grew up here. It smelled old, and like lichen.

Finished with the transplant, he dusted off his hands, pushed up his spectacles, and sat on his side. "Do you know what lavender means, Dory?"

I shook my head.

His throat worked, and he was silent a long moment. "Devotion." His eyes welled up, but I didn't know why the word made him cry.

I tilted my head. "What does 'evotion' mean?"

"It means—" Someone called from the house, stealing his attention. "Stay here," Papa said, climbing to his feet and moving toward the voice. "I'll be just a few minutes, then we can plant the next one."

In the wall of forest, birds flittered between branches. A frail beam of sunlight shone on a bent tree before hiding behind the clouds. I stared at the limb, noting the moss on its underside. I glanced around. In fact, all the trees had moss on one side—like it was playing peek-a-boo with the sun.

Curious, I plunged into the woods, observing the fungal growth as I went. Deeper and deeper, over slippery rocks and through decaying leaves and under crooked boughs. I wanted to know if the moss grew the same deep in the forest where little rays pierced. But I grew tired, and my feet and hands were chilled, so when I found a patch of sunlight warming a hollow log, I laid on it to rest.

I woke to someone sobbing my name and lifting me up, enveloping me in the smell of tobacco. I was so cold, and I burrowed into the warm whiskers on his neck, ready to fall back asleep. He toted me through the foliage and through the grass, until finally we stepped into a room with a blazing hearth. After laying me on a sofa by the fire, he hunched down and rubbed heat back into my hands.

I blinked sleepily, but there was something I still wanted to know. "Papa?"

He paused. "Yes, Dory?"

"Papa, what does 'evotion' mean?"

He smoothed a curl out of my face, then folded me into his chest and squeezed me tight, whispering into my hair, "It means I'll always come for you."

I surfaced from the memory with a shuddering breath, crossing my arms around my middle. Tears leaked from my eyes and trickled into my hair. I'd trade anything to relive that moment, to feel his warm embrace cradling me.

It means I'll always come for you.

I sat up, clutching the downy bedding beneath me. *And I'll always come for you,* I mutely vowed back.

I glanced at a clock on the wall: 3:30. Ashley had said to meet at the archives at five o'clock. Needing the advantage, I squared my shoulders, stood, and grabbed the door handle, determination evaporating my tears.

13

Dorothy

I had to ask five different servants for directions to the archives before I cobbled together a general sense of its direction, so by the time I arrived at the rusty metal door in the westernmost corner of the palace, it was nearly four o'clock. Apparently, not even servants ventured this far into the vacant wing.

I lifted my hand to knock, only to find the door slightly ajar, so I slipped inside, making the metal groan on its rusty hinges. The fragrance of glue and musty paper coated the air. Tall mahogany panels inlaid with glass lined both sides of the narrow room and seemed to stretch on forever into the gloom, where no candles burned on the display desks. Despite the decrepit door, the archives didn't have a speck of dust—the only thing out of place being the familiar figure hunched over a pane of glass who looked up upon my noisy entrance.

I bit my tongue, blood heating in frustration. "I thought you said five o'clock."

Ashley returned to the document he was studying. "Then why are you here?" His tone was playful, but his jaw was tight.

He'd come early for the same reason I had—because he wanted to be one step ahead.

He didn't trust me.

Just as I didn't trust him.

But I needed him to if Nicholas's plan was to work.

"I was feeling restless," I said.

"Seldom doth she have visitors," came a small, scratchy voice behind me, making me jump. "For who would call upon lonely little Jacintha?" A gaunt woman emerged from the gloom, hip jutted out to carry a stack of books like a baby. Kinky gray hairs escaped her high bun, a few plastered against her temple where they were caught in her spectacles. The warm glow of the candles failed to color her pale skin, making her shimmering eyes the only thing that differentiated her appearance from a corpse.

She approached Ashley like he was a pretty bird in a cage, slowly circling and examining him in awe. "The touch of magic, your face has. Fortunate man, that it rebuilt it so bewitching."

I frowned, a dozen questions buzzing on my tongue.

He remained unfazed, instead asking, "You are the girl who doesn't age? You are Jacintha?"

That seemed to amuse her, and she straightened. "Aye— though she ages now, doesn't she? Five hundred winters as a maiden of twelve, now wrinkled and forgotten like the rest of these tomes. But so gracious of Her Majesty to grant her refuge, when she couldn't stop her slant from keeping her young."

My toes curled inside my ankle boots. So that explained why she'd been holed up here since Victoria ascended the throne, and why she wasn't firing on all neurons. I hesitantly touched her upper arm. "Have they locked you in here?"

"Locked? Nay! Jacintha hath leave to quit the archives, though never the palace, but no one takes kindly to the strange girl who is not a girl. Too eerie. Too suspect. 'Tis much easier to find fellowship among her books—and so benevolent of Her Majesty to grant her a charge, that she idly wander not. So she abides here. And none visit. And now she is wondering what brings you lovers hither?"

As I dropped my hand, a lump hardened in my throat. "We aren't—" But then I remembered we *were*—or at least were pretending to be. "That is, it isn't—"

"What my fiancée means to say," Ashley cut in smoothly with a winning smile, "is that we are both fascinated by history and have come in hopes that you'll impart some of yours. We've heard you're an unparalleled storyteller."

That brought color to Jacintha's cheeks, and I frowned. I'd forgotten how charming Ashley could be; how easy it was to fall prey to his wiles. I cleared my throat and stepped between them, feeling the strange need to protect the old woman even though getting information from her was what we'd come for. "Five hundred years, did you say? That would put you right at the beginning, then—when magic was first discovered."

Her eyes widened. "Aye! She was there the day the three miners did chance upon the Variance. They opened the cavern and became the most powerful mages ever known when the magic bonded to their blood. What magic they couldn't hold spilled forth and found others—found *her* and kept her young."

"You knew them then?" I asked.

"Knew?" Her feather-light laugh hovered at the top of her throat. "Jacintha did not *know* them—they were much too important for her. But she oft heard the stories, the legends, the half-truths that are all but now forgotten." Her far-off look gradually neared, until she was studying us with a tinge of suspicion. "Why seek you knowledge of the mages?"

"We're archaeologists," Ashley supplied without hesitation, "hoping to find the Undercity. It's of great cultural significance and could vastly further our understanding of life at that time. We're looking at a few preliminary locations for excavation sites, but any insight into the mages would be invaluable." He ended his speech with another charming grin.

"Archaeologists, you say?" Jacintha's gaze landed back on me. "She knew not *women* do such things now."

"It's quite exhilarating," I said, tacking on a stiff smile. Too stiff. The woman still eyed me.

Ashley's arm slipped around my waist, and I sucked in a soft breath that I hoped neither of them noticed. "Especially when we dig together. The earth often resists, at first, but with a delicate touch, one can coax out even her most intimate secrets." He looked at Jacintha as he said it, but his head was turned toward me, his words softly falling on my ear in a double meaning.

Jacintha must've been a romantic, because she visibly warmed. "*Mayhaps* she can lend you aid. Aye, she remembers reading..." She turned and ambled off into the darkened book-ways, leaving Ashley to gradually draw away like nothing had happened, even though heat was curling up my spine.

In the silence, I grappled for composure. I wetted my dry lips, wishing away the blaze over my waist, left there by his touch.

Jacintha returned, gingerly carrying a slim book with deckled edges and a faded leather cover. "It's the story." She reverently set the book on a table and hovered a hand over it. "The story of it all."

I blinked. Of the mages?

Ashley nodded—obviously knowing something I didn't— and unclasped the cover. "There are so few records left of this era. How—?"

"She hid it." Jacintha grew a slow, almost unhinged smile. "When they did burn all the books during the Gloaming. She sought some token to bear witness of all that she's lost." Her smile wilted, and again that distant look returned to her eye. "How much she has lost."

Ashley opened the book, and I edged closer so we could read it in tandem.

The Tale of the Three Mages

Long ago, in a darker age, a terrible famine ravaged England. The lucky peasants received rotten scraps from a lord's table, while the serfs languished into bones for the hunting dogs to gnaw on.

Seeking to change their fortune, three men scraped away in a mine, following a streak in the rock deep into the earth.

But what they found was far more valuable than gold.

They cracked a secret pocket in the depths, and magic burst from the Variance into the world in a stream of blue so thick you could taste stars when it rushed down your throat. It bonded with the nearest blood, branching out until every particle of magic had found a vessel.

In the aftermath glimmered the Undercity—the pocket which had held the magic for thousands of years—now fully formed into an architectural masterpiece, and the three mages, powerful beyond all human comprehension.

Edric, gifted with growing plants.

Ranulf, gifted with forging metal.

And Simon, gifted with wielding water.

But unlike all the others who gained a slant that day, theirs imbued enchantment; each of their creations contained a deadly magic of its own. Edric grew a flower whose smell could heal a broken heart. Ranulf forged a metal ring that perceived when its subject was lying.

*Simon conjured a sprinkle of rain that stole a memory with
each drop on your head.*

*The mages quickly grew in prominence and were
granted titles, thrust into politics because of the vastness of
their power. But magic ran amuck, mercenaries led by the
slanted arose, and the country burned.*

*The world was beginning to look at England with
greedy eyes—for despite its strength in magic, it was fractured, and therefore weak.*

*On the brink of invasion, the mages proposed to King
Henry I that he form a secret division of the slanted whose
efforts would keep all abuse of magic in check, and the
Order of the Worthy was born. They charted all slants,
enlisted a legion to defend the motherland, and soon
harmony was restored.*

And the glory of London began.

"The Order of the Worthy," I said slowly, pointing to that
section while my mind reached for my history lessons. "Isn't
that the society that Queen Victoria dispelled upon her ascension to the throne?"

Ashley's eyes grew cold. "Supposedly."

Did he think they still existed? An organization that dealt
with the politics of magic was useless if all magic was illegal.
The Order had been replaced by the bluedusters—which was
probably what Ashley was referring to. We both returned to the
reading.

*The Undercity became the epicenter of all magical
dealings and the headquarters for the Order, trade flour-
ishing between above and below.*

*Years passed, and when the three mages discovered a
similar vein in a different line of earth, they knew what it*

contained—but more importantly, they knew the chaos it would unleash, if ever opened. The mages put a lock on the second Variance, so that only one truly worthy could open it, then constructed a map to it and hid it well, for though they risked attracting appetites for power, magic was already starting to fade through the bloodlines.

And England's need might be great again.

For now, the world would be safe.

The king began exiling slanted criminals to the Undercity, for no one could use magic there. It became a desolate place and anarchy reigned, seeing the rise and fall of countless cutthroat dynasties.

And with every passing year, the secrets of the Variance, the mages, of London and its glory, were lost to time.

When I finished reading, I frowned. Huge chunks of the story were missing. What had happened to the Undercity to transform it from a thriving borough into the unscrupulous Necropolis? Why hadn't this Order put a stop to it? What was this lock the mages had put on the second Variance, and where had they hidden the map to it?

By then, Jacintha had retrieved another book and placed it before us, this one slightly larger, with a clasp on the front.

"'Twas Ranulf's personal journal," Jacintha supplied.

I unclasped it and riffled through the pages, some of them loose, occasionally pausing. They were filled with drawings of women, flowers, jewelry, and geometric designs that had an ethereal feel to them. This metal forger was obviously an artist.

"You said you heard all the stories." I shuffled closer to Jacintha whose chin trembled beneath her dull eyes. "Did you ever hear rumors of a second Variance?"

Ashley's movements froze.

Jacintha didn't seem to notice, still in her melancholy

trance. "Rumors, aye. The mages came upon it, not long after they found the first. But they didn't open it. Nay, there was too much magical havoc as it was."

"Did you ever hear of a map leading to it?" I pressed. "The map the mages created?"

Ashley frowned, and he shook his head almost imperceptibly.

Jacintha's eyes widened. "You are not searching for it, she hopes?" Her frail, tremulous hand covered her mouth as she breathed, "*Death*. Death to *all* if the map pieces are unearthed and the second Variance opened."

I mentally kicked myself. Ashley was right; my digging was too obvious, too soon.

But Jacintha was no longer listening. Her focus cast about the room, voice rising. "So much power. So many ashes. The sun will ebb to black and the stars flicker and die."

The hair on the back of my neck stood on end.

"It cannot survive again, we cannot survive—!"

Ashley grabbed her hand, and she instantly cut off. Her eerie, luminous eyes gazed up at him, still frightened but desperate for human connection.

"We are not magic-seekers," he soothed. "We merely wish to know the history—from an intellectual standpoint. Such information will greatly aid in our research."

She blinked, and after a long moment, relaxed.

"Perhaps you should go lie down? I can ring for a servant to bring you tea. That'll settle your nerves, and you'll be radiant again in no time."

She nodded, staring regretfully at his hand still covering her own. "You have a silver tongue, man-with-the-magicked-face. But even silver tongues speak truth sometimes." She took a deep breath and pulled away, wandering off into the shadows once more.

Alone again, I said, "Sorry," referring to my bumbling attempt at gleaning information.

Ashley didn't comment, instead turning to a loose drawing in the journal. "I've seen this before," he said, voice low and thoughtful.

Bending over the desk, I cranked my neck to try and right the upside-down image. Three hexagons overlapped, with a circle joining them in the middle and intricate lines filling in the spaces.

Ashley knocked his head back in recognition, face clearing. "The hedge maze behind the palace—it's planted in this design."

I was about to ask how he'd possibly gotten an aerial view, when another thought stopped me in my tracks. "Are you saying the map resides in the hedge maze?"

"No." Ashley tucked the page back in the book. "Jacintha is the one that let it slip—map *pieces*. Three mages—three pieces of the map, each hidden using their magic. One of them was gifted with growing things. The hedge maze must contain his piece."

The scrap of gossip I'd overheard earlier squirmed in my ears. "Isn't it a spot for—kissing?" I barely managed to not squeak the word. I gulped, not wanting to think about leaving Buckingham grounds while alone with Ashley and his magic— let alone falling prey to a mysterious enchantment.

He smirked, but it came too late—almost...calculated in its delay. "You're welcome to stay behind if that makes you skittish, Miss St. James."

"I'm sure you would like that."

"I would." His palms planted on the desk so the tips of his fingers were only an inch from mine, his smile growing a dark edge. "I work faster alone. However diverting your company, you've only ever been a distraction."

My fingers curled in retreat, before I caught the action and pushed them back out. "But do you like being distracted, Mr. Gardner?" I forced myself to linger, to welcome his gaze, then cocked an eyebrow.

He swallowed. And after a sickeningly tense moment, to my surprise, he slowly straightened, a bitter look flashing over his features that swiftly disappeared.

You play the game differently now. You are changed.

For the better, I'd hope.

I think not.

But it was *he* who'd changed me; who'd turned me into someone I barely recognized.

I was in the middle of debating whether the moment counted as a success, when Ashley said, "Was." He crossed his arms over his chest. "It *was* a favorite spot for lovers. Guards have been posted at the maze's entrance since the beginning of Victoria's rule. The only entrance."

Chasing the logic, I frowned. "You won't be able to illusion us invisible unless we're off the grounds, deep in the maze. So how do we sneak in?"

"I'll workshop it."

I stepped around the desk to examine the drawing at a better angle. "What exactly is this enchantment?"

"That's the part I'm *not* worried about. We'll use your slant to wriggle out of any bind." Ashley leaned in, lowering his voice into something mocking. "What was it again? Being able to make a warm cup of tea anywhere?"

"My magic can only do cold tea, I'm afraid."

"Right—you said it wasn't useful."

"Perhaps we could use the tea to water the hedges, in hopes of curbing the enchantment."

"That would make your slant useful, which would also make you a liar."

"Not as bad a liar as some, Everett—Ah, I mean, *Mr. Gardner.*"

Our faces were close, our breaths mingling, our chests rising and falling to the same rhythm. Ashley noticed it too, because even though his smile flashed cheekier, the way he shifted away and returned to studying the journal was pointed. He was not interested in picking up where we'd left off. A wall stood between us—one which he was markedly, carefully maintaining, and which I had to discern how to scale.

"I still don't see how we are supposed to find a map piece in an entire maze," I said. It seemed more impossible than a needle in a haystack. We didn't even know what the map looked like, or whether it still existed.

Ashley thought a moment, and his stillness almost gave the impression that he didn't know what to do next—a thing I thought impossible. Then he pointed one more time at the drawing before shutting the book, a little too roughly for it being five hundred years old. "We look for the symbol."

14

Emmeline

The last time I'd been inside this house, whatever inch of wall space not eaten up by Mr. Joule's dynamic paintings had been covered in clocks. A constant ticking had followed me through winding hallways, and only after wondering about it all night had I been informed that Mr. Joule hopped on a new fad every fortnight, declaring it the peak of fashion.

Now, a few weeks later, his obsession had shifted drastically away from timepieces.

After showing me in, a butler bowed deeply and shambled off to inform Mr. Joule he had a visitor, giving me ample time to study the drapes embroidered with leeks. In another corner were wooden, vine-like pedestals, holding a ceramic cabbage vase and a glass dome protecting a rutabaga.

How shy Mr. Kelly knew someone like Mr. Joule—coveted painter and societal oddity—was a mystery.

Shortly, the small man appeared wearing a striped jade waistcoat with bright red, balled-up gloves popping out of his jacket like cherry tomatoes. A pale green silk cravat hung from his neck, its trailing, coiled ends mimicking the shape of squash vines.

Mr. Joule grew a frazzled frown that twitched when he came to a stop. "But where are the aubergines?" he demanded.

I blinked. "The...the what?"

"Might I say, what deviously shoddy service you provide. I've been waiting near twelve hours!"

He'd confused me for some kind of delivery girl. I glanced down at my outfit—a blue and cream polka dot number that, though a little dated, hardly cried *service trade*. "Sir, you're mistaken. I'm here to inquire about another matter."

"Is it a lengthy matter?"

I paused, unsure. Eccentricities aside, Mr. Joule seemed like a busy man who preferred to spend his time painting rather than answering impertinent questions from strangers. "It should only last five minutes."

"Could it be made to last for twenty?"

I frowned. Blinked some more. "What?"

He clapped and rubbed his hands, a wild glint entering his wide, wrinkly eyes, his voice threaded with a giggle. "I've just perfected the tea set. You shall join me!" He spun on his heel and streamed around a wood-paneled corner. After I'd stood speechless for a few more moments, a hand (nothing more of the man) reappeared and gestured hurriedly for me to follow.

I grinned and did.

"So, Miss Morgan," he began once we'd settled into iron chairs inside a stiflingly humid conservatory with creepers all about my feet, "what is it I can do for you?"

I cleared my throat, surprised he remembered my name as we'd only met once, and briefly. And also that, even knowing my identity, he'd still thought I'd been there to deliver aubergines. "I've been informed you have connections. Secretive connections."

Teacups constructed of curving, porcelain lettuce leaves filled with hot tea as Mr. Joule poured his mysterious concoction. Tapping a spoon against the bumpy green rim of his cup, he said, "You'll have to be more specific." Then he gestured for me to try the tea.

Remembering the purplish powder he'd scooped into the pot that had filled the room with a faint onion smell, I repressed a grimace. Red flakes floated on the surface of the steaming liquid. *It can't be worse than peppermint.*

I brought the cup to my lips and sipped. A hot, earthy taste coated my tongue, growing slimier and more acidic as it slid down my throat. My mouth shuddered on a gag. I was wrong. It was worse. "What do you know of a carriage service that uses no licenses?"

His wide eyes blinked at me while he swallowed from his cup. Too innocently. "Not much."

"I was told you could give me information about them."

"By whom?"

"Mr. Miles Kelly."

His face immediately brightened. "Ah, Kelly sent you! But why didn't you say so? Yes, I know of them. Use them frequently, in fact."

I sat back in my chair. "For what?"

"Odds and ends. Smuggling magicked paintings out of the country and things of the sort."

My eyes widened slightly at how openly he talked of his slant. He could be hanged if he mentioned it in the wrong company. If anything, it pointed to his enormous trust in Mr. Kelly.

"What about people?" I leaned in. "Is it ever used to transport people?"

"Oh, all the time. It's for disappearing *anything.*"

An odd way of phrasing it, but before me sat a very odd

man. If the black carriages provided the services Mr. Joule claimed, it was no wonder they hadn't turned up in the registry or in any of my searches. They were breaking the law.

Which meant they were dangerous, and any innocent nose-poking wouldn't be welcomed.

Distracted by these thoughts, I nearly took an idle sip of my tea but was saved by a rancid whiff jolting me back to my senses.

I would just have to be dangerous right back. *Sans* tea.

"How might I—?"

"Forget about ever discovering their headquarters, but if you want to get in touch with them..." He stood and disappeared through the conservatory door, only to reappear a few minutes later with a card in hand. He dropped into his seat and slid it over, tapping it with two fingers. "Here's my man. He's usually in the boxing rings at Elephant and Castle, south of the river. He'll get you an appointment. What were you planning on smuggling?"

A smirk crept across my lips as I stared at the little white card with bent corners. *An uncle,* I mutely answered.

But my smile quickly dropped when Mr. Joule said, "Never mind, we have so much else to talk about, and you've hardly touched your tea. Drink up! I have another pot brewing!"

15

Dorothy

Ashley wasn't just a person; he was a presence, almost ubiquitous in his ability to know things. And for that reason, even after watching him leave for the garden party half an hour ago, I trembled as I reached for the doorknob to his quarters. I half expected to find him lounging in a chair with a lazy smile, a cat watching a mouse scramble when she'd been caught by the tail. I sucked in a breath and plunged inside.

Inside was both warm and cool, fresh but slightly astringent in my throat. The bedcovers were disheveled and unmade, an empty water glass and half-eaten breakfast tray sitting on the nightstand. Pieces of clothing—all black—strewn the floor.

Working quickly, I checked in the nightstand, where I found a magnifying glass, a volume of Plato, two lockpicks, a timepiece, and several rumpled ascots. I checked the dresser drawers next, only finding clothes, careful to return everything to exactly how it was. Then I moved to less obvious places: behind curtains, paintings, and furniture, and under the rug and mattress, running a hand over every surface to check for hidden seams. I mainly found maps: large scrolls under the bed and crude drawings of routes—even a set of tiny miniatures in a box of cards within a secret desk compartment. Knowing they were probably what the Rook used to map his targets, I shivered.

But no bracelets.

After another half hour of searching, I was certain. Wherever Ashley was keeping them, it wasn't here. A painting hung backwards on the wall to display its plain brown backing, and, curiosity piqued, I peeked underneath to see why he'd turned it over.

Not a painting. A mirror.

Memories hit me—of him shaking and turning white as a sheet after glancing into a mirror at a factory. He'd barely been able to walk afterward.

I swallowed the questions and lowered the mirror. One of its sharp corners jabbed my finger and I hissed, watching a driblet of blood congregate on the tip. I sucked it away and slipped back out into the hallway, knowing I didn't have much time before Ashley would grow suspicious at my absence and come looking for me.

I hurried toward the garden party, smoothing my light pink chiffon dress, tucking brown curls behind my ear, and pulling on my evening gloves. A moonlit garden party was unusual, but so were all the events planned for the queen's seventieth birthday, replete with hunting bustards, a midnight ball, and culminating in a Shakespearean performance in a fortnight.

Torches lined the walk of Buckingham's backyard, leading the guests on a winding path speckled with purple petals, at the end of which towered an ivy arch. I stepped through, greeted by soft, trilling notes of harps, flutes, and piccolos. More torches lined the large perimeter, illuminating refreshment tables. June cherries dipped in crystallized sugar piled and glistened like jewels, next to fluffy sponge cake topped with rosewater whipped cream, and tiny quail eggs sprinkled in salt. Garbed in feathered tulle, glacé silk, and iridescent beads, guests mingled about the lawn, sipping champagne and playing quoits with poles of daisies.

To my right, a hedge wall loomed, its thick, centuries-old bushes rising well above my head. In the center of the wall gaped the opening to the maze, bracketed by a pair of ominous guards, shooting a shiver down my spine. We still didn't have a plan for sneaking inside, but with so many distractions before the guards, tonight was undoubtedly our best chance to act.

I scanned the guests for Ashley and, not seeing him, decided to amble toward the refreshment table. As I accepted a small dish of cake from one of the waitstaff, a group of tipsy matrons approached the other end of the table, speaking in low tones.

"...survived the fire all those years ago?" one said, adjusting the burgundy fabric around her bosom. "I heard it from my niece—it's circulating all around the *ton*."

"But how?" said the tallest of the group. "A little French boy—"

The last one snapped her fan shut. "He wouldn't be so little now. He'd be all grown and taking after his father, I suspect. The Renault family were known to have powerful slants. Magic ran thick in their blood—despite residing across the Channel."

The tall one wrinkled her nose. "But how could we tell if he *did* survive, if he never uses his slant?"

A laugh. "They also were known lawbreakers. Anthony Renault was, after all, ha..."

The group moved on, leaving me to wonder about the end of that sentence.

"Good evening, Miss St. James."

I turned. "Good evening, Mr. Brass." I'd assumed that only

the hundred-odd, invited guests were allowed at these events, but apparently being head of the Lightfoot Agency to the Queen granted special privileges. A shiny black tailcoat stretched his shoulders, and my gaze magnetized to the ornate steel buttons—a signature of his business. Which coat of Ashley's did the steel lion button found in my father's room the night he was kidnapped belong to?

I took a bite of my cake, warm vanilla hitting my tongue like a pillow.

Mr. Brass looked around the party and smiled even as he said to me out the side of his mouth, "Have you heard from Nicholas?"

I swallowed my heavenly bite. "Yes, he saw me settled into my quarters earlier."

Mr. Brass glanced back at me, and though his expression didn't change, a new spark entered his eye, and he seemed to analyze me with new intensity. "Did he now?"

"Is that... Is that against protocol?"

"Not expressly."

A stoic couple passed by, and Mr. Brass picked at the quail eggs and truffles on his plate until they were out of earshot again.

I eyed Mr. Brass, wondering if he had any information that could aid our search for the map, then turned to him. "What do you know of Edric?" It was one of the names we'd found in the archives.

He paused for a moment at the change in topic, then nodded. "One of the three mages. In his lifetime, he often expressed his regret over finding the Variance because it gave power to those ill-fitted for the responsibility." Mr. Brass tsked. "He wished there was some way to control it."

My face scrunched, not sure I understood. "Control what?"

"Those who had magic, and those who didn't." He sighed.

"It would certainly make our job easier. I can't tell you how many orphans I've seen abused; how many people left for dead because of slanting gone wrong. Sometimes it's an accident, but more often it's the power that gets to their heads." He glanced at me sideways. "Would you take people's slants away, if you could?"

I got the sense that I was being tested, and I weighed my answer carefully. "I hardly know. It seems justifiable in some cases. Like mine, when I couldn't control my slant."

Mr. Brass straightened and nodded. His slightly pleased smile prevented me from tacking on the other thought I had: that despite the inconvenience it'd caused in my life, I wouldn't know who I was without my slant. I'd feel empty, without identity.

So too, I imagined, would Ashley. Ashley had more magic than anyone I knew.

The gossip I'd just overheard, about a fire and a French boy from a prominent family, tickled my ears. In my father's lab, Ashley had confessed his mother died in a fire. Had he nearly died as well? It seemed silly to consider the rumors would be about him, and yet... Yet I couldn't stop the niggling feeling that it was a piece to his puzzle. And any information on the Rook's history could be weaponized against him.

"Do you know anything about the Renault family?" I asked.

Mr. Brass scratched his neck, brows slanting up in a hesitant, mournful grimace. "I... Unfortunately, yes. More than most, in fact."

I straightened.

"Working for the Agency, you'll learn the truth sooner or later, so I can relay the details. But I trust you understand the facts are confidential." He glanced around, then leaned in and lowered his voice. "Fifteen years ago, the Lightfoots got a tip that the Marquis de Avèjean across the Channel, Anthony Renault, had information about a second Variance. Not only that, but he had schemes to sell that information to the highest bidder. Even as a freshly minted agent, I'd climbed the Lightfoot ranks quickly, so I tagged along to France to stop the rumors."

My brow furrowed. "Why didn't the French government handle it?"

"Even internationally, magical matters are solely our jurisdiction, according to the Slant Charter. We captured Anthony Renault at his chateau and tried to cut a deal. He refused. We had no choice but to hang him.

"His..." A dark, slightly haunted expression twisted Mr. Brass's face. "His wife and family were supposed to be travelling in the Alps. We didn't know they were hiding in the house until he was already wriggling. At the time, strange propagandist reports were circulating about the Lightfoots—instigated by the marquis—that we were performing inhumane experiments on people, using their slants. A cult-like test to join our ranks. Though I was never subjected to it, I'm ashamed to admit that a few of our number had indeed performed these atrocities.

"The marquise believed her son would be better off dead than be taken into our custody, so she...she shot him, and herself, before we could stop her. It is one of the greatest regrets of my life. The French government requested we salvage the whole fiasco—to help them save face—so we set fire to the chateau and testified that the flames had claimed the entire Renault family. An accident."

My lips parted, horror turning my bites of cake to ash.

"Forgive me." Mr. Brass sighed. "Such things are distasteful to speak of."

"But..." I could hardly wrap my mind around such a nightmare. "That poor boy."

Mr. Brass gave a sad nod. "It's a tragedy the scale of which I've done everything in my career to avoid repeating." He inhaled, shrugging off the story. "I must be getting back to the office. Please pass along your progress to Mr. Hart, Miss St. James." He moved toward one of the games of quoits.

Trumpets silenced the twitter of conversations around the lawn as Queen Victoria appeared in a floral satin dress, a lace shawl draping her shoulders. Grandly for her small stature, she took her seat under a purple canopy, then snapped her fingers and said, "Percy."

An attendant's jowls waggled as he sprang forward and thudded his announcer stick against the brick path. "Esteemed guests," he said in a loud voice, "Her Majesty has a treat for you all tonight! It has taken several weeks of preparation..."

My ears tuned him out as Ashley appeared at my side and murmured, "Good evening, darling."

My insides balked at the endearment, falling so soft and natural from his lips. Eyes facing forward, I said, "Where have you been?"

He stuffed his hands in his pockets. "Gathering intel on the next piece of the map. But I think the real question is where have *you* been? You were late."

I kept my tone light, still staring straight ahead. "I was— primping."

Around us, guests drew closer to the announcer to better hear, but all I could concentrate on was the silence congealing between Ashley and me. When I could no longer bear it, I peeked at him from the corner of my eye, only to find him staring at my glove. I followed his gaze to the little spot of blood leaking through my white silk. The mirror.

I tucked the glove behind my back, and then we locked eyes. "Surgical scissors," I explained. Ashley's face was blank and he said nothing, but there was a knowing glint in his eye as he returned his attention to the announcer. The blood drained from my face.

He knows. He always *knows.*

But he would've said something. No, all he had right now were suspicions, which meant I needed to tread more carefully going forward.

Light applause brought me back to the torch-illuminated throng. Listening to the excited whispers around me, I gleaned what had been announced: a game.

"For centuries, lovers met here for their midnight trysts, and we wish to pay homage to that tonight, in a once-in-a-life-time opportunity to enter the maze." Delighted gasps broke out, forcing the announcer to raise his voice above the clamor. He raised his arm, from which dangled a rainbow of ribbons.

"Seven couples shall be joined by these seven ribbons. The first couple to retrieve their matching ribbon from within the maze and successfully return shall receive this fine silver trinket box. We realize more than seven pairs of you will wish to play, so in the spirit of forbidden love, plead your case to Her Majesty and you may be one of the lucky couples selected!" He banged his stick against the brick again, and the crowd erupted in a flurry of skirts and slicked hair.

Ashley pursed his lips. "Everyone will be watching the entrance for the returning couples. We wouldn't be able to slip in undetected unless—"

"We're one of the couples," I finished for him.

As one, we lined up with everyone else hoping to be bestowed with the honor. One by one, pairs were presented to Her Majesty. Occasionally, the Queen nodded her approval and Percy, the announcer, would join their wrists with one of the ribbons. First there were six ribbons left. Then five. Then four. I watched them dwindle as the line inched forward. Three more left. Two. Finally, we stood next in line. One.

Victoria smiled, her gaze lighting on Ashley when we stepped forward. "Well," she said, delicately tracing the turquoise silk in her lap. "Tell me—why should I bestow this last ribbon upon you? What makes your love special?"

"Is not every love special, when built on fascination and sacrifice?" Ashley began, an oddly soft tenor in his voice. The crowd slowly quieted. "In that way, I am no different from other men. I am not the first to travel the restless roads of the night, nor to burn with the heat of a thousand suns. But beside me stands my heart's compass, my soul's ballad, my life's dream. So pray, let me be weary. Let me burn. Let me prosper in this story a moment longer."

My face flamed. He didn't have to sound so...so beautiful, and...and *convincing*.

"What is love, Your Majesty, if not one grand story?" The party lay still, everyone bespelled by Ashley's words.

Victoria nodded, pleased. But her smile faltered when her gaze shifted to me, and I knew it was because while Ashley was suave and believable, I wasn't playing my part. I felt a subtle nudge from him on my arm. The Queen opened her mouth—to deny us.

I stepped forward. "If I may, Your Majesty. I... I disagree with Mr. Gardner." My voice sounded small and stilted at first, slowly growing steadier. "Our love was not earth-shattering like the ballads or stories of old."

"No?" She tilted her head, interest piqued. "Then what was it?"

"It was...quiet. And subtle, at first. An early morning spent tinkering in a lab, clinking tubes and drops of liquid, testing every reaction. But soon, yes, it burned hotter. It boiled over. Its heat could no longer be controlled or denied, much as I wished it could be."

Much as I wish to erase their burns now.

The entire lawn held their breaths, captured by our tale.

"And then I saw him and realized…I wasn't the only one who'd been testing it. Maybe it's that feeling—of wonder and seeing and holding your breath as you watch something explode—that turns chemistry into something *worthy* of ballads and stories."

I glanced at Ashley, but found I didn't have the courage to hold it, so I shifted my gaze to the Queen's feet while I finished. "Our…*love* may not be the most inspiring. It may not be perfect. And you may deny us this opportunity to prove it, Your Majesty, but one thing I know for certain. From the moment of our first meeting, I knew the answer to this complicated equation. For better or worse, our souls are bonded together, his and mine, and by something much stronger than a queen's ribbon."

A pit of shame yawned in my stomach, because—

It was true.

Every word was true.

Ashley held deathly still beside me, gaze burning into the side of my face.

The Queen's slitted eyes studied us a long time. "I think you are wrong," she said at last, and that was when I noted the mist in her eyes. "A love like that is earth-shattering indeed." She held the last ribbon out to Percy, who took it and approached us. Around us, cheers and applause resounded as my wrist was tied to Ashley's, disappointed sighs coming from those behind.

The game now had its players. We were going into the maze.

16

Dorothy

As Percy explained the rules, I felt Ashley's wrist against mine like a brand; the rest of me recoiled. He seemed equally uncomfortable with the contact, holding himself rigid. We stood among the other couples lined up before the maze entrance, listening to the last of our instructions.

"Heed the signs' warning you if you've ventured too deep into the maze. Each ribbon is hidden in a different section, so remember: You must retrieve *your* color. For every couple that does, a trumpet will sound. Last of all"—he paused for dramatic effect—"may the strongest love win!" He waved a red flag and the couples spurted forward with giggles and bright eyes.

We rushed forward with them and plunged inside. The dark hedge walls loomed twice my height, their thick leaves reflecting the moon. At every intersection, paving stones were set into the grass, one for every direction, mirroring a compass rose. Ashley led the way, taking a few turns like he knew where he was going.

Once the twittering of the other couples drifted away, Ashley slowed his pace and turned to me. Wordlessly, he untied the ribbon joining our hands. The second he was free, he took three steps back and cranked his neck, like he'd taken off a too-tight necktie and could breathe again.

"We should split up," he said, analyzing the green walls around us and avoiding eye contact. "We'll cover more ground."

I frowned. This felt like the archives all over again. Or maybe this was about what I'd said to the Queen. I couldn't care less about finding the map—but I couldn't get close to Ashley again and find the bracelets if he kept pushing me away.

"How would we alert the other if we found something?" I shook my head. "No, we stick together."

His eyebrows ticked up—probably because he wasn't used to me being so bold—but his mouth remained a thin, displeased line, and he still wouldn't look at me. "Fine. But we needn't stick too close." He turned on his heel and stalked around a corner, leaving me no choice but to follow.

After a dozen or so turns, we came to a turquoise ribbon tied to a hedge wall, which Ashley quickly retrieved. Handing it to me, he said, "First things first."

I stared at his retreating figure, too stunned to move. He'd known the Queen had planned this game and, given the guards, must've scouted from a window as they hid the ribbons before the party, and had memorized the path to it. In fact, he'd probably done so for all seven ribbons, since he couldn't have known which color we'd be assigned. All so we'd have a proper alibi.

It was so...*him*.

Something twisted in my heart, and I swallowed the wave of pain down as I followed Ashley again. Several minutes of navigating later, we came to a sign staked into the grass.

LEAVING BUCKINGHAM GROUNDS
TURN BACK NOW

Ashley didn't hesitate before stepping beyond it, while a distant trumpet announced that the first couple had retrieved their ribbon. A mist rose up from the ground, swirling around my chiffon dress as I walked. Despite the season nearing the height of summer, my fingertips numbed with cold. The deeper into the maze we delved, the thicker the mists grew, until the chill crept toward my palms. This must be the enchantment Jacintha warned about. The only reprieve was an uncanny warmth emanating from Ashley. *His magic,* I realized with a small amount of alarm. Now that we'd passed beyond the boundary that surrounded the palace, his magic might threaten to pull me toward him again.

As we walked, I edged farther away.

The hedge walls shifted like they were inhaling, then the white, biting fog gusted around me, sinking into my pores like needles. I stuttered mid-step, daunted by the breathing hedges and how bitterly cold I already was.

At every juncture, Ashley grew more indecisive, but he moved so quickly that his back often disappeared into the haze and only reappeared once he'd stopped at a new intersection.

Until it wasn't there at all.

My heart rate spiked, but I squeezed my arms around myself and kept walking, hoping he hadn't turned, and I simply needed to catch up. But after several more minutes, the hedges only stretched taller and the cloud around me thickened. My teeth chattered, which was when I realized: My vision had dulled, and that warm rush of his magic was gone.

I was alone.

The thick silence echoed like a bell. Pounding and tolling and turning my breaths into icy bursts. Wandering through the enchanted mist in a dress as thin and delicate as spun sugar made my skin convulse. Ice crept up my fingers, hardening them until I swore I heard them clack together. I was going to die out here.

Limbs wooden, I sprinted down the trail and frantically scanned the offshoots, but the movement did nothing to heat my blood. If anything, the chill grew sharper. The mist poured down my airways like an icy soup, freezing me from the inside.

Shivers wracked my muscles as I turned in a circle, searching for any signs of life. Down the hedge, something black rose up out of the fog. I scrambled back. A scream hit the lump in my throat and never broke free.

Ashley stood there, white wisps trickling off his shoulders. "Dolly," he said, his voice strained and loud. Nearing so quickly he appeared to glide on the mists, his fingers grazed mine, then quickly recoiled. His touch was hot. But his eyes remained wide and dazed, and it took me several beats to pinpoint why the expression was so alien.

He looked worried.

Ashley never looked worried. Controlled, prepared—yes. He never *had* to fret about anything because he was always two steps ahead; the ribbon still clenched in my fist proved that. Yet, every look, touch, and shared moment had all been a ploy to steal my family's bracelet—so why was he pretending to care now? What new game was he playing?

In the next moment, he locked the emotion down, breathing hard through his nostrils. Through a clenched jaw, he said, "You're freezing."

But I wasn't, now. The second he touched me, that familiar trickle of warmth spread through my core like a drug; his magic, lulling me toward him. The colors around me—my pink dress, the dark green hedge, the white moon, Ashley's black clothes and emerald eyes—seemed to expand and loom, so vivid they almost seemed alive.

I glared back at him, shrinking away, and the cold seeped

back in. If I wasn't careful, Ashley's magic was going to make me do something I'd regret. "I'm surprised you looked back at all."

Ashley paused. "I wasn't trying to lose you."

"You don't have to lie to make me feel better." And I tried to stop the next words, but they flew past my chattering teeth. "Like you've done so many times before."

His nostrils flared on an inhale, and he shifted out of his dark coat and settled it on my shoulders a little roughly, like he was angry at me for being cold. I warmed and thawed. My gaze fixed on his ascot, breathing in the space he'd stolen away. I could smell him. *Feel* him. Feel his hand on my face and his lips on my skin—

I dragged my gaze up.

As his pulsing green eyes bored into mine, his head fell to the side, slowly. His expression shifted. Darkened. "And you've never lied to me?" he muttered, tightening the coat around me.

I didn't feel guilty. I'd lied to him, initially, about the bracelet—before he'd stolen it—and I'd do it again. But now I was deceiving him about much bigger, deadlier things, and my heart thrashed in my throat at the thought of him uncovering them.

Struggling to keep my face blank, I whispered, "What do you mean?"

"A serving girl at a dinner party spilled soup on your dress —or rather, used her magic to *avoid* it."

Relief mixed with confusion over how he could know about an incident that had occurred before I met him. "What has that to do with—"

"She was arrested that night. Someone reported her." He walked away, and unwilling to leave the conversation there, I followed him.

"You think *I* did?"

Ashley's jaw clenched, but he stared at the ground. "Are you a spy?"

The question caught me so off guard, my jaw dropped and I struggled to form a response.

"Would you turn someone in for using their magic?"

"Of course not. I swear it wasn't me."

Finally, he looked at me, and he stared so long I felt all my lies start to wriggle like worms on my tongue. *I am a spy. I know who you are. I will bring my father back. I will outsmart you and bring you to your knees, even if it kills me.*

I couldn't say any of that, so instead I said, "But—it was still illegal."

"It shouldn't be."

"You'd rather have chaos?"

Ashley halted and faced me. "Do you hear yourself? Death is the penalty for using something you were born with? Regardless of what it is used *for*?"

Put like that, of course it sounded bad, especially given my history of not being in control of my slant for so long. But my ears rang with Mr. Brass's words, and I found I didn't disagree. By teaching others what Nicholas had taught me—to harness my magic—we could help those in the same predicament that I'd been in. That was what I'd wanted all along. "Magic is power, and power corrupts. We shouldn't trust that everyone with a slant won't use it for evil."

"Of course they will. And when they do, maybe they ought to hang. But it should still be their choice to make."

"Like how you choose to use *yours*?" Hostility coated the words, borne straight from the angry knot in my stomach, and I bit the inside of my cheek. I was venturing near dangerous territory. Letting on that I knew he was the Rook would ruin our whole operation; even endanger my life.

Don't mention the kidnappings.

Don't mention father.

Ashley's gaze cut down my figure then up, a dark question in them. I was supposed to be doing the *opposite* of making him more suspicious. But if I was to earn his trust, there were certain things that needed to be said between us.

I folded my arms. "You say you've never lied to me, but what about your scar?"

Ashley blinked, head slowly rearing back as realization washed over him.

"I saw it, on your collarbone," I went on. "I saw it that night in my bedroom while you were unconscious."

"I have hidden many things from you," he said quietly, brushing past me. "That is not the same as lying."

Secrets.

Secrets within secrets, and this constant game of tug-of-war to get a glimpse at them. I was tired of it.

We trekked the maze for several minutes in silence. The cold still burrowed toward my bones, but it was much more manageable when I stuck close to him. With every step, the mist thickened. At last, I said, "How did you get it?"

At first, I didn't think he'd answer, but then finally the low words came. "It's Greek. The *A* stands for *axios*, which roughly means *of weight*, or *of worth*." More walking, more silence. Then, "They call themselves the Order of the Worthy. They do not bestow their mark lightly."

"I thought they ceased to exist after Victoria ascended?"

His tone was flat. "They did not."

"So, you were part of them?"

Ashley gave a soft, mirthless chuckle. "I was a child. It was...given to me."

I frowned, trying to understand what he was saying. Someone had branded him? As a child? But where were his paren—

Dead.

I stuffed down the pity swelling up in my chest. He had no right to it. "And what does this order do, exactly?"

This time he didn't answer.

Another distant trumpet announced the return of another couple. After several more minutes of wandering, Ashley suddenly stopped at the next intersection, sighing. "We may need to call it for tonight and return later; your lips are blue and we've found no clues. How *could* we, when we can't even see our feet?"

"I can see my feet."

Ashley looked at me like I was mad.

I blinked. That's when I realized the trickle of warmth, the vivid colors... Something about Ashley's magic was heightening my senses and granting me the ability to see through the mist. My eyes widened, then caught on a paving stone at my toes. Unlike all the other stones in the maze, these had markings on them. "Do you see that?"

"What?" said Ashley.

"Markings on the stone."

That seemed to catch his interest. "Do they look like this?" Above his open palm appeared an illusion—glowing white lines forming the mage's symbol.

Fleetingly wondering how he could remember such an intricate shape and to such great detail, I studied the similarities between the floating emblems and the stone. "Mostly. It's missing these lines. Here, and here." I pointed them out on the symbol.

Ashley's eyes lit up as he ingested the information, then skimmed the hedge walls around us. He felt his feet along the grass until he found another stone, marking the start of a new path branching off. "Is there anything on this one?"

"Yes." Excitement vibrating in my fingertips, I drew the few lines in the air, and he copied it with his illusions to ensure the angles and position were accurate.

He shifted to the next path. "And here?"

We repeated the process until we'd come full circle. Then Ashley confidently pointed to a pathway. "This way."

"How can you tell?"

He drew the incomplete symbol in the air to his right. "This represents the direction we came from. And the stone I stand on"—he drew a few more lines to his left—"is the only one with these markings. Layer the designs on both"—he brought the glowing lines together with a burst and a smirk, obviously showing off—"and the symbol is complete." With a twist of his fingers, the lines whirlpooled into his palm and disappeared.

The playful way he used his slant was both boyish and annoying.

A few minutes later we came to another intersection. Again, I used my enhanced vision to view the pavers through the mist, and Ashley used his unparalleled memory to detect which lines were missing from the mage's symbol and which stone had them. Over and over, we worked together, until my stomach started to churn with something not unlike excitement.

It was working.

Right, then straight, then right, then left...

At last, after two more trumpets sounded, the hedge stretched into a long tunnel, at the end of which sat a clearing. The mist thinned to wisps, allowing me to see that the hedge grew in a ring. A path lined with white bricks that seemed to glow in the starlight wound its way up a slight incline toward the solitary structure standing in the center.

The stone gazebo had a gothic roof; its roman pillars were

draped in pink climbing roses. Even from a distance, their sweet smell coated my nostrils. I stepped into the clearing and immediately felt a hush roll over like a blanket, almost like I was stepping into a secluded cemetery.

Softly, I walked along the brick path. Once under the gazebo, I fingered a rose leaf until a glistening dew drop streaked down its petiole and soaked into my glove. I looked up to see arches in the roof that let in the moonlight. "Could the map piece be here?" I whispered, because I didn't dare speak louder.

"It has to be," Ashley replied, and I realized he'd followed me under the gazebo and was scanning the stone for clues. "This is where the paving stones led us." Then under his breath he added, "And it reeks of magic."

I squinted harder at the ceiling of the gazebo, decorated with delicate scrapes. "That's the symbol isn't it? There, in the center."

Ashley looked up and stopped. "It is. But I see no map." He centered himself under the design, drawing a path with his finger from it to the moon and then down to his feet. He cocked his head and crouched, pulling a knife from his boot. I had to circle around him to see what he'd found: Something sparkling in the limestone floor, the size of a half crown.

After a few minutes of work, Ashley managed to pry it loose. He held it up and squinted at it. "There are etchings. I think we must shine a light on it for the map to be revealed."

I eyed the opaque gemstone. "The map is...a jewel?"

"At least we know what we're looking for with the other pieces." Ashley stood, slowly turning it over in his hands.

The more I thought about it, the more it made sense. A gem was a lot more durable than a piece of paper and could be encased in a stone floor. How else would it have survived centuries? "I'm assuming you'll want to keep the gems with you."

"Not to brag, but I'm much better at keeping secretive things safe."

Bitterness snaked up my throat, an image of the bracelet inside my grandfather's statue resurfacing.

You've had a lot of practice.

You've had more secrets.

He was right, but I couldn't help thinking he wanted this arrangement because he still didn't trust me.

I felt an odd prickle at the back of my eyes before the roses grew impossibly pinker, as if no mist caressed their petals. Everything around me turned even more lurid, sharper. My blood flashed warm, and then I felt it.

His magic, tugging me forward. Slowly at first, and then more insistent.

I resisted, mind grappling for control. The magic yanked, and I gasped in a quiet breath, head swirling with sparkling stars.

He was still preoccupied with the jewel, profile strong, unaware of my internal battle. My gaze scraped down the hollow of his cheek to his lips, a knot of tension making me ache.

No.

It's the magic.

But I wanted it. More than anything, I wanted to taste his lips again, and my whole body seemed to throb with hunger. My eyelids drooped.

Something about this situation felt wrong, but that was a distant problem. All I knew right now was the smoldering sensation in my chest that threatened to consume me if I didn't draw nearer. *Him, him, him,* it insisted.

Lids falling, I inched closer, heady with his scent—warmed cardamom and smoke. I could feed on it...*live* on it. Warmth radiated from his skin, only centimeters from mine, even as he remained preoccupied with the gemstone.

The magic tugged again. *HIM.*

My lips brushed his jaw, and I couldn't help the way I immediately sighed.

Ashley stiffened. The jewel clinked to the floor.

I didn't care. The burning sensation had lost some tension, but now it was spreading. Building again. I opened my mouth and kissed his jaw a second time, farther down. The fragrance of roses and mist drifted around us, warming the air and making the moment glisten.

As if in a trance, his head turned until our noses brushed, kindling a deeper ache inside me. Then his fingers slid up to cradle my jaw. *Finally.* Moonlight skimmed his dark lashes as he stared down at me, his breaths shallow and heavy. Head swimming, I arched against him, a mute plea. He hesitated, then sucked in a breath and leaned down, just scarcely.

Firm hands fell to my shoulders and pushed me back.

Ashley's eyes were an ethereal green, but his mouth slashed downward, his brows set at a fierce angle. He swallowed, gaze flashing down my face again before saying darkly, "Do not do that again." His voice had a dark bent I'd never heard before— like he wasn't really talking to *me*, even though we were alone.

I blinked. Then blinked faster, shaking my head to reclaim my senses, and it jiggered loose the magic's hold. Slowly, air returned to my lungs. Blood returned to my face, and how it burned, realizing what I'd done. Worse, how much I'd *wanted* to do it—

No. It was the magic.

Only the magic.

And what was its aim? How would bringing me and Ashley together ultimately give him the bracelets? Or more power?

Ashley swiped the gem from the ground and pocketed it, throat bobbing. "Keep the coat," he murmured. Then he stepped out from under the gazebo and into the moonlight.

17

Ashley

Dust from the street rose up in clouds, coating my trousers every time I vaulted to the next rooftop. Below, Londoners queued at street pumps to fetch their daily water, or spit tobacco on the wooden roads of the less fashionable side.

Polina had insisted on meeting in person, even though it wasn't necessary, so the location was my revenge. The ballerina hated anything east of Holborn. Catching the navy uniform of a blueduster, I quickly flicked on an illusion, and his gaze passed over me.

My mind drifted to last night in the hedge maze, moonlight making Dorothy's curly hair glisten. She'd claimed she hadn't turned Wren in, and she had been so insistent that I'd given in and used my memory magic on her.

The mutation seemed to always worsen when I used my second slant to search memories. But in this case, I was glad I did, because I'd found that night in Dorothy's mind and confirmed the truth.

She was innocent.

The knowledge lifted a weight off my chest but filled it with something just as unbearable. Like a prickly, sticky ball rolling around and lurching at the mere thought of her. Thinking Dorothy was a traitor had been a bulwark to hide behind; my main argument for keeping my distance had just crumbled into nothing.

Now I didn't know what to think, and the new possibilities —the old ones—terrified me, because deep down I knew they weren't possible at all.

"*I didn't feel it,*" I'd muttered last night as we navigated out of the maze. After *the moment.* The mists had completely disappeared, the enchantment broken now that it no longer protected the map piece.

"*Feel what?*" Dorothy had said.

"*Feel the magic working. Not that time.*"

"*It's not you,*" she'd said quietly, brows furrowing. She hugged the hedge wall as we walked, her cheeks dusted with humiliation. "It's a progression of the mutation, you no longer sensing it. It means it's becoming more of its own entity. Less..." She seemed to connect the thought, then glanced at me sharply. "Less controllable.*"

I could've told her that. But sometimes magic was necessary, unpredictable as it was.

Or just habit.

Knowing the altercation had been my fault—not hers— filled me with shame, and a determination to limit our time together as much as possible so it wouldn't happen again.

Ahead of me, *The Southbank Serpent* crouched on warped timbers, its deep blue paint in need of a fresh coat. The inside smelled of turtle soup, which several patrons slurped at small tables. A quick glance at the walls told me a mirror hung on the south side—another habit—and I logged the information away.

I navigated up the stairs and into the second room on the right. An elegant figure did pliés near the window, the weak light catching her high cheekbones, along with all the dust motes twirling around her. "You are early," Polina said, her Russian accent muddying the words.

"In all fairness," I said, stuffing my hands in my pockets and shutting the door with my heel, "I didn't think *you* would be."

She chuckled and approached, eyes glittering in that familiar way that made my muscles clench. "Oh, Ashley." She fiddled with my waistcoat buttons.

I frowned and gently pushed her hand away.

"You are still ze same." She pouted, sashaying back toward the window, making the old boards creak. "Maybe I won't give you what you seek zis time."

"We made a deal."

She spun back. "And I never get what I want out of your *dealz*."

Because it was the magic making her want it. And it always would be. That was why I could never build something with any woman.

I'd thought—for one blissful moment, I'd dared hope—that Dorothy was different. Immune. That moment was all it'd taken for me to fall hard and fast, and now I was paying the price for it. I'd pay the price until I no longer drew breath.

I cocked my head. "Really? ...So you *want* me to tell everyone you're a Lightfoot Agent?" I said it lightly, but I knew the effect it would have on her.

Polina made an admirable effort to conceal her surprise, but the little twitches in her expression shifted through shock, denial, disbelief, then finally into disturbed acceptance.

She knew how. I had a hundred other people around London like her, whose sole job was to tell me things.

Until last week, I hadn't even known the agency existed and had only found it out through one of my informants. Being preoccupied as I was with the bracelets and then the map pieces, I had yet to do the proper digging into it, but I knew they were a Crown-sanctioned organization that handled magical matters. In other words, *hangings*.

A secret that big garnered me some leverage if Polina decided not to hold up her end of the bargain.

"Fine," she said at last, quietly. From under her skirts, she fished out a piece of paper and handed it to me. Unfolding it revealed a drawing of a crown, its peak curling into the mage's symbol. "It was constructed by one of the first mages—ze one that worked with metal. He made for friend who was exiling himself to Germany. The friend lived the rest of his life without his slant, it is rumored, since his magic couldn't renew at the source."

Ah yes. Magic was in the blood, but it could only go so long away from the Variance before it stopped working, and I'd experienced it firsthand whenever Bram's ship strayed too far around the world. That was what gave England the monopoly on magic; it wasn't just the people, it was the location.

And I'd wondered.

I'd wondered if it would work on me. To exile myself. If it would be worth it.

In the end, I couldn't abandon London. Not like Bram had. Even if I sailed to the edge of the world, I couldn't outrun the memories that haunted me. I'd rather go down in flames than live like a coward, because that was the only way to make the past mean something.

My parents' deaths, the people I'd lost... I *had* to make it mean something.

I studied the drawing, pleased that Polina had managed to unearth where the second map piece was hidden.

After everything with Dorothy the night before, I'd studied the etchings on the first gem for over an hour, unable to interpret them. Maybe the next piece would illuminate key information, but knowing where the second Variance was didn't actually matter, because I had no desire to open it—and I also happened to know Lark couldn't.

I folded the drawing and stuffed it in my pocket. "And where is the crown now?"

"I would not know zis thing. But it could be on display or in vault. Or your queen sometimes wears it."

"You'll get your payment the usual way." I turned to leave, then thought better of it and decided to do some of that digging. "Don't Lightfoot agents track down the slanted?"

She inched closer. "Yes. But I have no wish to hunt you."

My eyes narrowed. She knew I was slanted; it wasn't much of a surprise. I was so busy weighing whether to be wary I barely registered her still drawing closer.

One corner of her ruby lips lifted in a smirk. "At least...not in that way." Her eyes raked me up and down, and this time I did feel it—magic, draining. The air pulsed, an illusion shifting around Polina's form...changing her.

No.

I hissed and jerked back.

"You are lonely, Ashley." The Russian accent was gone. It was *her* voice.

"Stop," I whispered, panic rising.

Her irises cleared into a pale blue—so pale and hungry and pleading. And her lips. The lips I'd tried not to notice yet had somehow memorized every curve. They smiled invitingly.

A French garden smell wafted off her skin. My nostrils flared, mind clouding.

Dorothy rested three fingertips on my neck, and my heart

leapt to my throat in response. She was here. She was touching me.

She's touching me.

"I can fix it," she murmured, then covered my mouth with hers.

I stumbled back. Her hands buried into my hair. My back hit the wall, and I deepened the kiss, squeezing her to me. This. This was all I'd thought about since that night she'd patched me up in her bedroom. My mind tumbled and rolled like an ocean wave. Or maybe it was the euphoric reward of the magic spinning in—

Magic.

I shoved her off and gasped in a breath.

The illusion shattered. Polina stood before me, chest heaving, lips quaking. "*Asssshley...*" Dorothy whispered, and Polina started to morph again.

I hit the wall with my fist. "*Get out of my head!*"

The magic fled like a droplet of water against a blast of wind.

Inhaling deep breaths through clenched teeth, I fought for power over the illusion. I sensed the magic's discontent; the delayed, ireful way it obeyed me and slowly unhooked its claws.

I know what is best for you, it seemed to say as it meandered back to my palms.

You will see that soon.

You will.

I trembled and loosened my collar. The crevice in my chest widened, and the magic settled there like a black stain. A coiled snake. A weight that was going to drag me under very, very soon.

"What happened?" Polina fell back a few steps. Her eyes—

now lucid—widened and blinked as she took in my chaotic state. "You are angry."

"Not at you," I muttered. And I brushed past her and out of the room, before I could lose control again.

I raked a shaking hand through my hair and slumped against the wall in the stairwell, evening my breath. I needed to find the other map pieces and get the last bloody bracelet from Lark. At this rate, I wasn't even going to make it two weeks.

If the mutation took over completely... Historically, it had only happened once before, and I'd researched every bit of that occurrence. It had sealed up the Undercity and turned it into a black hole for magic—killing its host and hundreds in the process—and that was before London was such a grisly, burgeoning metropolis. An implosion with that radius today...might be cataclysmic.

My jaw pushed out. But it didn't matter—because it wasn't going to happen twice.

A conversation from one of the tables downstairs echoed up the stairwell, something about the odds of an upcoming pugilist match. Flashbacks of boxing with Bram on the foredeck flitted through my mind, every jab serving as a reminder of the promise made to my mother. I shoved the memory away.

Bram wasn't *here*. Though I was grateful he'd saved me—sharpened my skills and turned me into a weapon while hiding me from my enemies—there was no denying he'd take one look at the ship I was running and scowl. *This isn't what I trained you for, boy.*

But I couldn't take down the Order if I no longer controlled my own mind. I finished descending the stairs and wound around the chairs of the tavern, trying to order my thoughts, trying to plan my next move. A man at a tiny table watched me from above his pint, the dark trickle of porter dripping off his thick beard. I moved toward him.

"Not now," I murmured to Simmons as I brushed past. I didn't feel like dealing with any more updates at the moment.

His rough voice followed me. "Not sure as it can wait, sir."

I halted, then turned back, looking toward the far end of the room to appear more inconspicuous.

"He's made enemies." Simmons gulped from his pint, then set it back on the table. "Eight men are planning on jumping him tonight, at Castle Yard. By the look of them, he won't survive." Simmons dug a coin from his pocket and slapped it on the table before standing, donning his hat, and stepping out of the tavern.

I watched him leave and stood frozen for several more minutes. Then I clenched my teeth and sighed through my nose. I hated that I had this information. I hated that I still couldn't let the past go. That my magic was degenerating.

I knew where Miles was. It wasn't hard. My network kept close tabs on his comings and goings, and I told myself I'd given those orders only because I'd need the information later. Once I'd collected the last bracelet.

But even if I *wanted* to warn Miles of the ambush, he'd never remain in my presence long enough to listen.

Which really only left me one choice.

I pushed onto the street and walked a few paces before the bleeding hole in my chest made me slump against a lamppost. A memory from seven years ago swallowed me up.

MILES SHOVED *my face into the sand. Coarse grains stung my cheeks and spilled into my mouth, making me cough on the gritty, briny taste. With an iron grip, he pinned my arms behind my back, his weight settling on my hips. "Agincourt," he demanded.*

Sweat rolled down my temple, bare shoulders heated from both a half hour of wrestling and the scorching mid-day rays. "You think I'm made of syllables?"

"Say it."

My toes dug into the sand, angling for the brass sextant I'd buried earlier. Miles was superior at tussling, so I was constantly forced to innovate ways to give myself an upper hand. I left it here somewhere...

I groaned. "Remind me again why you chose that particular keyword to signal surrender?"

"Because you are French-born—"

"I find that offensive."

"—and surrendering is what the French do best."

"Turns out we're also top-notch at getting our spines crushed by seventeen-year-old Englishmen."

"I wasn't aware you had spines."

"You're just full of insults today."

"Take it up with your ancestors. Can't help it that we keep a stiff upper lip."

"That's just to hide all the bad teeth."

My left foot hit something solid, and I grinned, my triumphant exhale sending up a puff of silt. I gripped the metal between my toes, thanking every star for their dexterity.

There was a pause, and Miles stilled. "You're stalli—"

I kicked the sextant up and it whacked Miles's head, disorienting him enough that he slackened his hold. I wrenched out of his grip and twisted, hooking his neck and tackling him to the sand.

He growled. "You really"—he grunted through his teeth—"came to this spot hours ago and"—we rolled—"buried a sextant after we agreed to"—I straddled him and thrust his face into the ground, muffling the rest of his sentence—"no weapons?"

"We agreed to not being armed. You said nothing about the

beach." I cranked his arms into his back at a sharp angle, making him hiss. "Now what's that word you English are so fond of? Agercont? Argentin?"

To our left, a schooner inched by on the glittering water. Bram's whistle pealed toward us from The Hepzibah, signaling that they'd obtained the needed supplies from Naples down the shore and were ready for the open sea again. It was time to return to the ship.

I hopped off Miles and stood victoriously over him. "Guess I win, then."

He turned over and spit out some sand before glaring up at me. "Only because the sextant saved your stupid—"

"Sorry, can't hear you over the winning."

Miles rolled his eyes and retrieved his shirt from a few paces away. I did the same. In the distance, a sprawling patchwork of densely packed homes with terracotta tiles rose over the bay, and beyond it, the imposing shadow of Mount Vesuvius. After pulling on his linen shirt, he squinted, first at the sun, then at the ship. "Do you think they forgot Seymour when they were loading up?"

I scoffed. "How exactly does one forget a leopard?"

It had happened in the backstreets of Naples. After ditching Bram the second we docked, as we often did, the pair of us had followed a crowd to a dank backstreet of the city, where a wide hole in the ground covered by a metal grate had acted as an arena. Inside, dangerous animals clawed each other to death, speckling the cheering crowd above with gore. Entertainment reminiscent of ancient Rome but on a much smaller scale.

A leopard had prowled the pit, a champion beast from the whispers circulating the throng. Doors in the pit opened to admit three braying hyenas. The match was brutal and had ended with tufts of blood-stained fur littering the ground, and the leopard dead.

Miles stared at the carcass for so long, the crowd had dispersed and I was groaning in boredom. Only then did I glance down and see what he was so intent on.

Slowly, the leopard's chest rose and fell. It was alive. Barely.

Miles's tender heart couldn't bear it; he'd constructed a makeshift stretcher from some poles and a tattered sheet drying on a line and forced me to help him transport the animal. Approximately an hour later, he'd already named it. That was weeks ago, and while Miles had nursed it back to health, the leopard had been residing inside a borrowed cage, plopped inside the atrium of our rented villa. Living like a smelly king.

I cocked my head at The Hepzibah, already pulling farther away from shore. "You think they'll wait for us?"

"Nope."

We dove into the Mediterranean, letting the cerulean water wash away the grime on our tanned torsos as we lapped toward the schooner. My lungs burned by the time we reached the barnacled base of the ship, where a rope ladder waited.

Miles climbed aboard first, then turned to me, only a few steps behind, to offer me a hand up. I reached for it, but he withdrew it at the last second, eyes glinting with amusement. He shoved me instead. I fell backward, trailing laughter that broke off when I plunged into the sea.

When I finally sloshed my way on deck, I was ready with a quip and a way to get even, but stopped short when I saw his tense stance, his blanched, stricken face. I noticed everything else simultaneously:

The crew had gathered around a sailor gripping a white-bandaged stump where his hand used to be. His face creased in pain. A trail of blood connected him to where the leopard paced its cage, baring its teeth, red streaks staining the fur around its maw. To the other side of the cage, Bram bore a grim, determined expression, the one that made the hairs on my neck stand up.

"When...?" I began stupidly.

"When we were boarding." Bram's tone was clipped, but not unkind. He reached to his hip and unholstered his pistol, then approached us. He put the pistol in Miles's hand, which the younger boy held loosely. "Kill it."

Dazedly, Miles glanced from the pistol to Bram's sun-weathered face. "What?"

"Violence is all this beast has ever known, and if it lives, it will only grow more aggressive. The next time it attacks, we'll be lucky if it's only a hand."

My lips parted. I knew how much the beast meant to Miles. He'd spent hours salving its wounds, changing its bandages, and hand-feeding it scraps of venison—hours the leopard obviously did not remember, by the way it beat against the bars, snarling at Miles in a crazed rage.

It seemed too cruel to ask him to shoot something he'd named after his father. Rivulets of water trailed from my trousers and puddled around my feet. I stepped forward. "I could—"

Bram stopped me with a hand on my chest. "It must be Miles."

I gulped back my retort. Bram was using this as another test of some kind—trying to make Miles strong—and if I'd learned anything, it was that even though Bram's tests often seemed impossible, it was easier to complete them than to fail.

Failure meant grueling punishment.

Salt water dripped from my hair and pooled on my lips as I —along with the crew—waited in the slight breeze.

"Can you not do it?" Bram asked patiently.

Miles said nothing, still frozen. The column of his throat worked, eyebrows slanting up.

"Very well then. Perhaps some motivation." Bram nodded at

the sailor guarding the cage, who at the signal, lifted the lever and swung the entrance open.

The leopard leapt onto the deck, yowling in fury. Miles didn't raise the gun.

Adrenaline zapped through my limbs. Do it, I mutely urged. I volleyed between my friend and the approaching cat, and somehow I knew—Miles couldn't shoot it. He loved it. He was going to let the beast shred him.

The leopard leapt for Miles. I ripped the gun from his hands and launched in front of him. I fired three shots into the creature's skull. It fell to the deck, dead.

Miles stared at the spotted beast, face ashen, hands trembling.

A tense hush settled over the ship.

"Well done, Ashley." Bram approached with a reproachful eye, gingerly taking the smoking gun from my hands. I swallowed a hard lump. "For your bravery you have earned yourself twenty-four hours tied to the figurehead."

My gut recoiled. We were heading onto choppy waters, and there was nothing as loathsome as hanging slantways while salt water blasted you for hours on end; and if The Hepzibah happened to be caught in a storm, Bram didn't care if you half-drowned from the rise and dip of the bow. Twenty-four hours and not a minute less. But I couldn't forget the pain flashing in Miles's eyes, and I would do it again if I had to.

As the sailor with the bandaged hand was ushered below deck, Bram's attention shifted beyond my shoulder. "May you learn from this, son." His hand gently clapped Miles's neck and he gave him a stern look. "Sometimes the strongest mercy is to end the suffering. Some things are too broken to save." Bram dropped his hand and walked off.

Miles's eyes glimmered, the closest I'd ever seen him come to tears. We both stood in silence as the scene thawed and everyone *else returned to their duties, hoisting sails and tossing the carcass into the Mediterranean and swabbing up the blood. I tipped my head, a discordant note playing in my ears.*

Some things are *too broken* to save.

Then Miles's gaze cut up, and he looked at me, and looked at me, and the truth slowly inked onto my heart like a shaft of shadows carving an inscription:

Yes.

Some things are.

18

Emmeline

Lips pursed, I scanned the rowdy crowd around me, wondering if I'd made a grave mistake. *Oliver Cartwright* was the name penned on the white card in my palm; Mr. Joule's man in the black carriage service. And as fists pumped the air and spittle flew from red, dirty faces, I realized I had no physical descriptor to work with.

Magic pulled my face into a boyish resemblance, street urchin clothes hanging from my frame. I was grateful for the paltry disguise, as most of the fetid bodies surrounding me were male and hardly spared me a glance. Such would *not* have been the case if I'd come in my delicate satin polka-dot dress trimmed with Belgian lace. Liquor splashed down beards as men bellowed at the boxers in the center of the room, and it stickied the floor in foul puddles. Another reason I was grateful I hadn't worn a beautiful dress.

"Come on, Cartwright!" a man shouted into my ear.

I rubbed the ear on my shoulder and glared at him, before registering what he'd said. My eyes flew to the rubber ring. Joule said I could *find* him here, not that he was one of the boxers. Maybe because he was Mr. Joule's man I'd expected him to be like him: small, friendly, getting on in years.

Cartwright was the opposite: a towering specimen with thick muscles and a curled mustache that threw powerful jabs at his opponent.

And his opponent—

My jaw dropped as the crowd picked up the chant.

"Kel-ly! Kel-ly!"

A familiar bare torso—not that I'd studied it—or was studying it now—glistened under the sparse gas lighting as he approached Cartwright, fists raised. They exchanged a few blows, then Miles was thrown against the rubber ring.

And before he got his bearings and turned around, time slowed to a standstill as he lifted his head and we locked eyes. Even in the low light, I could see the confusion shuttering his eyes, followed by surprise. His eyebrows twitched, taking in my urchin clothes. I gulped. He scowled. Then Cartwright was on him again, ripping his attention away.

The way they moved—jabbing, dodging, bouncing on their feet—was a masculine sort of dance. Testing, poking, then striking hard when they found a weakness. They circled each other for what seemed like an age, and then something equally magical and devastating happened—Miles sidestepped and pommeled, moving so lightning-fast I only followed half his punches. He was beating his opponent to a bloody pulp. The crowd roared.

Stop! He's my only lead! I wanted to scream, even as my insides cheered along with the mob. I covered my mouth, transfixed until Cartwright collapsed to the canvas.

The second he was down, Miles's gaze whipped sideways, and I ducked, watching through various limbs as he skimmed the crowd for me. I inched backward and circled the ring of bodies, tracking Cartwright as two men gingerly pulled his limp body into a back room. Sticking to the shadows, I followed, keeping one eye trained on Miles who was being swarmed with fans.

I waited quietly in an alcove until I saw Mr. Cartwright's handlers exit the room they'd stowed him in, then ducked inside. Grimy wallpaper peeled away from the brick wall in generous strips. A pile of bloodied rags were heaped in one corner of the small space, giving the air a copper tang. On a bench opposite them, Mr. Cartwright slumped against the wall, eyes shut and one beginning to swell something awful.

I cleared my throat. "Mr. Cartwright?"

He didn't open his working eye.

"I'm sorry to disturb your rest, Mr. Cartwright, but I must speak with you."

He didn't so much as lift a finger.

Drat it all. I inched toward him, nervous energy giving me courage. I cleared my throat again, then gently patted his cheek. "Wakey-wakey."

Gah, why was that what came out? Childish. I needed to show I was in control of the situation; a woman—no, urchin (I'd nearly forgot!)—that commanded respect.

I thrust my shoulders back. "Now is not the time to be incapacitated, young man!" Then I hit his face much harder than I intended, immediately hissing and apologizing and wondering what kind of money there was in boxing and that maybe I ought to give it a try myself, but of course none of it mattered. He still failed to stir.

Then I heard a voice behind me mutter, "What are you doing here?"

I whipped around and, much to my growing dread, saw Miles Kelly—body battered, though thankfully shirted— standing in the doorway.

19

Miles

Raggedly boyish clothes hung from her frame, magic making her jaw squarer and her nose more angular under her brown cap. Same dark eyes, though. Same freckles and lips.

"You..." She frowned. "You spoke a full sentence just now."

I straightened, only just realizing that fact myself. Maybe her jabbering presence was beginning to break past my defenses. Or... "You look more like Emerson." And it was playing tricks on my brain. Either way, my tongue was miraculously weightless.

"Emer—oh." She rocked back on her heels, remembering the fake name she gave me in the alley after I'd caught her gambling, dressed exactly as she was now.

My gaze shifted between her, the slip of paper with Joule's handwriting in her hand, and the man I'd rendered unconscious, all the time ignoring that protective swelling in my chest I was beginning to associate with her. "He works for the black carriage company?"

She folded her arms. "I don't see how that concerns you."

"It doesn't," I said flatly, ignoring it again.

"Good." She arched a brow and made a go-away gesture with her hand, but her breaths were shallow and quick. She kept shifting her weight while gnawing the inside of her cheek.

She was nervous. And though I didn't know whether it was because of me or the hundred uncouth men in the other room, I did know one thing: She was woefully unprepared to navigate this seedy side of London.

That nagging, *caring* feeling burned hotter, making me flare my nostrils. "...But if it *did* concern me—what exactly is your plan?"

Emmeline arched her neck in that defiant, feminine way— so at odds with her currently boyish face—and put her hands on her hips. "And why would I ever tell you, knowing your *friend?*"

"I want to help." I could practically *see* the words as they left my lips, and I blinked at them, surprised they'd slipped out. But not surprised I felt that way. No, the guilt had been steadily eating away at me, one sleepless night at a time.

I could've stopped Ashley. I alone saw what he was becoming and had done nothing because of our friendship, our history, my hope that he was still good at heart. Now dozens were insane and Dorothy's father vanished, and all I'd wanted was to sail away from the mess I could've prevented. But that was before a chance to make things right had practically fallen into my lap.

And before I'd sent this girl walking straight into trouble.

"I directed you to Joule," I went on when she still appeared unconvinced. "I didn't have to."

"You didn't have to stab my cousin in the back either."

"You wake him up"—I pointed at Cartwright's slumped form, jaw clenched—"and what do you say to him? 'I know you work for a carriage company that's making deals under the table, could you point me to your headquarters so I can spy out the worker who chauffeured my uncle'? Their whole business relies on *not* being found, especially as they make a lot of powerful people very angry. You think he's going to offer that information freely?"

She opened her mouth, but I plowed on, feeling—perhaps for the first time—unable to stop the words from spewing.

"No, you thought to hire them and smoke them out, but you forgot they deal exclusively with the upper crust. Cartwright'll take one look at your clothes, laugh in your face, and then he's gone. These people—one whiff of someone digging, they vanish, and so does your only chance. You get one shot. That's how these things work."

Her cheeks reddened, and in the corner, Cartwright stirred. After a few moments she muttered, "I think I liked you better silent."

I snapped my mouth shut and swallowed, not disagreeing.

She huffed a sigh. "Fine. Give me your clothes."

I blinked. I hated the strange swirl I felt in my stomach at those words from her lips. "Pardon?"

"If I'm going to *be convincing* as you say, I'll need your clothes."

My feet grew roots into the floor.

When Cartwright stirred again, she snapped her fingers in my face. "Hurry, we only have another minute!"

But I remained frozen in confusion until she'd undone two of my vest buttons and wriggled one of my arms from my jacket sleeve. I jumped back. "All right!" I said, if only to keep her from pawing the rest of me.

I dressed down to my undershirt and trousers, then watched Emmeline slide into my jacket and shoes, which dwarfed her small frame. She looked ridiculous. That was, until she used her slant and her face morphed in front of me. Her face narrowed, eyebrows growing bushy and lips thinning until she vaguely resembled someone familiar…

Her father, Benedick Morgan.

My lips parted, but before I could question what she was doing, Cartwright sat up.

Rubbing his head, he asked groggily, "Who are… What are you doing in my dressing room?"

"My name is Benedick Morgan," she said, and I cocked my head. I never guessed her petite voice could go that deep. Her crisp, commanding diction came impressively close to the man's as she shouldered up to her full height. "I've made my coin in finance and shipping, but I also come from a noble, upstanding family line. Perhaps you've heard of me?"

"Mr.…" Cartwright's clouded eyes cleared, taking Emmeline in and obviously buying her disguise despite the ill-fitting clothing. I must've hit him harder than I thought. "Mr. Morgan. Yes, of course." Then he noticed me and frowned, then coughed. "You two know each other?"

"I have a job for the black carriage service." She handed him Joule's card to show him she could be trusted. My brows ticked up. So she'd planned one smart move.

But this kind of game didn't rely on *one smart move*. It relied on you making smart move after smart move without room for the smallest error, or you'd be beaten to mush and dumped in a back alley to bleed out. My nostrils flared, imagining the sight.

Cartwright worked his mouth, eyes darting shiftily between us and the card, before landing squarely on me. "I don't know what you're talking about." He reached for his boots under the bench, grimacing—probably from a rib I'd broken.

Black fog. He was denying her to get back at me.

"It's a small job, and I pay handsomely," Emmeline said quickly, still in her father's voice.

With slow, pained movements, he put on a white shirt and slipped it under his suspenders. "Sorry, sir. You have the wrong man."

"I'll lose," I found myself saying, then immediately berated myself. *Shut up, Miles.*

I had one week until I met Barnam, and only one match before then. Tossing it meant less money. Less money meant no ship. All for a girl who scowled at me, eyes bugging as if to say *What in blazes are you doing?*

I wished I knew.

I wished this situation—and everything else that had happened—wasn't my fault.

Swallowing the bad taste in my mouth, I said, "I'll throw the next match. Narrowly. But only if you'll allow...*Mr. Morgan* to hire your services." I'd pull a couple shifts at the docks, sweep chimneys, fetch water—*something*—to make up the money.

Cartwright studied the card again, his pursed, bloody lips slowly ticking up at the corners. He pocketed the card then stood, thumbs hooked under his suspenders. "We'll be in touch."

"Make sure to contact me at Nevin's apartments," she rushed to say. Then noticeably deepened her pitch. "On Warley in Bethnal Green."

He eyed her with an amused glint. But nodded.

Emmeline offered her hand to shake as a gentleman would do, but Cartwright brushed past it and out the door. Sliding out of her extra layers, Emmeline dropped her magic. I felt my tongue immediately tie itself in a knot, and I suddenly became aware of how tiny a room this was, and that it was rather hot.

"Thanks for your help today." Frowning, she shoved the jacket into my hands so hard I fell back a step. Her expression flashed with remorse, indecision, before it hardened. "But it's tainted with your guilt. So, in the future, just so we're clear—I don't *need* your help anymore, silent or otherwise. See you back at our flat."

I opened my mouth, but of course nothing came out, and she flounced out of the room before I could muster a stuttered retort.

I huffed a sigh, glaring at the empty doorway and working my jaw. "*My* flat."

I STEPPED INTO *THE DOLPHIN*. Steams of cooked eel met my nose along with the salty smell of oysters, and like always, only half a dozen candles lit the dim tavern. I expected my gaze to cut to the booth where I'd first seen Emmeline, gambling with a sailor and a chimney worker and getting out of her depth.

But my impending meeting with the Mole must have been looming larger than I thought, because my mind instead drifted to the memory of Bram on his deathbed, and the secret he'd uttered.

I sat in a chair next to Bram's bed in the captain's cabin. Ashley sat on the other side, gripping his godfather's hand with a fierce, devastated set to his mouth. Bram's leathery face lay stark against the pillow, but that starkness drained with every ounce of life slipping out of him. Ashley and I locked eyes, and in that moment, we both knew.

We were too far from port. This was to be Bram's last voyage.

Bram stirred, eyelids flicking open.

Ashley sat forward. "Bram? Can you hear me?"

Quiet reigned. Then his lips parted, and his head fell over to look at Ashley. "Leave me now." He slowly gasped in another breath. "I would speak alone with Miles."

We both sat in stunned silence. Ashley's face fell, and I could see how badly he wished to seek Bram's advice, make these last sentient moments count. Instead, these precious minutes were being granted to me, and we both knew I didn't deserve them. Bram should be asking to be alone with his heir. With his godson.

With the boy he had loved more.

"Leave," Bram said again. Ashley blinked, then slowly rose from his chair and shuffled out of the room.

Bram's glazed eyes stared straight ahead. "You will look after him?"

I nodded, tongue too thick to speak. It wasn't even a question, but I understood his need to ask it.

"Keep him from himself," he went on. "Or he will get lost in the knots of his mind."

I nodded again. And I waited, unsure whether I should call Ashley back.

Bram's shaky fist opened, a bit of silver gleaming in his palm. "The bottom drawer," he rasped. I looked between his face and the key, before gently sweeping it up and walking to his desk where I slid it into the lock. Inside was the last thing I ever expected to see.

A woman's filigree hairpin, crowned in flowers.

I relocked the drawer and held the object out to him, but Bram didn't take it. Instead, his lids fell softly closed. "Ashley has a twin sister."

The hairpin suddenly felt twice as heavy in my hand. My mouth parted and I slowly sank into my chair. "Why has he never mentioned...?"

"He does not remember her. The memories are missing."

My jaw went slack, and I grew as still as the man dying across from me. Finally, I managed to voice the quiet, fearful question. "Who took them?"

"Promise me," Bram croaked. His eyes fluttered, his breathing growing so labored that I flinched toward him. "...Promise...me...that you will keep this secret from Ashley. That you will find her. And that you will not let him see her until... until she restores..."

His chest stalled.

"Bram—"

His eyes flew open and landed on me. He wheezed in a painful breath. "Promise me!" he whispered.

"I promise," I whispered back.

"You have always...been good, Miles." A tear meandered down his cheek. "But Ashley...has always been great." Bram's chest rose and fell three more times before his skin grayed and he fell completely still. My vision swam and the boat lurched, and I yelled for Ashley over and over. And my last question burned at the back of my mouth, never to be uttered because the only person who could answer it was dead.

Until she restored...what?

The Mole was already waiting for me at the corner booth, his greasy hair plastered over his forehead and curling near his shoulders. He lapped at a mug of ale that was no doubt on my tab, and watched me approach.

"Wasn't sure 'f you'd show, Mr. Kelly."

"Neither was I," I admitted, sliding into the booth.

"It's about the girl. It was a doddle to find her for you before, and I don't know what you did to set her hair on end—"

My gaze batted to the side in annoyance. "It was not her I frightened, but her handlers. She was to meet me at Whitechapel where I would take her to a waiting boat, and yet somehow, all the wrong parties got wind of our plan. She never showed. By the time I got to her residence, it was abandoned." My fingers tapped the table. "Since we're casting aspersions, I might claim that someone sold me out."

"I take great umbrage!" the Mole said, hooked nose sniffing. "My work is clean."

I was tired and irritable. I sighed, trying to reorder my thoughts, but the Mole went on.

"Regardless, 'tis made my rummaging a lot more difficult. Ah've only just unearthed where she is now, if you'd like to know."

"It doesn't matter," I muttered. "I no longer need to contact her." I set a few bank notes on the table. "For all your trouble."

"Right shame, that." But he grinned, crooked teeth shining yellow in the candlelight. He stuffed the bills into his coat. "Well, sir. If ever you change your mind, I have the channels, and she awaits your reply."

I started. "She sent a message?"

The Mole slid a paper across the table. "Only this."

I unfolded the paper.

Where is Ashley?

I stared at the name, and the longer I stared, the more it seemed to bleed through the paper and ink out to the corners. The fact that her first thought was for her twin, and not for orchestrating her own escape, spoke to her character. But it did nothing to mollify the festering wound inside me.

Everything was always about him.

If the Mole was as trustworthy as he claimed, then it had to be someone on her end who had uncovered our plan to meet at Whitechapel. Someone had made her vanish. Someone had been keeping her a secret all these years.

But contacting her would make me start caring again, dragging me back into a fight that was not my own. Let Ashley solve it, if he was so clever. And that weight in my chest...that was a silly promise I'd made to a dead old man, who had called enough shots in my life already.

The Mole blinked his beady eyes at me. "Would you like to send a reply?"

I read the message one more time, before saying slowly, "No." I stood, signaling the end of the conversation. "No, I would not."

20

Dorothy

With shimmery charmeuse skirts flowing around my ankles, I descended the grand curving marble staircase, keeping my steps light to avoid waking anyone. No one was about except for a handful of servants, and Nicholas must've known that would be the case when he sent me the note last night. I'd recognized his script immediately.

Meet me under the willow tree by the south pond
Just before dawn

The air outside brimmed with a dewy scent and distant birdcall, the grass swishing underfoot as I traversed Buckingham's back lawns in the dim light. It was only a few minutes' walk to the bent willow, one side of its fronds dipping into the water, but the tree was situated outside of the palace's black hole radius, and far enough to evade prying eyes. When I stepped inside its protective covering, Nicholas was waiting for me.

His brown hair was styled but damp against his temples,

like he'd come from a swim. When he saw me, his eyes lit up, the freckle above his lip lifting as he smiled. "Morning," he said quietly.

I wasn't prepared for the little swirl of butterflies I felt at seeing his expression, so it took me several moments to formulate a response. "Hello."

The soft smile continued to play on his lips. "Your hair..."

I'd woken a little late, so I'd dressed without fixing it. "Oh..." My hair was always a curly, wild tangle in the morning, and I probably looked a fright. I quickly combed it with my fingers and wove it into a side braid and tied it off with a lucky bit of string I found in my pocket, face warming.

Nicholas swung the willow fronds aside like a curtain. "Shall we?"

Mutely, I stepped through the opening, scrubbing the heat from my cheeks. In the stillness, we walked along the pond's edge for several minutes.

"You remind me of my mother," Nicholas said at last, breaking the silence. He scooped some pebbles from the ground and glanced at me. "With your hair down like that."

"I hope that is a good thing."

"Very much so."

I studied his strong jaw and wet hair, wondering what his parents looked like. "I should like to meet her."

"I call her mother, but the truth is, I grew up in an orphanage." He said it with a hint of sadness.

"...Oh."

"The worst kind, where they beat us, or forced laudanum down our throats if we grew too unruly. They used to feed us rats. One of us was always vomiting or badly bruised or both, and for a long time, I struggled to believe there was any good in the world. I thought...maybe there was no point in living."

My lips parted as I stared at his profile, a surge of sympathy making it difficult to speak.

"Then one day, right as I was about to—" He stopped, shaking his head. "A fire spread through the building, and it changed everything. Mr. Brass found me among the ashes and brought me into his home."

Several puzzle pieces clicked into place; the loving way Mr. Brass regarded Nicholas, their closeness. "I didn't know he was your father."

Nicholas nodded. "More than my own blood. He made me see that there is right and wrong, and that one person standing up for their beliefs can turn the tide. That maybe...maybe I ought to live, after all."

As he skipped a few pebbles on the water's surface, I remembered Mr. Brass's words from the garden party. *I can't tell you how many orphans I've seen abused; how many people left for dead because of slanting gone wrong.* The thought spurred another one—one I hadn't considered before.

If something had happened to my father...I was also an orphan. I bit my lip. Would Brass and Nicholas extend the same kindness to me? Take me in as one of their own?

Something told me they would.

Nicholas inhaled a deep breath and turned to me, shaking off the serious conversation. "Enough about me. Are you ready for another session?"

The magic in my blood stirred, bouncing with energy that was eager to be used. That alone was evidence that my slant was getting stronger; it never used to react like that. I nodded, and Nicholas instructed me on how to push through the mental barriers to land further in the future.

I closed my eyes, blocking out Nicholas's expression filled with sad kindness, and followed his promptings. I dove into my mind, fingering the thousands of strings that wove my fate.

Choosing the right one was critical, because I couldn't hop between them, and neither did I have enough magic to explore multiple. But a common thread wound through them all, and I could see clearly what it was: my goal. To find the bracelets and capture the Rook.

I tugged on one and lurched into the future, people and settings zooming past in a blur. I stood outside Ashley's quarters, knocking. He answered it in wrinkled clothing, and we bantered about his appearance before I nudged the conversation toward what I was learning about the three mages—and the whereabouts of their magical objects. He gave a vague answer and deftly changed the subject. The vision winked out, and my magic spent, I returned to my view of the still pond, frustrated.

"How far did you go?" Nicholas asked beside me.

"About an hour, I think."

His face glowed with the good news. "That's incredible. Now that you know how, you can work on expanding your abilities on your own time."

I tried to put the failure of Ashley's exchange from my mind, because Nicholas was right. Considering my state a few weeks ago, my progress *was* incredible.

Nicholas cleared his throat, all business again. "Do you have an update on the bracelets?"

"I've not found them." I fingered the tall blades of riverbank grass as we continued walking. "Nor do I have any inkling where Ashley is keeping them. I tried searching his rooms but saw no sign of them."

Nicholas shook his head. "I, too, searched his rooms. He's not fool enough to keep them that near."

"But he wouldn't keep them too far, either." The problem was, there were a million places fitting that criterion.

"My agents are receiving reports of sightings of him around the town, but it's shoddy at best."

I nodded. "The second Variance map was split into three pieces, each piece constructed by one of the first mages. We found the first one five days ago."

Nicholas's brows raised. "Five days?"

"I know," I sighed. "I haven't heard from Ashley since, and I found it suspicious when he didn't attend the hunting party or the charity concert. People have begun asking me where my fiancé is."

"I bribed a few maids to keep an eye on his comings and goings, but according to them, he hasn't left his quarters at all. I wish I knew if it was another game—and he's slipping out a different way—or if he's locked inside planning something. Or if the maids are incompetent." Nicholas made a thoughtful sound in his throat. "Have you considered going to him? We only have nine days left for you to earn his trust."

My insides squirmed. I was doing an intensely poor job of that. "I wouldn't know what to say."

"You don't have to say anything." Nicholas cocked his head. "There's something about you, Dorothy. Something that makes a person certain they can trust you; like there's an extra measure of safety in you holding their secret too. People *want* to tell you things. Want to be close to you."

I could've imagined it, but as he said it, Nicholas seemed to inch nearer to me as we walked. I shook my head. "I don't see why."

"Because you're—" He sighed, and it ended in a soft chuckle. "*Good.* And you make a man believe he can be good, too. No one is immune to that kind of hope, not even the Rook."

Maybe I had been good, once. But it didn't feel like that anymore—and not because I'd chosen it. My ribs caved in, protecting my broken, bitter heart. I'd been forced to see the ugly side of the world, and I couldn't go back to being ignorant.

Ignorance is bliss.

Nicholas halted and turned to me, gray eyes drinking me in. "He doesn't stand a chance," he said quietly, and a warm heat pooled in my belly. "Just be yourself and he won't be able to help spilling his heart to you."

My lips parted. We weren't talking of Ashley anymore. My pulse thrummed with frightened anticipation.

"He'll feel like...he's drowning and will never breathe again unless he sees you." Nicholas's gaze wandered my face, and he swallowed like he was struggling for breath now. "Touches you." His thumb drifted down the side of my face and smoothed over my cheek, his voice turning impossibly soft. "...Kisses you."

Pink rays broke the horizon. Doves gently called and glided over the glistening water. Nicholas leaned in, warm lips brushing over mine, and after a moment's hesitation, I kissed him back. My skin tingled. When he pulled away, he looked different. Stronger and safer, and like someone who could fight the shadows for me and win.

But someone had made me feel like that before.

It must've shone in my eyes because Nicholas slipped his fingers to the back of my neck, his stare growing grave. "Dorothy, I'm not like him."

The ache in my chest grew heavier, crowding up my throat. "Are you not?"

"I know what I want." His thumb brushed over my lips, then his eyes flicked up. "I always have, and I would never do anything to hurt you. I am not hiding anything. What you see before you...is exactly what I am."

Something inside me broke at those words, and what

spilled out was relief. From the past, from the torment and anger. I collapsed against him, a single tear streaking my face as he clutched me to him, cradling my head. We didn't move for several minutes, the dawn embracing us as we embraced each other.

21

Emmeline

As I trekked up the stairs to the flat, I stared at the crisp paper gripped between my fingers, lips screwing to one side of my face.

Please fill out the residential address you would like
your goods delivered to this Thursday at eleven p.m.
Leave an envelope atop them with 20 pounds inside.
Extra fees to be charged for delivery outside London.

The note was from Oliver Cartwright at the Black Carriage service. Miles had come back from boxing yesterday and wordlessly set it on the bed, and that was when I knew I had several problems. One, I owned no illegal goods to transport. Two, I had no residential address I could send said nonexistent goods to, if they were picking it up from here. And three, I hadn't two pennies to rub together.

I'd easily found the solution to the money problem, albeit a painful one. The periwinkle dress Dorothy had sent me was both chic and extravagant, and I'd allowed myself the small luxury of trying it on once—just to feel the buttery silk slide against my skin—before carting it to market. Twenty pounds was a hefty price for a dress, but it would fetch at least thirty for the mustachioed man I'd sold it to, if he played his cards right.

Under my arms, I carried both my dinner wrapped in brown paper, and the solution to the illegal goods problem. I'd called on Mr. Joule again and drank four cups of eggplant tea in exchange for one of his magical paintings. He'd definitely gotten the better end of the deal.

But that still left no residential address.

When I stepped into the flat, Alice meowed and arched against my skirts, probably smelling the food. Miles sat in the corner in a white undershirt, changing the dressing on his bloody knuckles.

"Afternoon," I said.

He didn't even look up. I scowled and shut the door behind me, then set my packages on the bed.

Over the past week, the man had hardly said a word, and yet he was growing more irritating by the day. Perhaps because I was beginning to understand his silent language far better than I'd like. He didn't *have* to say anything.

He had tells.

Not looking at me meant he was annoyed. Shock made him turn away. Disgust made his upper lip pucker—oh so slightly. If he disagreed with me—which was frequently—he only stared at me with the blankest stare, capable of cracking stone. Worst of all, he breathed more deeply when he was angry, like he was trying to control it instead of getting snippy like a normal person.

George's tomb, I was sick of it.

I sank onto the bed and unwrapped my dinner—a Yorkshire pudding, but without the trappings of gravy and vegetables.

The cat followed me to the bed, meowing louder. "Ah, are you hungry? Does your master not feed you?"

Miles still didn't look at me.

Ha. Annoyed.

Just speak! I wanted to scream at him. How hard could it be? Instead, I was doomed to constantly analyze the minutiae of his body language.

Petting the cat's soft black fur, I crooned, "Poor, poor Alice."

Miles's jaw clenched, and even though I shouldn't, I felt a twisted sort of satisfaction.

Yesterday, when he didn't know I was outside the door, I overheard him call the cat *Captain*. But he could never bring himself to correct me, and I knew it irked him.

I took a bite of my pudding, then tore another piece off and offered it to Alice.

Miles stopped his bandaging. "Don't—"

I froze. His upper lip curled, eyes glued to the bready piece of food in my hand.

Disgust. He hated Yorkshire pudding?

"What was that?" I asked innocently.

Miles's attention shifted to me. His frown deepened, and he went back to his dressing.

But I was tired of the silence, so I said in my deepest Miles Kelly impression, "Captain hates Yorkshire pudding." I brightened my tone, reverting to my usual voice. "Don't be silly, *Alice* has never tried it." Then back down to Miles again. "But it's disgusting—it's all burnt on the outside and gloopy in the middle. I wouldn't give it to my worst enemy, let alone to such a noble creature."

I stood, offended at everything Miles wasn't saying that I had just said for him. "Well! *Some* of us can't afford to be picky, Mr. Kelly. Not all of us can *hit* things for a living." And with that, I tossed the piece to Alice, which she devoured enthusiastically.

Miles grimaced.

I fished out my second pudding and strode to Alice's bowl, ripping it into little pieces for him to nosh on. When I turned around, Miles held my note from the Black Carriage service in his hand; it must've fluttered to the floor when I stood.

I cleared my throat, panic stabbing my heart. "That's none of your concern. You're no longer helping me anyway."

Then, to my utter astonishment, his gaze lifted and he stared his blankest stare at me.

Oh ho ho! He disagreed?

"You're rude, and angry—and strong—and, and…fast, and strong—" Now I was just remembering how tightly he'd pinned me when I'd snuck into his and Mr. Gardner's flat a few weeks ago. The deadly dance he'd performed in the boxing ring. Face heating, I cleared my throat. "Which are all attributes not the least bit useful when sneaking around."

I knew I was being ungrateful—sacrificing a little pride was a small price to pay if it meant rescuing my uncle—but not totally unreasonable, if he was still loyal to his friend.

Miles's gaze never let up. And the longer he stared, the more I felt my resolve crumble; there was something so soulful and weighty about his eyes. So unpretentiously sure.

He *had* gotten me this far. And merited or not, I didn't want to go through life like Dorothy was now—distrusting everyone and everything. I'd rather be stabbed in the back than live with that kind of fear.

So again, in his voice, I said all the words he wasn't saying for him. "You need me, and you know it."

I huffed. "Fine!" I plopped onto the bed. "My plan is to send the Black Carriage service on a delivery, and I'll—*we'll*— be waiting at the drop off location. Then, we'll follow them back to their secretive headquarters where we'll access their records and find out where they've sent Uncle Geoffrey."

Miles nodded, then gathered all his dirty bandages in a pile.

I paused at the bursts of tingles sparking in my stomach. He liked my plan. *Nodding means approval,* I added to my mental list. Which seemed silly, given that nodding was the *universal* sign for approval.

"They'll pick up this illegal painting from here," I went on, snuffing out the odd sensation and pointing at the package on the bed, "but it's not as if I can tell them to deliver it to Dorothy's old home. So I haven't the foggiest idea of where to send them."

Miles glanced up at me.

I put my hands on my hips, arching one brow. "Oh, *you* do, do you?"

22

Ashley

I knew where to find her, and I'd been avoiding it almost as much as my own conscience. But I couldn't afford to delay any longer; I needed to get the map pieces to Lark, get my bracelets, and siphon out my magic before it consumed me completely. So, I came to the top of the grand marble staircase leading to the third floor, scooted my back to the wall, propped a twisted ankle beneath me, and waited, even though the pose made me feel every lingering bruise on my legs.

Nonchalance had a steep price.

A few minutes later, Dorothy appeared with a book in hand, returning to her bedroom completely alone as she always did immediately after breakfast. When she neared the top, she noticed me and halted, cocking an accusing brow.

"Where have you been all week?"

"Did you miss me?"

She finished ascending the stairs. "I think everyone did, given how many questions I had to answer about my absent fiancé. Didn't you read the itinerary?"

Ignoring the barb, I smirked. "I didn't hear a no."

Color rose to her cheeks. "And I didn't hear an answer."

Then her gaze caught on my temple, and I subtly moved a lock of hair to cover the tender flesh. A week ago, I'd felt like I'd gone ten rounds with a freight train, barely managing to stagger to a friend-of-a-friend's dwelling for help. Here on the palace grounds, I couldn't cloak the injuries in an illusion, so I'd hid away during the day, and snuck out for healing sessions at night, until they were mostly mended. But magic was limited, so some wounds, like the one on my temple, were still visible.

"I know where the second map piece is," I said.

Dorothy straightened. "Already?" A flash of panic hit her eyes, but when I blinked, it was gone.

Odd.

I unfolded the sketch Polina had given me and showed it to Dorothy. Like gears spinning, I watched her piece everything together, and tried to stifle my approval so it didn't show on my face.

She glanced up. "It's one of the gems in this crown. And you can crack the safe?"

"I thought we'd use *your* slant for that." I paused, gauging her expression after every word. "Metal bending? Walking through walls? Pyromancy?"

She tipped her chin up. "I can't use my slant in the palace. Now can you crack the safe or not?"

I pushed off the wall, covering my disappointment that her face had given me nothing. "I've yet to encounter one I can't. It's situated inside the royal vault, which is open to everyone. Since everything valuable is under thick glass, there aren't even any guards stationed. All we have to do is wander into the vault, keep a lookout, and we'll be out with our map piece in a matter of minutes."

Dorothy nodded, but she looked squeamish.

"Something wrong with that plan?"

She swallowed. "No. It's just... It's stealing. From royalty."

I shrugged. "Nothing I haven't done before."

She opened her mouth like she wanted to ask something, then shut it, deciding against it. The less she knew the better. "If someone sees us, they'll know who to start questioning once they discover something was stolen. Which means I'm useless for distracting another guest if you can't do the job quickly enough."

"Ah, but everyone is going shopping in the West End this afternoon." I tilted my head, unable to stop the smug smile pulling at my lips. "Or didn't you read the itinerary?"

Growing up with Bram as a godfather, I'd seen my share of jewels; every size, every color, and from all over the world. But there was still something special about the way the palace vault sparkled with past centuries.

A single gas lamp burned above the long rectangular room cut with center shelving, highlighting imperfections on the ancient brick walls and concrete floor. They ought to redo the room, if they wished to repel thieves. A good drill would make quick work of that wall.

Dorothy wandered to a corner of the vault where brown papers were carefully laid out on a table. "The Magna Carta, the Slant Charter... These documents are priceless."

Noting a corked glass of water next to the aging papers, I tsked. "Someone must've been thirsty."

She popped the cork off and brought the bottle to her nose. "It's odorless."

"Water tends to be."

"My guess is sulfuric acid. It's commonly used for document preservation."

I hummed a dismissive sound and turned away, if only to disguise the admiration wanting to shoot out of my eyes. So she wouldn't see my small smile that I wasn't strong enough to tamp. I'd nearly forgotten she was a chemist, like her father.

I'd nearly forgotten how impressive she was.

Her brilliant mind was the first thing that had attracted me to her, and she kept doing little things like this that kept feeding the unruly beast of admiration.

It was ravenous.

On the far end of the room, built into the wall, a safe with perpendicular levers and knobs bore Victoria's escutcheons, though the iron rusted in places. I knew straightaway it wasn't a key lock, and that the pin set in my coat was useless. But I'd come prepared. I knelt in front of the metal face and extracted the shim from my coat, then wedged the thin piece of metal under the dial to separate it from the combination lock.

The fact that the second map piece was in a vault and not somewhere like a vast maze veiled in an enchanted mist meant someone had already retrieved it from its original hiding place. It made our job all the easier.

From the document table, Dorothy asked, "How long do you think it will take?"

I spun the dial slowly, feeling for any subtle shifts of tension under my fingers. "Six minutes." The first number was four.

"Really?" She sounded surprised.

"Five, if you stop talking."

I spun the dial one way, then all the way back. Then twenty-two. Judging by its size, the safe probably had up to six sequences. With a knuckle, I softly tapped the metal. Click... click...*click.* Then fourteen. Two numbers later, my brows pulled in. Everything about the safe appeared normal, but there was something off...

Ear to the metal, I twisted the knob, listening for its heartbeat. Click, click, click...click.

Dorothy sucked in a breath. "Someone's coming—"

"One more—"

The metal cracked. The sound echoed off the walls and out into the corridor. I swore under my breath. It was definitely *not* supposed to do that. That must be what I'd detected—some modern defense mechanism. Although—

"Ashley!" Dorothy hissed, rushing toward me.

While the safe hadn't unbolted, the metal face had fractured open a gash the width of my hand. I peered inside, and the crown glinted back at me. *So close—*

Bootfalls thudded. They'd heard the crack.

I reached for my illusions and felt no spark before remembering I couldn't use magic. My stomach dropped. *Bloody silt.*

Dorothy and I ducked around the tall displays just as two guards marched into the vault. They beelined for the safe, exchanging a few urgent words when they saw the fissure. Their argument masked our sound as we circled out of the room and barely managed to squeeze into a closet down the corridor before more guards marched by.

Footsteps scuffled, and stern voices issued commands. "Lock the palace down," one of the guards ordered. "Interrogate the servants and make a list of all the guests who stayed behind. I want a full report of..." The words drifted off as they travelled down the corridor.

Our heavy breaths filled the silence. My awareness shifted to Dorothy, flush against me, and I was reminded of another time we'd hidden together, in a different closet—that one in the factory. Maybe she remembered too, because she glanced up and we locked eyes.

Time froze. A thin beam of light slashed from her cheek to her jaw, cutting across her round lips. Her chest pressed against mine, her exhale hitting the base of my throat. And as I watched the memory play out in her eyes, I remembered everything I'd dared to want, and every reason why I couldn't want it.

I couldn't, I couldn't, I couldn't.

We both blinked.

"We need an alibi," Dorothy whispered at the same time I said, "The West End it is."

Beaumont's Department Store was a grand building whose exterior was mostly windows paneled in a deep green. The inside smelled of cocoa and floor polish, and if you followed the red carpet up the mahogany staircase to the upper floor, you'd pick up talc-like traces of bath powder from the cosmetic department. Shopwalkers guided patrons around the carved wooden shelves and sculpted jars of lemon sweets, and planters bursting with waxy leaves hung over the long bar where you could sample chocolates or pay for purchases.

Some of Buckingham's guests had moved on to the Bond Street shops, but as Beaumont's sold everything from Japanese silk to peppermint sticks to violet perfume to cigars, most were content to wander the store and peruse its endless offerings.

Having agreed it was wiser to be seen by as many people as possible, Dorothy and I split up the moment we entered. I made quick work finding different guests, sliding into their conversations, and mentioning how long I'd been shopping and the purchases I'd made in the last hour.

After I was sure I'd laid enough groundwork, a string of pearls on one of the shelves caught my eye. I pretended to ignore it until, no longer able to fool myself, I gave in and inspected it. Dorothy had mentioned in the Necropolis how she had always wanted her own set of pearls. I couldn't buy them for her, that was out of the question, but I...

...I wanted to.

Not a good idea.

But they would look exquisite on her.

I pressed my lips together, eyeing the beads far longer than I should, hating that I was losing the internal battle. What was wrong with me?

From the other side of the shelf, a hushed feminine voice drifted. "...just sent word from the palace, and apparently there has been a break in!"

Mindlessly, I picked up the pearls, but inside me, every-thing stilled. My hearing sharpened.

A gasp followed, then a lengthy pause and a grave hush of, "The Rook?"

"No one knows."

A third voice whispered, "We shall all be kidnapped from our beds!"

"If he can get into Buckingham, he can get in anywhere."

"Not to worry," the original voice said. "Her Majesty just heightened security. And there are now to be six guards placed at the vault's opening, with instructions to let no one in but the Queen herself."

My mouth worked.

Two guards were distractible. But without magic, it would take a lot more planning to get past six. Which required more time. Ever aware of where she was, I glanced at Dorothy across the shop, only to find she was already looking at me, face grim. She must've overheard a similar conversation.

A figure stepped up behind her, and my muscles wound taut. Nicholas Hart whispered something in her ear and she turned, smiling softly.

An ugly feeling grew hooks in my gut, digging sharper the

longer she stared at him. My jaw clenched. I'd already taken a step before I realized what I was doing.

The female voices from the other side of the shelf turned the corner and, seeing my fingers curled around the necklace, drew near. "Mr. Gardner!" a young girl with bright red ringlets exclaimed. "Were you wanting to try that on?" She giggled and so did her friends.

The way they eyed me reminded me that I couldn't always sense my magic working now and needed to extricate myself as soon as possible. Yet, the memory of Polina flooded my mind; it seemed the more I resisted, the more of a foothold it gave the magic.

I didn't feel like being charming.

My knuckles were white as I set the pearls back on the shelf, but I pasted on a winning smile and turned to a boater hat next to it. "No, actually I was planning to try on this." I put it on, tipping it at a fashionable angle. Then I held my hands out as if to ask their opinion, mentally planning my escape the moment they did.

The girl's red ringlets bounced in excitement. "Oh, but you look so dashing! Does he not?"

Sensing a sale, a shopwalker with a pencil mustache and upturned nose neared. "Dashing indeed, if I do say so, sir. Perhaps you would like to see for yourself?" From behind his back, he pulled out a golden hand mirror and held it six inches from my face.

My gut lurched—

The hat tumbled from my head. And I locked eyes with my reflection.

23

Dorothy

I didn't hear the rest of Nicholas's sentence because my eyes snapped to the mirror the moment it materialized. Ashley froze, neck spasming like he was trying to look away. His face blanched, contorting in agony.

I acted without thinking. I flew to his side and yanked his arm, ripping his gaze from the mirror. The other shoppers stared on in stunned silence.

"Mr. Gardner is not feeling well," I pushed out, then pulled him around some shelves, struggling to support his weight. We hobbled through a side door, and out into a grimy alley covered in crates and soot.

Ashley broke free and fell to all fours, then braced a hand against the building. I stared wide-eyed, breaths quick, hands fluttering like they didn't know whether to help. At the mouth of the alley, a ruckus of carriages and hawkers kicked up dust, but the moment seemed still and quiet as I waited for Ashley to turn around.

I didn't want to ask if he was all right. He clearly wasn't.

But neither did I want to analyze why I'd been so quick to save him, when—when he *deserved* to suffer.

"What happened?" I said instead.

Ashley said nothing.

"What *happened*?" I repeated. The silence stretched on, until finally I could no longer stand it. "If I'm going to help you—"

"*Don't*," he bit out. He turned over, muscles shaking under ashen skin, sweat beaded on his forehead. Blood trickled from his nose, and he swiped it with the back of his sleeve.

I blinked, insides flashing cold. He looked like he was dying; all but his green eyes, which sparked behind a glare as he met my gaze.

"Get as far away as you can. Don't you get it, Dorothy? Lark is playing you. He doesn't know who kidnapped your father and never will, and you nearly froze, and now the royal guard is after us. You have nothing to gain, and everything to lose. And if your peril doesn't come from this dangerous game, it'll be *me* who—!"

He swallowed the rest of the words. With great effort, he scooted back and braced himself against the building. Then quieter, "It'll be my magic that destroys you. You need to get out before it's too late."

My heart pumped slower, stinging and flooding with quick, brutal images. A black feather amid the rubble of a broken statue. Another one atop my father's pillow. The only light that had warmed my lonely house—gone.

"It's already far too late," I whispered through the pain. He'd shredded the person I once was.

But the images kept flowing. Him shirtless against another wall. A gaping wound in need of dressing. Sweat-plastered black hair. Hooded green eyes pinning me. A hushed plea of

I'm so sorry, Dolly. Pink lips coaxing me toward the brink of ruin. Then pushing me over the edge—

I tore myself out of the memories. A guilty tremor wracked my hands, and I clasped them behind me, realizing this was the moment I'd been waiting for; the moment to slip in and gain his trust.

His shoulders slumped. His stare was bleak, defeated, yet it bored past my skull, past the horizon and all time and space, looking at something that wasn't there.

And finally, I dared voice the burning question that had been kindled that day at the factory. "What is it you see...in the mirrors?"

His answer was a long time coming, so long that I knew it was a secret he'd never spoken to another soul. Then his eyes swept up, and he pulled in a long, steadying breath, uttering only one word.

"Blood."

The admission hung heavy between us, metastasizing into horrible meanings. I swallowed and waited—waited for minutes that felt like days—for him to confide in me, using that trait of mine Nicholas had so highly praised, and eventually, I was rewarded.

"I can view memories," Ashley muttered like he was in a trance. "Sometimes. I don't know why." He shook his head against the brick, throat working. "I don't know why I have two slants, or why they're...slowly mutating into an untethered creature.

"When I look into a mirror, it is my own memories I see. Only they're—" He cut off like he had to swallow back bile. Shallow breaths wracked his chest. "They're *wrong*. It's the same scene of my mother dying, only her head is bent like a ragdoll or someone's torn open her chest—turned her inside out until I can't tell one body part from another. Her screams rattle my bones." He gritted his teeth. "And the smoke scalds my lungs, charring my insides, because everything I've ever loved is burning, but the blood is what I taste. Sharp and coppery. Like I'm drinking it and drinking it and drowning because I can't stop."

My lips parted, and my hand crept to my throat, where an uncomfortable lump had settled.

"The magic is an axe slicing through my skull and cleaving into my brain until my mind is only held together by a thread."

Ashley's eyes glimmered. "Every time I look into a mirror, the memory worsens. The trickle of blood becomes a stream and then a river and then an ocean. And it roars." He shook, from fear or rage or both. A tear trailed down his cheek. "And *roars.*"

Before I knew what I was doing, I crouched in front of him and laid a hand on his cheek. It was a touch that smoothed rippling waters. He stilled, dazed eyes finding me like he'd forgotten I was here.

I didn't know what to say. He deserved to suffer, yes, and yet I...I couldn't endure watching it.

"I'm sorry," I finally whispered.

The shadows cleared from Ashley's gaze.

Magic sparked and leapt to my palms—my own—and I knew. This was a crossroads moment, building toward something that lit an apprehensive flame in my stomach. Using the training Nicholas had taught me, I shut my eyes and dove into the magic. Glowing threads of futures twisted into a timeline, but one glowed brighter than the rest—so strong it burned my eyes. I touched it and saw what was about to happen.

"No, I'm sorry, Dolly," Ashley said. *"I stopped trusting you. I wish...I wish so many things were different."*

"So do I." I meant it.

"Can you forgive me?"

"For what?" Though I already knew.

"For"—he blinked quickly, lips tight, his hand folding around my wrist, and I thought he was going to say everything, *but instead he finished with—"anything."*

Could I forgive him for anything?

No.

No, some things were unforgivable.

And yet... His eyes were so desolate and tortured, mirroring exactly how I felt inside, that I found myself nodding.

For the first time, I considered...what if he was just a pawn in a much bigger game? What if he hadn't wanted to kidnap Father, but something—or someone—was forcing his hand?

Eyes on my lips, Ashley leaned in, then seemed to think better of it and hesitated.

Before he could pull away, I threaded my fingers through his hair and closed the distance. He reacted immediately, pulling on my waist, deepening the kiss, clutching me in a way that made me feel like I belonged there, in his arms, and nowhere else. And—

I jerked out of the future and slammed back into the present, where my hand still rested on his cheek. Only a few moments had passed, but my heart thundered.

Because I'd felt it; in this future, I wouldn't kiss him because of his magic, nor to gain his trust. I would do it because he'd slipped past my defenses. Because I *wanted* to.

I clenched my teeth. I was so pathetic and weak.

Weak, weak, weak.

"No, *I'm* sorry, Dolly," Ashley said. "I stopped trusting you. I wish..."

I sucked in a breath and yanked my hand away as the future played out before me now. Face flaming with shame, I whispered, "I'll see if everyone has cleared out from Beaumont's, and we can head back to the palace." But what I really meant was, *Stop stirring up these sick feelings—guilt and desire so thick I could choke. I won't betray my father, or Nicholas, the way you betrayed me.*

Then I stood and fled back into the department store before the future I'd witnessed could come true.

Out of the corner of my eye, I watched Ashley all the way back to Buckingham, swaying slightly from the bumpy carriage ride. Not knowing what to make of what he'd revealed, and all that had happened. All that had *almost* happened.

He sat sideways, legs long and crossed with an arm propped behind his head while he tossed and caught a coin with the other hand. His gaze remained trained on the bit of carriage wall above his boots, never deviating to the coin, or to me. He seemed lost to the world; perhaps again drowning in his memories.

Every smack of the silver piece on his palm felt like another brick in the wall he was building. *Re*-building. The thing he scrupulously maintained to keep himself apart, but which had crumbled the second he looked into the mirror.

Toss. Slap.

Brick.

Toss. Slap.

Brick.

My blood flashed warm, sensing his magic as it manifested in veils of red and orange, leaping in the center of the carriage. A column of flame. It danced with the shadows, licking higher. Why was he casting an illusion of fire? Did it have to do with those memories he'd relived?

Then a brush of heat hit my knees. My eyes widened.

Ashley caught sight of the blaze and froze. He slowly

uncrossed his legs and sat forward, eyes flying to me. A blur of red uniform and iron gate glided by out the window. And it—

Ashley's still-pale features screwed like he was trying to pull the magic back.

"No"—I reached a hand out—"stop." I pointed out the window. "Look."

Ashley followed my finger and when he relaxed, I knew he'd noticed what I already had. The illusion had been formed outside the black hole, but even on Buckingham grounds it was holding.

The carriage crunched to a halt and still we watched in silence for a whole minute as the illusion burned but didn't burn, before it finally fizzled and died. Our eyes snapped to each other.

"You weren't trying to use your magic just now, correct?" I asked.

Ashley sighed. "Of course not. But why should that matter?"

"I mean if you were trying, the illusion might last longer. Or, *not* an illusion." My talking sped up, synapses firing faster than I could form the words. "That must be why it's working on the grounds; because they're turning real. At least for a moment. Because of the mutation. And if you *began* an illusion outside the black hole, like this one—"

Ashley's face cleared. "We could use it to impersonate Victoria," he murmured.

Despite the confusion, the heartsickness—despite *everything*—a smile bloomed on my lips, because the thrill of the puzzle intoxicated me. The thrill of unlocking something together. "And get into the vault," I finished for him.

24

The Samaritan

The city never slept. By the time the ham shops and oyster rooms and pastry houses dimmed their lights, the pubs blinked their eyes open and roused with a bleared smile. Boisterous song and hearty ale spilled into the streets. And long before the rumpus quieted, the marketplaces bloated with donkey carts, rolls of carpeting, confectionery, and sides of bacon, ready for the godless hour that the bystreets drew potential customers.

The city did not rest.

But there were times, just after midnight when it sat in a lulled stupor, that a man could slip around unseen by all. The Samaritan knew this and hefted his load higher up his shoulder —another woman, this one from Southwark—and quickened his pace. The lull wouldn't last much longer.

Warm wind whipped over the Thames and leaked into the city, making the Samaritan lower his face to keep his mask on as he passed a church on Horseferry Road and darted onto Lambeth Bridge. The wind picked up, undeterred by the three tall spans suspended by cables that were beginning to rust.

Legend had it that St. Peter crossed here one dark night, on his way to consecrate the first abbey, and rewarded the fisherman who ferried him over with a miraculous draught of fishes. To commemorate the event, Londoners built a bridge and charged a toll. Why follow in St. Peter's footsteps when you could pad your pockets instead?

Luckily, the toll had ended a few years ago, otherwise the Samaritan would be forced to find a different crossing altogether, and he didn't fancy going several blocks north to Westminster. The incline of the bridge had him quietly huffing. With his extra workload during the day, as well as his increasing nightly excursions, his body was beginning to feel the strain, muscles twinging in exhaustion as he trekked on.

Halfway across, the wind shifted.

He didn't hear anything new. Or smell anything. But a sixth sense made him slow and straighten a second before the cold steel of a pistol barrel pressed into the back of his head. He froze.

"Going somewhere?" a soft, deep voice said.

His blood chilled.

It was *him*.

The Rook.

A cold sweat broke out on the Samaritan's neck. Not because of the metal against his skull. But because the Rook had seen the back of his head so many times in the light of day, and now only inches and shadows stood in the way of recognition.

That would be worse than death.

But a moment later, the angry fire in his chest chased the fear away.

The Samaritan changed his voice, making it higher, and scratchier, because the fury hadn't completely overridden his sense. "Out for a stroll."

No response came from the Rook, but a second later, fingers snapped and a shadow moved from behind one of the bridge's pillars. Wordlessly, the Rook's pawn—whoever he was —took the woman from the Samaritan's arms and disappeared.

What was he going to do with her?

His muscles wound tight, insides screaming in protest. But the gun pushed harder against his head, making the threat impossible to ignore.

"Two things," the Rook said, the wind quickly snatching the low words. "Who are you working for?"

"I work alone."

The pistol cocked. "You're lying. And if, as I suspect, you're working for the Order, you can tell them they've done an excellent job hiding in the shadows all these years, but their time is near its end."

With the echo of the cocking gun ringing in his ears, the Samaritan stayed silent. The Rook didn't know what he was talking about but contradicting him was fruitless.

"And the second thing?" the Samaritan finally asked.

"You'll never find the bracelets. So give up and stay away, or next time..." The Rook leaned in, whispering menacingly, "I'll pull the trigger."

His jaw pushed out. He dropped and rammed his elbow back. The Rook dodged the strike—but not the leg sweep that knocked his balance.

Just enough for the Samaritan to tackle him.

They rolled across the bridge. Limbs striking against bone and steel. The gun thudded and disappeared—magic. The Rook kept his face concealed in shadow—also magic. Blood dribbled through the Samaritan's lips, filling his mouth with a copper tang. All his training went out the window, his moves fueled only by rage—and that was probably for the best. The Rook would recognize his technique.

The Samaritan was stronger, landing harder blows.

But the Rook was faster; and he took the hits when he could have evaded them, using it as some strategy—

The Rook threw him so his head cracked against the ground. He hissed through his teeth. With one hand, the Rook yanked his collar and with the other, ripped off his mask.

The Samaritan covered his face, A fresh wave of adrenaline powered a flurry of heavy punches. Several landed, giving him time to wrench away. He scrambled to his feet and leapt for the rails.

The Rook hadn't gotten a good look at his features.

Yet.

He might not stay so lucky.

The Rook rose and spun toward him—

The Samaritan did the only thing he could and dove off the bridge, plunging toward the murky depths below.

25

Emmeline

I didn't think it possible, but Miles Kelly had both combed his hair *and* looked even more uncomfortable in my presence than usual. Maybe it was because we were going to see his mother. Maybe it was because I'd put on my best outfit—a tight yellow cambric with little white bows—and applied both lip salve and a dusting of rouge. Maybe it was because my hands held the sordid serial of *The Samaritan and the Rook! Episode 12: Crumbling Bridges.* Either way, across the carriage seat, his gaze kept wandering up my dress, over the black and white serial cover of a monster lurking near the uncompleted Tower Bridge, and catching on my face before assailing the window to his left.

It was completely ruining my story.

And I was right at the climax, too, when the Samaritan was about to plunge his blade into the wicked phantom's heart and throw him into the Thames. But—wait, no! The Rook had a secret knife hiding in his jacket! He slashed toward the Samaritan, grazing his lip, and—

I huffed and glanced up at Miles. "What."

Miles blinked at me.

"It's to help pass the time and distract me from your angry eyes."

He frowned.

"I know they're the sensationalization of violence and that they glorify supernatural or irrational belief systems, contributing to the harmful rise of superstition across society, and that participating in an escapist mentality can contribute to an unhealthy detachment from real-world traumas. But they're also fun."

His frown deepened, no doubt aggravating the angry red line splitting his lip—a gift from a boxing match, I presumed. It had been late indeed when I finally heard him slip into the apartment last night.

"Which isn't a concept I'd expect *you* to appreciate," I went on. "Though, I think it perfectly understandable if you didn't want to read all about your friend's ignoble exploits."

His jaw worked and he opened his mouth.

"And before you say anything"—*ha, if only*—"I know these penny dreadfuls aren't true." Settling back into my seat and pulling the serial up to cover my face, I mumbled, "I only wanted to see if you would defend him. Anyway, I don't know what's got your petticoats in a plait. It's not as if *you're* the Samaritan."

I sighed and read a few more paragraphs. But when I got to the cheap lithograph on the next page—a depiction of the Rook cutting the Samaritan's lip—I found that the statement was still softly echoing off the carriage walls, refusing to die. My face scrunched as I scrutinized the picture, then I slowly lowered the serial and peeked at the man across from me. At the line on his mouth, which suddenly didn't look like a boxing cut at all. He'd been gone from dawn to dusk every night this week. What could he possibly be doing with all that time?

I slapped the serial shut. What nonsense. I shook off the thought before it had fully taken root. What utter, silly nonsense.

The carriage came to a halt in the core of Cheapside, and I took in the tall stone building of Miles's mother's residence. "Here we are," I said in a sing-song voice.

"Just—"

I caught Miles's eye, and he stopped, swallowing whatever advice he'd been about to dole out. He shook his head, muttering something unintelligible, and disembarked to the street filled with zooming gigs, stiff bluedusters, and whistling newsboys.

Given his nervousness, I deduced his mother to be some matchmaker who'd see me as a potential love interest. Well, I'd have to disabuse her of that notion...maybe. I was unable to decide, too busy staring at the way Miles's coat pulled across his shoulders as we ascended the outer stairs and he rapped the knocker. A few moments later, a woman answered the door, a red knitted shawl wrapping her thin frame.

"Miles!" Mrs. Kelly smiled—a thing she used too confidently, given that her teeth were the same shade as my dress. But she seemed kind, possessing a willowy figure and brown hair that matched her son's. Other than that hair, he must take after his father, because he was much handsomer than the narrow-faced woman before me.

Miles cleared his throat, swallowed, cleared his throat again, then said finally, "Mother." And no more.

I took that as my cue. "Good afternoon, Mrs. Kelly. I am Emmeline Morgan. You may not remember, but I wrote to you some weeks ago about your son's residence? Might we step inside for a moment?"

Her attention shifted to me, and though her brown eyes appeared oddly dull, she nodded and cracked the door wider.

"Please." She led us into a modest sitting room, where stearin candles of every circumference decorated the mantle and the molding that divided the room horizontally. She left for a few moments, returning with a tea tray.

After setting it down, she clasped her shaking hands in her lap, her eyes darting nervously to something beside the pink velvet sofa she sat upon. She'd barely looked at me. *Not a matchmaker then.*

"This is a charming house you have," I said with forced cheerfulness. "I especially love the, um...candles. Everywhere."

"I like how they smell," she said. "And the incense too." Another peppery plum aroma slithered underneath that, one I couldn't name. Mrs. Kelly poured tea into the cups on the coffee table, brushing against some foliage dangling from a nearby plant stand. "Miss Thurston gave them to me. She's such a pretty thing. In fact, she inquired about you the other day, Miles dear."

I frowned. Miles shifted in his chair.

"Cream?"

I nodded. Miles said nothing. Mrs. Kelly again glanced to the side of the sofa, then gave me my cup. Since Miles showed no inclination for making this visit a productive one, I opened my mouth but was thwarted.

"You know she has been to Vienna? Came back so accomplished. You two were so close as children, and when she visited me the other day, she mentioned she missed you."

With white fingernails, I gripped the teacup handle and brought it to my lips. *Wrong—Mrs. Kelly* is *a matchmaker.* Perhaps her odd mannerisms were the reason for Miles's trepidation in bringing me here?

"Golden ringlets and rosy cheeks; she'll make such pretty babies. Do you think you'll start writing to her again?"

Babies? Writing? I wanted to gag. How many words had he

given her? And how easily they must've come, given how *close* they were. But—*babies?* Who blasted cared what her babies looked like?

"Is the tea not to your liking, Miss Morgan?"

I glanced up, only to realize I'd been glowering at my cup. "It's—fine." I pushed the ugly, confusing feelings down. "Mrs. Kelly, we were wondering if we might use your home as the address for a delivery we're expecting later this week. We wouldn't ask, except Miles's flat is hardly suitable and I'm..." I couldn't say *living with him*, so I finished, "I am between houses, at present."

Again, her eyes darted to the side of the couch, where a slender wooden pipe was propped against it. "Of course." She straightened. "How is it you are acquainted with my son again?"

I laughed nervously. "We are—colleagues."

It was a vague answer, but one Mrs. Kelly bought because she nodded in relief. "I am glad to hear that is *all* you are." I blinked. She turned to her son. "Miss Thurston has plans to stop by tomorrow, and she was so hoping to see you..."

I took another sip of tea, widening annoyed eyes at my cup while Mrs. Kelly's glowing chatter of Miss Thurston went on for several minutes.

Eventually she remembered herself and said, "Forgive me, where are my manners? Would you like some Yorkshire pudding, Miles dear? I know how you love it."

Relieved to be moving on to a new subject, I chuckled. "Quite a good—"

"Here." She grabbed a saucer and proceeded to pile it high with a generous slice.

I'd almost said, *Joke*, but the chuckle petered out in my throat. My amazement only grew when, instead of telling her how deeply he disliked the pudding, Miles silently took the offered plate, took a bite, and swallowed painfully.

He wasn't fond of talking, I understood that. But if he'd managed to tell *me* he hated it, why hadn't he informed his mother?

A strange warmth bloomed in my chest as I watched him choke it down. And for the first time, I began to understand how he could remain friends with someone like Ashley Gardner. He'd rather stomach something he found highly reprehensible than upset his own mother; he'd admitted duty was his motivator for helping me. The man was loyal blue, through and through.

I wondered if *Miss Thurston* knew he hated Yorkshire pudding.

What a stupid thing to care about. And yet I did.

Mrs. Kelly blinked rapidly and reached for the long wooden pipe.

Beside me, Miles sucked in a breath. "Mother."

My brows furrowed, confused why *this* would be the thing that made him break his quiet.

Mrs. Kelly stood. "I'll only be a moment," she said shakily, and rushed from the room, clutching the pipe to her chest.

Only then did I put the clues together. The dull eyes, the tremors, the odd smell not quite masked by the incense.

Opium.

My gaze swung to Miles, but he wasn't looking at me, his face pale—from embarrassment?—his mouth pinched tight. I couldn't help my surge of pity, even while I simultaneously scrambled for a conversation topic to detract from the stifling silence. Everything seemed either too insensitive, or too inane.

When I could bear it no more, I finally gave in and said, "Do you think Miss Thurston pretty?"

Miles stood. Without responding, he stalked out. I followed

him into the foyer, where he was sliding into his brown great coat, popping the collar with agitated movements.

"Oh." Mrs. Kelly descended the stairs with the pepper-plum smell wafting strongly off her clothes. "Are you departing already?"

Miles nodded, hesitated, then said, "I'll send a doctor by."

She grinned, exposing her yellow teeth. "You don't have to do that, Miles dear. I feel better now."

Again, he hesitated, then kissed her cheek. "Rest."

On the carriage ride home, I studied the man across from me carefully—his strong jaw and pensive stare. In the whole of our visit, he hadn't looked at his mother once, and I realized now that it was out of shame. Yet despite it, he'd still brought me here to help me. He took care of her—sending doctors, and likely food and clothes—while letting her believe she knew him so well, and I wondered why.

I wondered why watching him kissing the opium-addicted mother he could hardly stand, made me want to swallow him in a hug.

26

Emmeline

My jaw practically dropped when the carriage silently trundled down the narrow alley and then disappeared into a brick wall. From the darkened alcove notched into the street, I squinted out, but everything was dark and deserted, the only sound a few wind chimes blowing in a breeze.

Beside me, Miles said under his breath, "Blimey," but otherwise didn't show surprise. At our legs, Alice blinked up and meowed in agreement. I gave him a quick pat on the head, wondering for the dozenth time why Miles had insisted (wordlessly, of course) on bringing him.

The street was old and little used, nestled far northeast of the city center, and needles stabbed my feet from all the walking. The Black Carriage had carried Joule's painting from our flat to Miles's mother's house. We'd waited in some prickly bushes on her street, then followed it here, Miles using hand motions that indicated when to duck behind a cart, or into a doorway, or onto a side street, or hang back to avoid notice.

I would never tell Miles of course, but after several close calls where the driver had looked over his shoulder or turned abruptly, I never could've successfully trailed the carriage without him.

Magic pulled my face into a boyish resemblance again, the collar of my urchin coat scratching my neck. I finally regained my senses and snapped my jaw closed. I'd never traveled through a magical portal before, and though the idea didn't sit well with me, I mustered my courage, squared my shoulders, and stepped into the alley.

Miles gripped my arm and jerked me back as another Black Carriage materialized out of the brick wall. Forearm over my collarbone, he flattened me against the building, pressing a finger to his lips. Ebony horses with glistening coats pulled the contraption, their movements so eerily silent it was like watching a void glide past us, leaving a chill in its wake. Only someone's slant was capable of something like that.

I shivered.

The second the carriage disappeared from sight, Miles dove into the alley. My eyes widened when he didn't even hesitate, just stepped through the brick like he'd seen a hundred portals before. Alice followed without a backward glance.

I scowled after him. Traitor.

Crossing the portal made my skin crawl, and I immediately knew we were out of London from the air quality; it wasn't laced with smoke and rot, but rather leaves and moss. Before me, curvy, iron gates opened to a muddy courtyard, edged by a large U-shaped building comprised of dozens of carriage houses and stables linked together. The carriage from earlier glided into a garage.

In the center of the courtyard loomed a gothic house, its four stories painted black and slowly being strangled by ivy. Columns of bay windows supported concave turrets, and orange lights glowed within. Everything about it seemed pointy and ominous; a hub for dark dealings. The Black Carriage Headquarters—and somewhere inside, the records of my uncle.

Thick, gnarly woods boxed everything in. And inside these woods, to the side of the gate, shrouded in shadows, Miles watched the scene with a predatory stillness, documenting threats.

I quickly joined him, then fished the gold field glasses from my satchel. It was dark, but through the barrel, I made out a couple dozen guards. Smuggling must pay handsomely. "George's crypt," I cursed, then lowered the binoculars.

Alice meowed in agreement.

Miles slunk away and headed toward the portal.

"Hey!" I whisper-shouted. "Where are you going?"

"Back."

I stood and scurried after him. "Why? To do what?"

"Plan."

"But we have—" I circled in front of him and jabbed a finger in his chest, making him halt. "We *have* to do this tonight. I have gone down every avenue and braved far seedier places over the last month, looking for my uncle. Every day we delay is another day he languishes in who knows where. I did not work my patootie"—I deeply regretted the word—"off night and day, just to turn tail and run in the name of *planning*. The time for premeditation is over. Tonight, sir, is about action."

Miles looked behind him, and I could tell he was weighing it all. The guards, the carriages, the house, the escape route, the likelihood of success if we went in blind. His gaze cut to me. His lips thinned and he shook his head.

I put my hands on my hips. "How is it you stand so straight, Mr. Kelly? Without a backbone, that is."

He inhaled a deep, deep breath, his nostrils flaring. "Rage."

Hm. Maybe he'd only said that because "I'm a pigeon-livered coward" used seven too many syllables. But maybe I was the coward because I shrank under his withering glare and shuddered back a step.

"Fine," I muttered. "I'll go in by myself, per my original plan."

He inhaled a louder, deeper lungful through his nose—more anger bubbling under the surface—

"And for heaven's sake, stop breathing!" I spun around and, before I could think twice, darted for the house.

27

Miles

Black fog.

I was going to kill her.

I was going to manhandle her back through the portal to make sure she was safe, and then I was going to kill her.

Helplessly, I watched Emmeline dart across the yard, wincing every time her boot crunched on the ground. A guard turned a corner, and terror sluiced through my gut. She dove into the house, barely escaping his notice. I swore under my breath.

The girl had uncanny luck.

But I wasn't about to let her rely on it. I'd sooner dance with the devil in irons than abandon her.

Bloody, impudent little cove.

A small ball of black fur purred questioningly up at me, making me feel marginally better. In the weeks since I'd adopted him, I'd trained Captain to do a few tricks—clawing someone's eyes out among them. He'd help me with all the dirty work. I emitted a short, disgruntled sigh.

My fingers brushed my brown trench coat to check my

invisible arsenal. As usual, my pistol was there, primed and loaded; but I also had the hairpin, a shovel, a wagon wheel, and the glider. Not a very useful lineup in a situation like this, against dozens of black-market operatives, but now—thanks to *Emerson*—I had little choice but to make do.

After tightening my belt, which carried more ammunition, I slunk inside the gate, keeping to the shadows as I mapped the targets.

I'd counted eleven black-clad employees working with the horses at the back, eight more washing down and tuning up the coaches, seven milling about the yard, and three inside the house. Thirty, give or take. All armed. With two fingers, I gestured toward the carriage houses and Captain silently sprang into action.

As two men headed toward the house, I angled behind them and advanced. A Black Carriage was completely noiseless; it was part of what made their business so covert. As such, the yard lay dissonantly silent, with not a whispering voice or squeaky wheel. Which made this next part all the trickier. Bullets could only be used as a last resort.

I hooked an arm around a throat, then rammed an elbow to the second man's head. He thudded to the ground. Hands gripped my arm where I was cutting off air. Then they scrabbled lower to where he holstered his pistol. Too late. I'd already popped the gun out. I crashed the butt into his temple. He fell.

I inspected the gun—a .32 Iver Johnson—then tossed it into the bushes hedging the house. Cheap munitions for such an upscale operation.

The scuffle had been quiet, but in a completely soundless place, it was enough to draw three more men sniffing from the carriage house. I circled around the house, avoiding the moon's light and staggering their takedowns. One with the rope. Another by a quick strike to the neck. The third came while I was lugging the second body to the bushes, and he nearly got a round off before I wrenched his arm back, cracking it out of its socket. I smothered his scream of pain with my palm, then, desperate, used the shovel in my pocket to knock him out.

I hated these odds. I hated the silence, and secret organizations, and the lack of a plan, and the fear lacing my lungs, and nearly everything about the last hour.

And Emmeline. I hated Emmeline most of all.

The shovel's clang brought faces to the window, one of which lingered on the bush I hid within. The man squinted and unlatched the window, hand edging toward his holster. I emitted a short, low whistle. To my right rang a crash like glass shattering, drawing the man and his companions out into the yard. A few seconds later, a little shadow pawed up beside me.

I scratched Captain's head, grateful for his cunning distraction. "Good boy," I breathed.

Perspiration beaded my forehead, my knuckles smarting. An ache settled under my shoulder blades from all the fighting I'd been doing—first the boxing, and the late nights, and now this. Setting the shovel down, I jogged over to a stall on the opposite end, drew magic to my hands, and touched a Black Carriage. The massive contraption shrank down into something invisible on my palm, and I siphoned it into my pocket, then sprinted for the house.

It wasn't that I needed it, exactly. But if Ashley's luck had taught me anything, it was that opportunities only came once, and fortune favored the bold.

Captain and I had bought us—at most—a few minutes before someone found the bodies and sounded an alarm. I needed to get Emmeline out before we were trapped in this dead-end portal. I silently dove inside.

A pair of men played poker in a parlor off the entrance, the black chandelier above them clouded with cigar smoke.

Quietly, I slipped past them. I checked all the rooms on the ground floor and first floor, my panic rising, visions of them holding Emmeline hostage or pointing a gun to her temple making me sweat faster. More worst-case scenarios danced behind my eyes, making adrenaline shoot through my limbs as my search grew more frantic. Past oil landscapes and tasseled drapes, across burgundy carpet, under a frightened stag head...

After running into another man in the stairwell and scuffling while taking him down, I listened for sounds of someone coming to investigate. All was still. Satisfied, I took the stairs two at a time to the third story, finally finding her rummaging through a closet just off the landing.

Unharmed.

I heaved two desperate sighs. My knees buckled, and I grasped the railing to stay upright.

She found something and froze, face paling.

My gut twisted into a knot. "Is your uncle dead?"

"No, it...it's..." She glanced up, frowning. "It's my father. He's employed the Black Carriage service before. Regularly. He has a whole file." She blinked a few times then swiftly creased the papers and yanked on her collar to shove them down her shirt. I jerked my face away, wishing she'd chosen to store them somewhere else. Because now all my attention had shifted to that little glimpse and away from detecting threats. I raised my eyes heavenward in a plea.

I was reduced to being jealous of *paper*.

You're a moron, Miles.

My ears twitched at a whisper of sound and my defenses went flying up again. I scoured the shadows for movement. To my left, Emmeline continued on, oblivious to the noise and riffling through more files.

"Here it is—the day I saw my uncle." She scanned the paper in her hand, then pivoted toward me, an exultant gleam in her eye. "Cambridge! They took him all the way to King's College!"

I jumped and slapped a hand over her mouth while pushing her against the wall. My heart squalled in the silence, and not only because I was terrified someone had heard her. My quick breaths washed over her face, and her luminous brown eyes—which her disguising magic had left untouched—blinked up at me.

The line linking our hearts went taut. And suddenly all I could focus on, feel, hear, was the brush of her lips under my palm. The freckles dusting her nose looked like a tempting constellation—a thing that could guide me if I were lost at sea.

She melted under my touch, gaze delving into my soul.

I swallowed.

Ears perking, Captain meowed urgently. Someone was coming. I unhanded Emmeline and withdrew my Colt Peacemaker.

"Someone's knocked him out!" a voice said from a lower level. A scowling face peeped through the railing and landed on us.

I cracked two rounds off, splintering two balusters and making the man duck. Shouting passed through the men below. A thread of gun smoke whispered through my nostrils, metallic and like burnt oil. How I imagined heaven smelled.

Emmeline darted up the next flight of stairs. My gut sank, knowing what was coming. Outside, a bell rang continuously. Through a window, I made out dozens of man-sized shapes emerging from the carriage houses and swarming the building.

I backtracked up the stairs, firing anytime someone thought about getting too close, and finally rolling the wagon wheel down to knock them over like pins. When I ran out of the .45 ammunition in the chamber, I sprang after Emmeline, Captain on my heels, and into the topmost room and deadbolted the door behind us. Bullets whizzing through the wood stopped all thoughts of barricading.

Emmeline huddled in a ball under a desk, eyes round as compasses. "How are we going to get out?"

I stalked to the giant arched window and tested the handle. Locked.

Blast.

Quickly, I loaded six more bullets, spun the cylinder, cocked the hammer and shot. Glass shattered, and the lock blasted off. I threw the window open, then spun back and fired the remaining bullets into the door, downing a few men behind it. Cock, trigger, cock, trigger. The Colt smoked when I finished, the carbon steel barrel threatening to melt.

Emmeline jumped to her feet. "You're not serious."

I wished I weren't. I never thought I'd resort to this, especially without Ashley here to push me into it. But I had to save her.

More shots sounded from the other side of the door, metal burrowing through the jamb and flinging the first bolt off the door. When a hand reached through to work the second one free, Captain sprang forward, clawing the knuckles until they dripped blood and retreated.

I spun my Colt back into my pocket, and while there, closed my hand around something else—the glider. Emmeline tracked the move.

"Do you trust me?" I yelled, eternally grateful that she still looked like a street boy because now was not the time to stutter over words.

She swiped some hair from her frazzled expression. "Strangely, yes!"

The thugs must've reloaded because the second deadbolt blasted off, right before the door banged open and a flood of black-clothed men stormed the room. At my signal, Captain sprang from the desk, and I caught him with one arm.

"Then—jump!"

We leaped. I ripped my fist out and opened it. Below my palm, the glider sprang into being, wings spreading out like a massive eagle whose back we fell onto. Emmeline squawked and clutched my coat, turning my whole body into a raging fire. The wooden frame jolted from our weight, but we flew away from the house.

Emmeline was not like Ashley. She didn't know where to stand to balance the contraption, or how to steer, and her wobbly movements pitched the nose down into a sharp dive before it leveled out, costing us precious height. But it did the job, soaring over all the carriage workers flocking to the house and barely clearing the iron gate before it crashed to the ground, sending us rolling.

Bullets flew past us or ricocheted off the gate. Emmeline scrambled to her feet, clearly nursing her right knee. Captain jumped from my arms and sprinted through the portal, and we followed, the carriage workers close behind. With gunfire still ringing in our ears, London's streets sounded muffled as we dashed, the sky lightening to a heather gray. I had a hunch that they wouldn't dare tail us into the city, as they risked exposing their operation more than it already had been. My hunch proved correct, since the few Black Carriage workers that straggled through the portal kept such a steady, unsuspecting pace, we easily lost them in the winding streets.

To be safe, I steered us straight for the Thames and hopped aboard the first steamer crossing the river, Captain reemerging to scamper up the boarding plank just before they heaved it up. Only once we were securely tucked at the bow of the ship did I breathe a sigh of relief, bending over the water and gripping the metal to steady myself.

Emmeline fell back against the side rails, elbows pointing away from the ship. A rivulet of blood trickled down her cheek from a scratch she'd acquired sometime during the chaos, and ridiculously long strawberry blond strands fell out of her cap, betraying her gender despite her still boyish features.

A sudden chuckle burst out of her, and her eyes sparkled. She turned to Captain, who rubbed against her legs. "What a useful cat you are. That was close, wasn't it?"

But the knots tying me together didn't loosen. No, they wound tighter.

"Don't." I straightened. "*Ever.*" Rotating, I locked eyes with her, blood seething. "Do that." I pushed her forehead with a finger, a little too forcefully. "Again."

Her jaw dropped and she rubbed her brow. It was probably because I'd dared to touch her, a fact which I could hardly believe myself.

But the truth was, she scared the salt out of me.

Not just tonight. *Always.*

She made me feel alive. So dead to everything else. So— *helpless.*

So, so bloody afraid.

Her expression sobered. "We survived, didn't we?"

I frowned. She sounded like Ashley. I hunkered down, slipping my legs through the rails and letting them dangle above the river while I rested my forearms on a rung.

After a moment, she shifted, her back sliding down the metal until she sat on the deck beside me, facing the other direction. Seagull calls mingled with a boat horn in the distance, capturing Captain's attention. Paper crinkled as Emmeline withdrew the files she'd stolen. "I have to tell you something." She sounded strangely uneasy.

I stilled.

"Shipping. That's what the Morgan name is built upon. All

these years, as my father's wealth compounded, that's what he told me. What he told everyone. But these records span fifteen years of using the Black Carriage service, and shipping isn't illegal. It's what they were carrying."

Inhaling a shuddering breath, she finally glanced at me. "Opium, Miles. My father's been smuggling opium."

I blinked at her.

Her lips rubbed together as her eyes misted, and she waited expectantly for perhaps a whole minute. Her hands fidgeted, the movements growing more agitated until she finally said, "Have you nothing to say?"

I stayed silent.

"Look at the records." Emmeline held the papers out to me. "Do you know what this means? Benedick Morgan is the reason your mother is enslaved to an illegal drug."

"And why does that matter?" I muttered.

"Because it's wrong, and—and unfair! And I've been ignorantly reaping the spoils off the suffering of so many. I should've connected it sooner. Perhaps it's my fault that—"

"It isn't," I said firmly. I sighed. "My mother..."

Blast. I didn't talk about this. Or anything. This was partly why women made me so nervous. How did they put words to feelings so easily?

"It is pitiable, her situation. But she made her choice, long ago. So did your father. And those choices are not ours." It wasn't an elegant speech, but the contemplative way she stared at me told me it had done the job.

She nodded slowly, then turned away, paused, and nodded once more to herself. "Can I ask you something?"

My palms started sweating, but she forged on before I could refuse. She had a habit of doing that.

"Why don't you tell your mother about the Yorkshire pudding?"

Again, I said nothing, quietly tracing the frothing swirls the water made below my feet.

In my periphery, Emmeline squeezed her knees to her chest. "Because I'm sure you've had years' worth of opportunities to tell her you hate it, yet she orders it made specially in case you happen to drop by."

I swallowed.

From a young age, I'd always been quiet, watchful; a handy skill when you were counting enemies or mapping escape routes. But when it came to internal happenings, I remained as oblivious as possible. It was cleaner that way, and much less confusing.

Her question caught me off guard and plunged me headfirst into a jumbled mess of emotions I didn't know how to navigate. "I just..."

Maybe it was because I was looking away from those glittering, brown-black eyes that I managed to dredge up the memories—or because the gentle sway of a boat while staring out at choppy water put me more at ease than anything else could.

"One day I found a bird with a bent wing, lying in the road," I began quietly. "People passed. No one else seemed to hear its weak trilling. I took it home and splinted the wing—I mashed up worms and dropped them into its open beak. It died a few days later." I shook my head. "I kept finding them. Dogs, ducks, even mice. Some lived. Some didn't."

Captain arched into my side and rubbed his head against my leg, unafraid of the water beneath us. I felt, rather than saw, Emmeline put the pieces together—that he was one of my rescues too.

"My father was a well-paid sailor," I went on, "and my mother received enough income to live comfortably. Yet every month, I watched her blow it all on opium, leaving me to scrounge a few pennies polishing shoes or hawking discarded flowers—just enough to buy bread and cabbage. It was always worse at the end of the month, when her supply ran out. And one time she—"

No. I still couldn't talk about the reason words came so difficult when a female face was staring back at me.

Unexpectedly, my throat thickened. "Just as with the bird, I knew it was only going to get worse, and still, I...I couldn't leave her. I couldn't do *nothing*. Felt wrong."

We sat in silence for a moment, inhaling the industrial runoff and listening to the bell clanging from the approaching shore. Soon we'd dock, and Emmeline's face would return to its beautiful freckles and soft lips, and I'd go back to hiding the tangles I felt anytime she was near, or anytime I saw her on the street through the grubby window of our flat, or anytime I remembered the feel of stumbling on top of her with my hand caught in her hair, or anytime her name casually drifted into my mind. Which was always. And everywhere.

Soon the moment would fade. So I needed to get it out now —or it would never come out at all.

"There are many things in my life that are breaking—or *have* broken—and the chance of them ever becoming whole again is so slim, it hurts to think about. I know I can't fix them; but neither can I give up. So I'm stuck in the middle, trying, and failing, and trying again, and failing, because it's wrong to do anything else."

I swallowed, blinking quickly. I hated this feeling, and I remembered why I avoided analyzing emotions. It left me exposed, vulnerable. When I finally risked a glance at Emmeline, she was watching me with an empathetic tilt to her head.

"You feel that way about Ashley too," she said softly. "He's something broken you feel compelled to fix."

My tongue knotted, suddenly wishing I could take it all back. *No*, I wanted to say, but what came out was, "I know."

And suddenly I did. All my breath rushed out of me at once, freed by the admission.

"But you can't."

I swallowed again, eyes stinging enough to make me rapidly blink. "No."

She glanced down, fiddling with her hands. I'd never seen her unsure of herself before. "I left my own family a few weeks ago," she said quietly. "I didn't want to, but I couldn't live like that—holding on. Trapped. It hurts especially to think of Clarence, my brother; he's still young and innocent. Every day I wish things could have been different, and I question whether I made the right decision, but sometimes there are no true answers. Only the ones that hurt less."

Emmeline shrugged. "I'm not wise, like my cousin Dory, but if I were...I would tell you to let Ashley go. You don't have to fix him. Some things are just..." She shook her head, discarding what she'd been about to say. "Sometimes letting something go doesn't mean you've failed. In some ways, it's proof of how deeply you care. It will still hurt. But the pain only means that you loved, and in that, there is no shame. You only need allow yourself to move beyond it."

Her words sent a strange, warm tingle through me.

The steamer trudged across the water and docked on the other side of the river. We sat there, frozen for another minute; I was afraid that if the moment ended, I'd never feel this close to anyone again, giving voice to the things that haunted us.

Giving voice to anything.

A ship horn blared, warning passengers it was time to disembark. Emmeline sucked in a breath, and the moment melted. "So," she finally said, dragging the word out. She clambered to her feet and put her hands on her hips, one brow quirking down at me. "You have magical pockets."

28

Nicholas

I turned the corner on the gravel path of Hyde Park to find Dorothy leaning against a tree, hunching over something she held in her lacy day gloves. The aches of a long day's work sloughed off my muscles, replaced by a warm contentment that only swarmed me when she was near. Shade dappled her hat and shoulders, sun pockets shifting over her skirts as the branches above swayed in the breeze.

The last few days had been grueling. After Dorothy's unsuccessful attempt to lift the second map piece from the vault, Queen Victoria had heightened security around the palace, and I'd had to grease a lot of palms to keep our operation going.

Of course, Her Majesty didn't know the full scope of what we were doing—or even that the break-in had technically been under Lightfoot direction—because those were details she might not condone. Observing Mr. Brass had given me a solid appreciation for the political dance; it was all about knowing your power, playing to your strengths, and not revealing the ugly bits until everyone had already reaped the success.

Dorothy was so wrapped up in what she was looking at—a letter, I realized—that she didn't hear me approach.

"A secret correspondence?" I said above her shoulder.

She jerked her head over, but her expression didn't give way to surprise. Like she always expected a man to invade her space and whisper in her ear.

I frowned, unsure how I felt about that.

About Ashley Gardner coloring the lens through which she saw everything. Everyone. I pasted on a smile. I was overreacting. It would pass.

It would all pass.

"I was reading a letter from Emme," she said, waving the piece of paper in her hand, grin blooming, eyes sparkling in that way I found irresistible. "She's making excellent progress on discovering where Ashley's keeping my father."

"Is she?"

"Apparently he's hiding somewhere in Cambridge."

I stilled, then struggled to keep my expression neutral, because while I wanted to support her, the reality that her father wasn't ever coming back stared me sharply in the face. It had simply been too long, but I didn't have the heart to crush her hopes.

I changed the subject so she wouldn't notice my hesitation. "Polina asked me to tell you goodbye."

Dorothy's expression immediately screwed up in suspicion. "Did she?"

"She's being stationed in Paris until further notice and is sorry that you'll miss her."

Dorothy made a noncommittal sound in her throat.

I smiled. I got the sense she and the ballerina didn't see eye to eye. "And where is the Rook?"

Dorothy tucked the letter from her cousin inside her chatelaine purse. "Right now, he's testing out my theory, to see how long his illusions will last on the grounds if he starts them outside the gate. If we're lucky, it'll be long enough to sneak into the vault again."

I nodded. Selfishly, I disliked putting her in so much danger—both with Ashley, and with the Queen's guards—but as a Lightfoot agent, I didn't see another option.

The second she and Ashley discovered where the map pieces were and exchanged them for the bracelet, I was ready to swoop her out and perhaps...perhaps declare my intentions. Pieces from our recent magic sessions flashed before me.

Her progress thus far had been remarkable, and honestly, I could watch her do it all day. The power at her fingertips. The raw, clear exhilaration shining on her face every time she saw into the future. Not everyone was like her, using their magic for good. She wanted to help people, as I did.

And that kiss we'd shared in the dawn... I'd walked that memory so many times, it'd worn holes in my soul. I ached to repeat it—but to kiss her more deeply. Properly.

Thoroughly.

Her eyes follow him, a voice of reason whispered in my mind, echoing louder when I tried to ignore it. *At the garden party, at dinner...even in the department store.*

Her eyes follow me too, I mentally shot back, and it was true. I'd found her taking in the lines of my shoulders, the freckle above my lips, studying my hair in the breaths between exercises when our faces were close.

There was something unnatural about Ashley Gardner—that he could inspire such devotion in her even after she believed he'd kidnapped her father. It was another one of his tricks.

This—what Dorothy and I had—was real.

At my first London Science Society dinner, I'd lost a diamond cufflink gifted to me by my mother, and at the next banquet—a whole month later—I'd found an envelope on my chair, addressed to me. The cufflink was within. I'd looked up to find Miss St. James's face darting away with a blush, and a few inquiries later confirmed she'd been the one to return it to me. I'd stared at her all through dinner. Everyone knew Geoffrey St. James was strapped for cash, and the large diamond would've fetched a sizable price.

Her character was what first drew my notice, but then I started noticing other things; the soft crinkle by her eyes when she laughed, the careful pause that always preceded her words, how she favored gin over wine, the way she pursed her lips when she disagreed with a scientific opinion. The burning urge to know her better only built.

For months, I watched her across the table, waiting for my moment. The *right* moment to approach her...gain an introduction...call on her every Thursday afternoon to talk about science and everything else that lit her eyes...walk this park and watch the flowers blossom...step nearer...stare into her soul and find her lips with mine...

Mere months had passed, but to me, it had felt like eternity. I wasn't about to let a bleeder like Ashley Gardner steal that dream out from under my nose.

I helped Dorothy into the carriage, and soon we were on our way to the underground station at Paddington. The tunnels under the city were red-bricked and tubed, trapping in the smell of sulfur from the trains grinding past, as well as tobacco from dozens of pipes. Heat radiated through the underground, leaving the crowds flushed and my skin sticky.

I could feel Dorothy tensing beside me as we purchased our tickets and neared the train. My hand found hers and gave it a squeeze through our gloves. "You'll do well," I said. And I didn't doubt she would. She rose to every challenge placed before her.

Instantly, she relaxed.

We split. At the back of the line, Dorothy adjusted her plum teardrop hat and entered the private car where Lark's brother, Jay, waited. Lark had chosen somewhere public for them to meet but had arranged for a private carriage from Paddington to Gower Street for their conversation. For me, I stepped over a discarded newspaper with the headline, *"Samaritan Saves Another!"* and into the train, a few cars up.

Because we'd hanged a fair amount of people from his Necropolis—a place whose portals we still hadn't pinpointed— Lark didn't trust the Lightfoots. So, just as with the initial negotiations, Dorothy had to be the middleman. She would update him on their progress as far as finding the map pieces, and then after he left...

She would rewind time in the train car to let me hear the whole interaction, and I could pass all relevant information on to Brass.

It was only a ten-minute ride to Gower Street, but my knee bounced the whole time, my eyes shifted to every face, and I shuffled toward the back car when I couldn't take it any longer. If I was here to keep an eye on Dorothy, I didn't doubt Lark had also planted his own people.

He made me nervous.

Finally, the train rolled into the next stop, hissing steam and whistling its arrival. I slid into the back booth and watched through the window as Lark's brother exited the train and headed up the stairs to the streets. I slipped into the back car to find Dorothy standing to the side with her eyes closed, already concentrating on rewinding time.

As I bolted the entrance to the car behind me, her hands hit an invisible wall, and she dropped the magic.

A hollow version of her entered the darkened car. Sitting on a bench, an equally hollow man with white-blond hair crossed his knees and motioned for her to approach. He held his eyes in a widened state with a nostril slightly lifted, giving him a rapacious, hungry look. "So, you're Dorothy," he said.

Dorothy took a seat opposite him, looking surprisingly confident. "And you're Jay. The hotheaded brother."

He scowled, his red complexion turning apoplectic. "Did you hear that from Gardner?"

Dorothy froze and took a deep breath before finally responding, "No."

A bubble of annoyance frothed up my throat. *Why does it always come back to him.* The train jerked under my feet, continuing to its next stop even while the past kept playing out.

"Lark warned me about you," she went on.

"And I could say the same of you." Jay leaned forward. "Finding a new home is the only thing my brother wants more than humbling Ashley Gardner, so he was pleased when you offered him both." With the pad of his thumb, he stroked the underside of his jaw. "He's less pleased now."

"I understand his frustration that the map was split into pieces. But we have the first section, and we're working on the second."

"He wants to see the first piece." Jay held out his hand, expecting Dorothy to plop the gem in his palm right then.

"You will get your pieces all together." She lifted her chin. "And in exchange for the bracelet, per our arrangement."

"And what guarantee do we have that you're not making duplicates?"

I froze, mouth prickling before remembering he was a vision and couldn't see my reaction. I relaxed my shoulders.

We were a government agency, about to hand over a map leading to a massive magic source to essentially an underground mafia ring. We already knew where the second Variance was, and we would get to it first.

And then—

"We aren't."

I was suddenly glad Dorothy didn't know everything, because *lying* was an area in which she didn't excel. I could always tell when she bent the truth; she blinked too quickly and fidgeted with her fingers.

Clearly trained on picking up those tells as well, Jay sat back, satisfied. Their faces glowed and darkened as their past selves passed by gas lamps lining the underground tunnel, syncopated against the lights we were passing now. "Since you're taking so long, Lark believes you could use some... incentive. The Old Gal is hosting a ball in three days, is she not? Deliver the full map to him there, or he keeps the bracelet."

Dorothy paled. "Lark can't do that. He gave me two weeks—!"

"We don't have that anymore. The Necropolis is deteriorating faster than anticipated. You have three days."

"I *gave* Lark that bracelet. I made a deal—"

"Yes." A slow, maniacal smile grew over Jay's lips that, coupled with his wide eyes, made him look sadistic. "But it was with an Acheron." He stood and disembarked from the train.

The vision closed, and I looked over at the real Dorothy, impressed. Before a few weeks ago, she never would've been able to use her slant to dig that far back into the past. She'd come a long way in expanding her magic.

Dorothy crossed her arms and sighed. "I'm sorry, Nicholas. You trusted in my idea and it's backfired. I don't know how we're going to get the other pieces in three days."

I neared, hands finding her waist. "All will be well. The Lightfoots will double our efforts. In the meantime, find out all you can about the remaining pieces. It would be prudent to secure them before the Rook, if possible."

"But he's—" She shook her head. "He's always four steps ahead. I'll never catch up."

"You'll think of something. You always do."

A wan smile lifted her lips. "No, *Ashley* always does."

I bristled. Then chose my next words very, very carefully. "Do I sense a…softening toward him?"

Her eyes shot up and her answer was immediate. But also quiet. "No." The word trailed at the end, straddling the line between sounding certain and sounding like a question.

I didn't like it.

I didn't like that with her, there were always so many unknowns. I wanted to rip the Rook out of the picture completely. Make it so he was never a part of her. Be the one that made her heart pound faster.

"Just…" I inhaled. "…Don't forget."

Don't forget he's the Rook.

Don't forget me.

She blinked up at me, her blue-gray eyes so luminous I felt like I was drowning in them. And deep at the bottom of that sea was a rocky shore, a certainty that didn't move with the currents and made it a little easier for me to breathe.

"I haven't."

29

Miles

A month ago, if I could've predicted where I would be today, I would've guessed on the deck of my own ship, sails set for Greece—not standing in Ashley's and my old flat.

A table and chairs sat in the center, the sofa off to one side. Doorless closets had passed as our bedrooms, and the mantle still bore liquor bottles and throwing knives. It looked basically the same. As I half expected, Ashley had only taken his essentials, leaving the bulk of the possessions behind for me to claim. Like he knew I'd come back. I would've been annoyed, if not for the fact that I was only here because Emmeline and I were following our lead north to Cambridge, and for that, I needed supplies.

I'd asked a little girl next door to care for Captain until I could return and collect him. And I'd also hidden a little something in his collar, so that regardless of what we faced next, I wouldn't be caught so unprepared next time.

My feet wandered into my old bedroom, and from a nook in the wall, my hands pulled out the bill of sale Barnam had given me months ago. *The Midnight Gale* looked like a decent schooner, and with it, I wouldn't need as large of a crew; not to mention that, even with the extra shifts I'd been pulling, I was still short for the brigantine, and the deadline was in a few days.

For far too long, I stared at the blank line begging me to fill it with my name. A few strokes of pen. That was all it would take to break the chains tethering me to this place.

I let the papers fall to the mattress and turned away. Maybe because I had a dream and was sick of settling for less. Maybe because the chains were too much a part of me now, and I was afraid that if they crumbled, so would I.

A few minutes later, my pockets were full of rope, extra bullets, and food rations. I paused at the feel of the hairpin in my coat, the steel edges of my pledge to Bram. The thought of removing it was so foreign—unthinkable, even—but I'd already broken one promise, by abandoning Ashley. What was one more? Who cared if Ashley found her and went mad from the hole in his memories? Then he'd only be in the same shoes as the Rook's victims.

His victims.

He deserved such a fate.

And yet...I still didn't remove the hairpin.

My muscles wound up, giving me the strongest urge to hit something. Why was he always so blasted selfish? For being such a mastermind, able to see all ends, he was infuriatingly short-sighted.

So many years of my life wasted, following Bram and then Ashley as they pursued their purpose, never daring to find my own. Phase one had been to steal the bracelets in danger of falling into the Order's hands. Phase two was locating their base of operations. And phase three was burning it all down with them inside, a mirrored justice for what they did to Ashley's family.

We'd never made it past phase one before it all fell apart.

It wasn't about revenge so much as keeping the world stable. But since we were the only ones who knew the crimes of England's most secret society, it fell on our shoulders to set everything right.

No more.

Let it find other shoulders, because I was done. Done with saving Ashley and hunting bracelets and trying to unearth the Order and always coming second. I glared at nothing and spun on my heel.

I'd already stepped halfway out the door when I noticed something else and stopped in my tracks. An abandoned black coat of Ashley's hung on the rack, the same one he'd been wearing when he used my stolen slant to retrieve the statue from Dorothy's house. It should've been too ordinary to draw my notice.

But Ashley had few clothes, and they were one of the only things—along with his maps—that he always brought with him, whenever we moved bases. Eyeing the coat like it was a loaded gun pointed at my heart, I took steady steps toward it and slowly turned the pockets out.

Nothing. It was empty.

Could it be...?

After one more moment of hesitation, I reached for my slant and touched the coat again. What I found inside made my brows twitch down. I swallowed, lips tightening at the uncomfortable mix of emotions tugging at my chest.

It had to be a mistake.

It had to be...

But Ashley never made mistakes.

He had more secrets than I had thoughts in my head, and after knowing him half my life, he had probably only told me half of them. So why did understanding him matter now?

Emmeline's words rang in my ears. *It will still hurt. You only need allow yourself to move beyond it.*

Move beyond it, Miles.

I removed my hand without retrieving the item and stalked for the purchase documents lying on my mattress.

With quick strokes, I signed it, jaw clenched. Then I stuffed the papers in my coat and left the flat, feeling more confused than ever but vowing that I'd have a clear conscience at the end of this. I'd help Emmeline rescue her uncle.

Then I'd return to retrieve Captain and disappear forever.

30

Dorothy

I inhaled and shot up. Dim light and the leather spines of books met my eyes. My ivory sleeve was damp from my drool, and I used the cuff to inelegantly mop the saliva from my face.

After waking at an ungodly hour to practice my futuristic ability—which also resulted in future Ashley redirecting each one of my questions—I managed to expand my limit to seeing two hours into the future. I'd returned to the present cold and trembling, magic drained, but had quickly changed out of my nightdress and snuck down to the archives where I'd sifted through records all day. I must've dozed off.

It was always dark down here but judging by my rumbling stomach and the amount of wax puddling in the candle holder at the top of my desk, I'd missed dinner and it was nearing time for the firework display.

A lot of good all this work had done me. So much research, and I had gleaned very little information on the last map piece. My time would've been better spent tracking down the bracelets. Ashley hadn't been pleased when I'd passed along the information of Lark's new deadline for the map, but he'd understood we could do little about it.

I sighed and rubbed my eyes, straining to make it through the last section of Ranulf's journal I'd been reading before I'd fallen asleep.

> *Something is wrong with Simon. His eyes, brown all the years I've known him, now shine an eerie green. And he has tried to hide it, but I have confirmed that he now bears two magics: water wielding and dreamwalking. I know not what this means, but I do not think it a good turn of events...*
>
> *Water springs from his hands, unbidden, burning everything it touches like it is acid. And the dreams he walks...they soon morph into nightmares, the magics becoming increasingly volatile and unpredictable.*
>
> *I've tried to speak to him about it, but he will not hear me.*
>
> *It's almost as if...his magic now has a mind of its own.*

My lips pursed. I flipped the page and scanned the last few lines quickly, tapping my chin with the knuckle of my thumb. Ranulf's next entry was after two months had elapsed. Unlike his other logs, it didn't begin with any pleasantries.

> *It is so terrible to pen, I tremble as I write this. But it must be recorded, and I fear the task has fallen to me, as there are so few survivors.*
>
> *Today marks the fifteenth magical summit held in the Undercity, and from across the table, I could sense something was wrong with Simon. His neck kept twitching. He kept glaring at someone who was not there.*
>
> *I remember wishing Edric hadn't been absent that day,*

so I might have someone with whom to consult. That wish, I am glad, did not come to pass.

What happened next, I don't know how to describe. In the middle of a Roman Cardinal's speech, Simon closed his eyes and writhed, water pouring from his hands like a sprung dam. We all scrambled back from the table. Screams erupted.

The air glimmered. The ground shook. Everything on earth took a breath and gravitated toward Simon, as if he was the center of the universe. Green fire summoned all the air to him and then—

The magic collapsed.

Power rent the Variance, killing him and hundreds of innocents—all but a few. As I dug myself out of the rubble, I suspected it was my enchanted armor alone that had saved me. Along with the two other men who'd survived, we soon found we could no longer access our slants.

The Undercity is dead; a void no magic can pierce. Somehow, Simon caused this.

I have told Edric. He tries to mask his terror, but I see it in his eyes. He fears the same will happen to him. He has vowed to travel abroad, to test the theory that his magic will go dormant, unable to replenish itself at the source.

As for me, I will endeavor to construct something that will help the Undercity continue to function, but I fear it will never rise to the glorious metropolis it once was. Crafting intricate jewelry using magic-infused gems—cuffs, rings, bracelets, all with special powers—is all I am good for, now. I hope the nobility can make use of these gifts…

That was all. No more entries.

My attention jumped back to the bit about the green eyes. I thought back to Ashley's dripping green hands I'd seen through the slant gun. It sounded exactly like Ashley—and he'd even admitted in the alleyway to having a second slant.

Father's theory on mutated magic seemed to be true. And if it was, that meant…

Ashley didn't have much time left.

Was that why he wanted all the bracelets? He wanted to change out the mutation for someone else's slant? But whose? And for what?

"Jacintha has found something," Jacintha's voice scratched from the shadows, making me jump. I saw her crooked teeth first, white and gleaming, before the rest of her followed. I blinked at the tome she carried atop her kinked hair.

"Whilst you slept, she has labored ceaselessly to find another record. Anything for the maid with the angel lover." She plucked the book off her head like a crown and gently set it on the desk before me, next to the candle that reminded me I was going to be late. "Open it."

I did, and the spine cracked. My eyes caught on a yellow edge sticking out, and I flipped to that page, pulling out the fine vellum that bore swooping script. I read the six lines quickly, brow furrowing.

Writ in glass the key resides
Where each mortal frame abides
Nine dreams, ten dreams, twixt is where it wakes
The muse of kings must circumvent
Breach the pale and give dissent
Poor clock, war clock, chime unto the lakes

"It's a riddle," I said unhelpfully. I sighed, massaging my forehead. I thought after Ashley's clues, I was done with riddles.

"Aye. Penned in Simon's own hand. She found it tucked in between—"

I started. "Simon wrote this?"

"That he did."

I read the riddle again, slower. *Writ in glass the key resides...* It had to mean the third map piece. I looked at the next line, my gears cranking into a new speed at the prospect of answers, even as I distantly registered Jacintha stacking my mess of books and carrying them off to sort.

Where each mortal frame abides—that line obviously meant in the earth, where people were buried. Was the map piece in a grave? A shudder coursed my spine at the thought of dese-crating a tomb.

Then my eyes fell to the next line and I frowned. How did the gem wake between nine and ten dreams? What did that mean? Were the dreams something figurative or literal? I rubbed the damp section of my sleeve, wishing I hadn't fallen asleep midday and had more time to solve this.

My rubbing slowed. Sleeping. Of course! Nine dreams, ten dreams, twixt is when it wakes—between nine and ten o'clock. That must be the only time the gem could be accessed.

The next three lines absolutely stumped me, and for so long that I cast worried glances at the dwindling candle. *The muse of kings* could mean anything. Something abstract like power, or something more tangible like gold, land, or a specific thought leader.

Maybe their grave!

But my excitement slowly died, because no two kings had derived inspiration from the same historical figure. Or if they had, the grave would much likelier be in Greece or Austria.

I gnawed my lip then tucked a wayward curl behind my ear. Maybe I was going about this all wrong. Cranking my head to the side, I scanned the lines at a different angle. The use of homophones was common in riddles, and the second half of the riddle contained *four*. I mentally swapped the words.

The mews *of kings must circumvent, breach the* pail *and give* descent, pour *clock, war clock, chime unto the lakes.* It still didn't make much sense, but now I felt I had something to work with. Mews were the pens where falcons were kept, but through the centuries, as the royal family started housing animals together, it also came to mean stables.

The mews of kings—the king's stables.

My mind snagged on the word *clock*, because when the riddle was written, their timekeeping devices were rudimentary. The best they had were clepsydras, which measured time by the steady flow of water from one vessel into another...

Of course. Breach the *pail* of the *pour* clock. The water clock. Which would also tie in the phrase *war clock*, as clepsydras were most prominently used in wartime to keep battle schedules and military routines.

An electric thrum pulsed through my nerves as the last few pieces clicked into place—to give descent, and chime unto the lakes. The gem was hidden in an underground lake that could only be accessed between nine and ten by filling a hidden bucket that had remained in the king's stables for hundreds of years.

At least I hoped.

Jacintha again shambled out of the shadows. "You may study as long as you wish, but Jacintha must take her late supper now. Alone. Ever alone..."

A pang of pity filled my heart as I wished I could do something to help the woman. But as much as I wanted to stay, I didn't have time to visit with her. "Do you happen to know the time?"

"The ninth bell, I'd say."

The Queen's fireworks started at ten.

Once Jacintha had drifted away, I swiftly copied the lines into the margins of a nearby book. "Heaven forgive me," I muttered, and flinched as I tore the page out. Then I stuffed it into my dress and hurried upstairs and behind the palace.

The Royal Mews carried the sweet tang of manure, leather, and tack. In their lofty stone stalls, horses whinnied and shook their manes as stable hands brushed their coats into a velvety luster. My boots rustled stray bits of hay as I clacked my way down the stables, peering into stalls and inspecting the columns, but otherwise the place was kempt.

No sign of any pails or clepsydras.

The mews were a rectangle of spacious buildings, and I drew more than a few curious glances from stable hands while I painstakingly searched. One, while lighting the lanterns hanging from intermittent hooks, told me, "No more riding today, miss," which was a subtle nudge out the door. I found a few buckets full of oats, but the pail I was looking for would've had to be built into the structure, or the floor, if it were to last hundreds of years. A deep sigh escaped my lips when I'd come full circle without seeing a stone out of place.

Something was off. It could be that I hadn't searched the place thoroughly enough in the dim light, but I didn't think so. Either I was in the wrong place, or I'd misinterpreted something in the riddle.

Outside, ten bongs marked the hour. *Blast.*

I was late.

I wasn't accustomed to the constant upkeep of my appearance at the palace; if left to me, my hair would live in a side braid. A maid was already waiting when I scooted into the vanity's cushioned chair, determined to wrangle my brown curls into an elegant bun. Beatrice—my old maid—hadn't often been burdened with the same task. As the Science Society dinners occurred only once a month, they used to be my only occasion to dress sophisticatedly and step outside my home.

A winking light in the corner of the vanity caught my eye. Atop a little purple cushion rested a string of black pearls with an inset black diamond dangling from the center.

It was stunning.

My forefinger traced over the smooth orbs. When Nicholas had mentioned getting me pearls, I imagined his choice would be more classical. Instead, he'd selected something dynamic, unorthodox, adventurous—all the things I'd been aspiring to be. A smile bubbled to my lips, knowing that he must see those traits in me.

The maid noticed my examination and said while scraping a pin against my scalp, "Looks like you have an admirer, miss."

Nicholas had always been so incredibly thoughtful. "Did he leave a note?" I asked.

"No, miss."

"Did you see the person who delivered them?"

"No, miss. The jewelry appeared there this morning."

Gradually, my smile slackened as another conversation tickled in my ears. *An innocuous girl like Dorothy St. James doesn't have a string of pearls,* Ashley had disbelievingly said in the Necropolis. Heat flooded my face as I imagined him clasping the dark jewelry around my neck, tenderly, fingers grazing my skin like they'd done while lacing up my dress. I gulped.

The stunning piece looked like something he'd pick out. And if he had, it said a lot about how *he* saw me, not Nicholas. Mixed emotions swirled in my stomach.

If it was from Nicholas, wouldn't he have mentioned it or left a note? Ashley, however...

Wouldn't have.

I blinked the thoughts away. This was too absurd. Nicholas had *promised* to buy me a set of pearls; meanwhile why would the Rook remember a passing comment I'd made over a month ago when he didn't care about me and never had?

They couldn't be from Ashley.

But when the servant girl asked if I wanted to wear the piece to the Queen's firework display, I glanced at it one last time, saw his black hair gleaming back at me, and slowly shook my head.

31

Ashley

The sky exploded. Bursts of red and blue fire showered down in celebration of Queen Victoria's seventieth birthday, and her pinched face under an awning seemed rather unimpressed by it all. Around the lawn, a hundred guests oohed and aahed in between sips of their champagne. When it had rained earlier, everyone had worried the downpour would postpone tonight's firework show, but the weather had cleared before dark, and now the vegetation reflected the display off their glassy surfaces.

A shadow darted in my peripheral. My hand was halfway to my boot before I caught sight of the end of a cat's tail as it dove into some shrubbery. Ever since the bridge, my nerves had been on the brink of snapping. Something about the masked man had seemed different that night...

For the dozenth time, I scanned the crowd for Dorothy and forced my muscles to relax. Not seeing her, I approached the Queen and her guards with a deep bow. "Good evening, Your Majesty." I rose slowly, analyzing every detail of her dress so I could get the illusion just right—the gold stripes, tassels, and lace—then slapped on a smile and shifted my attention upward.

Queen Victoria snapped her fan closed, the creases on her face shallowing a smidge. "Ah, Mr. Gardner. Good of you to grace us with your beguiling presence. Where is your fiancée?"

"Left to powder her nose. I don't know how I shall survive."

The truth was, I was supposed to escort Dorothy here, but after waiting for half an hour in the hall outside her chambers, she still hadn't shown. So, I'd come alone to get the appropriate respects taken care of so we could crack on the moment she materialized.

Tardiness muddied arrangements. And though I wasn't superstitious, I'd never had a plan play out well that began late.

"Let us hope she returns soon, then," Her Majesty said, brows lifting.

I glanced over my shoulder. "There she is now." I turned back to the Queen whose expression looked on the cusp of amusement. "The air returns to my lungs." After bowing in departure, I wove toward Dorothy who was deep in conversation with four other female guests, not wanting to admit that my lungs did indeed feel fuller with her in my sights.

Keep it together, I told myself. *Keep up the façade. And keep her at a distance.*

My steps slowed as the group's discussion met my ears.

"...your father reported missing," a girl with blonde ringlets said. I recognized her voice from the exchange we'd overheard during the procession the first day. Later she'd been introduced to me as Lady Cynthia, daughter to the Duke of Cabourne. "You must miss him terribly, and all his...eccentricities." Cynthia finished with a sweet simper, but I knew Dorothy hadn't missed the dagger.

My jaw tensed. *Gads.* Why'd they have to bring up her father, of all things?

With her back to me, Dorothy said, "He has many endearing quirks, to be sure, and perhaps that's why I feel so protective of him." Her tone was even, but her clicking fingernails at her side told me that fending off the society wolves made her nervous. "Just as he is of me."

"Isn't that why he hid you away in that house? Then the moment you spring onto the scene, you have a fiancé in tow," Cynthia went on, eliciting nods from the other girls. "And it's none other than Mr. Gardner—*the* undisputed bachelor of the Season—even though the rest of us don't know two things about you. Rather fortuitous, Miss St. James, wouldn't you agree?"

My hands curled into fists.

Dorothy flushed. "The courtship was sudden—"

"Indeed! One must wonder what Mr. Gardner sees in a baronet's daughter when he could clearly set his sights higher." Jealousy threaded the words, and she squinted in that haughty, aristocratic way. "Tell me...what *were* you doing in that house—and with your father missing?"

I traversed the remaining distance to sidle up to Dorothy. "Trying to politely avoid my advances, no doubt." I slapped on my most captivating smile, hoping to strangle the group with charm. As one, they turned to me with doe eyes, like they hadn't just been tearing into their peer. "We met by chance, in a bookshop. I couldn't leave her alone after that—couldn't help myself." *True enough.*

I turned to Dorothy, my gloved hand folding over hers and making a soft rush of awareness settle there. *So much for keeping her at a distance.* "But I won her over in the end."

Her breaths quickened at the touch, so slightly. So did mine. I hated that I noticed both. Then, to my wonder, she relaxed into me, giving my hand a faint squeeze as an even fainter smile touched her lips. The oxygen froze in my lungs.

Stop, I commanded time. *Just keep her like this.*

Looking at me like we belong together.

With effort, I dragged my gaze away and stepped in front of her, surveying the group. "Now if you'll please excuse us, my fiancée and I have more people to greet." The title tasted like honey on my tongue, and I wanted to say it again, pretend it was real if only for another moment. Instead, I pulled her away, our fingers laced.

We mingled a little longer, first with a woman in a towering wig, then a balding man who spoke too loudly with his good ear tipped away from the explosions, and lastly, with a gaggle of rosy-cheeked debutantes.

"You look lovely tonight," I murmured halfway through. It was a silly statement because she always looked lovely, and I blamed our still-intertwined hands for loosing the thought. More colorful blasts popped in the sky. Acrid swirls of gunpowder thickened like a fog, and I stuffed a cough.

Dorothy paused and glanced at me, mouth working like she was debating how to respond—no doubt wondering if I was still continuing the charade. I wasn't.

"Then it's a shame I shall shortly look like the Queen instead," she said.

"She looks arguably lovelier."

"One might think you wish *she* was your fiancée, Mr. Gardner."

"I admit it freely. It would be a foolish move to turn down the title of Prince Consort."

"And you do not make foolish moves, Mr. Gardner," she said with mirth while looking around the crowd.

"No, I do not, Miss St. James." *Besides being near you.*

According to our plan, halfway through the fireworks, Dorothy slipped away from the smoke and drifted into the dark. A few minutes later, I followed. I met her by a pond, a spot beyond Buckingham's black hole radius.

It had taken a full day of measuring and tweaking, but I'd finally secured a doable route. My illusions, when conjured off the grounds, held for three minutes and forty-six seconds. If we sprinted, it took two minutes and four seconds to get to the vault. That left one minute and forty-two seconds to extricate the crown from the safe, hide it in my evening jacket, and get out of the sight of the guards before the illusion broke.

Dorothy bent over, rummaging with something under her skirts. I tried very hard not to look but caught a flash of a red and white striped paper tube.

My brows inched into my hairline. "As entertaining as the guards might find a display of exploding skirts, I'm inclined to think it's not something our reigning monarch would do."

"The firework," she said, straightening, "is for when things inevitably go wrong. A distraction, just in case. I can't plan for everything, but I can certainly try."

"Ah, so *that* is your slant—seeing the future."

She glanced at me sharply, then seeming to catch herself, quickly looked away. It was so similar to another moment between us, when she'd been lying about her grandmother's jewelry set containing the magical bracelet, that I reacted without thinking.

I dove into her memories.

Returning to her mind felt like cool water rushing over blistering skin. Cards of memories lay scattered on a table, gently swirling, one limned with gold and pulsing. I touched that one and fell inside, eager to solve the mystery of her slant and finally know.

But I wasn't ready to see the both of us in the alley from only a few days before. I watched, hypnotized, as she leaned in and kissed me.

Longing arced through me, an ache that clawed at me as the kiss unfolded; I could practically taste her lips on mine.

Taste her kindness, her fierce loyalty to her father, her hope for a better world—and it was intoxicating. I wanted it all. I wanted *her*. But somewhere, distantly, I recognized this wasn't real; rather something that could have been...

That was why her mind had been difficult to navigate before. She had memories of things that had never happened. Memories that didn't belong to her. She really did see the future.

I reeled.

My grip on the memory slipped, and I came crashing back into my own body. I fell back a step. Reality felt different, like gravity had loosened its leash, or a lens in my eye had a hairline crack.

"Shall we begin?" Dorothy said, oblivious to the world tilting.

I looked at her, and when she shrunk back, I realized I was scowling. Because seeing that memory had shifted everything, and a million thoughts nagged at me to sort out why.

She'd seen the future. Or *a* future in which we shared a kiss. But then she'd chosen a different one.

But it had still been possible.

"Ashley?"

I was taking too long to respond. We were losing time. And yet—

Had it been the *pull* working on her and she'd resisted?

Was this happening all the time, my magic threatening to shackle her like a slave, until she had no choice but to use her slant to anticipate it? Would she soon turn into Polina, and Wren, and all the others? Limp and mindless beyond fulfilling my desires?

My magic rushed to circle my palms, and there it whispered faintly, *You are lonely, Ashley.*

My gut clenched and I fisted my hands. I stepped away,

breathing in the dark and unable to speak because of the acid inching up my throat.

"Ashley?" Dorothy said again.

"It's going to be tight," I finally managed, proud of how light the words sounded. Another moment and I'd schooled my expression and could face her again. I turned back and, without a hint of the storm raging inside me, arched my eyebrows. "Are you ready?"

32

Dorothy

I gripped my pale pink satin dress, the ribbons crisscrossing my bodice suddenly too constricting. Nicholas's question rang in my ears. *Do I sense a softening towards him?* I wanted to say no. But I wasn't so sure with the way my heart had soared earlier.

When those women had peppered me with impossible questions, Ashley had stepped in with a dark smile, twisting his words so easily and making me remember it wasn't the first time he'd rescued me. And why would he do that, if he didn't care at all?

Memories played behind my eyes, rebelling against the idea, and I came back to my senses. Those kinds of thoughts weren't just alarming—they were dangerous. I pried them back and stuffed them down, down, down.

As he waited for my response, Ashley glistened in the darkness, his haunted eyes seeming to emit a green light of their own. "Are you ready?" he repeated.

Foot tapping nervously against the grass, I turned my focus to our mission: retrieving the next map piece. I technically had no reason to be nervous; as a Lightfoot, I worked for the Queen —but the Queen's guards didn't know that. They might act before I had a chance to explain. And since it would ruin the whole operation, I wanted to avoid blowing my cover in front of Ashley, if at all possible.

I wondered if Ashley had ever felt like this, at first. Or Miles. Or if they'd just been born with a knack for risking life and limb.

I took a deep breath and said, "I'm ready." Then I turned back toward Buckingham, preparing to sprint.

Fireworks crackled in the distance.

Ashley twitched his hands and the glittery feel of an illusion swept over my skin. I shrunk almost a foot, my frame widened, and my dress transformed into a cream-and-gold silk, a twin of the Queen's outfit tonight.

I ran.

Behind me, I could hear Ashley follow a few seconds later, and I knew he wore an illusion of a red-uniformed guard. He quickly caught up, and we soon approached the limestone palace. Once inside, we decelerated to a royal walk and I held my breath, trying to hide my panting. We passed a few servants who bowed in deference, bolstering my courage.

It was working.

Right before we turned the corner to the corridor where the vault entrance was situated, Ashley consulted a timepiece, and I knew by the pleased pull of his lips that we had shaved a few seconds off. My nerves smoothed.

Four officers lined the wall of the vault, faces stern, while two held their spears over the entrance, blocking the path. I raised my chin as we approached. Stopping in front of the spears, I snapped my fingers. I had no idea if Victoria usually snapped her commands, but I'd seen her do it at the garden party, so it seemed like a better gamble than trying to mimic her voice.

The gamble paid off because the guards uncrossed their spears. When Ashley tried to follow me, they wordlessly blocked his path. I spun around, blood draining from my extremities because this hadn't been part of the plan. Ashley was supposed to be the one to retrieve the crown from the safe.

Ashley knocked his chin up. *One minute and forty-two seconds,* his eyes seemed to say.

Right.

I hurried to the back of the vault in what I hoped was an adequately dignified way. I peered into the hole in the rusty iron safe. A sword, leather books on magic, and brooches peered back at me, and when I finally caught sight of the crown toward the bottom, my palms started sweating.

My arm wasn't long enough.

But we couldn't fail—whether or not we succeeded, word would get out that Victoria had visited the vault, and then the *real* Victoria would crack everything down. We wouldn't obtain the whole map, Lark would keep the bracelet instead of returning it to the Lightfoots as agreed upon, and I would have let everyone down.

My father, most of all.

I spun around, looking for inspiration. Maybe I could use that spear to wedge it up? But with how narrow the crack was, it would take a lot of maneuvering, which would eat up time I didn't have.

Think, think...

My gaze fell on the documents spread out on the table in the corner, arranged exactly as they had been before, and the clear bottle of—

Sulfuric acid.

My head snapped back to the safe, an idea sparking once I

realized the iron had rusted. I quickly bent over and pawed my skirts, unclasping the paper firework tube and ripping a hole in the top, praying this particular pyrotechnic had enough aluminum powder to create a thermite reaction.

Without proper measuring tools, it would be dangerous, but I didn't have time to come up with anything else. I poured the powder generously over the crack, trying to not spill any inside. I'd only read about this experiment in books, but if it worked properly, the reaction would reach around 3000 degrees Fahrenheit, and I didn't want to destroy the crown—or anything else in the safe—by accident.

I retrieved the bottle of sulfuric acid, took a deep breath, and uncorked it. Every precious second ticked heavily in the back of my mind.

It's either this or nothing.

I poured some acid over the crack and leaped back. Fire spit toward the ceiling. Smoke and steam crackled. I glanced over my shoulder, praying it wasn't so loud the guards felt the need to come investigate. Orange, molten iron poured toward the floor, the crooked smile of the safe yawning wider by the moment. A smile which I mirrored. It had worked.

I snagged one of the spears and navigated around the splotches of lava dotting the floor. The safe face gaped wide open, but its edges still burned, so I didn't dare reach in myself. I hooked the crown and brought it out, quickly fastening it to the garter under my dress that had held the firework and shoved down my skirts.

I was grateful for the illusion—still intact—or it would've betrayed the flush that swarmed to my face. I walked briskly toward the exit, feeling the seconds pound down and praying I still had enough of them left. My throat dried and my stomach squirmed as I approached the exit. The guard's spears parted.

Please.

I clasped my hands in front of me and lifted my brows regally.

Almost there.

I nodded to the guards as I passed.

Just a few more steps.

I turned right, and Ashley fell into step behind me, still illusioned as a guard.

Just a few more seconds.

We passed the last sconce illuminating the carpeted corridor and entered the shadows. I exhaled a slow sigh of relief. It cut short at the feeling of the crown wriggling down, the garter sagging. I hadn't secured it tightly enough. My pace quickened. I could readjust once we were out of the guard's sight. Only a few more steps—

Thud. I froze, and so did Ashley.

As one, all six guards turned to us.

I bent to retrieve the metal band. Ashley stiffened beside me, and too late I realized a queen wouldn't have stooped for her crown. She also wouldn't be hiding it in her *dress.* Pulse in my throat, I locked gazes with one of the guards.

The illusion flickered and died.

The guard's eyes widened. I could only hope the shadows concealed our faces well enough.

"Bloody silt," Ashley muttered.

All six red coats scrambled forward.

Ashley yanked me around the corner, and we broke into a run.

33

Ashley

The shouts of the guards followed us into the night. Overhead, an almost-full moon cast long shadows on the wet grass as we circled the palace toward the entrance.

"What about hiding that way?" Dorothy said breathlessly, pointing to her right then bending over.

I shook my head. "Fenced. We need to get off the grounds."

In the distance, a cacophony of barking rose into the air. Her eyes widened.

Dogs.

Bloody lovely. "*And* to move faster."

I grabbed her hand and ran. A crowd of Londoners had swarmed the gates to watch the fireworks, and I used that distraction to evade the guards as we navigated through, cut across Green Park, and plunged into Mayfair. This late, the main streets were abandoned, save for flickering gas lamps and stray cats. The baying grew louder.

I could illusion us invisible, but I couldn't mask our scent.

Dorothy didn't complain as we flew through side streets and squares, but her breaths grew more ragged, and I could tell she was losing steam. I needed to find a way out of this mess and quickly. My eyes snagged on things we passed—signposts, barrels, wads of castoff textiles, shards of pottery where a jar had broken, a discarded length of rein that had snapped off a bridle.

Nothing I could use as a weapon.

A loud growl made me glance over my shoulder. Twenty feet behind, the dog leading the pack had gained on us.

Clink. Dorothy ripped her hand out of mine. The crown had fallen to the street. *Again!* I wished for Miles's pockets.

"Leave it!" I snapped.

She turned back for it, and the dog leaped for her, mouth frothing.

I yanked her behind me in time to ram my knee into the creature's skull. It hit the ground with a yelp, then barked louder than before.

With wide eyes, Dorothy stared at me, breathing hard. Disbelieving. Her expression morphed into horror as the dog got to its feet. "Conjure something," she shouted.

"Whatever illusion I cast—" *I don't know what will happen,* I wanted to finish. It was already growing too volatile. Anything dangerous enough to chase away the dogs put her in peril too. Which I'd sworn I'd never do. I jerked my head, no.

"If you don't, we're dead." More dogs' barking grew louder, echoing through the slick, empty streets. We had seconds. "*Do it now!*"

The terror in her voice wrenched my gut.

I slammed my eyes shut. I couldn't remember the last time I'd had to concentrate on casting an illusion, but I channeled everything into the magic now. I imagined every detail, every sound and texture and smell. It built and roared up my spine, sparkling and feverish and so leaden my bones were fragmenting.

Then I let the wild magic loose.

In a circle around us grew up six dark shapes, slowly morphing into four-legged beasts as tall as my shoulder, with glossy gray fur and wet black snouts. Their massive claws clicked against the ground, their guttural growls like grating rock, their soulless eye sockets glowing embers. Through their mouth and nostrils breathed fire and smoke. It reflected in the puddles on the cobblestones, casting the whole street into shades of orange and red.

Hellhounds.

And they were—*real.*

Dorothy's jaw dropped, eyes shooting from the hounds to me, and I deciphered the message shining in them because I'd seen that fear before—in Miles. *So much magic.*

The Queen's dogs reached us and the hellhounds leapt forward, cutting into the smaller beasts. Blood stained the ground, and the air curdled with the smell of charred flesh. My gut clenched—not because the hellhounds were wreaking havoc.

It was because I hadn't told them to.

"We need to leave," I urged Dorothy. I had no control over this magic. I reached for her hand, but she pulled back.

"Wait." Her eyes were fixed on where she'd dropped the crown.

Pistols cracked as the guards sprinted onto the scene. Several rounds sunk into a hellhound's flesh, before it collapsed. More bullets whirred past us, one shattering the panes of a gas lamp. Two hounds sprang to attack, just as a few drops of rain *plinked* to the streets. They tore into a guard, teeth ripping flesh as he howled.

Dorothy leaped into the fray and swiped the crown, pocketing it in her dress. In those few seconds, thunder cracked, and the heavens poured. Liquid sluiced down my clothes, soaking me in moments.

Seeing their mangled companion, the remaining guards shouted and scattered down alleys. Hounds followed. Snarls and blasts and flashes of light echoed off the buildings through the rain.

Dorothy's slippery hand grabbed mine again and we turned —straight into a hellhound that hadn't followed the others. I raised my ankle and unclipped a knife from my boot—not fast enough. He bellowed. The fire from his chest singed my face. Smoke clouded my lungs. And my heart lurched as he sank his fiery teeth into Dorothy's leg.

She shrieked.

"*No!*" I slashed at its neck. The blade glanced off its short fur, but it released Dorothy to turn and snarl at me. Throat, belly, eyes, mouth—those were the weak points. I rolled under the beast, slicing at its abdomen, but even there, its hide was too thick. The hellhound swiped at me, legs stamping. I moved with it, narrowly avoiding it crushing my lungs.

Fighting an animal wasn't like fighting a person. There was no overpowering or outrunning it. It was vicious, its reflexes too feral to anticipate or counter. The best you could hope for was to stay one step ahead long enough to kill it.

First, take out the legs. An overhanging signpost caught my eye. Then I remembered the severed reins and a plan formed.

The beast's bloody teeth snapped onto my sleeve, black saliva dripping onto my hand. I sliced its snout. Blood streamed over my cuff. It howled but retreated, pawing at its face. I sheathed the knife, rolled away, and sprinted across the cobblestones, tossing a glance over my shoulder to make sure it followed.

It did.

I scooped up the discarded reins, praying they would be

long enough. I ran up the brick building—one step, two—and launched for the signpost, using the momentum to swing up until I stood on the iron bar. The creature hurtled toward me, leaping up the building with fire spewing from its mouth. The blaze licked my rubber soles.

Next, the maw.

When it fell, so did I, and I landed on its back. It growled, jaws snapping as it writhed and spun. I wrapped the reins around its mouth and held fast. Fire built between the cracks in its teeth, and I knew it would singe through the leather in a few moments, regardless of the downpour.

I had seconds.

Now the kill.

Blood slicked my hands as I fumbled for the knife in my boot. Flames shot through its teeth, burning the reins—

I plunged the knife through the beast's eye. It yelped and staggered, lowering enough for me to grab a stone from the ground and pound it into the hilt. The blade drove into the hellhound's brain. With one last roar, he slumped to the street and moved no more. Rain pummeled his short fur, fizzling when it turned to steam.

My chest heaved, and I swiped at the water pouring into my eyes. Slowly, I got to my feet. When I finally turned back, my heart stopped. Fear lanced my insides. Dorothy, dress bloody and wet curls strewn over her face, lay lifeless on the cobblestones.

34

Dorothy

Fire spread from my thigh, searing the flesh on my leg. Then ice followed; a bitter bite that turned my bones brittle. Fire, ice, fire, ice. I free fell into a roiling abyss, black as pitch and thick with churning smoke. I couldn't open my eyes.

I tried to scream.

My throat collapsed.

Behind my eyes I saw stars, streaking the sky and plummeting to the earth. But they were dark. Pellets of power and destruction, pelting my face.

Help me.

Tears of agony leaked from my eyes.

Someone, help!

I pulled in a breath.

Anyone.

A black shadow passed over me and lifted me off the hard ground, and I thought it must be Nicholas. Warm arms cradled me to a strong chest, and I sank into that security, jostling when my rescuer broke into a run.

I felt like a little girl who'd wandered into the wood after planting lavender with her father.

Nicholas knew we were going to steal the crown from the vault tonight, and he'd come to save me. Relief spread through my body like an antidote, easing the pain just a little. He wasn't Ashley. He wouldn't leave me broken.

Fire continued to stab my leg. Whistles pierced the night—the guards still hunting us. With every jarring footfall pushing my eyelids apart, I caught pieces of buildings blurring past. Darkened windows; soaked handbills on the cobblestones; a street broom propped against a wheelbarrow quickly filling under the deluge. Then came the gentle shushing of someone sweeping through foliage. I pulled in another breath, deeper this time, and smelled it, even through the rain:

Cardamom. Warm and spiced and bringing a pain of another kind.

And all I saw was lavender, and all I heard was a voice echoing, *I'll always come for you.*

The abyss beckoned, dragging me deeper and away from the scorching anguish. But it couldn't be Ashley and all his secrets. He'd had every chance to save me *before.* To shelter my heart.

It jiggered loose a memory I'd almost forgotten: my father's last words to me, uttered on a dark street moments before his kidnapping. *They are all takers, Dorothy. Every one of them. They'll steal your mind, your magic, your heart, your soul. It is what they do. But it is only a good man who will give them back to you, and until he does, don't believe that he's good at all.*

The last thought I had before the darkness claimed me, was that Ashley—the Rook—could *never* be good. He'd never come for me. He had taken all those things.

And he'd cut them into pieces.

Darkened images flashed through my mind, head spinning too fast to tell if they were dream, illusion, or reality. Gray stone walls towered overhead. Black feathers rained through an open ceiling, brushing my cheeks in their descent. Sapphires glowed against a silver backdrop, hovering in the air. They touched my thigh and I screamed.

The dull throb travelling through my leg woke me. I moaned, eyelids fluttering open. Above me, murky clouds drifted past stars and trailed a light sprinkle behind them, and a shadowed face watched me. A haze clouded my eyes, lingering no matter how many times I blinked.

Then I heard a soft, careful release of air—not my own.

"Nicholas?" I breathed.

The figure stiffened.

I sucked in through my teeth at the pain, then managed, "M-My leg. The guards—"

"You're safe." If I hadn't recognized the voice, there could be no mistaking who it belonged to when he shifted forward into a patch of moonlight, illuminating his high cheekbones, straight nose, and pink lips. I'd seen it so much recently, I'd almost forgotten how painfully beautiful his face was.

Poetry, I'd once thought. Still thought.

Magic.

Ashley.

"Ashley..." I said weakly, inexplicable tears pricking my eyes. And I didn't know what emotion they were born from, only that they came suddenly, half delirium.

"You're safe," he said again, quieter, almost to himself. And he was wearing that foreign look again, the one that made his brows slant up but his eyes darken, like he was going to both splinter apart and burn the world down at the same time.

Heat fogged my head, mind shorting out like a disconnected electrical current. I was lying flat on a hard surface, raised above the floor like a table. An altar.

I was inside a church.

Rainwater and sweat soaked my corset, making it cling to my skin, and I shivered under the slight breeze washing through the open ceiling. Jagged moonlight shone around me on the altar, cutting itself on the broken stained-glass lancet windows. Ivy and wisteria crawled along the walls and traceries.

"Wh-where are we?" I finally managed in a whisper, wetting my dry and bloodless lips.

"I'm not sure," Ashley said, and I was certain he'd never uttered the phrase before.

Light fingers grazed my forehead, and I traitorously leaned my face into his calloused hand before I could stop myself. Wretchedly raw, I stared up at him, watching a water droplet trickle down his temple, watching his jaw clench, hearing his cautious inhales—like each one pained him—but most of all, feeling the pad of his fingers softly push a curl off my face in a trance, like he was unaware he was doing it.

His hand blazed a hot trail down my face to rest on the side of my neck. It oriented me; the fire, pain, and fog melted away as I became conscious only of his touch.

"I told you," he said, voice thick with torment. His throat bobbed. "I told you to get out while you still could—that my magic would destroy you. I'm sorry, Dolly."

My throat worked. "Stop." But I was directing it more toward the two warring parts of my heart, anger rising above the pain. Shakily, I tried to rise, but the world whorled and my thigh burned like acid, and when I whimpered, Ashley pushed me back down.

"Don't get up. I'm sorry, but I need to take the tourniquet off."

"Stop being *sorry.*" Vision flashing in and out, I took three deep breaths. I shook my head against the stone. "I don't need you to shoulder every burden and act like it's all been your fault, and then use it as a pitiful excuse to push me away."

"...It *is* my fault—"

"I asked you to conjure something. If it was reckless of me to trust you, then it's a decision *I* made, and I won't have you save me from the consequences."

I don't want you to be sorry, because then the rage recedes. I want to hate you.

Please, let me hate you.

"I *trusted* you." Tears leaked from my eyes and hit the altar, the pain and the fever freeing my tongue, the weight of our past pummeling me. "But I was blind. And so, so foolish. And my heart won't stop breaking."

Then I whisked away to a bookshop, a ballet, to fingers lacing up my dress and a closet in a factory, a darkened art studio and a fevered Ashley sitting against my bedroom wall, kissing me tenderly enough to spark dreams.

Each image redirected a fresh wave of pain from my thigh to my heart.

"It is not your fault," I whispered. "It is *mine.*" For having been so ignorant, and innocent, and trusting. *You're right. I have changed. And I hate how I am, but I don't know how to be anything else.*

Not while I can still see you. Not while I'm still broken.

Ashley watched me in silence, face dark and unreadable. With a hesitant touch, he thumbed away a tear lingering at the corner of my eye, then seeming to remember himself, pulled his hand back, rubbing the moisture between his fingers. I rolled my head over, the smell of soil and ivy filling my lungs with every injured breath. When his attention shifted to my skirts, I registered what he'd said earlier.

If my leg had required a tourniquet, I must've lost a lot of blood, and the rest of it flooded to my face at the image of him tying it on. Gently, he lifted my lacy petticoats which were discolored with huge brown patches, eyes averted. Perhaps I was too numb to sense Ashley's nimble fingers working the knot, because all I felt was a release of pressure before he lowered my dress with a dirtied bandage in his other hand.

He stared at the red trickling his palms for a long moment— my blood—before his gaze cut up and he swallowed. Hard. "I have to tell you something."

More than your *blood is on my hands,* I thought he would say.

"I stole the bracelet from your grandfather's statue." As he watched me, every inch of him waited with a tomblike stillness, all except a muscle in his jaw. "I wouldn't have, except—I need it. And there's no other way."

Even through the fever, the words were enough to make me freeze. "Why are you telling me this?" I breathed, afraid of what he might confess next.

A token for a token.

And that thought was quickly chased by a torrent of others: *Please don't say it.*

Do.

Tell me you had no choice in all the kidnappings.

That you had no choice but to take my father.

That you're holding a force more dangerous at bay.

That the magic is controlling you—something.

Anything.

If I can't hate you, let me love you.

His voice pitched lower, and he grabbed my hand, squeezing. "Because you need to stay far, far away. Don't trust me. Don't trust anyone. And I can help you find your father, I just—I need time. I must do something first."

"Do what?" I wished I didn't have the courage to ask. I wasn't sure I was strong enough to hear the answer.

Why offer to bring Father back when he hadn't bothered with any of the other victims?

All of Ashley's secrets and games—what was it all leading to?

Ashley's mouth sealed closed. Black flickered behind my eyes; something—whether the loss of blood, or magical bite wound, or crushing fatigue—was pulling me under, trying to force me to rest.

"I..." Half a thought formed, but ultimately dissipated when it failed to connect. Anvils rested on my eyelids, and it took all my concentration to keep them open.

Ashley bent forward, smoothing stray locks off my forehead. "Rest."

And I almost obeyed, until a realization pierced through the fog and made me clutch his sleeve in desperation. I dragged myself into a sitting position. "The last map piece," I said urgently. "With an injured leg, how am I supposed to..." The words slurred, my tongue so heavy each one was a labor to form. "We need to discover where to search and retrieve it. The ball is... It's tomorrow night and if Lark doesn't have it..." My muscles went slack.

"Shh." His arms slid around me to stop me from falling, one hand tangling in my damp curls.

My gaze stumbled onto his lips and clung there; it was the lifeline I didn't know I needed, and if I looked away, I would drown. I was in his arms, and it struck me that I might never be again. I cupped his jaw, intending to bring his mouth down to meet mine, but he caught my wrist and tucked it against his mouth. Not in a kiss, but still tenderly, like he needed my skin on his lips.

"You will be well by morning," Ashley soothed, soft voice so at odds with his darkening face. "I swear it. As for the last map piece...I already know where it is."

Of course he did—and my anger tried to rally, but against my will, I sighed, and my eyelids drooped closed. He lowered me down, falling slowly with me to the altar, and I imagined that he clutched me tightly there. That he held me for a long time. I sank deeper, and deeper, and his lips skimmed my ear, his final whisper echoing in the welcoming darkness.

"And you will not be helping me."

35

The Rook

To most people, even those who'd been raised on its streets, London and its smokestacks was a foreign beast. Beautiful, but formidable to gaze upon and navigate. By its nature, unknowable. But the Rook had achieved the impossible, for he had tamed it. He knew every building and alley and smokestack by heart.

Or so he had thought.

Cool summer breeze ruffling his hair, he gazed at the abandoned church, in awe of its lethal beauty. In awe that before last night, he hadn't known it existed. It looked as if it had remained untouched for a hundred years, but ever cautious, he'd staked it out all day. It wasn't on any map; no one came. No one knew to.

He'd been searching for such a place.

Stained glass crunched underfoot as he walked its roofless halls. As if by divination, a rook flew overhead and landed on an arch, cocking its head and turning to look at him. After a moment, it cawed in approval, then flapped away, a black feather fluttering to the stony ground.

Reverently, the Rook picked it up, twirling it slowly in his fingers, before digging out the crown from his deep pockets. He'd already loosened the topmost gem from its setting—covered in etchings, just like the first one—and now he used the feather shaft to finish prying it free.

He now had two pieces of the map. But not without cost.

Unbidden, the sobering events from the night before flashed in his eyes. He'd never felt so terrified. For that reason alone, he hadn't wanted to return to this church, but...

With all the Lightfoot agents sniffing around, his usual hiding place had recently come under suspicion, and he couldn't afford to be cornered now.

Not when he was so close.

He turned on his heel and drifted out the entrance, feeling a hardening in his chest that he recognized as stubbornness. He was climbing the heights, teetering on the edge, sweating at the realization of how far he could fall. But it was far too late to turn back now.

The church already hid last night's secret within its ivy-riddled walls. By the end of the night, it would be hiding five more.

36

Dorothy

Something soft and warm cradled me, making my bones melt with comfort like a butterfly nestled in a cocoon. A thought tickled the edge of my mind, pulling me up for air when all I wanted was to wrap myself tighter.

I fluttered my eyes open.

Burnished gold rays tickled the lacy curtains and splayed patterns on the white blanket that covered me. Mint green wallpaper flooded my vision, and it took me several disoriented moments to realize I was in my quarters at Buckingham and not in my bed at home.

Uncle Benedick's home, now.

By the cast of the shadows, it had to be after noon at least, and I frowned, wondering why I had slept so late...

I bolted upright, the memory of last night unfolding before my eyes like a play. Breaking into the vault, running from the guards, my scream as Ashley's hellhound sunk its teeth into my leg—

I threw my blankets off, pulling my nightgown up and over my thigh, holding my breath in preparation for the ugly sight.

In awe, I released the pent-up air and traced a thumb over the curving swollen lines. They tingled, a dull ache responding to my touch, but the wound was otherwise healed. No more than a nasty scar.

How...?

Nothing but magic could've made my leg whole so quickly. Yet, though Ashley had promised to heal me, his slant was illusions and—somehow—being able to see memories. Not medicinal. I'd need to ask him at the ball tonight how he'd managed to—

The ball.

The last map piece!

My gaze shot to the wall where a ticking clock hung. 5:15 in the evening.

A hazy memory from last night cleared. Ashley had admitted that he already knew where it was. *You will not be helping me.* Which meant he was searching for it now or biding his time until nine o'clock when he could access the underground lake.

Either way, he was cutting me out of the picture.

Outmaneuvering me.

Again.

Teeth gritting, I sprang to my closet, throwing on the first dress I found and braiding my hair with nimble fingers. He wasn't going to win so easily.

He wasn't going to win again.

I was so busy bustling through the door that I didn't see the servant bearing a note on a silver tray until I'd nearly bowled her over. "Urgent message for you, miss," she said with a clumsy curtsy, extending the tray.

I thanked her, about to tear the paper open when her eyes widened.

"Did you hear about the monsters, miss?"

My thigh tingled. "What monsters?"

"Hounds." She paled. "Dozens of them as tall as buildings, straight from hell, ravaging the streets all last night. Killed several of Her Majesty's personal guards. And they are saying —" She slapped a hand over her mouth, then, after glancing around, finished in a whisper, "They are saying the beasts were made by dark magic. By the Rook."

Strangely, the rumors were close to the truth. Remembering the moment in the hallway when Ashley's illusion had fallen away, I rigidly crossed my arms over my stomach. Had the guards recognized me? Were they looking for me now? "That's an awful lot of magic for one man. Has anyone else been implicated?"

"The guards didn't get a good look at any faces, miss. But Her Majesty has tripled the sentries for tonight's ball."

My shoulders relaxed marginally. As the maidservant bustled away, I ripped the note open, already resuming my brisk walk, but stopping short when I read the contents.

Come to the agency

The message was typeset, so I couldn't tell from the handwriting whether Brass had sent it, or Nicholas. A frustrated sigh burst through my lips. They likely wanted to scold me for last night's disastrous events, and they certainly deserved to, but...now? When I hadn't a moment to lose?

I glanced between the balustrade and the hallway that led to Ashley's quarters, hesitating only a moment before dashing down the stairs, praying this urgent meeting—whatever it was about—wouldn't take too long.

AFTER MILES OF INCHING, dusty London traffic, it was a relief to finally break through the congestion and rumble swiftly down a country road. Once I arrived, I paid the hansom cab driver and dove into the agency building, consulting a clock above the desks as I went. 6:06. Three hours until sunset and Ashley broke into the cistern. Six hours until the ball.

Maybe enough time.

Maybe just.

On the third story, I rapped at Mr. Brass's door, turning the golden knob at his invitation to enter. "What's happened?" I asked before I'd even fully stepped through.

Mr. Brass sat behind his desk, steepling his fingers. "I could ask you the same question. The day is nearly gone and only now do you appear. I take it you haven't seen this morning's *Times*?"

"Last night, I ran into some...complications. I was injured, and I overslept—"

"You are injured?"

I started at Nicholas's voice, coming from where he stood by the window. With combed brown hair and a freshly shaven jaw, he looked very put together—the opposite of what I must look at the moment.

His gaze raked over me, lips cutting a fierce angle like he had a bad taste in his mouth. "Tell me how," he breathed darkly.

"I am better now." My hand gripped my dress and folded the fabric over my thigh, as if shielding it from his attention. Somehow, I sensed that if he knew the extent of the injury, it would only hurt my case.

Nicholas pursed his lips, dissatisfied, then withdrew a folded newspaper from his vest and set it on the desk. Able to read the headline from this distance, a pit opened in my stomach.

My entire middle squeezed, tighter and tinier until it was a little lead ball, sinking to my toes.

Five? But how? When had he—

A voice was speaking, but it sounded garbled, like I was underwater. Last night, I'd almost dared believe... How had Ashley managed to do this in one night?

Why?

"Dorothy."

My gaze snapped up, realizing Nicholas had repeated my name several times.

He was leaning over the desk, staring at me through the tops of his eyes. "He conjured the beasts to distract us, then pulled off a mass kidnapping right under our noses. He played us. *Again.* And this time gambled with your life." He straightened. "I don't feel comfortable with you continuing the mission."

"What?" I blurted. The shock hit two seconds later, followed by a wave of indignation that made my hands clench. "But we were successful. We got the crown. We got the second map piece."

Nicholas shook his head. "There's too much risk."

I huffed. "I—"

"He *hurt* you. Maybe it's because he knows we're onto him and is leading you into a trap. Maybe you can't earn his trust because he *has* none." He combed a hand through his neat hair, mussing it. "We must retreat now, before the last map piece is discovered and the Rook collects all the bracelets. It's the only way to thwart his plans."

"And forfeit the bracelet we gave to Lark? We can't—we're too close!"

"We could lose everything," Nicholas said calmly.

My open palm slapped the desk. "I can do it. He already knows where the final map piece is. Let me help him search, and I'll convince him to tell me where he's stashed the bracelets. He's so close—so *close* to telling me." All the things he'd admitted last night were proof of that.

Nicholas's mouth worked, then he turned his head to the side, muttering to Mr. Brass, "Father, may I speak with her alone, please?"

Understanding softened Brass's eyes, and he rose, giving Nicholas's shoulder a squeeze before striding out the door and closing it.

Nicholas met me with a look that made my lungs squeeze—all disappointment and concern and something else that felt black. "Tell me you want to continue because you want to best him, not prove his innocence," he murmured.

My brows came together, mouth pinching. "*What?*" I breathed.

"Because if all this is borne from a need to *win*, well... That, at least, I may forgive."

I blinked, but before I could form a defense, he went on, softer than before.

"I've seen it, Dorothy; his influence over you grows stronger. Every day you grow closer to believing his lies, and it's like you..." He wet his lower lip, shaking his head. "...It's like you can't *help* it."

I looked away. "I can..." were my feeble words, but they rang hollow.

Nicholas stepped forward, a gentle finger tipping my chin up and forcing me to meet his eyes. "It's his magic. It's forcing you to have feelings for him when you know you shouldn't. And it's too dangerous for you to go on."

Were my passions the influence of his slant? Could that influence grow even when he wasn't near? My emotions had only continued to burn hotter—despite all that had transpired—so...perhaps it was true. "I admit, he has managed to...draw some sympathy from me. But that is my own shortcoming, not his."

Nicholas's finger dropped, and he scowled. "Even now you defend him."

"No!"

Please, I was on the cusp of saying, *please let me explain.* But Nicholas's voice rose before I could.

"As long as you remain near him, it will be like this. You will fall under his spell while denying you have, and I will wonder, and *wonder* if I have not made the most terrible decision. If I am not the author of my own agony."

My eyes prickled. "I am not under his spell, nor do I wish to prove him innocent. I want justice for my father."

"And what of what I want?"

"I can't *lose* my only chance—!"

His hands shot toward me, eyes frantic as he pulled me closer. "I can't lose *you*, Dorothy!"

My mouth fell open. The moment dangled from a thread, suspended and spinning.

Nicholas exhaled a shaky breath, then closing his eyes, rested his forehead against mine, whispering, "What happens when he conjures dragons next? What then? Please." His thumb tenderly traced my jaw. "Please understand why I am asking this."

My heart tugged me toward him, its labored beating heavy with an indescribable ache. And in that moment, I truly didn't know what I wanted. If I'd never met Ashley at all, the romance between Nicholas and I could have blossomed naturally. *Would* have. There was no question I was drawn to Nicholas, and always had been…but was that because he promised me safety?

No. I had feelings for Nicholas that went below the surface. Falling for him just felt different.

And those *other* feelings, the ones for a man who'd opened my cage but clipped my wings…those I couldn't trust.

In the silence, I swallowed twice before slowly nodding. I did understand. And I even agreed with him.

After a moment, Nicholas stepped back, his touch sliding down my arm to squeeze my hand. His jaw worked, like he found his next words bitter to say. "As his fiancée, you'll need to attend the ball tonight at his side, to avoid the whispers of the *ton*. But don't tell him what you know and don't help him search for the last piece. We'll stay on at the palace through the end of the week and decide our next step from there."

Another nod from me. Another squeeze from him, then he let go and headed for the door.

Stopping in the doorway, Nicholas turned back with soft, understanding eyes. "With all you have sacrificed, no one could doubt your loyalty and courage. There is nothing more for you to prove." He lingered, his direct gaze stressing his point, before disappearing.

I ruminated for a few minutes before working up the energy to walk out of the room. The past few weeks, Ashley had been doing what he did best: lulling me into a charmed sleep. These kidnappings were a grim awakening; a reminder that I still couldn't trust him. I never could.

No matter how compelling his lies, he was still the Rook. He still had my father. And I couldn't believe I'd almost forgotten it.

As I descended the stairs, my thigh burned slightly,

reminding me of all that had transpired last night. Ashley had confessed about stealing my family's bracelet—and from what appeared to be guilt, of all things, verifying he had a conscience. If he'd entrusted me with that information, he might divulge more if I only pressed.

As my hansom cab jostled me back toward London, Nicholas's words replayed over and over in my mind. He'd said I didn't need to prove my loyalty or courage—and I *had* been courageous, daily facing my father's kidnapper.

But my loyalty... That felt less certain, and I despised myself for that fact.

Maybe it was about winning, after all. Because when I thought about Ashley wriggling out of our trap as Nicholas wanted, my nails dug into my palms until I'd nearly broken skin. I wasn't ready to lose. I wasn't ready to lose my father, lose all the work I'd done, lose Ashley—

"No," I whispered through my teeth, willing the word to be true. It *was* true.

My mouth set in a determined line. And I'd have to beg Nicholas for forgiveness later, because heaven help me, I had to prove it.

If not to everyone else, then to myself.

37

Dorothy

From my quarters, I retrieved a slant gun, which I hooked under my dress, as well as the riddle I'd jotted down on the ripped book page. It was just after nine. As I sped toward the archives, I jotted over the homophones, nearly bumping into a set of velvet drapes, a bust of Prince Albert, two collies, and a butler on my trek.

Writ in glass the key resides
Where each mortal frame abides
Nine dreams, ten dreams, twixt is where it wakes
The ~~muse~~ mews of kings must circumvent
Breach the ~~pale~~ pail and give ~~dissent~~ descent
~~Poor~~ Pour clock, war clock, chime unto the lakes

Circumvent... Perhaps I needed to inspect the outside of the stables? Other than that, I couldn't decipher what I was missing.

Jacintha said she never left the archives, but she was nowhere to be seen when I arrived. I headed straight for the section that held information on the century when magic was born, pulling books that might be relevant and stacking them on a desk.

I combed through them, scouring the lines of succession, mentions of the mages, information on clepsydras, and old maps of London. I turned a page and grabbed a magnifying glass, studying an illustration of the walled square mile known back then as the City, but it marked no stables. What was now brick terraces and shops used to be fields and hamlets. Few structures from centuries ago still existed today.

Back then...

I wanted to slap my forehead for the oversight. "Stupid," I muttered. "Of *course*."

The old mews from five hundred years ago wouldn't have been at Buckingham—it hadn't yet been built. I'd gone to the wrong stables. I moved the magnifying glass across the fields until I found it, a tiny speck near Charing Cross: The Royal Mews. I flipped to a current map, lining up the corresponding location until my finger froze. Modern day Trafalgar Square.

Slamming the book shut, I checked the time again. 9:41. Nineteen minutes to find this underground lake. I swung around the desk, mentally apologizing to Jacintha for failing to clean up my mess, and ran out of the archives. Trafalgar Square was only half a mile from the palace, but it was large and would take time to search.

Here I was again. Racing against Ashley, trying to outsmart him. And the feeling was oddly...

Not comforting. But familiar enough that it shot sparks through my feet and made my breaths deepen with excitement.

The fountains at Trafalgar Square quietly sprayed water into their granite pools, while not far from them towered Nelson's Column, glinting in the night. A hansom cab clattered down the street. Two couples strolled the parameters, enjoying the evening air and both eyeing me—a girl out late without hat, gloves, or chaperone—curiously when they passed. Otherwise, it was deserted.

If I found the entrance, I'd have to wait until there was no foot traffic to open it. I couldn't chance someone witnessing.

Carefully, I walked the square, scouring for anything out of place. Thousands of feet passed through here on a given day, which meant the clepsydra—and the entrance to the underground lake—had to be disguised. Discovering nothing, I wandered toward Nelson's column.

As the column had been constructed only a half-century ago, the builders must've built in a new mechanism with which to access the lake. Or at least I hoped they did.

Bronze plaques, cast from captured French canons, adorned each side of the base, depicting four key battles from Lord Nelson's naval career. When I got to The Battle of the Nile, I stopped and squinted up at the scene. A wounded Lord Nelson, held up by his men, heroically commanded his ship. A shirtless officer hunched below him, and the young man's shoulder was sculpted a bit too sharply to be natural. It was such a small detail—practically undetectable—and yet... A quick glance around revealed that the couples had left, and I was alone.

I hiked my skirts and ascended in an unladylike climb, due to the massive steps. I thumbed over the bronze shoulder, then pushed it in. Grating rock filled the air as a small fissure opened in the ground behind me. Inside the hole lay two stone bowls with the diameter of a saucer. One bore a tiny slit in its side while the other was situated below it, meant to catch the runoff.

I grinned. The clepsydra.

With nothing to transport the water but my cupped hands, I ran the twenty paces to the fountains and painstakingly filled the upper cup over several trips until it overflowed. More grinding echoed, this time accompanied by the sound of gears as the granite stones lowered one by one to create a staircase that wound down into the pitch black.

If I weren't so worried Ashley had already found the map piece, I might've stopped to lament how often I'd had to plunge into the dark lately. I gripped the cold iron railing and began my descent. The stairs closed behind me—perhaps signaled by the emptying of the clepsydra?—and goosebumps prickled my arms, praying I'd be able to open them on the return journey.

Complete darkness closed in.

Dripping echoed from beneath, marking my progress as it grew louder and was joined by a chorus of others. The air swirled cold and wet, coating my lungs with a strange mixture of mildew and mint. The railing grew damp and coarse against my palm, the top chipping off in patches where the iron had oxidized. With his slant having to do with water, it seemed strange that Simon hadn't considered a non-rusting metal when concealing his map piece.

After I'd descended what I guessed to be a couple hundred feet, the quiet clang of metal stairs gave way to the gentle scrape of stone. Bits of grass and dozens of little glowing mushrooms sprang up between the stones; the caps were iridescent blue like the magical particles one saw through a slant gun, bright enough to illuminate a landing with an archway held up by Grecian pillars similar to those in the Necropolis.

Above the arch was chiseled a foreign phrase that I strained to read.

Μόνο οι άξιοι θα επικρατήσουν

One of Ashley's clues for the Samaritan's identity had forced me to study Greek using books from my father's library. I had enough grasp of the language to roughly translate it into

Only the Worthy may prevail. Tingles coursed through my limbs, suddenly stiff and cold.

There was that word again. **Αξιος.** Worthy. I thought of the A on Ashley's collarbone and stepped through the arch. Thousands more of the blue glowing mushrooms speckled the floor and walls, brightening the chasm in an azure shimmer.

I hadn't exactly bothered to be quiet with my descent, so I wasn't too surprised to find Ashley standing inside, leaning against a pillar with his arms crossed and his eyes unreadable.

We plunged into a tense, almost awkward silence as we just stared at each other. Squirming under his gaze, I straightened my shoulders. "I do not give up easily, Mr. Gardner."

"So I see." His voice was deeper. Tired.

"I thought you admired that quality about me."

"I can admire something and be terribly inconvenienced by it at the same time."

"Are you concerned you will lose?"

"You and I are not in competition. I was to find the last map piece *for* you, Dorothy, and now you endanger us both by coming."

I bristled at the accusation. "What's that supposed to mean?"

His mouth snapped shut. When it opened again, it was to ask quietly, "How's your leg?"

"Miraculously, nearly healed, thanks to you."

His eyebrows twitched down, and he looked like he was about to press for more, so I quickly changed the subject.

"The map piece is somewhere in this cavern? Any inkling where?"

Ashley stuffed his hands in his pockets and tipped his head toward the nearest column. "I thought I'd follow those markings." The same mage's symbol from the journal and the hedge maze engraved the pillar. Beyond it, another pillar bore the same.

Colonnades lined the vast chasm, reminiscent of ancient Greece, rising out of a shallow pool of water. Upon closer inspection though, the stone floor sloped sharply a few feet from the edge, making the depth of this underground lake unknowable.

The musty air was full of magic, reminding me that if the other map pieces had been hidden by their mage's enchantment, some danger probably lurked in the water here.

Which made following the symbols tricky.

I glanced around. "Look." I pointed down the stony shore, where a small boat was tied to one of the pillars, resting on the glassy surface. If it had been here all these centuries, it must be enchanted to not decay somehow.

"Yes, I noticed. How thoughtful of Simon."

We trekked several yards toward the boat, and my trepidation grew with each step. Maybe it was because I was used to Ashley's genius touch, but this all felt too convenient. There had to be something more sinister at play.

Ashley grabbed the rope and began unwinding it from its anchor.

I cleared my throat. "We're going to use it?"

"I don't have a spare dory in my pocket. Do you?" He smiled like he'd cracked a joke, but his mouth carried a bitter slash to it.

Not knowing what to make of his comment, I swallowed my misgivings and stepped into the boat, careful not to let my dress touch the water. As I settled into my seat, I mopped my dewy face with one hand.

Venturing out onto an underground lake in enchanted waters was not my first choice. If Ashley's magic decided to flare up again, there was nowhere for me to run.

And then what would I do?

His influence over you is growing stronger. Nicholas's words echoed in my mind. *It's like you can't help it.*

Ashley pushed the boat off and expertly hopped inside. Using the oars, he navigated us deeper into the cavern, but his paddles were slow, as if he too were wary of the water.

I gripped my hands tightly in my lap. If we were on the cusp of finding the last map piece, I had to discover where he was keeping the bracelets. Which meant dangerous probing.

I licked my lips, then said carefully, "How *did* you heal me last night?"

Ashley stroked the water a few times before answering. "Magic."

"But healing isn't your slant."

"So it isn't. Quite the sleuth you are."

I bristled at the mild jab but didn't let it show. "I know I was fevered and disoriented, but for a moment while I lay on that altar, I swore I saw something blue and glowing. Something like sapphires. I think you used a bracelet to borrow someone's slant and heal me."

His eyes slid to me, but he said nothing.

"It wouldn't surprise me if you'd known of someone nearby who could help," I went on. "You've always had fortuitous connections. I only want to know if I'm right."

His strokes of the oar slowed then stopped.

I leaned in slightly, voice soft. Coaxing. "You can tell me anything, Ashley."

His stare was guarded, but his throat bobbed. He wanted to. He was so close, and all I had to do was—

His gaze cut away, down to the water. "We're here."

I looked up to find that the symbols on the pillars didn't continue, then followed Ashley's gaze. Glimmering at the bottom of the pool was a gem identical to the other map pieces, but because the water was crystal clear, it was impossible to tell how far down it lay.

And that's when I noticed it: the piles of bones scattered on the lake's floor, half a dozen soulless skulls gaping up at me. Gooseflesh prickled on my skin. These people had already attempted to obtain the map piece—and had died trying.

"What do you think the water's enchanted with?" I said, cautiously peering over the edge.

"Only one way to find out." Ashley stood and shrugged out of his coat.

My eyes widened. "Don't—"

But he dove off the side, barely making a splash. I held my breath as he emerged, waiting for him to exclaim in confusion at his surroundings, or for his flesh to melt off his bones, but nothing happened. His brows ticked up, and he shrugged his shoulders.

"Appears to be fine."

"Don't *do* that," I breathed, turning my head away.

But he must've overheard because he paddled back and, grasping the lip of the boat with one hand, smiled faintly up at me. "Were you worried for me, Miss St. James?"

"Not at all, Mr. Gardner."

"Then how do you explain your dilated pupils?"

I glanced back at him. "There is very little light in this cavern."

His grin widened, and my gaze fixed to his pink lips. "Especially when I dove into the water."

I leaned over the brim. "And you seem to have left all your sense down there."

He chuckled, giving me a peek at his straight white teeth. Then he glanced up and the sound fizzled out in his throat, like he was just realizing how close we were. His eyes darted to my lips—so quick. So quick, and light, and barely there at all, that I was certain the low light was playing tricks on me.

My blood flashed warm, sensing his magic as it began to manifest—

Ashley shoved the boat away, creating waves and sending me rocking. Then he took two large backward strokes until he hovered over the map piece and dove, kicking his legs to plunge deeper.

My exhale in the newfound silence was slow. Last night, he'd touched me instinctively, eagerly; now his barriers were firmly in place, and I didn't know what to make of the reaction. If I didn't keep the newspaper headline at the forefront of my mind, I was going to fail.

The bracelets. I had to get him to tell me where the bracelets were.

A moment later, when I checked on Ashley's progress, he'd listed to the side. My gaze jumped back to the map piece—the complete opposite direction. He zigzagged through the water like a streak of lightning, with no seeming pattern or destination.

Since laying eyes on this cistern, a sense of dread had lurked at the back of my mind. As I watched Ashley swim farther and farther away, that dread grew, until I'd paddled halfway to him before realizing I'd even picked up the oars. When I neared, he was close enough to the surface that I was able to use the wood to poke his leg. He latched onto the oar and followed it to the surface.

He gasped in a huge breath, his exhale fogging in the chilly air. "It's pitch black."

"What do you mean?"

"The enchantment. Once I'm submerged, I can't see a bloody thing. I can't tell up from down. It's like walking in a nightmare; no logic or physics to guide you. I'm not sure I would've found air again if you hadn't pulled me up."

That explained the bones. Those men had kept on swimming, desperately clawing for the surface even while their efforts only drove them deeper.

"If you had a light to guide you—"

Ashley nodded, grasping the boat. "I'm sure that would pierce the enchantment. But what light doesn't go out even when underwater?"

Not a torch, nor a gas lamp. Certainly nothing I could think of—short of something magic. My mind drifted to the glowing surrounding the cavern, sparking an idea.

Summoning magic to my raising hands, I turned them in a circle until they hit a wall. I dropped the magic and a vision of the past sprang to life. A weave of ripples crisscrossed the water, past and present muddying the surface. Far to the left, an identical boat bobbed, another Ashley and another Dorothy conversing about what they should do.

The real Ashley looked at me, one eyebrow quirking.

I'd just shown him my slant.

"My slant deals with time," I said by way of explanation. "Past, present, and future." Without thinking, I lifted my skirts and retrieved the slant gun strapped to my leg.

Ashley clucked his tongue. "Anything else under there I should be worried about?"

"Oh, definitely." I unscrewed the slant gun compartment and dumped out the cartridges onto my lap. Three small cylinders sloshed with a filmy gray liquid. I popped the cap of one.

Ashley watched me, half-fascinated. "What are you doing?"

"Slant gun cartridges are filled with lumagenic acid. The acid, when it collides with magical particles—" I dumped the acid on my palm and a luminescent blue light spread over my hand. "Glows," I finished, smiling.

Ashley lifted his eyes in fascination, and for a few moments, I forgot how to breathe.

Until he asked, "For how long?"

My smile faded. "A minute. Maybe two."

Ashley nodded and stroked backward, then after filling his lungs as deeply as they could go, dove under the surface. Hand tingling with the thick, oozing glow, I plunged it into the water, knowing it wouldn't wash off easily. Ashley must've been keeping time in his head, because he re-emerged only a few seconds before the light on my palm dimmed and winked out.

No map piece.

"How far down is it?" I asked.

"Only thirty feet, I'd guess." Ashley folded his arms on the rim of the boat.

I raised my eyebrows. Only? Perhaps that wasn't deep for someone raised on the sea, but for me the feat would've been impossible.

"And I made it down," Ashley went on. "The tricky bit is that it's somehow encased in the floor—as it was in the maze—and I have to try and pry it up."

"Why don't you take the next cartridge? It will cast far more light if it's on *your* palm while you're swimming—"

Ashley was already shaking his head, his arms tensing. "I won't use my magic. Not after last night." His eyes met mine with meaning.

Not after the hellhounds bit me.

My stomach swooped, even as I knew that statement, too, was a ploy. I slowly nodded, using the enchanted water to scrub the acid from my palm, which had started to tingle painfully. The acid was not meant for topical contact. It took a bit of work, but my hand finally rubbed clean. "Then we only have two more tries."

Ashley watched me as I worked. I could've sworn I'd disguised the pain, but I must've winced at some point because he edged toward the bow and fished in his coat pockets, finally tossing some fabric at me.

I stared at the black leather gloves. They were the second thing of his that he'd insisted I wear, and my cheeks warmed at the intimacy. Did he use these during his kidnappings? Had these gloves handled my father? I swallowed hard. "It might dull the concentration of the magic—"

He sighed. "Put them on, Dorothy."

I was beginning to realize he only called me Dorothy when he was tired. He called me Miss St. James when he was being cheeky, or intentionally distant. And Dolly... I didn't know why he called me Dolly. All I knew was that when he did, it was always with reverence and a hint of wonder.

The gloves were warm and supple against my skin, despite dwarfing my hands. At Ashley's signal, I rewound time again and dumped the acid on the glove. It glowed as brightly as before, and when Ashley dove, I plunged it under the surface and he descended.

I watched in amazement at the expert way he darted through the water.

"It's loose," Ashley said once he surfaced and his breath had evened again. Water dripped over his eyes.

Again, I rewound time, then popped a cartridge cap off the cylinder. "Can you get it this next time?"

He stroked backward, preparing to dive as he eyed the last cartridge clutched in my hands. "I'll have to."

I didn't like those words.

But before I could insist on a different plan, he'd disappeared, making me hurriedly dump the lumagenic acid on my palm and thrust it back into the lake.

Down, down, down he went, and even though blue light shone brightly from my hand, the water seemed to darken, as if sensing that its treasure was about to be stolen. Ashley was a dark blur, arms moving as he worked at something. Every second was an hour, scraping by so slowly I was certain he'd lingered too long. A cold sweat broke on my temple.

He wasn't going to make it.

Slowly, his form grew larger and larger as he rose, following my dimming palm like a beacon. Hope bubbled in my chest.

Almost there.

A little faster. A little—

The light on my palm faded into nothing.

My nerves jolted. He was only a few feet under the surface, but still too far for me to reach from the boat. Too far to pull up with the short oar. Quickly I stood and slipped over the edge, keeping my head above the water while sucking in quick breaths as my body adjusted to the chilly temperature.

Gripping the boat with one hand, I extended a leg down. *Please.* I kicked farther down. My foot brushed the top of Ashley's head, and a second later, his hand wrapped around my ankle, making me gasp. His touch traveled up my dress, a map leading him to air. His head broke the surface, and he panted, shaking out his black hair. "I got it," he whispered, a handsome, open-mouthed smile splitting his face.

Before I thought better of it, I mirrored it. "*We* got it."

"I was the one risking my neck," he chuckled playfully.

"I'm just as wet as you are. And your neck happens to like being risked."

"Just as your pupils like to dilate when it does."

I splashed at him. "For the last time, it is very dark in here."

Then, as we treaded water, a strange silence settled

between us, discordant and uncomfortable and slowly pilfering the smiles from our faces. Only then did I feel his hands about my waist, my own hands clutching his shirt. Our breaths mingling. When had that happened? The warm tingle of his magic seeped into my skin, urging me closer.

I resisted, about to let go when he uttered, "Yes. I used a bracelet to heal you."

My breath froze in my chest, my lips parted.

"With a bracelet, you can steal someone's slant for a few hours. And I had a friend who...who let me borrow theirs."

"*A* bracelet," I whispered, trying to tread carefully while feigning ignorance, even though my heartbeat galloped in my ears. "You have others besides my grandfather's?"

"I have six."

"And Lark's will make seven."

Ashley said nothing.

I licked my lips, edging closer to him. "It's dangerous to keep them on your person like that. You should find a safer place."

His gaze lifted and locked onto mine, green electricity arcing and pulsing through my irises. My stomach turned, acid coating the root of my tongue because I was a terrible liar and maybe this had been a terrible idea.

I know what you're doing, his eyes said. *I know because I've done it to dozens of others.*

I'd never learned the art of subtlety.

"You've seen what we've done," I fumbled, groping for a way to turn the focus back on him. I retreated and gripped the boat once more, my middle cold where his hands had been. "In the hedge, and with the vault, and with the hounds, and even down here in this cistern, we find a way through. Not because of you, or me, but because of both of us. *Together.* If you weren't so obsessed with working alone, you'd realize we make a good team, Ashley Gardner. You'd realize—finally—that you can tell me anything." My hands shook when I finished, surprised to find that I meant every word. "That you *always* could."

He remained silent, studying me with that dark, poker-faced expression that made my nerves jump.

"But it will not do," I went on, voice rising and echoing off the pillars. "You insist on staying in the shadows. Nothing anyone does will *ever* be good enough to earn your secrets."

"You play the game too," he muttered, and those five little words made me seethe. "You pretend like you're an open book, but you too have riddles."

"Ask me anything, then!"

"What is Lark giving you?" He fired the words before I'd finished my sentence, and my mouth snapped shut. "In exchange for finding the map, he will bestow me the last bracelet, but what are you getting? What drives you this time? I try to reason it but come up short—because Lark doesn't have your father, I *know* he doesn't."

My lips parted. *Because you're the Rook.* Shivers—from the cold water, or this conversation—coursed my skin.

"Neither can Lark help you, because he is not the Samaritan. So why? Why are you so desperate to find the map? Or here's another one." His voice grew quieter now, deadly. "Your slant deals with time. And in the alley outside of Beaumont's, you saw a future where you kissed me—so tell me why you chose a different one, and I will tell you where the bracelets are."

Horror scraped my insides. When he confessed he saw memories, I'd stupidly assumed he meant his own, and now I was learning he'd been within *mine.* "You went into my *mind?*"

A bit of color rose to Ashley's cheeks—something I'd never

seen before. But he only looked at me. Regretful, but so, so determined.

I reeled with both anger and fear. My present magic used to automatically alert me when someone was slanting nearby, but now I had to activate it. I'd have to maintain it in Ashley's presence, just to be sure he wasn't delving into my memories again. "Why would I make any kind of deal with you, when you have no scruples about invading my privacy?" I snapped.

"Then don't take the deal." His head cocked back. "Though I hadn't pegged you as one to be so afraid."

The veiled insult skewered deeper than it should have. Because I was *not* the cowering girl he knew before.

What else had he seen in my mind? Had he seen Nicholas, or the Lightfoots? Perhaps not if the kiss was what he was questioning me on, but even that... What could I say? I wet my lower lip, searching for an answer. Finally, I opened my mouth and said, "I..."

"No." He dug inside his vest, and the silver band he retrieved made me slowly drift back. The truth ring. "Answer with this on, and I will do the same. A secret for a secret."

Our quiet, chilled breaths filled the space.

Water dripped down Ashley's face as he continued to stare at me intently, adding softly, "A token for a token."

Here was my chance.

One little sentence, and I'd discover where the bracelets were.

But telling him that I'd been ashamed to kiss him, ashamed because I should not still carry feelings for my father's kidnapper... That was as good as the end. Once I confessed what I knew, he had every reason to kidnap me like the others, or do something far worse—

I took too long to respond, because Ashley retracted the ring and slipped it on his own finger, face shuttering closed.

"As I thought. Even you have secrets you treasure."

"There was a time I would've told you them all, without hesitation. And do you want to know what changed?" *You took everything from me.*

"*No*," he said, jaw ticking. "I don't. I don't want you here. I don't want you in my life. I never did."

The ring glowed blue. Truth. I reached for my present magic and waited for the rush of warmth, the signal that he'd illusioned it—but it never came. And then—

My raw heart gave a horrible twist, and the pain made me suck in a little breath. Was it really so easy for him? To ignore every shared look, breath, touch, every moment where we'd bared our souls, and treat it like it was nothing? Like...*I* was nothing?

Why isn't it so easy for me?

My eyes prickled, and I ground my teeth, desperately trying to shove the tears back down, because this was not supposed to happen. I wasn't supposed to care anymore. I wasn't supposed to fail. *Again.* Nicholas wasn't supposed to be right.

I wasn't supposed to love Ashley Gardner just as much as I hated the Rook. Especially when he clearly didn't love me back and never had.

"As your fiancé, I will fulfill my duty and escort you to the ball. I will play one last game." He gripped the edge of the boat, knuckles white. "But then I am finished." Dark images guttered through his eyes, and they flickered by too fast for me to decipher a single one, but they hinted at sadness. A deep, ravenous heartache. "I am finished with it *all.*"

38

Dorothy

To the sound of eleven distant, deep tolls from Big Ben, I marched up the stairs to my quarters, my waterlogged dress plopping sporadic drips on the carpet. Heightened security had made gaining re-entry to the palace take twice as long, where I'd been forced to claim I'd been caught in a downpour to explain my appearance. My skin shuddered from the cold, and my muscles quivered from exhaustion, and my mind replayed the moments in the cistern over and over and over.

I thought of the Lightfoots and how I'd let them down. I thought of Nicholas and how angry he was going to be with me for disregarding his orders. I thought of the feather on my father's pillow.

And the longer I thought, the more I felt that feather stab into the fleshy part of my throat and twist. With every fiber of my being, I prayed Papa was still alive, but in practice I could do nothing. Nothing except gain the Lightfoots' help by making his kidnapper pay.

I'd tried to be so clever—concocting a plan, venturing into the Undercity and striking a bargain with Lark, solving every puzzle and attempting to earn Ashley's trust while keeping my heart far from his reach. It had been a fool's hope.

In the end, I still lost.

In the end, Ashley still won.

In the end, my father was still missing, and I was still *broken*.

I'd let my foolish, misplaced feelings cloud my judgement, just as Nicholas had warned, and the clock was running down. An hour wasn't much time, but maybe it was enough to fix all this. I *had* to believe I could still fix it.

In the center of my chambers, the same servant girl that had attended to me before rocked anxiously on the balls of her feet. At my entrance, she turned so quickly the pins in her pale low bun nearly came flying out. "Caught in the rain again, miss?"

Again? I almost replied, but realized that after healing my wound, Ashley must have secretly returned me to my quarters last night, then sent a message for a servant to come change my dress. I nodded.

"If I may, miss," she went on hesitantly, wringing her hands, "the ball is not too far off, and there is little time to ready you—"

"Yes, yes," I said in a weary voice, slogging toward the dressing screen. The absolute last thing I wanted right now was to dance on my feet for four hours, but I had to make an appearance.

"Do you know what color Mr. Gardner will be wearing?"

"Color?"

The maid pointed to the invitation, lying open on the vanity. "It's a themed ball. Every couple is supposed to match."

I nodded, wishing I'd inspected the invitation closer and had asked Ashley when I'd had the chance. "Just a moment." I turned and marched out my door and down to the East Wing.

When I turned the corner, I slowed. Ashley's door was cracked slightly open. On impulse, I rested a hand on the doorframe and leaned in, spying through the crevice.

Ashley stood in his still-damp trousers, white shirt untucked and sleeves rolled to the elbows. With agile fingers, he worked the buttons while striding across the room, pulling the wet shirt off and tossing it over the bed.

My stomach lurched, eyes quickly tracing the strong lines of his chest and abdomen before I could stop them, as well as the brand on his collarbone. This was a bad idea. I couldn't tear my gaze away, seeing memories in every hard line of his skin, feeling a yearning ache the longer I stared.

"You can't run from me forever," a feminine voice within the room said.

Ashley froze.

So did I. Because the voice sounded eerily familiar.

Ashley raised his head, leveling his stare straight ahead at the wall. "I told you to leave me alone."

A woman stepped up behind him, curly brown hair softly falling over one shoulder. She touched a hand to his bare back, and he tensed. She shifted, allowing me a good look at her profile. "But you don't really want that, do you?"

My lips parted, needles pricking my skin. It was—

It was *me*.

No—an illusion. But then why had he felt her touch?

"Poor Ashley." She traced a few delicate shapes on his back with a finger. "All these years, without anyone ever understanding the burden you bear. Always apart, always alone. But now you don't have to be; that's why I'm here."

"You're not her," Ashley said tightly.

"Look at me."

After a few moments when Ashley didn't move, she repeated herself, magic laced through her voice. *"Look at me."*

Ashley jerked halfway around, grunting from an invisible battle, then finally turned and glowered at my likeness. The loathing streaking his face made me recoil. It was the look of power, and darkness, and unbridled rage.

It was the look of the Rook.

And it was unearthly, the sight of us facing each other down. Tingles migrated my spine.

How was Ashley's magic manifesting when we were inside Buckingham? Was it possible the mutation was becoming stronger?

"How dare you," Ashley muttered through clenched teeth. "How dare you use her against me."

My thigh burned, the bite still fresh.

The hellhounds. They'd had their own minds and will—more reality than illusion—and suddenly I understood. The events of last night had cracked the wall holding his magic at bay, and it was manifesting. Uncontrollable. Sentient. Not as much *magic*, as—

Real.

"All you have to do," the other Dorothy said, smiling softly, "is give in. Give me control and I can make your deepest desires come true." Her hand traced Ashley's shoulder over and up to gently cup his jaw. "You want to." She bent in, tugging his neck down to her level, breathing, "*So badly* you want to."

His eyes rolled closed, and for half a breath he leaned into her hand, before his eyes flashed open and his hand shot to her wrist, shoving her away. "Touch me again, and I will end you."

She chuckled lightly. "You can't kill me. I'm a part of you."

"Then you'll die with me." He shouldered past her, grabbing a black shirt draped over a chair on his trek to the window and jerking it on. My mouth dried. He'd said the words callously, with no premeditation, like he was well acquainted with the idea.

The illusion turned and locked eyes with me through the crack in the door, making me suck in a breath. It'd known I was here the entire time. A slow, wicked smile spread over her lips, and her finger curled, beckoning me inside.

My insides jolted forward, compelled by the magic. And then I heard its voice in my mind. *Come. You can convince him much better than I can. Come, come, come.*

I resisted, pulling back. But outwardly I remained frozen, unable to move an inch. My knuckles on the doorframe whitened.

To him, the magic coaxed, tugging on me, coiling and curling—

He needs you.

My breaths came quicker, muscles spasming.

And you need him.

Just one little kiss.

NO.

"No," I whispered. I jerked back, pulse pounding in my ears, and fled back down the hall.

I didn't stop shaking until I was safely back inside my room. My gaze wandered my surroundings in a haze, unfocused, catching only scraps of mint-green wallpaper, a maid's worried voice, my squished toes inside my boots. The ringing in my ears slowly cleared.

"...the ball, miss."

My eyes cut to the clock on the wall. 11:30. Half an hour until it commenced, and I hadn't even begun readying myself. Jeweled cosmetic containers on the vanity drew my notice, and something about them gave voice to a niggling thought at the edge of my mind.

I can make your deepest desires come true.

Magic was always loyal, and mutated magic had your will but not your morality. It would do anything to make your deepest wish a reality—even if it meant conjuring an illusion of a girl.

You can convince him much better than I can.

Now you endanger us both by coming, he'd said in the cistern.

What if... What if what Ashley wanted most of all wasn't the power of the bracelets, or taking people's magic away, or gaining a new slant?

What if it was me?

All this time, I'd been searching for Ashley's weakness, exasperated when he didn't appear to have any. Despite his cold treatment, despite our past, despite everything—or perhaps because of it—what if...*I* was his weakness?

In both the present and the future, he anticipated my move, or deflected, or turned the dagger back on me. *Give up,* his eyes had said during that first carriage ride—what they had always said. *Give up before your heart breaks even more.* But he'd taken my father from me, then dared to make me fall in love with him. There was nothing of my heart left to break.

That gaping hole in my chest, the chaos of his magic, me— they were all powerful tools to be used in finally defeating him. If I could just figure out how...

"Yes," I replied to the maid distantly. She'd asked if I was ready to be dressed for the ball, and only after she scurried out of the room did I register that she'd also asked if I'd like her to fetch some smelling salts. I must've looked as peaked as I felt.

In her absence, I stood abruptly and rushed from the room, hastening outside and toward the pond, where I could use my magic. Once there, I raised my hands, peering into the future one last time. A carousel of color and sound whirred by as I pushed further than I ever had before, driving my slant to the brink until it was utterly exhausted.

The scene that unfolded was unfocused, at an indistinguishable location. But Ashley stood before me, black hair reflecting the moon's glow, and as I stared at him, helplessness pulsed in every one of my veins. It had always been there, but now I could no longer stop its torrent.

Then I felt it: His magic swept around me and seized control of my feet as I ventured nearer, my hands as I gripped his shirt, my tongue as I murmured something in his ear. I was completely overtaken, drowning in magic without hope of ever breathing air again. Ashley turned his nose into my neck and melted with relief—before his features screwed in anger. He thrust a hand into his pocket—

The vision shuttered closed.

I walked back in silence, thoughts churning. Slowly at first...then cranking into a breakneck speed, steps quickening up the stairs and into my chambers. Squaring my shoulders, I strode for my vanity and scrawled a hasty note, not bothering to sign it, then flagged down a servant in the hall. Once it was securely on its way, I turned back just as the maid from earlier re-entered, smelling salts in hand.

Eyeing the cosmetics on my vanity again, I sat down. I traced a finger over a jeweled jar before opening it and liberally applying the rouge to my cheekbones. Then using a thin wooden skewer, I rimmed my eyes with kohl. I unwound some silk paper and smeared dark red lipstick over my lips, my movements methodical. Feature by feature I coated in a mask, thinking of Polina as I did so.

You are not just his weakness, a voice warned at the edge of my mind. *He is yours. This will not just break him. It will break you too.*

I banished the thought with every stroke, whetting my resolve into something razor-sharp.

Then let it break me.

When I finished, I didn't recognize the woman staring back

at me. Her beautiful lines. The striking set of her eyes. I looked like *him*.

I looked like the Rook glaring at his magic.

My attention shifted to the maid in the mirror, who'd been frozenly watching me the entire time, eyes growing rounder with my transformation. She snapped up and nodded toward the leftover lipstick abandoned on the vanity. "Would you like the red dress then, miss?"

"No," I said, knowing which color Ashley would be wearing. What he was always wearing. Touch light, I lifted the dark pearl necklace with the ebony center diamond out of its case and tied the clasp. It rested heavily on my neck like a yoke, chaining me to my one and only task, a thing which had always been inevitable:

To give in to Ashley Gardner's magic.

To let him win.

And to make him fall.

"Tonight, I shall wear the black."

39

Ashley

I scuffed my feet against the carpet, trying to ignore the weight of the map pieces in my breast pocket. Only a few more hours until the gems would leave my hands, replaced by Lark's bracelet, and the evening looked to be smooth sailing. All I had to do was crack a few jokes on the sidelines, occupy myself by dancing with every girl but my fiancée, and *voilà*. Purgatory over.

Music and laughter, so faint it tickled my ears, spiraled up the staircase. Everyone was already at the ball, and Queen Victoria was likely poised delicately atop her chair, formulating the best way to scold her favorite couple for arriving late.

A door behind me creaked open. I turned around with a droll joke on my tongue but stopped cold.

Dorothy stepped into the hall, candlelight glittering off her full black skirts like thousands of stars, dancing in a way that had to be magic. Onyx silk gloves came above her elbows, almost grazing the gossamer bell sleeves resting off her shoulders. Her collarbone was bare, save for a string of black pearls sleeping against her pale skin. The ones I'd left for her.

My pulse spiked. But my eyes weren't finished taking her in.

Half her hair loosely twisted back into roses, while the other half cascaded in soft brown curls that fell past her necklace. My breath caught in my chest, the striking lines of her eyes, brows, and burgundy lips making me wonder how I'd ever once thought her only pretty. She was perfection.

Dread coiled in my core. Purgatory was far from over. And the only word I could think of was—*No*.

It pounded like a mallet with each of her whispering steps toward me.

No, no, no, no, no.

Yes, yes, yes, my magic hummed. It zipped to my palms, and I yanked it back, desperately trying to leash it. But some dripped through the cracks, fingers trying to hold water. Little illusions of smoke raced toward her feet, parting happily around the wake of her dress. She kept her neck poised as she approached, gaze too trained on me to notice my magic stealing loose. Not once did she break eye contact, and the hunger there, the unchecked desire, nearly crumbled my carefully constructed dam.

Come back, I ordered the magic.

But it's her, it's her—and she wants you—

Dorothy stopped in front of me, the fragile hem of her sparkling black dress brushing my boot. "Shall we go down?" she said softly.

Come. Back. Sweat beaded my temples as I tugged at it, pulling the magic toward me inch by agonizing inch.

I tried to swallow but hit a boulder in my throat. I opened my mouth to say something, but then all that came out was pained, heavy breaths. Her face glowed brighter, lovelier, calling me like a siren song. And her lips—

COME BACK.

The answer came faintly, the one I'd been dreading since the day I learned of the mutation.

No.

My heart rammed into my gut. My skin flashed cold and hot at the same time. And then finally, I managed four quick words carried on a hoarse breath. "I can't go down."

"Yes, you can." Her beautiful lips smiled, and the coiled dread in my stomach constricted because in that moment, I knew.

I wasn't going to last the whole night.

She slipped a hand around the crook of my elbow and leaned in to whisper in my ear, drowning me in her French garden scent. "You are Ashley Gardner, and you can do anything." Then she led me down the stairs and to my doom.

The wisps of smoke trailed her skirts all the way until we heard the rumble of the ballroom. To my relief, they seemed to dissipate under the bright light streaming through the arch up ahead, and I wrestled the magic back behind my defenses. I had to keep it at bay.

We halted under the arch, where stairs spilled into a red-carpeted hall. Laughter and waltzing notes from stringed instruments floated on the air, thick with perfume. Enormous gilt paintings hung on the walls. From the ceiling dangled crystal chandeliers, illuminating the rainbow of gowns twirling around the floor.

Everything in me screamed to flee, unable to shake the sense of looming catastrophe, but nerves of steel rooted me to the floor. If I didn't give Lark the map at this ball, I'd never see the last bracelet. Without it, I had weeks, at most.

With it, I could rip the magic out *tonight*. Once and for all.

I searched the room for a white-blond head, praying Lark was already here and we could make the exchange quickly. Three thorough scans yielded nothing, and I muttered a curse.

No Acherons.

Dorothy's hold on my arm tightened, and my magic rushed through my blood to congregate there. "What was that?" she said.

"Nothing."

"Still keeping secrets from me, Ashley?"

My name on her tongue was a caress. My ears tingled, every awareness heightening, the magic trying to twist my neck to look down at her. Knuckles cracked as I fisted my hands, staring straight ahead.

"I have nothing to hide," I lied lightly, carelessly, the complete opposite of the tumult raging inside me.

She leaned in and my muscles tightened. "We both know that's not true."

The map pieces in my breast pocket grew heavier. My gaze cut to her feet, sliding up her dress and reaching her sleeve before I caught myself and shot it forward again. I inhaled deeply through my nose.

I needed a bloody drink.

Glances followed us as we descended the wide stairs; I couldn't tell if it was because we were arriving late, or because of Dorothy's striking black dress, or because they could all see how hopelessly ensnared I was.

Praying food might distract Dorothy long enough for me to form a plan, I steered us straight to the refreshment table, even though my own stomach was squeamish. Chocolate truffles rolled in gold dust sat next to tiny sandwiches shaped like moons.

I forced a truffle into my mouth, and I'd never eaten anything that tasted so much like sand.

Well, besides sand.

Thoughts of Miles and the beaches we'd explored all around the world inevitably cropped up. I snagged a glass of champagne and downed it in one gulp, washing away the taste of sand and memories. I'd made my choice and had to live with it. Or die.

My magic clawed against my skin in Dorothy's direction, trying to escape the cage I'd put it in. Ever aware of where she was.

I clenched my jaw and trained my gaze on the Queen at the far end of the hall as she nodded to her bowing guests in a graceful yet unapproachable way. Instruments played their closing notes and couples drifted to the sidelines. Ladies checked their dance cards and were approached by gentlemen who whisked them away.

The first few haunting piano notes of a waltz acted as an omen.

Dorothy cut in front of me and filled every inch of my vision. I froze. She stared up from under her lashes, eyes sparkling with the glow from the chandeliers, wide and luminous and innocent like they used to be. Before I'd ruined them.

"Dance with me."

The soft plea echoed in my bones. The magic wrenched me toward her so hard, my arms practically fell around her, fingers gripping her waist. I dragged in a breath, begging myself to deny her—deny myself—but different words tumbled off my tongue against my will. "Whatever you wish."

I didn't recall leading her to the floor, maybe she led me, but suddenly we were standing in the center of the room and her gloved hand met mine as the other slid to my shoulder, and I forgot everything I ever knew. Luckily my feet remembered, and we stepped in time, movements slow and small because I couldn't manage anything more.

When we waltzed around a turn, she pressed closer, making my nostrils flare. She was so clearly not herself. I had to get away from her—get *her* away from the magic. To save her the humiliation of being abandoned mid-song, I'd wait until the dance ended. I only had to last a few minutes more...

Dorothy blinked up at me, a small smile on her lips. "You look very dashing tonight, Ashley."

Gads, I can't do this.

Anywhere but her. I had to look *anywhere* but at her.

Breaths heavy, I rubbed my ear on my shoulder, trying to loosen my black silk necktie. I knew I should say something back, make a little meaningless quip, but it was all I could do to fumble through the steps and not gather her to me.

"But then, you always do." Her gaze bored into the side of my face.

Concentrate on the magic. Rein it in.

Her hand on my shoulder slid over to my neck, her gloved thumb brushing over my Adam's apple. Little sparks burst through my fingertips, yellow and hot and fizzling in the air.

Rein it in!

"Will you not look at me?" A thread of hurt laced the words.

I licked my suddenly dry lips. The deep, sorrowful piano notes kicked into an allegro, thudding and tinkling until my pulse pounded in rhythm. Then my traitorous eyes glanced at the woman in my arms, and to my hope and horror, she was still beautiful.

My footsteps slowed, entranced.

Soft curls fell out of their pins, one by one floating down to cradle her face. My eyes widened at the illusion, as her hair came completely unbound and swirled around like a breathing thing.

Yes, the magic whispered.

Amid dancing couples, I eased to a halt. A bell tolled in the back of my mind, a warning that someone was going to take notice. But I could only stare into Dorothy's wide, innocent eyes while knots tied around my vocal cords. A curl lifted and reverently swept over her lips. Touching them the way I ached to. Heat pooled in my gut.

She gasped in a little breath. The sound was a crook around my neck, tugging me down...down...the curve of her mouth blotting out everything else.

Yes, it hissed.

Down...down...I trembled with desire. And I—

I couldn't do it.

In the middle of the ballroom, I dropped my hold and launched away, spinning back—

Only to be stopped by her fingers on my wrist.

"Where are you going?" she asked. Her touch slipped under my sleeve and slid up my forearm. It was only her glove on my skin, but my body didn't know the difference, and I quivered.

"For some air," I croaked.

"You'll be back soon?"

I jerked my head in a motion that could hardly be described as a nod, too full of sensation to manage anything more. Then I ripped away and fled the room.

By the time I'd made it to the gentleman's anteroom, the magic's urgency had dissipated and breathing came easier, especially after I'd generously slackened my necktie. I didn't like the idea of hiding out here until Lark arrived, but if my magic wasn't going to behave, I'd do what I had to. I raked a hand through my hair, mussing the waves that I'd attempted to style for once.

Various card games were in motion around the room, men in tufted leather chairs lethargically sifting their cards like they'd had too much to drink. Lamps with green glass shades lit my path as I shifted into the space, hoping for a book and a quiet corner. I didn't particularly care for reading, but a novel in front of my face would signal that I wished to be left alone.

"Mr. Gardner."

I stiffened, recognizing the voice, and stopped.

"Care to join in?"

Stifling the glare before it materialized, I turned and met the gray eyes of Nicholas Hart who sat at a table, smiling faintly above a deck of cards.

"I'm a little busy, at present." I stepped forward again—

"Busy abandoning your fiancée?"

My step cut short. I tipped my head back, mouth working. "Maybe I fancy a game after all." Watching him steadily, I slid out of my evening jacket and draped it over the chair opposite him and sat. I bit my gloves off and tossed them to the table.

The two other men at the table vacated their seats, angling behind Mr. Hart as if they expected to be entertained. A quick glance confirmed I'd seen them before: men tracking the Rook, but never getting close enough to pin down his identity. Through some recent digging, I'd discovered they were Lightfoots. The irony of me sitting before them now while they remained totally oblivious was not lost on me.

Their presence also confirmed what I'd long suspected—that Hart was in league with them.

I locked a steely expression into place. This game was potentially just as dangerous as dancing with Dorothy, but in a completely different way. Try as I might, I couldn't erase the image of Nicholas Hart smiling down at her in Beaumont's. Of her smiling back at him.

"What are we playing?"

"Sleight," he answered with a look of triumph.

With fingers nearly as agile as my own, he shuffled and

dealt us each seven, while I watched for fake cutting, scratched cards, or sleeve-touching—anything that smacked of foul play. When he finished, he set the deck in the center of the table and paused. "Perhaps we should make things a little more interesting. You know what these are?" He dug something out of his waistcoat and held up two identical rings.

Their rubies looked slightly dull, but I instantly recognized the metal work as being constructed by Ranulf, one of the first mages. Without moving my head, I glanced around the room, gauging how common it was to bandy about magical rings. No one gave us undue notice; even the men behind Mr. Hart didn't react. "I thought magic didn't work at Buckingham."

"*Slants* don't work. And these..." He rolled one of the rings between his fingers. "They're more enchantment than magic. They're vice rings, constructed by one of the first mages. It inflicts pain on the wearer, and it was first used in barbaric religious rituals, meant to cleanse the masses of evil. When that failed, it became a favorite medium for torture."

He lobbed one onto the table where it rolled to a stop in front of me. "We both wear one. First one to crack before the game ends, loses."

Wearing an enchanted ring from someone I didn't trust was a fool move, but my competitive streak surged to new heights, and I tipped my head in acquiescence. In rhythm, we slid the rings onto our fingers. Sharp pain sliced up my hand like a hot blade. I struggled to keep my face like stone. Slowly, the feeling ebbed to a painful ache that crawled past my wrist.

Nicholas leaned back, smiling, somehow knowing I hadn't expected the sensation to be so strong. My feet dug into the floor, right before the agony in my hand seared open again, making my breath come tight. Nicholas lifted a brow. "Ah, and one more thing about the rings: If they sense anger, the pain intensifies."

"So I noticed," I muttered, picking up my cards and organizing my pocket folly, two jacks, and a spark. It had potential, but it was far from a winning hand. I shoved the irritation down, focusing on the greater game I now played: riling Nicholas Hart.

I didn't know the man well. Not personally.

All I knew is that I hated him.

"How did you come to possess these rings? As a lowly journalist, that is."

"I am not without my connections." He drew first, taking his time before he tossed a velvet queen to the table.

I logged the card away then scanned the Lightfoot agents behind him. "These *connections* of yours are very generous, granting you security. Or worried you can't manage any...trouble...on your own."

Hart inhaled through his nose and sat back, face a mask.

"And what need does a reporter have for muscle?" I drew, then discarded. "The stories you're chasing must be dangerous. Either that, or you talk a big game to distract from the fact that this table is lopsided and it's clear who's the bigger threat."

His brows lifted, unfazed; something which earned him a few begrudging points in my book. "I do face danger, as it turns out—constantly. You know nothing of the squalor I see daily. The deaths on the streets and the gore inside orphanage walls that could make even the blackest heart bleed with pity."

I shrugged. "Sounds like a one-man job to me."

"Then why aren't *you* working to save London, if you're so plaguing good at it?"

"Because I'm tired." Which happened to be true. The pain from the ring leached up my forearm and dug hooks in my elbow. "And because it seems like you four"—I let the word dangle a little—"have it well enough in hand."

The slow way Hart blinked at me told me he was

unamused. "Perhaps we could use your expertise, seeing how you somehow managed to build a silk empire, despite coming from nothing, and *nowhere*." After throwing down a card, he went on. "A little suspicious, wouldn't you agree, the way everyone clamors to be in the company of a mutt?"

I clucked my tongue. "I'm actually quite personable once you get to know me."

"Shame I never shall."

Did he detest the thought, or was he implying something more sinister? I analyzed his taut body language, his gaze as sharp as a steel blade.

Both, I decided.

Hart leaned forward, voice lowering. "So much wealth, yet so little character. I've never met a man more undeserving of a woman."

Dorothy's name, unspoken, echoed in the air.

Pain spiked up my bicep, slashing open my veins and making me want to scream. This time, I managed to keep my expression like stone, even as my forehead beaded with sweat. But it was nothing compared to the pain of knowing he was right.

I did my best to tamp the anger. "You mean the woman you pathetically stare at like a wandering pup?"

Nicholas's face didn't react, but his pallor blanched. His ringed hand shifted like it bothered him.

Through the pain, I grinned. *Found his sore spot.* "Hoping she'll look down and take pity on you?" I needled.

His nostrils flared, but he cocked his head nonchalantly. "Maybe Dorothy doesn't notice me. But she does notice other things—things that perhaps you'd rather didn't come to light?"

My brows twitched, white hot pain making the bones in my hand tremble. I tsked. "Just 'Dorothy,' is it? Awfully forward, speaking of my fiancée like that."

"She doesn't *belong* to you."

"For your sake"—my voice softened, chilling to a glacier—"you'd better think she does."

We locked eyes and held there for half a minute, the space between us glimmering with sharp edges.

Nicholas threw down a four, giving him a Fortune Slip—the second highest play—and a likely victory. He gradually listed his head to one side, amusement humming in his throat. "Is that a threat?"

"It is." I slowly rearranged my hand and drew my last card. "And you're wrong. Dorothy is remarkable and intelligent, but there is only one thing she really notices." I glanced up, a rueful smirk pulling at my lips. "*Me.*"

The word had the desired effect, because fury flashed in Nicholas's eyes before his jaw clenched and a sound escaped his lips—not a grunt, not a whimper, but something in between.

I leaned over the table, tossing the winning crown ace on the pile and smirking at the man across from me. I stood. The game was over. "I am all she will *ever* notice."

And I hate it.

I hate that I don't know if it's real.

The pain roared and tore across my shoulders, scraping the flesh it traveled to. I stood paralyzed for a moment before I ripped the metal band off my finger, panting. With a slight tremble in my hand, I let it fall to the table where it thudded and rolled to a halt.

I whipped my evening jacket off the chair, allowing the anger to pulse freely now as I stalked across the room, Hart's gaze searing my back. In a far corner, I settled into a tufted leather chair and swiped an abandoned newspaper from a coffee table.

The headline made me pause.

THE ROOK BREAKS HIS SILENCE
HELLHOUNDS TERRORIZE STREETS WHILE FIVE
NEW FEATHERS FOUND ON PILLOWS

I frowned, then turned the page and read a different article. Two pages later, the men who'd stood behind Nicholas passed behind me, whispering to each other on their way to their own chairs. I caught only snippets.

"...strong suspicions..."

"...where the bracelets are..."

"...sure?"

"In the morning, we'll..."

Folding down the newspaper, my frown deepened. My eyes found a clock on the wall, confirming that I'd stayed away from the ball too long. I ducked out of the anteroom, pulse rushing as my mind pieced the information together.

They could have been referring to an abandoned warehouse or my old flat, but I couldn't take that chance. I had to move the bracelets tonight.

I stepped back into the ballroom, muscles tight as I braced for the tug of magic toward Dorothy. It remained eerily dormant. But that didn't stop me from being assaulted in other ways—the shrill violins, the scent of powder and velvet, the whirls of heat radiating from waltzing couples. I spotted a white-blond head standing near a potted fern in the corner and bee-lined toward it, pace stuttering only when the man turned and revealed the hooked nose of Robin. Not Lark.

At least Lark hadn't sent Jay. The ill-tempered Acheron would've likely caused a scene.

"Not here," Robin said off-handedly as I approached, never glancing my direction. He took a languorous sip of champagne before setting it down and strolling around the corner. I waited ten beats before I followed him, through various hallways to a terrace where the cool air hit my face. Rectangles of light patterned the stony floor, streaming through the French doors.

Robin angled back, fishing through his suit pocket then extending a hand. A silver band of silver lions and four-pointed stars rested on his palm, the sapphires gleaming.

I stilled.

Something swelled in my chest, a foreign emotion punching the back of my throat. And it had been so long since I'd felt it, blindly groping but always finding it just out of reach, that it took me a full minute to pinpoint what it was.

My lips parted.

Hope.

Robin looked bored, like he wasn't holding my entire fate in his hands. It took a heap of restraint to not summon my magic and use a little sleight of hand to whisk it away. Or do it without the magic. Instead, I dug the map jewels out of my breast pocket.

The exchange was unceremonious, a few seconds of swapping hands and it was done. The map was gone, and I had my life back.

Without hesitating, I threw the bracelet against the terrace, pleased when it didn't crumble into the loamy, spongy matter the Artifice used to forge counterfeits. I wouldn't put it past Lark to try a trick like that, especially when someone like the Artifice lived only a few levels down.

Robin only raised his eyebrows. As I stooped to retrieve the bracelet, he said, "Is it so hard to believe my brother would be honest?"

"It'd be a first."

"He's a man of his word."

Stuffing the piece of jewelry into my jacket, I stood. "He's desperate. Not the same thing."

Robin's lips cut a disgusted diagonal. "He *will* keep his

word, especially when it comes to you…a man he's sworn to kill."

I paused, then glanced up. A dark smirk pulled at my mouth. "He's at least fourth in line—not the best odds for him." I hopped over the stone railing and fell fifteen feet, rolling when I hit the gravel walkway.

Perhaps it was the pull of magic or perhaps it was my own stupidity, but I couldn't stop my feet from circling the palace and slowing when I stood in the light of the ball. Couples danced across the windows and disappeared into the stone, none imagining I watched them; that I stared longingly at a girl with curly brown hair in a deadly black dress.

My hands curled into fists, unsure what the next move was for the first time in my life. Because what would I say if I approached her? That everything was my fault? That I needed her more than I needed blood in my veins? That only by being worthy of her lonely heart could I ever heal my own?

I couldn't say any of those things.

The minutes ticked by. Dorothy danced and glittered and I took my fill, knowing I could stand there, drinking her in through eternity, and it would still never be enough.

With one last painful, memorizing glance, I turned and slipped into the night, facing the future rather than the past. Facing the direction I had hope.

Ready for the magic to be gone.

Ready for the peace.

The relief.

Finally.

40

Ashley

In the darkness, I retraced the six miles from the night before, the distance not seeming quite so far now that I wasn't hyperventilating while carrying Dorothy's limp body to safety. Stone buildings gave way to farmland as I followed the road west, until I found the little-used trail. It meandered through a pocket of woods, thick with mist. I slowed when I saw the arches of the roofless church spearing the fog. The night cocooned the scene in silence and the cold smell of decay.

I stepped through the opening arch and followed the hallway past tarnished candelabras, ripped tapestries, and the echoes of worship. Inside the main hall, I veered toward the back corner where I'd stashed a change of clothes, quickly abandoning my evening jacket and waistcoat.

Haunting beauty encompassed me; oaken pews, once polished to a deep sheen, now rotting; the peppery aroma of soil; stone murals of birds in mid-flight; the altar, smooth but cracked under the weight of heavy vows; ivy dripping down crumbling stone walls that leaked moonlight. I was halfway through fastening the buttons of a new shirt when I heard a rustle and paused.

Someone was here.

I flattened into the shadows and stilled my breath, drawing magic to my palms as a last resort. Then I waited. Several minutes ticked by.

Starlight glittered off Dorothy's dress as she stepped into the hall, her face open in quiet wonder as she took in the surroundings. She probably hadn't been lucid enough to notice them last night. I remained frozen in place, the war inside me raging as to whether to approach her or not, and I was angry at the universe for putting me in this position once again.

That war clamored to a feverish pitch when she neared the bracelets' hiding place, and it made the decision for me.

Rolling my sleeves to my elbows, I steadily slipped up behind her and murmured, "How did you follow me?"

Dorothy halted, the hairs on her neck raising like I'd caught her off guard—even though I hadn't taken special care to be quiet. Then I realized I was close enough to notice those hairs and eased back a step.

"I wanted to speak with you," was all she said.

My magic tugged me toward her, but not nearly as strongly as it had at the ball. I'd had time to rebuild my defenses. But I wasn't fool enough to believe I could last forever. "It couldn't wait?"

Slowly, she turned around. She took me in, and for the first time I felt self-conscious under a woman's inspection. Naked. She lingered on the haphazard way my shirt was tucked into my formal trousers, and then on the last few shirt buttons I'd failed to fasten.

I resisted the urge to straighten my appearance, because I knew the movement would betray my flayed nerves.

Dorothy lifted her eyes, which burned with hot emotion.

"You're planning to leave tonight." She inhaled quickly. "I came to ask you to stay."

"For how long?" My gut squeezed. Blast. Wrong thing to say. Wrong thing to *want*. Wrong thing to think about—about how she'd uttered those words right before she'd kissed me in her bedroom. My tone darkened. "Until the magic destroys *both* of us?"

She stepped carefully toward me. "For as long as you will."

I swallowed. Looked her up and down. Swallowed again. The air between us charged with wanting.

I can't, I said, but couldn't make my mouth form the words, because every shred of me wished it wasn't true. "And what if I decide to leave?"

A plea swept over her expression. "Then at least kiss me first."

I pulled in a breath that was half hope, half agony, because what had prompted her to say that? Was that really what she wanted, or was it my magic's influence? Panic ripped through me as I grappled for control. Some of it seeped onto my face.

Emboldened by my reaction, Dorothy stepped toward me again. "Please," she whispered, a desperate ache behind the word.

The panic steeled into anger, pulling my muscles taut. "I *won't*." I backed away until I stood at the head of the church behind the altar, wanting to impale myself on the colorful shards of window behind me rather than live in this moment. "So *leave*." I was speaking to her, to the magic, to me, to the universe, to whatever thing would listen.

Silence rang off the walls for several minutes while we stood on opposite ends, as frozen as statues. Both of us too afraid to disturb the delicate balance that suspended us there. Dorothy tipped her head back and gazed through the jagged ceiling, starlight glancing off her cheekbones.

"This is a beautiful church," she whispered. "I think in another life I should've liked to have been married in a place like this. Not when it was imposing and flawless, but like how it is now. Wild and holy and broken." Her gaze fell to softly land on me. "Like us."

I fell back a step. "Us." The word landed painful and bitter on my tongue, because it was one that could never mean anything.

"If you will not kiss me, then I ask only one thing of you before you go." She clutched the black pearls at her sternum, and when her wistful gaze fell, her lips faintly parted, anguish twisting her features. "That you take that truth ring out of your pocket—but we make no bargains. No more questions or transactions. No shadows or games. Just truth offered freely, like vows on this altar." She came to stand on the other side of the stone altar. "You owe me that much."

I owed her something, yes, but this felt like too steep a price. Too many secrets I couldn't afford to share.

But because I was a fool, I reached in my pocket and pulled out a bit of silver that twinkled under the moon. Because this might be the only way to know, once and for all, if she'd come here because of...something real. I stared at the truth ring for a lengthy moment before fitting it over my finger.

"You were right"—my jaw clenched as I glanced up—"in the cistern. I have difficulty trusting people. I give a piece here and a piece there, but I can't give someone the whole picture because that's the same as locking me in a cage."

Overwhelmed by a sudden onslaught of memories, I shook my head. "Once, I was completely at the mercy of someone—a man who took everything from me—and I promised myself I'd never be helpless like that again. I'd anticipate everything." The ring glowed blue, the truth set free. I hesitated, holding it back, but my shoulders slumped and I admitted, "Then you came along." *And I am helpless once more.*

I stood there, and stood there, damming up the other truths that wanted to spill out, before finally setting the ring on the altar between us.

After some hesitation, Dorothy picked it up and slipped it over her slim finger. "From the first moment I saw you," she began quietly, "all I wanted was to know you. Every piece. Even the ugly ones."

Every action that had stained my heart black flashed through my mind.

"Your warnings only made me more curious because I never wanted some of the truth. I wanted *all* of it." The bitter twinge of her mouth was at odds with her glimmering eyes, like the confession had forced her to delve too deep. Down where it was painful, for some reason. "I still do."

The ring glowed blue, before she surrendered it and placed it back on the altar.

And I was assailed by the urge to fulfill that desire; to have her view every dark part of me and still stand there, unafraid. An impossible dream. I picked the ring up, taking my time putting it on.

"The bracelets are here," I said in a low voice. My eyes darted to the base of the stone, where they were hidden. "Inside the altar. Tonight, I'm going to use them to strip me of my magic and then—then maybe—" My eyes darted over her face before I swallowed and glanced up, tracing the rafters. "So many things I've been aching to tell you..." And suddenly it was too much to gamble, pulling her into everything and praying she'd emerge unscathed. I had to put everything right first—it was the only way we stood a chance. I bit back the rest, shook my head, and set the ring back on the altar.

No more truth.

No more pieces.

I couldn't.

Dorothy scooped up the ring and put it on her finger, stepping around the carved stone until she stood only a breath away. My wariness grew as she neared. What more could she possibly reveal?

Her hand lifted, faltered, then settled on my collarbone where she'd stitched me up in her bedroom, and in the depth of her gaze I glimpsed the soft innocence of that memory—an expression so utterly her.

But Dorothy's next words broke that illusion.

"I want you, Ashley," she whispered, glancing up. "I want to be with you."

The ring glowed blue, but my heart stopped dead in my chest—because I'd felt a flash of magic. My eyes widened, mouth thickening in fear. "*No.*"

She blinked and inched back.

"No, you don't." I shook my head. "You only think you do."

"I know my own—"

But I couldn't listen. I couldn't watch this nightmare unfold again. I stumbled back, trying to put as much distance between us as possible. A bleak edge colored my voice. "Take the ring off. *Leave.* You're not yourself and you don't know what you're saying—"

"Yes, I do." She rushed forward and caught my wrist, climbing my arm until she held my shaking head between her hands, and I hated the way I instantly stilled. Instantly, desperately, pathetically wanted to believe her. Her thumbs swept away black locks off my forehead, hands looping around my ears to cup my jaw. "Yes, I do," she said softer, gently pulling my face down an inch.

Magic burgeoned in my chest, pressure building until it felt like it was shooting out of my fingertips, my eyes. It mixed with my eddying thoughts until I could no longer think. Nothing but—

What if...maybe...?

"You need to stop," I breathed. "I'm not strong enough—"

Her gaze fell, voice quieting. "I don't need you to be strong. I need you to love me." In my peripheral, the ring glowed blue.

No. You need me to not *love you.*

Slowly, her hands swept down my neck, fingers hooking under my collar. "You're lonely," she murmured.

My blood iced over, a warning ringing in my bones. Those words...it was how it always started. *Stop!* I screamed at the magic. *Make it stop!* But I wasn't moving, ensorcelled by the spell that only she could cast over me. "Dorothy..."

"And I can fix that." The ring glowed blue.

Is it her or the magic?

"Don't say that." An animalistic sound rolled in my throat, short and low and pained. A sound that revealed how close I was to breaking. "Whatever you do, *don't* say that."

She arched onto her toes.

I froze, leaned away slightly, and froze again when she grazed her lips over mine. A feather-light temptation. All breath left my body, my mouth burning. My insides wound tighter than a cable.

Her gaze slid up and locked onto mine. "Then stop me from saying it."

I stared at her for a dozen agonizing heartbeats, glancing frenziedly between her beautiful eyes. My breaths shallowed.

I can't.

I can't.

I can't.

I can't.

But I desperately wanted to.

Then everything snapped.

I pushed her back, hand meeting the wall. Our bodies followed and I crushed her into the ivy, my lips capturing hers in a rush of need. Sliding once, twice, deeper—

It all cascaded out, every emotion and memory since that day in the bookshop crumbling my walls beyond hope of repair. I could only watch in horror as the flood destroyed everything.

She opened her mouth to mine and when she moaned softly into it, the sound rumbled through my every sinew, awakening senses I never knew I had. They sparked and scattered at the taste of her, eager for more. And I gave it to them. With every shred of anger and confusion and longing, I kissed her, begging her, *Please, please, please.*

Please let this be you.

Her hands buried into my hair and she impatiently kissed me back, seeming to answer, *It is, it is, it is.*

I lived. For one, glorious moment, I soared above the bitter truth and into a twilight glistening with every secret desire. The air pulsed with a lush pink hue, mists of sparkles floating down and springing up roses where they touched the ground. The illusions surrounded us in a garden, one that grew and budded with our kiss.

Then the kiss morphed into something different; softer and achingly familiar. My mouth slowed, relishing the bevel of her lips, turning more chaste as the moment stretched on. Kisses I poured every one of those dark secrets into. And they whispered, *I want to call you mine. I want to cherish you like this every sunrise, every sunset, until the end of time and then beyond. Let me sleep by your side so I know that you're safe. Let me hold you in my arms during those long nights. Let me tell you every truth, let me give you every piece. I don't want you for this moment. I want you forever, Dorothy...*

Forever.

I pulled back, breaths broken and bleeding because I

couldn't keep doing this. My fingers slid up her neck to cradle her jaw, and then I kissed her forehead, sweet and slow, our souls gravitating into a tender orbit until I felt them brush.

Her shuddering sigh hit my collarbone—like she'd felt it too —and it sparked foolish hope in my chest. Could it be that she wanted this just as much as I did? The roses bloomed open, shades of pink and white intertwining. Love and purity.

When my mouth moved to the skin below her eye, it was wet. Salt skimmed my lips as I covered her tear with a reverent kiss. I lingered, breathing in the different notes that flavored her skin—a French garden, and lavender, and something else wild and intelligent and hungry that drove me completely mad.

Threading my fingers to the back of her head, I held her, our faces pressed close, pulse ragged because I no longer had the courage—the willpower—to let her go. I was lost in the shadows, and if she couldn't find me, no one else would, and for once in my life I wanted...I had to be found.

I had to be found by *her*.

And maybe I'd never forgive myself, but I was about to gamble it all. Because losing everything was better than being trapped in this hell of *What if?*

I pulled a cold bracelet from my pocket and slipped it over Dorothy's wrist. She blinked dazedly, first at the gleaming sapphires, then up at me. "Take my magic away." I didn't recognize my voice—the raw prayer inside it. "Do it. Not one more moment. I cannot bear this not-knowing for one more moment."

Shock suspended her for another few beats before she dutifully lifted her hand bearing the bracelet to my neck. Magic jolted out of me, and I swayed a little at the release of pressure.

Dorothy shivered, eyes rolling back. I knew what she was feeling: tens of millions of cold, heavy sparks racing in her veins and filling every crevice past bursting. Skin that wanted to rip open from the strain.

I clutched her, drowning in guilt and love and fear. "Do you love me, Dolly? Is it *you*?" My breaths came heavy and quick while simultaneously not coming at all. Nothing but certain words from her lips would ever give me air again.

The moment stretched on, and devastation tore through me. Dread. A wreckage that couldn't be undone. "I don't want this," I whispered, "unless it's really you. I can't do it if it's not. Please—" My voice broke. I clawed her waist a bit closer; a reckless move of possession. Hope. "*Please* say it's real."

Dorothy's hand, still bearing the truth ring and now the bracelet too, pulsating with my magic, settled on my chest, rising and falling with every one of my anguished breaths.

Her lashes were wet and more tears leaked down her face, the memory of their taste still fresh on my tongue. Then those luminous gray-blue eyes glanced up, scintillating with a heartache that rivaled my own. "It's always been real," she whispered back.

The ring glowed blue.

She broke out of my arms, crushing roses under her heels. And with her other hand, she aimed a pistol at my heart.

41

Dorothy

Ashley didn't move for a full half-minute. His eyes pulsed with disbelief, his kiss-swollen lips taking an agonizingly long moment to part. Then his frame went slack like a puppet freed from its strings, and finally, he whispered, "Dolly...why?"

Because I finally found your weakness...

And it's me.

My vision before the ball had shown my failure, but it had also shown me that losing myself to Ashley's magic would push him past his breaking point. When he'd reached into his pocket, he'd been about to pull out a bracelet; I'd known it in my bones.

My hand tightened around the gun's grip, willing it not to shake even as tears clouded my vision. "Because of my father."

Behind me, the scrape of Lightfoot boots echoed in the church, the faces of agents appearing in the broken-glass windows as they surrounded the Rook. A man with no more tricks up his sleeve because I had stolen his slant.

Nicholas appeared at my side, hand bracing the small of my back. He'd gotten the note I'd sent him, and had played his part. I knew if Ashley overheard the Lightfoots talking about a place they were certain concealed the bracelets, that he would move them, leading us to their location.

And all I had to do was follow the siren song of his magic.

Ashley's gaze magnetized to Nicholas the moment he appeared from the shadows. His face flashed with anger, panic, then understanding as it settled on where Nicholas touched me. Opening his mouth, he took half a step—before a Lightfoot agent clubbed him from behind and he fell to the stone table.

Nicholas asked me something, but I didn't hear it. I stared at Ashley's unconscious form with a tear trickling down my cheek, unable to scrub the image from my mind. Because it was fitting, him sleeping there; my sacrifice.

I'd done the right thing.

So why did it feel like it was my soul, lying broken on the altar?

42

Emmeline

Out the window, sunny green hills mottled with trees and dry-stone walls rolled by. A three-hour train ride north to Cambridge was an awfully long time to spend in a dining car across from a man who inspired burning feelings in my chest whenever I looked at him.

I tried to ignore the impressions, but it was difficult when every brush of our knees made my stomach clench. For some reason, all I could think about was how—in excitement—I used to attack our postal worker in Shropshire whenever he brought me the latest serial of *The Samaritan and the Rook*.

I was confused as to why my subconscious thought the memory was relevant. It wasn't as if I wanted to attack Miles Kelly.

His shoulders held steady, a force of their own that couldn't be influenced by the slight rocking of the train. On them rested his signature brown trench coat, popped collar framing his chiseled jaw. His warm brown eyes didn't mindlessly gaze out the window like every other person on the planet would do.

Instead, they remained calmly trained on the door like he was waiting for an enemy to walk through.

Sensing my study of him, he glanced at me.

I cleared my throat. "Cambridge is a large campus, I believe. Where do you think Ashley is keeping my uncle?"

Miles didn't answer, and it was a full thirty seconds before I remembered.

Right. He didn't speak to me. Not when I looked like a girl.

He'd been so free with his confession on the steamer, I thought we were making progress—maybe even becoming friends. Clearly not.

My mouth worked, gaze dropping to my travelling boots. I shoved my confusing emotions down. Who cared if he didn't speak to me? It wasn't as if he was able to communicate with any other girl.

Except Miss Thurston.

"Well," I said brightly, but it sounded forced even to me, "you know how his mind works. I'm sure you'll have some inkling once we arrive."

"I can't pick locks," Miles muttered, eyes trained on the door again.

A wave of pleasure at his words—not those words particularly, just *any* words from him—washed over me. Maybe he *was* getting over his speech impediment. But then I heard everything he wasn't saying: Ashley had always been the one to break into places. No wonder Miles hadn't wanted to waltz into the Black Carriage headquarters without a strategy.

Hmm. That did put a damper on things. Maybe because I'd witnessed the skill with which he boxed and shot, I'd assumed he excelled at everything else too. Sunlight streamed in through the window, creating a golden outline of him against the blue velvet of the bench seat.

I scowled when my stomach clenched again.

Fisting my glove-clad hands in my lap, I said sharper than intended, "Why do you keep watching the door? It's not as if Ashley is aware we're coming."

His gaze shifted to me once more, and for the first time, I saw a glimmer of uncertainty there. First Dory and now him. Why was everyone so cowed by Ashley Gardner? The man couldn't know *everything*.

I shrugged a shoulder, aiming for nonchalance. "No one knows what we're up to. And even if they did, they wouldn't dare touch me while you've got that monstrous glower in place."

Miles's jaw tensed, and as his hand drifted to his coat, his glare hardened further on the door. Then he uttered so low I was half-certain I imagined it, "They'd *better* not."

And suddenly I knew why the image of our postal worker was relevant.

I did—very much, as it turned out—want to attack Miles Kelly.

On the lips.

My eyes widened. George's crypt, this was terrible news. *Well done, Emmeline. Not only have you managed to pick someone who hates you, but a man who can't speak to you at all. Smashing.*

Oblivious to my warming cheeks, Miles rested his head back against the cushions, exposing his Adam's apple and tanned neck. (Why was it preposterously attractive?)

I jumped to my feet. His lips parted—the stupid things.

"I need some fresh air," I blurted before I could say anything else, and rushed out of the car.

Out in the corridor, I breathed a sigh, feeling the weight of his stare burning through the door. In a cubby next to the compartment that held our luggage, I fished through my bag, wobbly fingers closing around a bottle of rosewater. Pumping with my hand, I spritzed three sprays on my neck, breathing deeply, gagging but not caring.

A conductor shuffled by. He slowed, nostrils hiking at the cloying scent as he eyed my hunched form and crabbed hands. My face burned hotter. How I must look. Like a crazed woman, sniffing perfume in a misguided attempt to wrangle my emotions.

Well, that was exactly what I was.

Attempting to salvage some dignity, I straightened and cleared my throat, and when he finally moved on, I stuffed the bottle back in my bag. Not trusting myself to return to Miles's company yet, I strolled toward the back of the train, passing through several cars identical to ours before stopping in the rear car, thick with cigar smoke. A man operated a bar in the corner, and passengers sat at four different green-wooled tables, tossing chips, shuffling cards, and racking dice.

A thrill shot down my spine.

Gambling.

"Still brow-beating the young rummies?" a round man in a gray suit chortled from the table closest to me.

The bespectacled man across from him chuckled and nodded. He had a high, intelligent forehead, and the open leather case stuffed with academic papers at his feet bore a collegiate coat of arms.

He was a professor at King's College.

"I daresay they deserve it," the spectacled professor replied good-naturedly. "Even if it means setting up displays hours before they arrive. The dean was tired of sloughing out of bed in the pitch dark to open the gate for me." He tapped his breast pocket.

My eyes narrowed at the gesture, gut telling me he had a key on his person. A hazardous idea started to form, one Miles would definitely not approve of.

Judging by the huge stack of chips in front of the professor, he was not only experienced, but doing well for himself, which likely indicated he'd be more willing to take risks. I watched him for a moment, and when he scratched one ear, I smiled.

But he wasn't experienced enough to not have tells.

Noticing my presence, the barkeep approached with a bow. "Excuse me, miss. This is a gentlemen-only car. I must ask you to leave."

Thinking of Miles's bag next to mine which housed a spare set of clothes, I blinked innocently. "But of course." I grinned. "That shouldn't be a problem at all."

43

Miles

My knee bounced, unable to put the man with the bowler hat from my mind.

Back at Victoria Station, as we were boarding the train, he'd glanced up, scanned the crowd, passed over us, then returned to his newspaper, flipping a page. It was a normal enough action, but some small detail about it had made it seem practiced. His beady stare had seemed too knowing.

I didn't recognize him, and I hadn't seen him board. Still, coupled with the dozens of other male passengers who seemed too eager to mind their own business, it was enough to put me on edge. Ashley—and I, by extension—had made a good number of enemies, and even Emmeline had gone up against the Black Carriage service. We couldn't afford to let our guard down. I reached for my slant and checked my pocket for the thousandth time, ensuring my pistol was still present and loaded.

Invariably, my eyes drifted to the seat Emmeline had vacated, wondering again why she'd left in such a hurry. I consulted my pocket watch. She'd been gone twenty-nine minutes.

Too long.

I shot to my feet and poked my head out into the hall, looking both ways. It was empty.

My muscles tightened, and I stalked down the car, narrowly resisting the urge to storm into every dining compartment and turn everything inside out. I didn't have reason to completely panic.

Yet.

After ten more minutes of searching, I finally made my way to the caboose, nerves frayed to a thread. Tobacco hung heavy in the air and poker chips clinked, informing me this was a gentleman's space. She wasn't here.

I turned away but halted. Pivoting back, I narrowed my eyes at one of the tables, where two figures sat playing poker. One was a middle-aged man with spectacles, and the other was young. White shirtsleeves and a leather vest dwarfed his smaller frame, but they were well-made. And I knew because they were *mine*.

My fist tightened.

I took one angry step forward, then froze when he slapped a card on the table, because I recognized the way he moved. The way *she* moved.

Emmeline.

Only, her eyebrows were dark and bushy, her nose had doubled in size, and her mouth had widened. With the bulk of her strawberry blonde hair tucked into a cap, a few ends peeked out and swept over her forehead, giving the impression of short hair. As if she heard me think her name, she glanced up and locked eyes with me. And then she *smiled*.

I frowned, legs stiffening. Black fog, the girl was trouble.

A few bluedusters had milled about the station, but while I

hadn't seen any of them board, that didn't mean she was safe. Cambridge was less than an hour away, which meant her hands would still show residue from slanting when we arrived. And there would doubtless be bluedusters there.

What? Emmeline mouthed, and that was when I realized I was bugging my eyes at her.

I swallowed and looked away, knowing she'd be caught if I kept staring.

I felt a sigh heavier than the train fill my lungs, but it never released because I was too angry. She held her cards with the most stoic expression I'd seen her wear, but an unmistakable fire danced in her eyes, and in a few short minutes, she'd managed to accrue four impressive stacks of chips. Begrudgingly, I admitted she had a knack for it. A strange warmth made my chest expand, and my lips twitched.

Impudent little cove.

"Kelly, is that you?"

I turned to find Nevin sitting at the bar, chewing nuts through his crooked grin. I straightened. My landlord was the last person I expected to see, gesturing to the wooden stool beside him. And now if Emmeline dropped her magic and she turned back into a woman, we'd definitely be in trouble.

As I slid into the seat, he said, "On my way to see my brother who lives in King's Lynn. What're you headed north for?" His breath reeked of peanuts and ale.

I resisted the urge to glance back at Emmeline. "Business."

He chuckled. "All right, keep your secrets. But blow me that you're still walking after the beating you took."

I frowned. Boxing matches could be brutal, and my opponents had been growing increasingly antagonistic from me dominating the winnings—but inside the ring I only ever took a few hits, and outside it, a spew of hateful sentences. I hardly called that a beating.

Unless...

A strange emotion sparked to life in my chest—one I wouldn't analyze. It couldn't be. "When was this," I muttered.

Nevin rubbed his jaw. "Ten days ago, give or take? I was walking along Castle Alley, on my way to the bank early that morning, when I seen you. Before I could call a greeting, eight figures emerged from the alley and jumped ya. Pummeled you until you were black and blue, sayin' something about how you'd never box again once they was through."

My lips pursed, and Nevin turned for another handful of peanuts, but I glommed onto his shoulder and pulled him back. "Are you certain? Are you certain it was me you saw?"

"Ey!" Nevin grinned and clapped my arm. "'Twasn't that dark. It was you I seen, clear as anythin'." He straightened, expression sobering. "Course, I wanted to help, mind, but I was in an awful hurry."

I barely heard him, mind reeling. Throat suddenly thick, I nodded, not trusting myself to speak. There was only one person I knew who could make himself look exactly like someone else.

And he would never take a beating for me.

Would he?

Movement at the other end of the car caught my eye, pulling me from my swirling thoughts. A man at a corner table stirred, staring me dead-on from under his bowler hat.

The man from the station.

My gaze magnetized to his hand, reaching inside his coat.

Blast.

He whipped out a gun and aimed at Emmeline. I shot forward and tackled her from her chair.

44

Emmeline

There I was, winning enough money to rent the Queen's jewels, when five hundred pounds of muscle (or what felt like it) threw me to the floor. I hit my shoulder and screeched.

The boom from a gun split my ears, then the window behind my seat shattered, raining down glass. The car erupted into a frenzy.

Miles grabbed the leg of a table and threw it in front of us on its side, spraying chips all over the ground—just in time for it to block three rounds of bullets. The sounds of men scrambling toward the exit met my ears.

"Why is he shooting at us?" I managed, heart racing. For one horrifying moment, I thought Miles wouldn't be able to answer me—before I remembered I still looked like a middle-aged man.

Thank heavens.

Back braced against the table, Miles whipped his pistol out of his brown trench coat. "There are five of them," he ground out. He arched up and let off a round, then ducked back down. "Four."

My eyes widened. "He knows, then? That we're onto him?"

Miles swung around and fired five more shots, cursing when he must've missed. Gunpowder smoke filled my lungs.

"The *snake*," I seethed. Mr. Gardner was taking everyone I loved. First Uncle Geoffrey, then Dory, and now—

"It's not Ashley!" Miles shoved bullets into the chamber. "Ashley wouldn't do this."

I fisted his jacket and pulled him toward me. "You mean send men to kill you?"

He cut my hold, blazing eyes catching on mine. "*Yes!*"

And for some reason my doubts melted away, because one thing I had learned about Miles Kelly: When he was certain of something, it might as well be cast in stone.

He shook his head. "They're Black Carriage workers. Or maybe—"

An explosion tore through the side of the train and drove us to the floor. More glass sprinkled onto my cap, and ash-edged playing cards. I peeked around the edge of the table, jaw dropping at the carnage. Fire licked shredded curtains and broken chairs, behind which two men poured something black into a tube.

They were making another bomb.

Miles swore again, coming to the same conclusion. "If they don't kill us, they'll sever us from the rest of the train. Either way, we're sitting ducks." Before I could ask what we were supposed to do, Miles shoved me toward the caboose platform behind us. "*Go.*"

I didn't hesitate.

As I sprang through the rear exit, four more gunshots blasted—Miles covering me—and then he joined me, slamming the door shut. Sparks sprayed as he rammed a metal bar down and bolted it.

I turned toward the tracks whizzing under the train, world tilting. Wind whisked my cap off and within seconds it lay abandoned on the tracks, a hundred yards behind.

"How are we going to jump—" I turned back to find Miles calmly climbing the train.

To get *on top* of it.

He swung up, then wordlessly extended his hand down to help me.

I felt like sighing. Why was *up* always the answer?

But I ascended the metal ladder. My long blonde hair lashed my face like tiny whips. I wobbled to my feet, grinning while the train earthquaked beneath me. As the adrenaline whooshed through my torso, I understood how this kind of danger could be addicting. "Now what?" I shouted above the roar of the tracks.

Miles crouched on top of the speeding train, looking around and stalking forward like it was solid ground. The collar of his trench coat flapped against his cheek. Stalking back, he said, "How high can you jump?"

Beyond his shoulder, a stone bridge loomed, larger and larger. The train would pass underneath it within seconds.

My eyes went round, air puffing out my cheeks in disbelief. Then the panic shot through my blood, all excitement draining.

I changed my mind. It was not addicting.

"Not high. Not high *at all*. I am not jumping from this train just so I can dangle from a stone bridge and plummet to my death! You promise me right now that is not your brilliant plan!"

"No." Miles glanced behind his shoulder, where two heads peeked above the rim of our car—the men shooting at us had caught up. He turned back. "I'm planning to throw you."

"What—?!"

His hands closed around my waist. The head of our car plunged into the tunnel. A bullet ricocheted off the stone. He launched me into the air and my middle collided with the stone bridge. Air exploded from my lungs.

My face contorted to its original form, magic utterly spent.

Wheezing, I scrabbled for purchase. I slunk backwards, heart dropping to my toes. Finally, my fingers hooked around a jutting section of rock, and I gasped in a colossal breath, arms burning. My whole body trembled, funneling all my strength into holding on. The clatter of the locomotive receded as it sped down the track. I made one feeble attempt to hoist myself up, but my hands released trickles of sweat and slipped off.

Time slowed. I squeezed my eyes shut. I screamed.

And the last thought I had was that this whole train debacle —the gambling, the shootout, the bomb, the bridge, and me falling to my death—would make an excellent penny dreadful, and it was a shame I wouldn't be alive to read it.

A hand clamped around my forearm, and I jerked when it stopped my fall. My head whipped up to find the glorious sight of Miles Kelly heaving me up and pulling me over the lip of the bridge, scraping my clothes against the rough rock.

Heartbeat still frantic, I collapsed to the ground, kissed it, and immediately spat away the tiny pebbles sticking to my lips. I slowly clambered to my feet, mentally piecing together what had happened. After throwing me into the air, Miles had travelled through the tunnel and hurled himself over the bridge on the other side, narrowly dodging the gunfire. Then he'd run across the bridge to hoist me up, just in the nick of time.

I looked at him then. He stood there, chest heaving, sweat rolling from his temples, gaze zipping over every inch of me. And that was when I saw the blood dripping from a hole torn in the upper arm of his coat. He hadn't dodged all the bullets.

I could tell by the amount of blood and the way he held his arm that it had only grazed him, but—but—

My stomach churned, a strange ache making my heart twist painfully.

He didn't notice the wound at all. Too absorbed in *me* to care that he'd almost *died*.

I clenched my teeth, limbs shaking. Then I stormed across the small distance between us, opened my palm, and as hard as I could, smacked him across the face.

Being a brick wall, his head barely turned an inch, but it shook him from his panicked assessment of me. He blinked. His mouth parted.

"If you ever need to save my life again—" My lower lip trembled, a flood of tears blurring my vision. "*Don't.* Do you understand?" Then I crashed into Miles and squeezed, burrowing my face into his vest.

His arms hovered above me, not daring to return the embrace, and he didn't speak, because my face had turned back into a girl again.

But I wanted him to.

"I wish it didn't matter," I breathed, the confession quiet enough that I knew he wouldn't hear. "I wish you would talk to me. When I'm *me.*"

When I drew back, his brows were pulled in tight—and I couldn't tell if it was because he was still assessing my injuries or because he wanted to know what words I'd mumbled into his vest.

But I would never know. He'd never utter a question to Emmeline Morgan.

I fell back another step, tamping down the tight sensation spreading through my sternum. "They'll be looking for us now."

Miles blinked and straightened, glancing around like this

was his first moment on earth. He dusted off his brown trench coat, stalked to one side of the bridge, and then the other, peering over the edge like he was gauging something.

Once I was sure I had my emotions in check, I cleared my throat. "I suppose you're not in the mood for any good news, then?"

Miles's gaze cut to me.

From within my vest pocket—or Miles's vest, as it happened—I withdrew the professor's keys, dangling them out in front of me. "The keys to the Old Building at King's College," I announced, tipping my chin up. "Gambled for in an effort so honest, it's enough to make even a scary man proud."

Miles was silent for nine whole seconds, then he scoffed. And at the end of it, right before he turned away, I swore I caught an inkling of a smile.

45

Ashley

I stared down the barrel of the pistol, magic still siphoned into the bracelet glowing on her wrist, and yet all I could do was think about how beautiful she looked.

She'd done it. She'd beat me at my own game.

Fool. You're a fool and you've lost.

You've lost.

"Dolly," I whispered.

Tears trembled in her eyes, but her full lips were set in a determined line.

"Why?" That was all I could manage. Nothing else came. No thoughts in my head except the fool and the why and the feeling of free-falling from the highest precipice, floating, plummeting, swinging between the taste of her lips and the steel pointed at my heart.

She gulped in air, but her fierce aim on the pistol never wavered. "For my father."

A figure pushed past the ring of men, staring me down with steely eyes. He'd meant for me to overhear. He'd set the trap, along with Dorothy. And Dorothy—

I AWOKE TIED to a table in a room that was white walled but dim, lit by a single lantern, and when I reached for my magic, only a cold snuff greeted me. To my left, a separate table bore various metal and wooden torture devices, some I'd even fraternized with in the past.

Time ebbed. Manacles chafed my wrists and ankles from being tied up for days. The sound of my breathing echoed in the quiet little cell, and outside of a man I'd nicknamed *the Questioner*, no one else entered it.

He'd come on three separate occasions, the shadows obscuring him completely, asking the kinds of questions I would never answer because I was too busy nursing the angry ember burning faintly in my chest.

Are you working alone?

Who are your connections?

And most importantly, *Where is the bracelet?* Then after getting no satisfying results, he'd left, presumably to let my resolve weaken a little further.

I adjusted my shoulders, grunting in discomfort because I'd long lost the feeling in my arms, shackled above my head. The manacles made me think of Miles, and being locked up in Bedlam's dungeon, back when he'd trusted me. I'd been ignoring the guilt rotting in my stomach, but being tied to a table, going days with no food and little drink, I couldn't ignore it any longer.

I shouldn't have stolen his slant. I shouldn't have been pulling several bracelet heists behind his back. But in a twisted sense, I was glad he was gone. Like I was glad Bram and my parents and Dorothy and *everyone* were gone. Let them all think whatever they wanted about me.

I was always destined for destruction, to take the Order down with me. This way, they didn't have to watch.

And Dorothy...

If I let my thoughts linger on her, the memory of her treachery fanned that ember into a bonfire, so I didn't let them. I kept them low where they'd sear the deepest, slowly turning my heart to charcoal so I didn't have to face the truth.

Footsteps sounded outside the door, growing louder. Several pairs. My mouth dried, vision sharpening with the fear of facing this next part alone. I'd never done it alone before.

Maybe I was a fraud.

Maybe I was only brave because in the back of my mind, I knew Miles was always there to get me out of whatever mess I'd created.

Not anymore.

Not ever again.

Two men who were built like oxen entered the room. One bore an eye patch and the other had greasy black coils that fell past his thick shoulders. I heard the Questioner follow them inside, slinking into a darkened corner.

"Oh good," I said dryly. "An audience."

"They're not here just to watch," the Questioner said.

"Naturally. I expect applause."

Steps methodical, the two intimidating figures circled the table, shadows slowly shifting over their faces. The Questioner began with the same statement he'd made a few days ago. "Only five bracelets were recovered at the church, plus the one you'd recently obtained. And yet, you had all seven in your possession."

For the thousandth time, I thanked every star I'd taken that precaution. A grin pulled at my mouth. "Outsmarted even in victory?"

A long silence followed, and his voice sounded tighter when he said, "Not for long."

"Hate to disappoint you, but I don't have a history of breaking." *Not yet.* I glanced over to see the man with the black curls picking up a metal rod. "Aw, not the whip?" I tsked. "The whip is my favorite."

He brought the rod down on my shoulder.

Sweet fire. My vision flashed white. I coughed, the pain suffocating.

"Where is the last bracelet?"

He hit me again. I heard a crack.

Bloody, bloody silt—

I broke my promise to myself and groaned.

"Where *is* it?"

My eyes rolled back. I couldn't breathe. "It's not...that you won't find it," I panted, feeling the blood drain from my head. Sweat pebbled all over my body. "It's that you *can't.*"

The Questioner waited pensively like I'd told him a riddle, but I hadn't. Only one person could retrieve the bracelet, and he'd left all my broken pieces behind, just as he should have.

He'd never go back to our old flat and find it.

"I'll be the judge of that," the Questioner said, then a finger emerged from the shadows and motioned toward the thumbscrews.

The root of my tongue grew thick, skin prickling. The Questioner must've seen my fear, because he hummed a chuckle, causing a ball to harden in my gut.

Straps tightened over my arms, and my hands were yanked

up, stretching me farther on the table. Against the pain, I forced myself to say to the man with the eye patch, "You can maim those. I never use the things anyway."

Then a red-hot agony ripped through my thumbs.

DAYS PASSED, alternating between the sharp, blinding pain and the muffled, throbbing aftereffects. Sometimes on the table, sometimes on the ground, on my knees. Racks, ropes, metal and blood. The dull pain was worse—because it went on and on without reprieve, intense in its constancy; at least when the lackeys beat me, there was some variety.

It felt like months, but I knew it was a week at most. Then when I couldn't physically sustain any more, they brought in a healer who would close my wounds, slanting my bones back into place, and it would start all over again.

Through everything, the Questioner didn't laugh or gloat. He didn't get his hands dirty or yell. He hardly moved at all.

All he did was stand in the corner, cloaked in darkness, and repeat the same question. Never a different one. Never angrier than the last time. Just the same question while two men beat me in between using a bracelet to siphon my magic away every few hours.

"Where is the last bracelet?"

I tipped my head back, making a trickle of blood slide down my cheek to meet my neck. I pulled in two deep breaths through my mouth.

"Where is the last bracelet?"

I thought of Bram. Everything he'd trained me to do. I wondered what he'd make of me now. Brought so low. Having failed so utterly. Over a decade of work swiped away, and all because I'd had the foolish sense to give my heart to the first woman to not fall at my feet.

A current of anger rose up in my chest at the thought of Dorothy, and I pushed it down.

I didn't want to think about her.

"Where is the last bracelet?"

With all seven bracelets, someone's magic could be removed completely. Such power shouldn't be in the Questioner's hands. Because he'd use it.

I was a dead man walking anyway. Might as well save England in the process.

"Where is the last bracelet?"

I bit down on the salty tang of blood.

I'd never tell him. I'd never betray Bram like that or my dead family or *myself*. I'd built my entire life—reduced as it was—around the idea that the world was in danger. I'd sweat, bled, pored over maps, walked the city until my feet blistered, charmed my way into circles both high and low, planned until my mind spun webs, and I couldn't close my eyes without tasting the freedom. Years and years of toil.

Leather cracked—once, twice. Pain striped across my back. *Snap! Snap! Snap!* I choked on nothing.

"Where is the last bracelet?"

It couldn't be for nothing.

Bloody silt, *I couldn't let it be for nothing—*

46

Dorothy

The air reeked of grinding metal and drying fish on muddy banks. Steam from the little boat puffed into the air, joining the smoke that rose from the button factory's stacks, sprawling along the edge of the Thames. I squirmed in my seat, covering my nose with a handkerchief in an effort not to gag, while Nicholas seemed unbothered as he steered the small steamboat from the rear.

It felt strange, returning to the button factory, where Ashley and I had hidden inside the armoire in Mr. Brass's office. Three large cormorants flapped out of the water and took to the skies, no doubt headed upstream where the pollution hadn't killed all their food.

Instead of steering us toward the factory docks where heavy shipments were unloaded, Nicholas angled us into a tunnel on the opposite side of the sprawling structure, hiding the waterway traffic from view.

"I didn't know the Lightfoot Agency had so many different headquarters." My voice echoed off the stony walls, even while the steam puffing out the boat's central tube condensed on them. I took a lungful of the dewy air, noticing dim lights burning up ahead. Now that I'd completed my...mission... Nicholas had suggested I move on to my next task in the Lightfoot Agency.

Aching for anything to keep me distracted, I'd readily agreed. It had been several days since...*and* since I'd had any word from Emme. My mind was hanging by the thinnest thread.

"The printing shop is really an outpost for the lower-level agents who do all the grunt work and menial tasks. Most never learn about this place. Think of it as the inner circle."

The tunnel widened into a large room with a dozen lamps, glowing next to five sets of double doors atop a platform on the far side. Nicholas navigated us parallel to it and shut off the engine before winding the boat's rope around a hook anchored into some concrete steps.

My boots scraped as I ascended, and I avoided shallow puddles as I stepped farther onto the platform. The five domed doors—more like gates with their golden gothic bars—each had a button to the side, making me squint. Electric elevators, modern and expensive. Above each entrance gleamed a shiny plaque.

The Eternal Council
Division of Operations
Inquisitions
Department of Applied Science
Circle of the Worthy

I stared longest at *Inquisitions*. It sounded like a euphemism for *torturing chamber*, but I shuddered and didn't ask. Because that night at the abandoned church, I'd counted the bracelets the Lightfoots had recovered, and one was still missing. One Ashley had been clever enough to keep separate from the others.

Nicholas headed straight for the *Department of Applied Science* elevator and pushed the button. The contraption lit up as its gears rotated and droned. While we waited, I glanced at Nicholas out of the corner of my eye. His sharp jaw wore a shadow, and his gray eyes were hazy with fatigue.

The impression disappeared when he caught me looking at him. He smiled. "Are you nervous?"

"Yes," I blurted. "You say that it's a great honor to learn of this place. I'm still uncertain why I've been invited."

A bell chimed, and Nicholas pulled a lever that caused the elevator doors to rattle open. We stepped into the contraption while my gaze hunted for the gears and electrical boxes that made it run.

"We have many fine agents," Nicholas said as we began to descend. "You've been invited because you have proven your loyalty in the deepest sense. Not many agents—fine as they are—do."

In the deepest sense...

I bit my lip.

Nicholas shuffled over to me, and the light overhead flickered like it was on the same electrical current as my stuttering heart. Nicholas stooped a little, watching me with those concerned, earnest eyes. "If you hadn't found those bracelets and betrayed the Rook...you wouldn't be standing here right now. Perhaps not ever."

"Really?"

"I felt much the same way, at first; like I didn't actually merit it." He smiled again, softer. "But that is not the case here. I cannot tell you how proud I am."

I smiled back, and though it felt a little wobbly, it was mostly genuine.

Weight fell back into my feet as the elevator halted, dinged, and Nicholas opened its doors to a labyrinth of marble hallways. The Lightfoot offices I'd visited, while orderly and professional, had a chaotic spirit within their walls—probably because of their need to pivot with any new information. Here, business was conducted in a steady, nearly quiet way. These agents strode past with calm, confidence, and focus. All traits I currently lacked.

Nicholas nodded to and greeted the Lightfoots we passed but kept a brisk pace and didn't bother introducing me even when they cast curious gazes. At the end of the hall, Nicholas opened a door and gestured for me to step inside.

I smelled the mahogany first—deep and earthy, and lining the spacious room from floor to ceiling. Books and scrolls of parchment filled most of the shelves, the others tastefully decorated with cloches, model contraptions, and miniature busts of scientific minds.

"Is this Mr. Brass's official office?" I asked.

"It's mine, actually." After a beat of silence, he prompted, "What?"

I shrugged. "This room, this place. It's as if you have a whole separate life."

He sighed, scrubbing a hand over his face. "It's *government*. There will always be things too classified for me to divulge."

I nodded, disliking that truth even as I recognized the necessity for it.

"Unless..." he began hesitantly, then seemed to think better of it and shook his head.

"Unless what?"

"Well, there is an inner circle even deeper than this—where you could be privy to *everything*—but Brass doesn't think you're ready."

I digested the information, then said slowly, "And what do you think?"

He tilted his head, his gray gaze penetrating my soul. "I disagree. But I also think it's best for you to take things one step at a time right now. Now, are you ready for your task?"

It was just like him to give an answer so considerate and gentle. Sometimes it felt like he saw me more clearly than I saw myself.

Nicholas unlocked the top drawer of his desk and retrieved a bracelet, making me blink in surprise. It was one they'd recovered from the abandoned church.

"The bracelets temporarily steal magic, but they do it permanently if you have all seven. Once we have that capability, we don't know where the magic goes. Theoretically, it automatically transfers to the person removing it. That's where you come in."

He produced a glass vial the size of his thumb and held it up. "We need you to find a way to contain a person's magic inside this. Un-bonded and stable." The glass clinked as he set it on the desk between us.

I blinked some more. "I...I wasn't aware Her Majesty had plans to strip citizens' blood of magic. Isn't it...painful?"

"It has yet to be done. But I can't imagine it feeling pleasant." At my uncomfortable expression, Nicholas frowned and added, "Magic, as leverage, is the future."

"But that's exactly what Lark Acheron does—hoarding cuffs to control who can and can't access their slants in the Necropolis. It creates tyranny."

He came around the desk and sat, bringing himself to my eye level. He scooped up my hands. "Think about it, Dorothy. Some people don't deserve to have magic. Look at the Rook. Look at the way he used it. On so many. On *you*."

I cast my eyes downward.

"Think how many people we could have saved if we'd removed his slant. How many *more* we could've saved if the magic had been given to a Lightfoot agent."

My eyes darted along the marble floor. What he was saying made sense...

"If the Queen were able to remove the slants from criminals and then store them for a time when the country was in need of them, the benefits to a government would be exponential. They may be used for espionage or covert missions or trapping thugs who deserve to be behind bars. Doesn't England deserve that kind of assurance? Don't you want to be part of all that?"

Raising my gaze, I nodded, though it felt more for my benefit than for his. He was right. He was always right. I picked up the bracelet and the vial, examining both. "I'm not an expert on the bracelets. What makes you think I can solve the problem of harvesting and storing slants?"

"We have reason to believe the magic will respond to a chemical reaction. Bonding and un-bonding, tapping into the genetic code of magic—isn't that what you and your father were working on?"

Then, as if sensing the painful turn of my thoughts—as was always the case when my father was mentioned—he dropped my hands and stood, not waiting for my answer. "Our science department is still getting off the ground. We're devising a more suitable laboratory for you to work in, but until then, I hope this office will do. Make a list of materials you require for your experiments, and I will personally see to it they are provided. And"—he peeked at a pocket watch before snapping it shut and tucking it in his waistcoat—"I'm fearfully late for a meeting. I'll be back at seven to take you to The Savoy for dinner." He edged toward the door.

I felt the color rise to my face at the casual mention of an evening out. Together. So official. "I'm hardly dressed—"

"You look lovely." He grinned and left.

I pushed my confusing mix of emotions aside and turned to the bookcase, immediately sifting through them to find titles that would be helpful: books on energy conversion, lumagenic acid, and a book from Miescher on nuclein. First, I formed a tall stack on the desk, then slowly started picking my way through, cataloguing different methods to try, along with a list of supplies.

I dove into the work with such fervor that my vision whirled with potential formulas, the loud scratches of my pencil filling my ears. On the third page of my scribblings, the lead snapped, forcing me to stop and hunt for a replacement.

There were no writing utensils atop the desk, nor in the first two drawers. When I opened the third, I stopped cold, shoulders twitching up. Though the drawer was thin and shallow, it was filled to the brim with black feathers. The ones he'd collected from the Rook?

"Ah, those."

I guiltily glanced up to find Nicholas stuffing his hands in his pockets as he entered. I looked at a clock on one of the shelves, surprised to see three hours had already passed.

He approached and gingerly picked up a feather from the top of the stack. "Every one of these is a feather that a Lightfoot agent encountered. I've kept them to remind me not to underestimate him; to always know what I'm up against."

But as I stared at the pile of black feathers, all I could see was Ashley's face. The look in his eyes as he realized I'd betrayed him.

Nicholas leaned over me and gently closed the drawer. "I hope you're hungry. I hear pheasant is the special tonight." When I said nothing, Nicholas ventured, "Dorothy?"

"Can..." I licked my lips. Why was I asking this? But I had to know. It was killing me not to know. "Can you find out what they've done with Ashley?" Nicholas's face fell and darkened, and I rushed on. "It's just that I feel terrible, and—"

"It's no longer my jurisdiction. And knowing will only make you feel worse."

"I understand that, but...please?" I glanced up at him. "For me?"

Concern etched Nicholas's brow as he studied me. Something in his posture hinted at resistance; he didn't want to do me this favor. But then he seemed to melt as he fell further into my eyes until finally, he gave a slow nod. "It's going quite a bit up the chain, so I can't guarantee an answer, but...I'll ask."

47

Emmeline

I'd always wanted to be a spy.

A thrill sparked up my spine as I readjusted my very scholarly-looking spectacles with fake lenses. After losing our luggage on the train, Miles had scrounged up some formal long coats and trousers for us to blend in, and with me slanting my face to look like a handsome twenty-something, we strode past some patrolling bluedusters and through King's Gate onto campus.

The flying buttresses of the chapel harpooned the sky, the gothic carvings and glinting rose window making my jaw drop in awe. I'd never thought of myself as an academic, but staring at the majestic building before me gave me the strongest urge to study Latin.

It took me several moments to realize Miles had continued across the manicured lawn. I sprinted and caught up with him, taking two steps for every one of his.

"What are we looking for?" I asked.

"Anything suspicious," was his simple reply.

After getting some directions from a highbrow man in robes —a professor, I guessed—we wove our way to the Old Court Library. There, after a few hours of digging, Miles found a map of the campus and spread it on a table to study.

Cambridge was enormous, with thousands of possible places to hide an uncle. More than ever, I was grateful our lead had narrowed it down to a specific college. Miles studied the map intensely, a scowl darkening his forehead.

"You think you can memorize it?"

He shook his head. "Never been good at that. It was always Ashley who..." He never finished, and the sentence hung between us like a black spider dangling from a web, neither of us brave enough to venture nearer to it.

"We'll start here," he said, pointing to a section west of the library, "and make our way down slowly."

"So that's it, then? You're just going to go room to room, dorm to dorm, until you've ruled everywhere out?"

He arched an eyebrow. "You've a better plan?"

I bit my knuckle, eyes tracing the black lines on the map. "It's a large campus, but there are over five hundred students, all of whom know every nook better than we do. One of them is bound to have seen something. We could ask them."

Miles's upper lip puckered. Disgust. "All five hundred?"

"*I* can do the talking."

"I don't like this plan."

"And all you have to do is smile."

"I like it even less."

I put my hands on my hips, knowing it broke my disguise and made me appear girlish, but not being able to help it. "Listen. It's a cinch once we find where the students recreate, where they let their guard down, or maybe share a pint. Comfort is the father of a loose tongue."

"Those areas," he stressed, "are likely to be in their little unions and clubs—exclusive."

"Then you're lucky *one* of us is so charming." I beamed and batted my lashes. When he said nothing, I added, "Me. I'm the charming one."

Miles groaned.

In town, I purchased a dress from a quaint little shop. A few hours later, I found Miles on a bench outside the chapel and plopped in front of him with a twirl, a broad grin splitting my face. "Guess where I've come from?"

He watched me evenly. Ah, right, I wasn't in my boy-face.

"The Backs," I supplied. "They're scenic walking paths that run along the River Cam. They're behind—"

Miles's brows lifted. Hm. So he knew where the Backs were.

"*Anyway*, after running around and meeting several dead ends with my inquiries, I finally met a group of men practicing their rowing. The middle one—his name was Alex—had the dreamiest eyes! And he was so clever too. He cracked this joke about my ankles and how cute they were standing up on the banks—"

I cut off when I noticed Miles scowling. My smile faded. "Well, I suppose you had to have been there. But the group of us talked for a long time, and they were generous enough to answer all my questions. Alex was particularly thoughtful, inviting me to dinner tonight—"

Miles's glare darkened and he scoffed.

"—Gesundheit—in order to discuss the matter further. I really wanted to say yes, if only to—"

Miles's breathing loudened.

"All right, no need to get angry!" I said defensively. "I declined, naturally, since we'll have investigating to do tonight —especially after I tell you all the information I gleaned."

I watched the wind tease Miles's warm brown hair. Even if I'd never muster the courage to touch him like that, it was comforting to know that at least Mother Nature wasn't intimidated by his menacing gaze.

Then I sat forward, settling onto my knees in front of him and growing warm and confused when his face seemed to relax. Was it my nearness? Or was he looking at me like a stray cat, in need of a home?

I could feel the heat rising to my face and stuffed the thoughts down.

"A new class opened about a month ago," I began, "on the Strand campus, featuring a cutting-edge professor. Only a handful of elite students got in. They come and go at all hours, and always in a pair, like the lectures are happening around the clock. One of Alex's mates thought the whole setup suspicious, and tried sneaking into the classroom, but was caught and expelled." Lowering my voice, I waggled my eyebrows with meaning. "No one's seen him since."

Miles blinked, unenthusiastic.

I cleared my throat and straightened. "I think the college fabricated the whole story so the faculty wouldn't ask questions. Today marks the last week of classes. With the emergence of this mysterious class in the middle of the semester, I'd bet all my money—which isn't much, I grant you—on these so-called students being *guards*, shielding a professor—my uncle— that no one's ever seen."

I sat back on my heels and held my hands out in a gesture that said, *It's only natural to be impressed,* while I waited for his verdict.

Miles's mouth scrunched—I really shouldn't be looking at his mouth—but then, slowly, he opened it and—

And—

And absolutely nothing happened. Because I still looked like a girl.

I stood and dusted off my dress, trying to mask my disappointment. "I'll show you where the classroom is."

MILES SPENT all day scoping the area and noting the times students came and left, to see if he could find any weak points, while my job was to map our escape route. Using the key I'd pilfered from the man on the train, I tested locks all over the campus grounds. With the constant flow of students peering on, it took all day to discover it unlocked the little iron gate on the south side, a section rarely used, given the overgrown dandelions.

We hunkered down for the night at the *Riverfin Inn*, a few miles north—far enough away to avoid suspicion. Their lumpy mattresses left sores in my back, but I was grateful for the separate rooms so Miles didn't have to listen to me toss and turn. The next day, he did more scoping to ensure the schedule was the same while I learned the layout of the town, finding the swiftest route to the inn.

By the third day, Miles confirmed he was ready and that we would stage the rescue that night. Then he disappeared all afternoon, presumably to prepare, but I didn't ask how, and neither did I follow him; a few bluedusters had started poking their noses around the area.

It wouldn't look good for a girl to be caught on premises where girls were strictly prohibited.

Instead, I holed up inside a dusty old shed a few yards from the building—our designated hub. Judging by the cobwebs over the trowels, clay pots, and pruning shears, the gardening shack wasn't in current operation. Through the shed window, I carefully watched the lone shuttered window that belonged to the mysterious classroom. When night fell, I swore I saw the profile of a bespectacled man cast against the candlelight, there and gone.

When Miles returned close to midnight, it was with jam and a few slices of bread, as if he'd heard my stomach growling from wherever the devil he'd been. He mutely set it on the filthy table beside me then situated himself by the window a few paces away, muscles taut. Every few seconds, his gaze darted to a timepiece in his palm, then he'd scan everything again like a hawk, every field of his vision suspect. He knew when the guards changed and was biding his time.

After scraping the little jam lid open, I dumped the contents over the first piece of bread and wolfed it down in three huge bites, moaning at the sugary tang of strawberries. It was inelegant, but I didn't care. Aware of the sticky residue on my face, I licked every trace of jam off my lips, only to glance up and find Miles's eyes glued to my mouth.

I blinked and froze. How incredibly selfish of me. "Did... Did you want some?"

He jerked his head away so quickly, he looked positively guilty. Which he should. For not bringing me food sooner.

Picking a few crumbs off my skirt, I hummed and mumbled to myself, "Doesn't like Yorkshire pudding *or* bread and jam." I took care to devour the food more quietly, only smacking twice more. When I finished, the song of crickets chirping outside filtered into the little shed, the summer air—even in here— humid in my lungs.

Miles stared out the window again, the moon casting a cold hue around the angles of his face. There was a stillness to him—

a surety—that I envied. Then my eyes fell to his shoulder, where the bullet had grazed a few days ago, and I swallowed. I hadn't even seen him bandage it.

Try as I might, I couldn't shake the image of that blood.

Here he was, about to risk his life again without a second thought, and I was to stay behind. To just *await* the outcome. And even though I knew it was the right thing—he could act so much quicker without me—the anxiety in my stomach bounced around until it had created so much friction, I was going to explode.

"How big of items can you store?" I blurted. "I'm sure it can't be as big as a house. Have you ever tried storing a house?" I bit my lip, waiting for a response even when I knew it wouldn't come.

Miles glanced at me, then turned back to the timepiece, batting me away like a pesky mosquito.

"And certainly, you mustn't put anything alive into your pocket? I imagine it wouldn't come out the same. Entrails everywhere. You ever try that?" Hopefully if I kept talking, he wouldn't notice that my hands were shaking. That I'd started to sweat.

That all I wanted to do was ask him not to go.

"No, Miss Morgan," I said in my best Miles impression, "because I am not a half-wit." I brightened my pitch. "Good to know! And while we're on the subject of Miss Thurston"—why the devil was *that* slipping out?—"you never answered if you found her pretty." I brusquely stood, disturbing enough dust motes to make me cough. "Of"—I coughed again, and it helped deepen my voice believably—"of course she is pretty. She is the prettiest creature I've ever beheld!"

I cleared my throat. "Well, not that it matters, but...you have my blessing." I blinked rapidly, even though those couldn't be tears welling in my eyes. It must be those blasted pervasive dust motes. "You should marry! Truly, I'm sure you two will be very happy together, being so well matched. You'll make beautiful babies, just as your mother said!

"Miss Thurston will feed you Yorkshire pudding every day, but that will only be because she is so friendly with your mother, so one really cannot fault her. And you can breathe at *her* when you're angry, but I'm sure she'll like it because that's the kind of annoying—er, patient—person she is."

Miles's jaw clenched. Tighter and tighter. He glanced at the timepiece again—then back to the window.

I started pacing the floor. "And you won't ever quarrel over cats or who sleeps on the floor. No, you'll both be sleeping on a bed." I stopped. My face flamed. But everything was spluttering out, and it was too late to stop the flood. I resumed pacing. "As—as married people sometimes do. Not that I know anything about that!

"And you'll be strong for *her*, and thoughtful of *her*, and protect *her* when she imperils herself—which will be never, because unlike me, she is sensible. But you'll talk. Oh, how the pair of you will talk! Going on about boats and guns and oceans and dreams. You'll spill everything in your scary little heart to her because she's so beautiful that you won't be able to—"

Miles spun toward me so abruptly, I halted and the "help it" died in my throat. His mouth pinched. His eyes blazed. And his cheeks were redder than cherries. That was all I noticed before his hands clasped my head and his lips fell on mine.

My spirit left my body, entranced by the soft, insistent press of his mouth, the gentle scrape of his stubble against my face. Was that leather and salt I was smelling? Something subtle that was turning me to pudding. And his lips tasted of anger and strawberries (or maybe mine did, from the jam).

Too soon he broke the kiss and pulled back, half-gasping. Then he glared down at me and said, "Just shut up."

He turned and darted for the college building, his timing impeccable as he disappeared through the doorway just as a student turned the corner. In a daze, my fingers grazed my lips, unsure what to make of the fact that even though I looked like me, Emmeline, he hadn't stuttered at all.

48

Emmeline

Agonizing minutes ensued.

Miles had discussed no plans with me, nor had I any way of knowing whether he'd been caught. But if it came to it, I'd slant my face and storm in after him, if only to escape the relentless pitch of my emotions. Worry when I remembered where he was. Heat when I remembered the kiss. Fear when I remembered his bloody shoulder. *More* heat when I remembered *the kiss*—

Goodness me, that needed to stop.

After maybe ten minutes, I resumed pacing—which was how I bumped into the little bundle of papers on the floor by the window. I scooped them up. My hopes, twirling and sparkling minutes before, now drooped and sank back to earth. I studied the sailing vessel's blueprint for a long time but studied the paper beneath that even longer, my disbelieving gaze going in and out of focus.

It was a bill of sale.

Miles's name filled the bottom line in bold black ink. Had

he accidentally dropped these when he kissed me? Why did he need a boat? Where was he planning on going? Would...

...Would he take me with him?

My dreams of travelling reignited with a fury—picturing lazy days on the ocean, and Miles at the helm, and my fingers tousling his hair just as much as the breeze, and him kissing me every night under the milky way.

But he'd never mentioned this ship, and that small, stupid little fact was enough to make those hopes sink back into oblivion.

A siren alarm shrieked, making me gasp and look up. Lights sparked in the main building. Two figures darted across the lawn, one obviously slower than the other. I quickly folded the papers and sprang out of the shed, meeting Miles and my uncle—

My uncle.

I stopped short of them, crushing under a wave of relief.

Uncle Geoffrey seemed unsurprised to see me, and I guessed Miles had mentioned I was waiting outside.

"This way," I said, pointing behind me.

Uncle shook his head. "But they always keep the back gate locked; only a handful of people have keys—"

"We're one of the handful."

The siren grew louder, a commotion stirring inside.

We ran across campus and unlocked the little gate, slipping away just as the first guards posing as students ventured outside. Miles took the lead, guiding us behind a stack of buildings.

I turned back to my uncle as we dashed. "Are you well?"

"What?" Pure confusion wrinkled his face. Then it cleared. "Oh, yes. Quite. Don't worry about me, dear."

"Well, we *have* been. Especially Dorothy. How could she

not? When she found that black feather on your pillow, she nearly died of fright."

"Black feather?"

"And she's been looking for you ever since. She found out the Rook's identity by accident and—"

Uncle Geoffrey halted, making me halt with him. He held up a hand. "You—You think that—?"

Miles kept going, silently urging us to keep moving, but ultimately stopped too, grimly tracking the shadows behind us.

Uncle's brows knit so closely together they formed a bushy gray caterpillar on his forehead. His wide brown eyes blinked at me, and he panted, "The Rook is not who's been kidnapping everyone."

"What?" Miles and I chorused, loud enough to wake the entire town.

Uncle Geoffrey chose that moment to grip his sides, glance heavenward, and catch his breath, and I'd never had a stronger urge to shake a feeble man's shoulders until his teeth rattled to the cobblestones.

He looked back to us. Hands trembling, he pushed his spectacles up his nose, and there was no mistaking his words this time. "The Rook is not the one who kidnapped me. It was the Samaritan."

49

Ashley

The stone floor beneath me dug into my joints, chains jangling as I shifted my weight. Long enough for me to bring my hand to my mouth, the chains allowed luxurious freedom of movement. The cell stank of sweat and blood.

After the healer had slanted my flayed flesh closed, I'd been given a steaming plate of roast and potatoes, and some clean water. The next day, a similar pattern followed. The healer entered the cell, slanting away my aches and bruises and bloodied lip, and more food was set before me. Slanted healers were common, and while each one could treat a variety of maladies, each healer excelled in their unique area.

This one specialized in bones.

By the third day, I felt mostly whole, which was what made a chill creep up my spine. A sixth sense told me they were planning something far more terrible than shattered bones, but my exhausted mind couldn't conjure it.

Nothing could be worse than what I'd just gone through.

Ominous footsteps thudded in the hall, a rhythm full of sickening purpose. The door to my cell creaked open and the

Questioner filled the doorway, face covered in shadow—all but his upper lip which curled in disgust. "Get him up," he ordered, and the two guards behind him jumped to obey.

A *click* preceded the metal bands at my wrists falling away.

I cracked a smile. "What, not even a warm hello first?"

The guards hauled me up, and my feet wobbled on the smooth ground, uncertain how to balance my body after its ordeal. It took a few moments for my legs to rediscover their strength, and while they did, I ignored the Questioner's amused aura. He seemed content to wait, and that somehow made me hate him more.

Once I was ready, I shuffled after him through dank, winding tunnels that I quickly memorized, the guards prodding my back whenever I slowed too much. The air carried a wet metal smell, and a methodical rumble shook the ceiling; a machine, like the ones in the button factory I suspected we were beneath.

Finally, the Questioner stopped in front of a solid steel door that looked much like the door to my previous cell. He turned around, a glinting gray mask covering his features. Slowly, he lifted his hand and stripped it away, revealing a smirk.

But I'd long known his identity.

My brows lifted, unimpressed, and I said dryly, "Let me guess. You're going to torture me some more." I shook my head, sighing. "You've always been predictable."

His smirk faltered, a lightning bolt of anger flashing in his eyes before he recovered. "No, Mr. Gardner. Today is your lucky day." Keys jangled in the lock.

Prickles of unease scuttled up my neck.

The Questioner—the Samaritan—opened the door behind him, the painful brightness of the room beyond not quite concealing the freckle above his smiling lips. His hand latched onto my wrist, the glow of the bracelet around his own wrist fading as my magic funneled back into me. "Why bother torturing you, when *you* can do it for us?"

He let go and stepped to the side at the same time hands from behind shoved me into a room constructed of mirrors. The door slammed shut and an ocean of air lodged in my lungs. I saw my reflection, face specter-white and already slick with sweat. Icy horror clawed to life like a plague of locusts, drinking my blood and devouring my flesh.

Then my legs gave out and a scream ripped from my throat.

50

Ashley

My mother dragged me into her bedroom, squeezing my hand so tightly that it was bloodless when she finally released it. In her other hand, she held my father's pistol. She bolted the door, her elegant snowy dress, which once fit right in with the carved French dressers—the four-poster bed and brocaded drapes, the oil-painted ceilings and intricate molding—was now frayed and covered in soot.

It had been a month since the Order of the Worthy had stormed our chateau and hanged my father for refusing to tell them the location of the second Variance. One month of them keeping her locked up while they experimented on me, testing my slant.

"His magic isn't strong enough now, but it will be in a few years," I'd overheard one of the men say when they thought I was unconscious, in between their psychological sessions. I remember shuddering in terror but could never remember all that had happened.

"Finally," Sullivan Brass had responded. "We'll keep him

locked up—and the mother too, so we can persuade him to open it when he's ready."

After digging around in my mind and draining my blood for tests, they'd seared an A into my collarbone and left me alone, placing a guard outside my room. My mother's frantic face was the next one I saw, and I was pulled upstairs, never knowing how she'd escaped them or slipped past the guard.

"My precious boy. I won't let them do this to you too." Her cold, dry hand slid down my cheek. "You are resilient. If only you survive...at least then you may avenge us all."

I nodded, never realizing that the tiny movement would enslave me for the rest of my life.

"Right here." She touched the folds of my jacket covering my heart. "Make it bloody. So there's no question."

Somehow, I knew exactly what her plan was. I hunkered down against the wall beneath the window, relaxing my muscles to get an idea of how the illusion should look.

She backed up several paces, and even in all the terror, even with her mottled dress and unwashed hair and dirt-stricken face, I remember thinking how noble she looked.

"Don't you move." Her voice trembled, and so did the gun. Tears of love welled in her dark blue eyes—the same color as mine, before the mutation took over. "Don't make a single sound, no matter what happens, Ashley. Promise me."

I nodded again, but she couldn't see because the illusion was already in place. To her, I already looked dead.

The pistol cracked, shattering the window above my head. Shouts came, then. Rapid pounding that shook the frame of the entire mansion, until the door splintered off its hinges and a storm of men flooded in, the gun still smoking in my mother's hands.

My vision spiked red at the memory. Distantly I could feel my limbs spasming, smell the viscous, dark magic pullulating the room. My neck shook from trying to look away from the memory. But everywhere I looked, I saw my reflection.

At the front of the men, the narrowed brown gaze of Mr. Brass took me in—the slumped form of a little dark-headed boy, whose magic had manifested far too early. I shrunk back but kept the illusion steady like I'd promised, making my eyes appear closed, making my skin appear paler, making a blood stain crawl across my jacket.

His attention cut to my mother. "You," he whispered before grabbing her by the collar. "He was our key!" With the heel of his palm, he struck the side of her head.

She crumpled to the woven carpet, then turned over, defiance in the set of her lips. "You may have destroyed my family. But you won't destroy the world too."

Bullets fired. Nine of them, straight into her chest. Her gasps of shock. Blood staining her white dress. Her body hitting the floor. And scalding tears running into my hand over my mouth, trembling from holding back my screams.

Claws sank into the memory, pulling, *shredding* my mind—ripping my mother's mangled body until she was unrecognizable. I shrieked.

"Someone's carriage is coming—"

Mr. Brass swore. *"There's too much evidence. Burn it all."*

"And the boy?"

"He's dead. Leave him."

It happened too fast—the kerosene they splashed over the bed and drapes, trailing out into the corridor; the lantern they shattered on the floor, sending up a wall of flames. When the roar of the fire drowned out the sounds of the retreating men, I let my sobs loose, crawling to my mother's corpse and reaching for her bloodied hand.

My parents were dead, both murdered while protecting me.

The room glowed orange, the legacy of Anthony Renault, the Marquis de Avèjean, crumbling down.

Château des Corbeaux—Castle of Rooks—was burning.

Smoke scalded my throat. Timbers collapsed nearby, shooting sparks that caught my clothes. Caught my mother's hair, flames devouring her delicate face and charring it black.

I screamed.

And screamed.

And I screamed, until my throat caved in on itself, and something slimy and rancid touched my cheek. Vomit. The magic dug deeper, inking its way south toward my heart like a meandering snake. I clamped my hands around my throat and squeezed, trying to stop it—trying to stop *seeing*—but everywhere I looked were mirrors.

Flesh melted off my mother's bones, the foul smell turning my stomach. Her eye sockets gaped up at me, soulless and empty. Blood melted down the walls of the chateau, splattering us in a red rain that rose into a tide. It pulled me under, and I gulped and gulped and gulped and gulped and—

I squeezed harder.

Until at last, my vision speckled black and my eyelids slammed shut, and I slumped down, into a bitter relief that swallowed me whole.

51

Nicholas

I closed the door to the mirror room, a room constructed just for Ashley Gardner after I'd seen the way he'd reacted to his reflection in Beaumont's. Shrill roars shook the metal at my back, haunting and soul deep. Even more unsettling than the fevered shrieks of those who'd lost their memories.

And he deserved it.

A warped sense of satisfaction curled through me at the sound, and I shifted down the hall.

The Rook deserved it *all*, after the trail of black feathers he'd left for me over the last two years. Toying with me, taunting me, flaunting his victories in finding each clue first. Always one step ahead.

Not anymore. Now I was the one with all the cards; I had him cornered, I had nearly all the bracelets, and most of all, I had Dorothy, and I was going to torture him with every single one until he was begging for it all to end.

I headed for the Department of Applied Science and strode inside. Hundreds of sealed pint jars lined the far wall, all filled with congealed blood and labeled with two things: a name, and the concentration of magic found in their blood. None of them high enough. A few microscopes of varying strengths sat on a nearby table. Dressed in a white lab coat, Alden stood before one, examining the newest sample, while Brass waited off to one side for the verdict.

The downturn of Alden's lips clued me into his findings, but I still prompted, "Well?"

Alden shook his head and straightened. "I'm sorry, Mr. Brass, Mr. Hart."

"All of them?"

Alden nodded.

With a burst of a sigh, I shoved my fingers through my hair, frustration making my mouth pinch.

Even if he managed to acquire all the map pieces, Lark couldn't unlock the Variance without someone whose magic was powerful enough to do it. But neither could we. And we needed to find someone before he did—hence, why I'd had to increase the number of kidnappings.

"Does that dosage of magic even exist anymore?"

Brass worked his jaw but said calmly, "We've not yet searched everywhere."

"But we're running out of time." Concern laced my words. "If only that French boy hadn't been killed." Fourteen years ago, months before Brass had adopted me, he'd discovered one person whose slant would be powerful enough once their magic matured—a boy. But he'd tragically died, and even after searching all these years...

He'd been the only one.

My eyes tracked over the jars of blood. Most of the abductions had been lower-class, uneventful, but a few names dislodged memories. "Once word gets out that the Rook has been captured, we'll have no one to draw the fire for the kidnappings."

"Then word will not get out," Brass said amicably. His cool-headedness was a trait I'd often admired and drawn strength from. He was a gentleman, a chess-player, wise, unoffendable, and ruthless. A blanket statement like that meant a hundred bribes, blackmails, or disappearances—a logistical nightmare—and yet his face was like calm waters. By camouflaging the truth and then leaking it to the penny newspapers, we'd managed to drastically sway public opinion in our favor.

We could do so again.

"I'm tired of working so quietly." I felt guilty for the admission, but it was true. All the secrecy was beginning to wear.

After half a glance from Brass, Alden cast his eyes down and wordlessly left the room, ever subservient to the head of our Order. In the reigning quiet, Brass asked, "Is this because of Miss St. James?"

I didn't respond, because we both already knew that it was.

"You are second in command. You cannot afford to show weakness, and especially not now. She is not ready."

"She is nearly. Give me a few more weeks to win her over."

Brass's head tilted. "You have it. But if she's not on our side by the time we are prepared to open the Variance, you must cast her off."

I nodded, but his eyes narrowed because he must've sensed my reluctance and the way my mind was already making loopholes.

"Check on how the SID gun production is coming along, will you?" he said, referring to the new slant identification devices. His tone remained even, but I could tell he was disappointed in me. And he should be. I was too soft when it came to her. "Marian won't be able to wipe all five tonight, but I'll have someone drop the first one in the usual warehouse, and you can take it from there."

From the corner of my eye, I watched him approach me

slowly until he was speaking quietly into my ear, "And let me know when the Rook cracks."

I nodded. He left.

Brass was anxious to find the last bracelet; we all were, as our success hinged upon the ability to redistribute slants using the bracelets. Stripping magic from the slanted in London and bestowing it upon those loyal to the Order—those who were worthy—was what drew me to Sullivan Brass in the first place.

No one at the orphanage had been slanted, no one but the administrator. But instead of using his magic to light our hearths on freezing nights, he laughed while singeing our hair, melting our skin, the alcohol heavy on his breath. I was one of the lucky ones who remained relatively unscathed.

My brother was not.

He'd killed Edmond, but not before disfiguring him past all recognition and burning the orphanage to the ground.

I exited the lab then pivoted right, picking my way down the network of marble corridors to the Division of Operations. Memories filled my vision, tinged in red.

It had taken a few months to track the orphanage administrator down, but I'd gotten my satisfaction when after we'd tested his blood and wiped his memories, I'd dumped him into Bedlam's to rot. He lasted only a week before his own insanity killed him.

My past had taught me precisely one valuable lesson: Not all those with power deserve it. And some people who were powerless—like me, like Edmond—*did.*

Assembly tables organized the Division of Operations, chemicals and cartridges at one end, and the rest of the equipment for the SID gun, like cuts of metal and lenses, at the other. Order members worked diligently constructing both. After a quick conversation with the foreman overseeing production, in which he informed me to expect the completion of our first gun as early as tomorrow, I snagged one of the unfinished devices from the table and tested its weight in my hand.

It was lighter and sleeker than the first prototype. That one had worked beautifully, easily tracking an invisible Rook through the fog, but I'd lost it after he'd stabbed me and ripped it from my hands. I set the SID gun down and rubbed my shoulder where the scar was still tender.

Brass had offered more than enough compensation to Geoffrey St. James for his research on magic stamping—the ability to not just see blue magic on someone's hands, but to fingerprint it and follow each individual trail. But when Dorothy's father adamantly refused, I'd followed orders and abducted him.

It was drastic but necessary.

Since we needed the brilliance of Geoffrey's mind to recreate his formula, he couldn't be drugged into submission. But while the other abductees were held in a cold cell with little food, I'd made sure, for Dorothy's sake, that her father had received every comfort.

And after every assurance that we would keep his daughter safe, Sir Geoffrey had finally recreated the research he'd intentionally burned, a formula that detected magical particles for a full six hours after they'd been used, as opposed to the one hour the old guns detected. Now we could track down the slanted far easier and begin redistribution.

No longer in need of the chemist, Brass had wanted to dispose of him. Instead, I'd convinced Brass that if we let the man continue playing with beakers, we may yet find another use for his genius—but was secretly relieved to spare Dorothy the heartache.

One thing was for certain, though: We couldn't turn him loose. Hence why I'd sent half a dozen Lightfoot agents to take care of Dorothy's cousin, when she'd come uncomfortably close to finding him.

I snapped out of my thoughts when I noticed a dark-headed girl standing in the doorway, looking over her shoulder, fixated by the distant sound of Ashley Gardner's screams.

"Marian," I said, gripping her arm and pulling her around the corner.

She jumped but complied. "Who is that?" The din of Distributions receded as we walked—and so did all other noises.

"He's none of your concern." I let her go. "I was about to come looking for you. Alden finished with the testing. All negative."

Her bow-shaped lips parted like she wanted to say something, but she swallowed it.

My brows pulled in. "What is it?"

"I can't do all five at once," she said.

"Brass knows the limits of your slant. He wants you to get started on the first one right away, and I'll return him tonight. Yes?"

She nodded.

Like me, she'd joined the Order as a child, but unlike me, she'd hardly left this inner sanctum under the factory. She was too valuable for Brass to let out of his sight. Not for the first time, I took in her wavy black hair pulled back into a bun, and her glittering dark blue eyes, trying to pin down who she reminded me of.

She noticed my study of her and her brows pressed together. "Are you well, Nicholas?"

I shook off the thought and sighed. "I'm tired."

Then Ashley's screams fell silent, the corner of my lips quirked up—not in a smile, but rather a dark sort of pleasure that couldn't be replicated. "But I think I just started feeling much better."

52

Emmeline

U ncle Geoffrey didn't slurp (he was much too refined for that), but the way he elegantly shoveled the brown stew into his mouth made me wonder if his guards had been starving him. Judging by his waistline, however, it had been the opposite. Physically, he'd never looked so hale as he mopped up the last rivulets of soup with a chunk of bread. He, Miles, and I sat before a flickering candle in an upper room of the *Riverfin Inn*, and in the dim light, I noticed the extra creases near his eyes and his sagging, haggard face.

Nothing much had been said after Uncle's shocking declaration, mainly because Miles hadn't thought it wise with the guards so close. So we'd used a stolen Black Carriage from Miles's pocket to take us to the inn where we purchased a private room and steaming dishes. It was nearly three in the morning. Which meant that for two unbearable hours, I'd bitten back the boiling questions bouncing between my teeth, threatening to bubble over.

Now, bellies full, we sat around a table, and the first question shot out. "What do you mean the *Samaritan* kidnapped you?"

"Keep your voice low, dear." Uncle Geoffrey pushed his spectacles up his nose. "It may be early, but even walls have ears."

My face lowered and I nodded, duly chastened, even as my impatience mounted with each millisecond.

Miles remained void of expression, and he said in an annoyingly calm voice, "Perhaps start from the beginning."

Uncle nodded. "Yes. Yes, that would probably be best." He grimaced at the ceiling, as if recalling something unpleasant. "Years ago, at a convention, I lectured on the relationship between chemistry and magic. It was revolutionary to the field because up until that point, everyone believed that magic dwelled in the air and was bent to the will of the one slanting.

"I posed a new theory: that magical particles bonded with blood, and it was these same particles that a slant rinsed out and repeatedly used. Afterward, a man named Sullivan Brass approached me; he was extremely interested in my work. Not only that, but he wanted to fund my research."

Uncle sighed, pushing his spectacles down and rubbing his eyes. "I may be a baronet, but the title never guaranteed a farthing. I was a penniless man with a wife, a child on the way, and an unrelenting dream to change the world. It was my chance to revolutionize the scientific field, and I took it."

He replaced the spectacles on his nose. "I was a fool. After years of toil, I discovered lumagenic acid—a compound that illuminates magical particles. I didn't learn Mr. Brass was employed by the government until after the work was complete, and by then, he'd already taken my findings to the Crown. Engineers used my research to create slant guns, and...well." He shook his head. "Society changed. More people hanged. Because of me."

A tremulous note entered his last sentence, and I laid a comforting hand on his sleeve. "Those deaths were not your fault, Uncle."

"I couldn't... I couldn't let the same happen to my only daughter."

While Uncle Geoffrey composed himself, I mentally tacked on the part he'd left out: *So I hid her away.*

He picked up right where my thought left off. "And sequestered away as she was, who was I to deny her, when her keenest interest was in continuing my work? Any findings we made would stay in my lab and go no further. So I thought."

He leaned forward and folded his hands on the table. "Sullivan Brass had planted a spy within London's Science Society to keep an eye on me, and his name was Nicholas Hart."

My eyebrows ticked up. "That handsome Lightfoot agent that Dorothy's—!" I barely caught myself and shoved the words back down, mind racing. I didn't want to worry him right now by bringing up the fact that my cousin was working for the man.

Uncle nodded. "Yes, the one who'd captivated her attention. Somehow, he got wind that I was on the verge of another breakthrough, this time the ability to fingerprint magic. Mr. Brass approached me again, demanding the research.

"He offered me money, at first. I emphatically declined. He sent me notes. I burned them. He grew increasingly aggressive until he appeared on the steam yacht that night, threatening to take everything from me if I didn't yield. That's when they took me."

"That very night?" I asked. He nodded again.

Miles stared evenly at something above Uncle's shoulder, like none of this information fazed him.

"I held them off for a few days, but then they started threatening Dorothy and I..." Uncle shook his head. "I delayed where

I could. The first several batches I made were flukes, and I kept insisting on more and more equipment. Knowing that my best chance of being found was by being transported, I convinced them I needed a more academic setting conducive to my endeavors. They happened to have connections here on campus, so they complied, but the second I disembarked from their Black Carriage, I sensed that their patience had run thin.

"I feared the worst, I feared I'd never get out, I feared they'd target Dorothy if there were any more delays, so I...I recreated the formula. What they plan to do with it, I know not."

I stood and paced along the wall, no longer able to remain motionless with all this new information swirling inside me. "And where does the Samaritan come into play with all this?"

"While being held in Brass's facilities, I overheard many things—about this supposed Lightfoot Agency that, at its heart, is something else entirely—"

I stopped pacing. "What do you mean?"

"It's a front for a secret society, age-old and festering into treason with each passing year. They call themselves 'The Order of the Worthy.'"

Miles flinched—only a slight movement from the corner of my eye, but I caught it. The thought flickered through me, *What do you know?*

But Uncle Geoffrey continued before I could ask.

"If you'll remember, the legend of the Rook materialized three years ago, only back then, he was stealing strange objects from the *ton*. It wasn't until several months ago that the kidnappings began, and it was all this Order's doing—the abductions which they lay at the Rook's feet by leaving a black feather, and the rescues, which they claimed were the actions of a 'hero.' And they made sure to leave open padlocks in their victims' pockets so the whispers would differentiate between them."

My eyes widened, and I emitted quiet splutters, voice raising pitch. "So besides those first few years of burglaries, the Rook is completely innocent?"

"No," Miles said, glaring at the wall and offering nothing more.

"I believe," Uncle Geoffrey went on, "that he continued stealing objects—what, is still a mystery. But never people. He's not the one that's been driving them insane."

Miles still scowled at nothing, but now his gaze had lowered to his lap. His nostrils flared and his blinking stuttered.

"That's not all, I'm afraid." Uncle leaned in, gray brows tilting up while he lowered his voice. "A few days ago, I overheard a few of the guards saying the agency—this Order—had captured the Rook. Whoever the bloke is, I feel sorry for him. He'll crack one way or another." Uncle inhaled a wobbling breath; his eyes glistened, his lips trembled. "Everyone does."

My mouth parted as I wondered if Dorothy had anything to do with Ashley's imprisonment. Then my gaze snapped to Miles, whose face was like stone but who was breathing very, very hard.

"Miles—" I reached a hand toward him.

His chair scraped as he brusquely stood. He made no excuses, offered no insight or opinion, just strode into the adjoining room.

In the quiet, I lowered back into my chair at the table and explained, "He knew him."

Pity swirled in Uncle's warm eyes. "Ah. Forgive me, I did not know."

A few scuffles sounded beyond the wall as I imagined Miles settling into his bed, and then all was still. But I doubted he would sleep. Not with news like this.

I knew his sleeping patterns too well.

Uncle's wrinkled hand reached over to grip mine in my lap. "Emmeline, where is Dorothy? Is she safe?"

I inhaled a deep breath, unsure what to say and what to let Dorothy explain herself. She was associating with Nicholas Hart, but I didn't believe her to be in any real danger from him. At least not yet. And I didn't want to trouble Uncle Geoffrey further, right after going through such a harrowing ordeal.

The best course was to get him far from the college as quickly as possible and contact Dorothy. She'd know what to do.

"She was safe when I left," I said honestly. I forced my face to brighten, and though it felt strained, it also felt genuine too. "She will be so relieved—I know I am."

He squeezed my hand again, tears spilling onto his cheeks. "I am so thankful to you, my dear—and Mr. Kelly. I owe the both of you a great deal."

After that, we both agreed to get some rest.

Uncle Geoffrey retreated through the adjoining room door, and when his mattress squeaked, I blew out the candle. It emitted only a few curls of smoke against the shady morning, and they followed me to my own mattress. I laid down on my side, wishing for Miles's strong, sleeping presence. It was our first night in separate rooms since the start of this ordeal, and I didn't realize how empty I felt with a slab of wood between us.

Like I suspected of Miles, I wasn't able to sleep at all. Which was why I heard it a few hours later: a door shifting open.

My knees curled into my chest, and I blinked away the moisture threatening to pool. No steps sounded in the hall, nor the soft release of hushed breathing—but like a little candle flame winking out, leaving me to face the bone-chilling dark alone, I somehow knew he had gone.

For good.

53

Miles

I stepped onto the wooden planks of *The Midnight Gale*, inhaling a fortifying breath and knowing I'd need dozens more to get through this morning. A mist off the sea hovered over the harbor and stretched its fingers toward the railing of the ship, trying to escape the dawn about to break. The Port of Boston at Lincolnshire—where I'd arranged to meet Barnam— was eerily quiet.

From the moment of Geoffrey St. James's declaration, a war had raged within me all night, slowly killing me from the inside.

Ashley hadn't committed any kidnappings.

But he'd lied to my face; stolen my slant.

With how everything had played out, he knew I'd believe the worst of him and had let it happen. Black fog, he'd *orchestrated* it, making me hate him so I wouldn't realize he was actually cutting me loose. So many things he'd done behind my back.

Including taking a brutal beating intended for me, without any expectation that I'd ever discover it.

Anger simmered low in my chest. Maybe I ought to listen, give him what he wanted, because it was too much. Too much to ask me to go back.

And Emmeline had seen my conflicted mood. She'd found the contract I'd signed for the ship and knew I was leaving.

Her lips had been so soft. Everything I'd dreamed they'd be.

And I had to leave because I couldn't bear to look at her ever again.

A figure across the deck noticed my presence and turned. "There you are, Kelly," Barnam said. "I had half a mind you wouldn't show." He paused, taking in my eyes which I didn't doubt were red with exhaustion. "Are you well?"

I said nothing and inspected the deck, following the railing all the way up to the bow. *The Midnight Gale* was small for an ocean vessel, and over fifty years old, but it was sturdy and clean, and, most importantly, *mine*. I couldn't wait any longer. I had to get out now. While I still had my wits about me—while my sanity was still winning that war.

"A beauty, isn't she? Stocked with all the items you requested. That is, if you have the money."

I sucked on my teeth, hesitating, though I didn't know why. Ever since Bram died, this was all I'd wanted, what I'd spent every waking moment dreaming about. Ignoring the uncomfortable pang in my chest, I dug out the wad of cash from my magical pocket and placed it in Barnam's hand, then waited as he counted the bills.

Once finished, he grinned, catching my hand in a firm shake. "Pleasure doing business."

He walked down the plank, and I stood alone on the deck, mentally compiling a to-do list before the *Gale* could embark on its first voyage with me at the helm. Assembling a crew came first, obviously. I'd already sent messages to some old mates that had sailed with Bram, but until they responded, I could pick up a few hands here in Lincolnshire or London. My eyes lifted to the sails flapping in the slight, salty breeze, knowing they were my key to freedom from the past.

Finally.

"I don't believe this."

I stiffened, recognition making blood rush to my face. Slowly, I turned around to find Emmeline hopping down from the boarding plank and putting her hands on her hips. Morning beams danced on her strawberry gold hair, the updo matted and loose from being slept on. Her cheeks had a lovely color to them—from the brisk walk here, or the anger swirling in her dark eyes.

"You're really going to do it. You're *actually* going to leave."

Excuses leapt to my knotted tongue, but I couldn't speak. Not with her looking so beautiful and feminine in the morning light. I switched gears, saying, "Ch..."

"Sneaking off early in the morning so you don't have to face me is a shocking and cowardly move—one I didn't expect from you, of all people."

It was like lifting a slab of granite with my jaw, but I finally managed, "Ch-Change."

Her eyes widened a little, lower lip pushing out in stubbornness. "You want me to morph into Emerson so you can argue with me? Well stone me, if that isn't a bit rich! You'd like that wouldn't you?"

My mouth worked, no sounds coming out—it was all I could do to give a pathetic nod.

Her face tightened. "I have a better idea, Miles. Why don't you learn to speak to *me*? If you can make your lips fall on mine, you can bloody well manage a few words with them!"

"I..." My breaths shallowed, trying to contort my tongue over the vowels they'd formed so many times. Sweat trickled down the side of my face to meet my trembling jaw. *Just say the words. Just say the words.*

I panted, giving up with a shake of my head.

Emmeline huffed and crossed her arms. Then still glaring at me, her face altered into the little street urchin boy I'd come to know. "You were going to leave. Without saying goodbye. Without saving Ashley."

The effect was instantaneous; the muscles in my mouth relaxed. I straightened and loosened my collar. "Ashley is capable of saving himself."

"It sounds like this time, he's not."

"He doesn't need me." *You have always been good, Miles. But Ashley...has always been* great. My voice quietened. "He never has."

"You have to go back and fix your friendship, Miles, because like you said, it's wrong to do anything else."

Now I glared back at her, muttering darkly, "I didn't tell you that so you could use it against me."

"I'll use whatever I please if it will get you to do the right thing!"

"And why do *you* get to decide what's right? *You* were the one who told me to let him *go.*"

"I know..." She flushed. "I know. And I was wrong. Blast it all, can't a girl get it wrong sometimes? I didn't know the whole story, and I'd gamble that neither did you—"

"Maybe he didn't do *everything* I thought he did, but that doesn't make him innocent. If he still hoards his secrets—as I know he does—then he is not my friend."

"You're right, he is more than that. He is your brother."

The words were an anchor dropping on my chest. I fell back a step, a barrage of memories hitting me next. Sun blisters on the open sea. Wrestling on a Mediterranean beach. Running for our lives in Copenhagen. Sleeping under the stars on Cairo sandstone and hearing his firm voice tell me, *From now on, we are brothers.*

"He..." I swallowed. Then I shook my head to dislodge the memories, shaking harder when they clung fast. "I'm *done*," I muttered, half-turning away mostly to convince myself that this was the right path. "I'm going back to the only place I've ever belonged."

Hurt flashed in her dark brown eyes. "No, Miles Kelly. You're going back to the only place you've *chosen* to belong. You intervened with that boxer, and at that creepy Black Carriage house; you even endured tea with your mother, though you were clearly out of your skin. You've helped me every step of the way, and whether it was to clear your own conscience or something else entirely, I don't care, because through it, I came to see you. The real you. Clearer than I've ever seen anyone.

"You helped me rescue my uncle. More than once, you have saved my life." She huffed. "And you belong *nowhere*? As if there is not a place by my side?" Dawn pierced the horizon and glinted off her welling eyes.

A dagger slid into my heart. I raised a hand. "Em—"

"I understand the reasons why you think you need to leave. Truly, I do. But I suppose I thought that between Ashley, and" —a tear dashed down her cheek, making that dagger twist— "and *me*...that maybe you had more reasons to stay."

I inhaled to say something—I didn't know what, exactly, but *something*—

But Emmeline dropped her magic, and as her face feminized and freckled, the words died in my throat. Arms hugging herself, she spun around and stalked down the boarding plank, and I watched her retreat with a squeezing chest, unable to even tell her goodbye.

54

Emmeline

Come to Father's house. Alone. Don't delay.
-E

I set my pencil down and slid the message into an envelope, hastily scrawling Dorothy's name on the front. The message was vague, but after unearthing so much mystery about the Samaritan and the Rook—and after my heart had taken such a beating from he-who-couldn't-speak—I'd learned that in this city, you couldn't trust anyone. I didn't want Dorothy to accidentally let slip where her father was.

Workers wove between columns that made the grand space look more like a bank than a postal service. Pencils scratched, tongues licked gluey stamps, papers shuffled and passed hands, and the man behind the long counter stared at me with glassy eyes.

"To the palace, please," I said, sliding the envelope across the counter.

The man lifted his brow. I felt every speck of grime coating my skin and dress, keenly aware of the grass stains and muddy patches and my stringy, greasy hair. But couldn't he tell my garment had once cost a fortune?

My facial structure alone!

"Yes, truly," I said, annoyed. "And it's urgent."

He blandly smacked his lips. "That'll be one shilling and fourpence, miss."

My jaw dropped. "One shilling and four!" A few customers glanced toward the outburst, and I cleared my throat. In the most dignified voice I could manage, I added, "Send it collect."

The man rolled his glassy eyes and handed the envelope to one of the couriers waiting behind the counter, allowing me to spin on my heels and exit the building. I approached the carriage waiting in the street with drawn windows and instructed the driver where to take us next, before gliding inside and settling in the seat across from Uncle Geoffrey.

As the carriage rumbled onward, Uncle Geoffrey removed his spectacles and rubbed his eyes with tremored hands. Setting the glasses back on his nose, he said, "I am so anxious to see my Dory. Has she been well?"

I inhaled thoughtfully, remembering how beside herself Dorothy had been after the kidnapping—the lack of appetite, the sleep deprivation, how she'd fallen hard for London's phantom, and had accidentally joined a secret government cult to get revenge on the man who'd betrayed her, but who, as it turned out, was basically innocent.

Tight air wiggled through my lips. I chuckled much too brightly. "She has indeed."

Uncle nodded in relief, blinking rapidly as if holding back tears, and in that moment, he looked more drained than a raisin. He needed some chicken soup and a long nap, and for myself I was itching for a hot bath. More than ever, I was grateful we were nearing our destination.

Getting Uncle Geoffrey back to London without Miles's

help had been more difficult than I'd anticipated. I had only pennies, and Uncle Geoffrey had just been released from an extended hostage-like situation, and yet we needed to outrun the news of his escape reaching Lightfoot ears, so a leisurely day-long journey had been stretched into a harrowing twenty-four hours. We'd changed horses at every stop, which allowed us to both lead a circuitous trail in case anyone was tailing us and let me gamble for more coins to pay for food.

Half an hour later, the carriage rolled to a stop. We'd arrived. It was a great risk to appear at Uncle's house—who knew if the Lightfoots were already watching it?—but there was nowhere else *to* go. And once Dorothy arrived, we could plan our next steps.

"Wait here," I instructed Uncle before disembarking, clutching my briefcase, but the command wasn't necessary. He'd stay confined to the carriage until I could sneak him in under the cover of darkness. In the meantime, I had other business to finish.

Hands tightening on the smooth leather of the handle, I marched up to the Georgian white stucco home and rapped the knocker. Moments later, the door swung open to reveal a maid whose eyes quickly widened in recognition.

"Hello, Beatrice," I said, pushing past her into the checkered foyer before she could awkwardly allow me in. "Would you please tell my father I am here?"

Her eyes darted nervously, but she bobbed a quick curtsy and scurried away. On the sideboard, a vase of purple bugles wafted their minty scent, and below them sat a tall stack of calling cards; Father hadn't wasted any time in his social climbing.

"I told you," a cold voice echoed down the hall. A few seconds later, my father emerged in black evening wear with his hair slicked back, dressed for an evening out. "I told you to never show me your face again."

I smiled. "Yes, I know you think it's hideous, but you see, I'll be needing Uncle Geoffrey's house now."

Father's glower didn't soften a bit. "How dare you."

"You'll need to expeditiously pack your—"

"You turn up here making demands, after all you've done to disgrace this family?"

"Actually"—I opened the briefcase and handed my father the record I'd carefully stored—"you make demands all the time, even though—funnily enough!—you have also done your fair share of disgracing. So, I think I've earned some leniency."

He scanned the page, expression blank.

"You can tear it up if you like, that's just a copy. But wouldn't it be a shame if the *ton* were to discover you had transactions with *smugglers* like the Black Carriage service? Dealing in illicit substances, no less. I shudder to think of the rumors! Mr. Morgan, a criminal? The toast of London will not dare utter the Morgan name for fear of dirtying their mouths."

His lips thinned and his knuckles gripping the page whitened. "You *dare* blackmail me—!"

"I have gotten daring indeed, during my time away; I know you will not be, but you ought to be proud. Now. I seem to have not made myself clear. I will be living under this roof now, which means you have precisely one hour to vacate, or I take this paper to the gossip circles. And if you dare dream of detaining me, I have a runner on standby, ready to release the information unless I contact him in twenty minutes."

Father's nostrils flared, wrath glimmering in his cold blue eyes. But after a lengthy, deathly pause, he called tightly, "Marie! Clarence!"

Footsteps sounded upstairs. At the sight of my brother appearing at the top of the stairs, my furrowed brow uncreased.

His strawberry-blond curls still flopped into his eyes, but it looked as if he'd grown a foot in the month I'd been away. My mother trailed not far behind him, and when she caught sight of me, she stopped, face lighting up—briefly—before looking to my father in trepidation.

"Pack your things," Father said icily.

"No, no, Father, you misunderstand. You aren't *all* leaving." I breathed in the victory, relishing the euphoric feeling. Then I smiled sweetly and put a hand on his shoulder in a gesture more affectionate than any he'd shown me. "Just you."

55

Dorothy

I dug my fingertips into my temple as my heels clicked down the hall, squinting against the morning sunlight streaming through the windows. It was my last day at the palace, and though the celebrations were to culminate in a dinner gala and Shakespearean performance this evening, I'd woken with a pounding headache that informed me I wouldn't be attending. If I avoided more whispers and questions about my missing fiancé, all the better, so my maid had packed my bags and sent them along to my flat.

I'd barely slept this past week, from all the thinking.

From all the trying *not* to think.

Every attempt of mine to dive into Lightfoot work ended with me listlessly staring into the distance, heart bleeding and unsure how to stanch the flow. I'd gotten exactly what I wanted, and yet it didn't feel like it.

When I reached the end of the hall, a palace servant stepped into my path with a note. "A message for you miss, if you'd like to collect."

Luckily, I had a few shillings jangling inside my dress

pocket, so I paid the servant and unfolded the paper. I read Emme's words twice. Then read them again. If she'd hidden a message inside them, I was too tired to decipher it, but the brevity—something Emmeline wasn't exactly known for—hinted that something was wrong.

Why else would she have gone to her father?

I stuffed down the tangle of nerves and ventured outside to the palace gardens. Nicholas had asked to meet with me before I took my leave, so whatever Emme needed would have to wait a few more minutes.

The air smelled like rain, even though I saw no proof of it, and the overcast sky was a non-threatening shade of pearl. A warm breeze brushed my cheeks as I trekked to the pond, where Nicholas's arms stroked across the water's surface with impressive speed.

I stopped near Nicholas's coat and boots which sat discarded on the banks and waited. After completing another lap, he noticed me and swam over, ultimately breaking out of the water with an open, out-of-breath smile. "You're early," he said, ruffling his dark wet hair so it flung drips everywhere.

I dragged my eyes up, trying not to notice the way the wet fabric clung to his form. "Perhaps I should come back later?"

"No." His smile softened as he sloshed out of the pond and stared down at me. "No, now I get a few extra minutes with you." He gestured to the willow tree a few paces away, and we walked toward the fronds. "How is your research coming along?"

I hesitated, then answered, "Slowly. I've been studying a bracelet, but I don't understand the temporary bond it creates, much less how to funnel it into something so that it will stay. I'm unsure why you recruited me for the task when I can't seem to make sense of the science."

"Nonsense, you're brilliant." He halted and turned to me,

gaze wandering my face. "You've always been brilliant." Then his eyes scraped down to my lips and stayed there, long enough for him to swallow, long enough for me to realize I still felt raw, and...unkissable.

Ashley's kisses still burned.

I cleared my throat. "I'm taking my leave before the gala this evening. What is it you wished to speak with me about?"

Nicholas opened his mouth like he wasn't ready for the conversation to move on, but he paused, shook off his thought, then rubbed the back of his neck. "It's about our conversation the other day. I made inquiries, as you requested. It was difficult information to obtain as I'm not allowed anywhere near Inquisitions—a conflict of interest, you see—and the department heads like to keep things close to the vest."

His voice deepened and slowed. "There is no easy way to tell you this." He turned his earnest gray eyes on me, pity swirling in their depths. "...Ashley Gardner is dead."

My heart yanked, teetered, then fell and cracked in my stomach.

"It was an accident, during questioning. He wouldn't divulge where the last bracelet was, and...they pushed too hard."

Dead.

It was an ugly word that meant nothing and everything, and the mallet in my head struck harder. My throat clogged, the backs of my eyes burning from holding back tears. One stole down my cheek before I could stop it, and I quickly batted it away, but Nicholas saw. I felt the weight of his gaze for an unbearably long moment.

Finally, he said softly, "It's all right to cry, Dorothy."

"No, it *isn't*." I swiped at another traitorous tear. Grief pricked my chest, digging and spreading its heavy poison. It broke through my ribcage. I clutched my stomach, bending slightly, unable to breathe. Why was this so difficult? I'd wanted revenge, and now I had it.

But now that I had it, I wasn't sure I could bear it.

If my feelings were truly an invention of his magic, like Nicholas had once suggested, why would I be this broken? When his magic no longer *existed*?

"Maybe he deserved to die," I breathed, barely managing the words, "but to meet death in such a terrible way..." I shook my head. I couldn't do this. From our first meeting, we'd been at opposing ends, but Ashley...he'd also helped me. Saved my life. Loved me, in a way I'd never been loved before.

And I'd foolishly, recklessly, fiercely loved him back.

Nicholas retrieved his coat from the banks and settled it on my shoulders, and as he squeezed it around me, I relaxed, marginally, drawing comfort from his familiar scent. It was nothing definable, it just smelled *safe*. Safe from every heartache.

"You feel the weight of that life—even one so despicable— because you have a conscience. But do not carry this burden; give it to me. Hm?" He cupped my cheek, his damp hand mingling with my tears. "Give it to me," he whispered again.

When my gaze finally lifted to his, his head bent, and he kissed my cheek, slowly, following the watery trail to my jaw. A spark lit in my core. It would be difficult to move on, but with tenderness like this, with the careful way Nicholas handled me, I hoped I could.

I exhaled and managed a nod.

He lingered, and I sensed his desire to go on, but he was reining himself in, afraid of pushing me too far. Gradually, he pulled back. "Let me take you to breakfast. You can eat a feast, and afterwards we'll find you a book to take your mind off things. Something scientific and frightfully dull."

Through the war of emotion, I chuckled—about to tell

him of Emme's desire to meet me—when my eyes raised and fell on his collarbone. On the way his shirt there clung to his skin. On the scarred lines underneath, visible through the wet fabric.

An *A*.

The pounding in my head thundered louder, and I blinked, struggling to grasp a thought that kept slipping.

"Let me don my boots," Nicholas said, squeezing my hand then breaking away, "and then we can go."

In a daze, I watched him approach the shore where his boots waited. I caught the thought and it unfolded like a book falling open. The clues Ashley had given me for the Samaritan.

He is an orphan.

Nicholas told me himself he was raised in an orphanage, but I hadn't realized it initially because he'd mentioned his father at Joule's party.

He'll be at Joule's party.

Maybe Ashley's clues hadn't been lies or misdirection. He'd always claimed he was telling the truth, and maybe he was right. Because—

The pen of Zeus marks his flesh.

A rush of hope whipped through me at the thought that even if by accident, I'd finally *found him*. I'd found the Samaritan. But that relief was soon consumed by more burning questions.

He had the same scar that Ashley did, in the exact same place. It was the marker Nicholas had hinted at, for those in the inner circle of the Lightfoots. Ashley's dead voice rang in my ears.

They call themselves the Order of the Worthy. They do not bestow their mark lightly. I was a child. It was...given to me.

Overhead, the clouds darkened, the breeze chilling and whispering a secret in my ear that I couldn't make out.

What had the Samaritan to do with the Lightfoots—or this Order?

Disturbed by the questions, I wrapped Nicholas's coat tighter around me, fingers catching on its large buttons. They were beautiful steel lions that...

I stopped cold, my blood turning to ice.

I recognized these buttons.

Breath frozen in my lungs, I felt down the front of the jacket until I found it: an empty space where a button should be but wasn't, because it had been dropped in my father's room the night he'd been abducted. My eyes were wide, but my vision blurred, my head shaking as though it could erase the horrible truth.

"Ready to go?"

I jumped and my head shot up to find Nicholas, boots clad, approaching. His face fell when he noticed my expression, and yet I could do nothing to change it. All I could do was breathe in needle-like air that sliced up the back of my mouth. My grip loosened and his coat fell around my ankles.

His eyes grew concerned, and he approached. "Is everything all right, Dorothy?"

Liar.

Deceiver.

All this time.

All this time it was you—

"Yes," I whispered, gaze focusing in and out. I fell back a step.

He took a careful step forward. "Then you are ready to go?"

"I just—" I fell back another step. "I need—some air—"

His brows stitched together. He took another step forward. "We are outside."

"I know, I—" I needed to act normal. I needed to get away. I gulped. I needed to not look at my father's kidnapper. "I—I don't feel well. I haven't for a few days."

The black rook feathers in his office. They weren't ones he'd collected from crime scenes; they were a stash for him to *use*.

Nicholas's palm pressed against my forehead—perhaps to gauge my temperature—but I gasped and flinched away. He frowned.

I couldn't force my eyes up. "Please, I...I need to go lie down." I turned away.

He put a hand to my back. "Let me accompany you back to your flat—"

"No!" I scooted away and spun back, fumbling for something to cover the sharp word. "I've already interrupted your morning, and I need to be alone anyway." Not looking to see if he followed, I walked briskly toward the palace, mind spinning, world tilting.

The Samaritan was the one kidnapping people. Nicholas— the Lightfoots—must be performing some kind of experiment on the slanted until they went insane. And then he was returning them, acting the hero and laying the blame at someone else's door. Someone—

Ashley.

A sick, dark pit opened beneath my feet.

Ashley.

"No, no, no, no, no, no, no, no," I mumbled, stumbling blindly forward. My boots hit the gravel drive, and both a moment and a year later I reached the gold swirls of the iron gate. A guard eyed the tears pouring down my face but didn't break position.

Bile inched up my throat as I burst onto the streets and wandered aimlessly down them. I didn't know where I was going, just away. Away from the awful truth. I careened endlessly forward until my feet felt like they were bleeding.

Strange details clawed for my attention. The calloused hands of strangers, muck slinking up shop walls, hems drenched in manure, puddles of alcohol and urine, my foot smacking into a protruding stone and driving me to my knees. My hands slapped the cobblestones. And suddenly I couldn't ignore it any longer, and I splintered into a thousand hemorrhaging pieces.

Ashley had not kidnapped my father.

And I had sent him to his death.

THE SUN HAD SUNK low in a burnished sky by the time I found my way to my old porch steps. My feet ached but so did every part of me, and I plodded inside, not ready to face my relatives, not ready to face anyone, but not wanting to be alone anymore.

The house looked exactly as I had left it, only darker and emptier, and I wondered if Emmeline had departed after I'd failed to respond to her message. That thought was put to rest when she poked her head into the foyer a moment later. "There you are." She sounded relieved.

I stopped, unable to move another inch. "Emme," I said, and my voice wobbled.

Her mouth dropped open, eyes rounding as she quickly assessed me head to toe. That was when I caught a glimpse of my appearance in the mirror near the door: my red, dirt-stricken face, my snarled curls, my ripped and sodden dress.

She rushed to me, hands fluttering around my person like she was searching for broken bones. "Are you well? Are you whole? George's crypt, Dorothy, did someone die?"

"Yes," I whispered. I sucked in a breath through lips he'd kissed. Flares of pain radiated from my flayed heart, but I shoved them down just so I could breathe. "I killed him."

Emme's face froze, then she nodded slowly like she knew everything. "Do you want to talk about it?" she asked quietly.

I shook my head, because I couldn't yet. Not without crumbling completely. Instead, I said, "Your father. Where—"

"He's gone. You need not worry about him." She hooked her arm around mine. "I have something to show you." She led me down the hall and into my father's lab.

Bees hummed in the air, a waft of lavender shoring me up. Familiar items filled the room: leather books, half-filled beakers, tubes and pans and potted plants and labeled jars. My eyes wandered to the other side of the worktable, where Father had always stood, muttering to himself as he hunched over his scribblings, and—

And there he was. Scratching something in his notebook as if he'd never left. His gray hair was combed, spectacles perched on his nose, but the new beard he sported was what made me realize I wasn't in a dream.

Father looked up, dropping his pencil when he caught sight of me. With rapid blinks, he came around the worktable, mouth and hands trembling. His warm brown eyes filled with worry, and he held out his hands. "Dory," he said, and it was the most loving word I'd heard a soul utter.

I choked on a sob and fell into my father's arms.

56

Ashley

When I finally regained consciousness, I did not remember to keep my eyes shut.

This time, I had no voice to scream with.

"I CAN'T DO *it if it's not real.*"

"*It's always been real.*" *The ring around her finger glowed blue between us.*

With her intoxicating scent in my nose, I glanced up into a mirror, tall and oval and gold plaited. My reflection was not my own. Nicholas Hart stared back at me, a slow, cunning smile curving his lips as he pulled her tightly to him.

No.

"*It's always been real,*" *she whispered again.*

Still looking at me, he angled his jaw and claimed her mouth with his, kissing her slowly.

I blinked and I was chained to a wall—no longer in his body but a few paces away, watching him tangle his hands in her hair and mumble her name.

NO!

I threw myself against the chains until my wrists were bloody. I hated that I did, hated that this torrent of fury and hurt could coexist within me when I no longer wanted anything to do with her. The kiss went on and on, and pain stuck like a hot blade in my chest, slowly crumbling my heart to ash.

THE THIRD TIME, I jerked awake in a cold sweat but kept my eyes shut.

It was the height of summer, but in whatever pit they were keeping me, the room was freezing, making me spasm with shivers. Someone entered and wordlessly tugged at my vomit-crusted clothes, and I instinctively illusioned smooth skin over the brand on my collarbone. The stranger left me my trousers, a bucket handle clanked, and a rag swished across the floor as they cleaned up the mess, then left.

How much time had passed? How many days? While my mind and chest throbbed, the rest of my body didn't feel as sore as it had when I'd been tossed in here. My tongue was gritty, and a raging hunger spread through my belly.

I rolled over on the hard mirror beneath me, the bare skin of my back shuddering when it met the cold surface. Somewhere overhead hung a light, too bright to be natural, making me see scarlet behind my eyelids. Magic.

Upon thinking the word, the black stain in my chest seemed to wake from its slumber. It had grown. So large that I could no longer distinguish which parts of me were me, and which parts were *it*. My bones seemed to shrink from it in fear, and I knew.

One more.

One more episode like the last one, and it would break free.

My ears twitched at the sound of light footsteps. Was the mysterious janitor returning? Hinges creaked and a draft of air washed over my face. The door shut, and a second later, the rim of a cup met my lips. Poison seemed like a welcome relief at this point, so I didn't recoil.

"Drink," a soft, feminine voice said.

I scrambled away until I hit the mirror wall. I opened my mouth, but it was so dry and hoarse, I couldn't form the words I wanted to say. *You need to get away from me. Tell them to send someone else.*

Again, the cup pressed against my lips. "Drink."

They knew about this too. They'd sent a woman and the magic was going to break loose—

"You have nothing to fear. I am a friend. You will die if you do not drink."

My throat bobbed, and I managed one scratchy word. "Good."

"No."

I flinched at the fierceness in her voice.

"You *will* drink. And you *will* live."

It was that intensity that made me go still for several moments, and ultimately not resist when she once again offered me the goblet. The water glided down, bringing instant relief to my vocal cords and throat. It must've been a deep cup, because she'd brought enough for me to completely quench my thirst.

I wiped my mouth with the back of my hand, asking hesitantly, "Who are you?"

Somewhere in another room, a distant scream sounded. "I must go," she said. "I will return when I can." The door squeaked open, then shut.

I MUST'VE LAIN there for hours, avoiding all thought in between fitful scraps of sleep. It was a noble effort, but I could only put it off for so long before my mind inevitably drifted to the one place I wish it wouldn't.

Dorothy had sent me here.

She'd betrayed me. Thrown me to the wolves. And while part of me burned with anger for it, a secret part of me understood.

She thought, along with Miles, that I'd kidnapped her father. Even though I'd done the opposite, going so far as to track him down through the Black Carriage company and send her a telegram with instructions that his route would pass through Lincoln's Inn.

And if that was why she'd aligned herself with Nicholas, that meant she was oblivious to his crimes and could be in danger. Initially I hadn't told her about him so she wouldn't be caught in the middle of this magic power struggle. If I'd known she'd continue a friendship with Nicholas—anything substantial, anything *real*—I would've told her his true identity in a heartbeat. It could've easily been her sitting in this dungeon instead of me.

Even if she hadn't knifed me in the back, I deserved this anyway. And in the end, I was grateful she'd given me the fuel to hate her.

How deep did her loyalty to him go? How entrenched in the Order was she?

The door scraped open again and my eyelids twitched, wishing I could tell who it was without opening them. My answer came a breath later when the feminine voice from before whispered, "We must be quiet."

Carefully, I analyzed the magic coiled in my chest, waiting

in dread for it to stir. It didn't. For some reason, it sat cold and dormant. Maybe the *pull* wasn't working because I couldn't see the woman, but I didn't dare voice that—I hardly dared think it —for fear it would wake the magic.

"Who are you?" I repeated the question from her last visit.

She was silent for a long time, then at last her answer was, "You don't know me. But you should."

I sat up, clucking my tongue. "That's an odd name. And rather long, for my tastes—"

"Marian. My name is Marian." She gave a humorless chuckle and under her breath added, "And you are still the same."

I frowned, wishing now more than ever that I could see her. Nothing about her voice jiggered any memories, and I didn't dare use my magic to slip into her mind.

"And why are you here, Marian?"

"Because I don't want you to die."

I clucked my tongue again. "A lovely sentiment, but that's not what I meant. What are you doing *here*? This is the Order of the Worthy, rebranded as the Lightfoot Agency, is it not? Pretending to do the Crown's bidding while plotting the tyrannical restructure of magic." I scoffed softly, the brand at my collarbone suddenly itching.

She said nothing.

"Do you ascribe to that belief?" I pressed. "That some are worthy of magic, and others are not?"

"If I do believe it," she said carefully, "it is not with these men in charge."

I cocked my head. "If you don't back Mr. Brass and Mr. Hart, then again I ask—why are you here?"

"Because I have no choice. I attempted to leave once before, but...I was caught. And punished."

A sour taste settled in my mouth. I pushed it down, not

really in the mood to feel pity. Scooting until my back hit the wall and settling my forearms on my knees, I said, "So you are valuable to them. And what is it you do? Build the fires for the branding pokers? Polish Mr. Hart's mask?"

I thought maybe I'd been too insensitive, but then she made a sound in her throat that nearly qualified as a chuckle. A second later, a new thought sparked, one that made everything click into place.

"You're the one erasing the memories," I murmured, testing the theory on my tongue.

She went still, and the quiet stretched too long for it to be false. Her quiet inhales filled the space, and she cleared her throat. "Mr. Brass doesn't want them remembering their time here, so I use my slant to do what he asks." Her voice thickened. "I don't mean for them to go insane—all those people. But in order to take a person's memory and have them not sense its bereavement, I must replace it with something else. Hide the emptiness *within* something that already exists in their mind."

"You mean you're transferring them? Into what?"

"Any tangible object, so long as it's in enough of their memories. But the problem is, if they see that thing in real life, it breaks the dam, which breaks the mind. And then they scream."

A chill raced down my spine. The kidnappings, the madness—it went so much deeper. And I'd been taking the blame for all of it, even though I had a fracturing mind of my own.

"Over the years," she continued, "I've experimented so many ways, searching for things that are both commonplace to the person yet will never be encountered by them. Thimbles, shells, hair combs, canisters of blacking, cufflinks, coins."

"So, it's not just seeing the feather you transferred the memories into. It's seeing any feather at all."

"Exactly. It's a tricky balance, and one I don't know that I've ever managed to strike. They all go insane anyway." Her voice softened. "Well...except the one."

I took a stab in the dark. "Geoffrey St. James?" I held my breath as I waited for her answer, and I didn't know why. I shouldn't care anymore.

When she answered, it was stilted like she'd been jarred onto a new train of thought. "No. I never slanted on Sir Geoffrey. They moved him some weeks ago—to where, I know not."

That was right when Dorothy's uncle had locked her up.

Distantly, I wondered who Marian was talking about if it *wasn't* Geoffrey St. James, but in the end it didn't much matter.

A sniffle echoed off the walls. "I never asked for this," Marian went on, her voice trembling enough that I imagined a tear trailing down her face.

An apology rose to my lips, even though it wasn't my fault, even though there was nothing I could do—but maybe because I, too, understood what it was like to be dealt your fate. There weren't fingers quick enough to steal different cards.

I'd tried.

"I've stayed too long." She rose, the swish of her skirts brushing air against my face as she moved toward the door. But it never opened. "Nicholas has promised that you will remain here until you confess, or until..." She didn't need to finish.

I pulled in a long breath through my nose. "And you think I ought to confess."

"I think..." She paused, then shifted her weight. "I think you should do whatever it takes to stay alive."

My fingers cracked from fisting so tightly. "What is the *point?*" I tried to stop the rage swelling to the surface—Marian was a stranger, and not the real cause of my anger—but I'd been pushing it down so long that it spewed out before I could claw it back.

"I built a purpose from shadows and blood, honing it day after day, year after year, and for what?" I spat the word— "*Failure.* With everything I set out to do. My dreams, if ever I dared have them, have shattered, and their pieces are strewn across the sea. My magic grows wilder, my mind is cleaving in half from trying to stop it, and because of that, I've lost everything I've ever cared about. Only two things are left to me: a chance to die *not* by my magic, and a pillar of spite the size of St. Paul's. So, spare me your opinion on what I should do. I will not confess. I am not *worth* saving."

Some things are too broken to save.

My angry breaths rattled in my lungs.

No noise came from the door for perhaps a whole minute. Then I heard the tiniest inhale. Followed by the tiniest whisper.

"*Everyone* is worth saving."

My jaw pushed out, the backs of my eyes prickling.

"Especially you, Ashley Renault."

My lids nearly shot open before I clamped them shut just in time—but I sat forward in astonishment—

The door squeaked open and shut. Marian was gone.

My mind sprinted, trying to remember who she was, but jamming whenever I came close to an answer. Slowly, I sat back, reeling in the silence, the echoes of her final sentence ringing in my ears.

Because I had not been called that name in a very, very long time.

57

Dorothy

The morning dawned red. Ironically, it matched my eyes, which were dry and scratchy from spilling so many tears last night. When Father wasn't in his lab, I ascended the stairs and stepped into the great hall, a knot unwinding in my chest at the sight of his bearded figure inspecting one of the vases. He was still here. It hadn't been a dream.

When was the last time I'd seen him in this room? I thought back, realizing it was only two months ago, though it felt like a lifetime. He seemed shorter now; a brokenness that cut so bone deep he hunched to keep it from hurting.

I imagined I looked the same.

In just a few short hours, he and Emme would travel to the seaside where they would strategize how to fake his death. It was the only way Brass and Nicholas would cease searching for him—a man who knew too much—once they received word of his escape. They probably already had. It was too dangerous for him to remain in London, and too suspicious for me to accompany him. I'd be forced to act like he'd never been here at all.

But Father believed that once things settled down, I'd join him, and I inhaled a fortifying breath, praying he'd listen to what I had to say.

"I need to talk to you, Papa."

He turned, gaze falling over my side braid and blue vest dress like he was making sure I was real too. Fresh tears welled in his eyes. "Anything, dear," he said, a little blubberingly, and sat on a chaise lounge beneath one of the tall windows. I joined him. The smooth velvet under my palms felt like the tiny lavender petals I used to help him crush using the mortar and pestle, and it soothed me.

"Last night, when you told me about the Lightfoots and your entire history," I began, "and then I told you of everything that had transpired here, I..." I bunched the fabric of my lap. "I didn't confess everything."

My father's face pulled in, and already I could feel the emotion climbing my throat. "I didn't tell you that I joined them, and that during these last few weeks, I helped them capture the Rook." I couldn't bring myself to look at his face, but I felt him go still.

"Dory," he breathed. "But once you join, you can *never* leave—"

"I didn't want to worry you, but also I—" I rolled my lips together. "I've wrestled with it all night. What they're doing—their plans to strip ordinary people of their magic and redistribute it—we both know it ends with one of their own atop the throne. Someone must stop them. And part of me knows that it must be me."

Who else? No one outside of myself, Father, and Emme knew of their plans. Perhaps Miles Kelly did, but Emme had curtly informed me he'd left the country. And *I* was the one Nicholas and Brass already trusted. If I could find a way to twist that to my advantage...

Father shook his head, fear creeping across his wrinkled face. "If they discover your plans, the Lightfoots will kill you, Dorothy. And they might not stop at you—"

"I know. But all of London—England—the *world*—hangs in the balance. If no one has the courage to stand up to them, the Thames will flow red from the carnage. I'm telling you this, not so you may talk me out of my decision, but because I want your blessing, Papa. I need to do this."

Ashley's face swam in my mind's eye.

I must *do this*.

Father frowned and stroked his beard. I still wasn't used to seeing him with so much facial hair, but it strangely suited him. "If this is about revenge—"

"It's not." And it was true. The blame for Ashley's death couldn't be laid at anyone's feet but my own. Tears flowed freely down my face now. "Not anymore. I've been so blind, Papa. Blinder than you could possibly know—all because of my hate. And though I won't walk that path anymore, that doesn't mean I can't seek justice. Some way to atone for..."

My insides crumpled and I rested my head on his shoulder. "I'm done hiding. Done cowering. And if this means the end of me, I won't meet it resigned to the shadows. I will meet it in the light."

For a long while we sat there in silence, my quiet sobs filling the space. He rubbed a comforting hand along my arm, then at last, turned his nose into my hair. "After I lost your mother, all I wanted was to protect you. I see now that I was wrong. When did you become so brave?"

I gave a watery chuckle. "I don't *feel* brave. It's all so terrifying."

"The right path often is."

I breathed, relishing the hints of tobacco and ether that smelled so like him.

"Take your chance, Dory, dear. Risk it all." Father pulled away and squeezed my hand, his usually warm brown eyes deathly solemn. "Do what I could not."

58

Ashley

"Get him up," Hart said, not disguising the anger in his soft voice. "And put a shirt on him."

A moment later, a soft wad of what felt like linen hit my face. I slid into the shirt, fingers stiff as I fumbled with the buttons. Before I'd finished with the last one—and for what felt like the thousandth time—iron-like grips hauled me to my feet. Black still lingered behind my eyelids, but my vision swam, my head weightless.

The world rocked beneath me, knees buckling no matter how many times I ordered them to lock. The firm grip on my arm prevented me from pitching forward, and a moment later, the polished head of a cane was shoved into my hands. It was sturdy hardwood, which meant it wouldn't break easily. I adjusted my rocky balance and finally managed to stand on my own.

Like clockwork, a hand locked around my wrist, the way it always did when they were siphoning away my magic. They weren't taking any chances.

"Hurry it up," Hart snapped. "Brass wants him gone within the half hour."

I tilted my pounding head. "Finally had enough, eh?"

"You," Hart said through his teeth, but again it was soft—it was always soft, and chilling, "will not utter another word."

I could feel his hatred like a knife poised over the base of my throat, ready to plunge through. But he couldn't yet. They had something special planned, otherwise they wouldn't bother going to all this trouble.

I didn't speak, but not out of compliance. What more could he possibly do to me?

No, it was simply because I had nothing more to say.

A thick bag tugged over my head, and for the first time in over a week, I opened my eyes. Little pricks of light peeked through the thick, dark fabric, and the tightness in my chest waned as I inhaled a lungful of humid air. It was beautiful, the light. Something I hadn't been certain I would see again. I exhaled slowly, molding my core into stone, and peace.

This was the end.

I was ready.

I'd greet Bram. My parents. I'd apologize for letting them all down. And maybe there had been a way to win and I'd failed, but I'd die knowing that I'd given it my all. That at least here, at the end, I'd thwarted the Order from ripping away people's slants.

Because they would never find the last bracelet. I'd made certain of that.

Someone snapped their fingers, and a second later, I was being prodded forward, out of my cell, with pressure on my arm guiding me when to turn. Footsteps echoed down the halls, and I counted four sets—five and a half, with me and the cane.

I knew the moment we stepped outside because the noise

scattered, and I caught a whiff of fresh air and manure under the sack. A horse's whicker sounded to my left. I stumbled up some steps and hunkered down inside the carriage. Two other men entered after me, but I couldn't tell if Hart was among them. The carriage rocked forward.

My mind drew a map of the city, routing the roads leading away from the button factory while simultaneously noting every time the carriage turned or angled on a fork. Precisely nineteen minutes and twenty-two seconds later, when we came to a halt, I knew exactly where we were.

I frowned. I supposed it gave a nice sense of *dénouement*.

The carriage door swung open, and with the help of my cane, I disembarked, legs shaking even more.

The bag ripped off my head. In the east, the sun had only begun its ascent above the metropolis of London, but I still squinted against the light, eyes taking several moments to adjust. A spiked iron fence rose before me, ornate and ominous. I caught the back of a man's head as he pushed the gate open, making it groan loud enough to disturb the birds resting in the trees above.

Through the gates was the grave I'd robbed; another bracelet that I'd beaten the Samaritan to. They'd brought me to a cemetery.

Convenient. They wouldn't have to haul my dead carcass more than a few feet.

Hart shoved me forward. The cane caught my fall, but I got the message and kept on walking, following the mystery man in front of me, with Hart and what I assumed were several Lightfoot agents bringing up the rear.

Next to the coarse granite headstones which were slick with morning dew, puffs of dandelions sprouted in the grass. My boots scattered the seeds, but I had no more wishes to make. Stone angels, cracked but beautiful, prayed for me as I passed.

I prayed too.

We trekked several yards into the cemetery before the man ahead halted and turned, letting me get my first good look at his face. A teardrop scar dripped from one eye. It had been fourteen years, but even without his telltale mark, I'd relived my memories enough times to recognize my parents' murderer.

The inner peace I'd cobbled together split open. Fury tore through my chest. I instinctively reached for my magic, but it was gone. Stolen. Often, I'd seen the man who'd taken everything from me around the *ton*, but always from a distance, biding my time and playing my cards right. Hundreds of times I'd dreamed of finally having this face-to-face, but never had I imagined I would be weaponless. Defenseless. Hopeless.

Sullivan Brass smiled—an amiable, gentlemanly smile. "You've proven yourself a formidable opponent, Mr. Gardner. It was a pleasure competing with the Rook."

I said nothing. I looked in his eyes and saw the flames of my childhood home. The nine bullet holes in my mother's body. I kept my face blank, blank.

Behind me, a hammer cocked, then four more. A firing squad.

"Perhaps we will play again soon?" Brass said.

My eyebrow twitched. My eyes darted to the side, wondering what he was getting at, why they weren't shooting me already. Then I glanced over my shoulder to find Hart's steel barrel wasn't pointing at me, it was pointing at...

Brass shifted to the side, and behind him, through the mist...

I fell forward. One step. Two.

A hundred feet across the cemetery, above the unmarked

grave that had held the fifth bracelet, a silhouette stood rigidly in the dawn, brown trench coat flapping. A man I never thought I'd see again, pistol pointed at Brass, and looking for all the world like he wanted to shoot everyone here.

My lips parted on an inhale. "*Miles,*" I rasped.

59

Miles

I made myself look at his ashen skin, and the half-dead glaze to his eyes. He leaned on a cane, stooped like his injuries cut deeper than bone. Guilt and love and pity slammed into me all at once.

Ashley caught sight of me and froze. He said my name. Only a few seconds later, I was relieved to see his gaze dart to my coat, because it meant his mind was still sharp enough to realize what I was about to do. Even if it brought the bleakest look to his face I'd ever seen. He was already shaking his head, and the graveyard was so still I heard him murmuring even with the distance. "No...no."

I absorbed the stances and positions of the surrounding men, including the one aiming his own pistol at me, who I assumed to be Nicholas Hart. Then my hand tightened around the wooden grip and I looked to the man with the short beard and teardrop scar. Mr. Brass—the one I'd arranged the meeting with. "My slant stores items inside pockets, which can only be retrieved by me," I said in a loud voice.

Without wavering my aim, I demonstrated by reaching into

my coat and pulling out a large chest on the grass, then depositing it back inside. "What you seek is also within my coat. Kill me now, and it disappears forever."

Brass's head tilted, intrigued. "There's no need for that, I assure you, Mr. Kelly. I am a man of my word."

In my periphery, the slow shake of Ashley's head turned frantic. "Miles, don't."

"This is how it's going to work," I said above him. "You tell your agents to back up a dozen yards. You send the Rook over, and once he's safely behind me, I will toss the bracelet to you. We both back away slowly, we both leave with what we want."

A breeze crept into the cemetery, carrying a hint of the river.

"I will call all my agents back but one," Brass returned. "And I will send the Rook to you, but when he reaches that headstone"—he pointed to the largest cross in the cemetery, halfway between us—"you will toss the bracelet to us. If you're bluffing or fail to throw it far enough...we shoot him."

I scanned the men, knowing immediately that Hart—the one who'd shoved Ashley—leaned too far forward. I wouldn't get any better deals. I'd just have to throw the bracelet far enough, and pray Brass was good at catching. Because if it hit the ground—

I nodded in agreement.

The other four agents retreated to the street, out of range.

"Don't do this," Ashley pleaded. With his free hand, Hart pushed Ashley forward again. And he came. But it was painfully slow. Not because he couldn't manage, but because this time he knew there was no winning. He was giving me every chance to turn back.

A strange calm settled over me, steeling my nerves, sharpening my focus. I inhaled and exhaled.

Ashley's hobbled gait neared the midway headstone. I

reached into my pocket and withdrew the silver bracelet, where it winked in the sunlight on my palm. The last one. The most precious magical artifact in England—the world—and once Brass had all seven, unlimited power.

Devastation tore across Ashley's face. "*Please*, Miles—"

"I can't help but wonder, Mr. Kelly," Mr. Brass shouted, tone conversational, "why you'd make such a fool's bargain?"

My gaze held Ashley's, memories shifting through me and clogging my throat. Cairo, Paris, beaches, wooden swords, wind, salt, freedom. For good or ill, Ashley's friendship had been the making of me, and it took standing on the deck of my own ship to realize it would *un*make me to throw it away.

"There must be an angle I'm not seeing. What's this all for?"

Ashley knew I'd find this last bracelet in his coat at our old flat. He'd always known. But he thought I'd leave it behind just as I'd left him. Moisture filled my eyes, and Ashley reached the cross.

He was wrong.

My mouth set and my eyes swung to Brass. "For my brother." And I flung the bracelet across the yard.

Brass raised his arm and caught it. Hart's aim shifted to Ashley anyway. I didn't think. I shot. Hart's gun spun out of his grip, blood pouring from his hand. He yelled in pain. I leapt to Ashley's side and dragged him backwards as the Lightfoot agents streamed into the cemetery, pistols cracking.

I fired twice—downing one of them—before ducking us behind a massive headstone. Blast. With all the dust ups recently, I was running low on bullets—something that was hard to replenish this side of the pond, as not many shops carried the long rounds used in American iron.

"Run, or fight?" I panted.

As one, we peeked back over the headstone. Like a void

stretching across one half of the cemetery, shadows on the ground gathered and spread, swallowing the graves, trees, and men in a black ink. The last thing the darkness consumed was Mr. Brass's amiable expression. It must be *his* magic. Shadows.

A bullet hit the headstone, narrowly missing us and shooting up a spray of mineral dust. I raised my Colt—but had no targets, only a blackness where they used to be. The earlier calm completely evaporated and full-fledged panic knocked into me.

Ashley turned, the same panic shining in his eyes. "Run."

60

Ashley

We scrambled out of the cemetery, both Miles and my cane supporting me. Bullets rained around us, shattering shop windows and puncturing carts piled with vegetables. Debris burst from every side.

"You could really lose some weight," Miles huffed.

"I *have* lost weight. You've just become frailer."

He scoffed. "I've been boxing."

"I know."

"I *know* you know."

I dared a glanced over my shoulder. Lightfoot agents spurted from the black void in pursuit. At least we no longer had to worry about Brass's shadows. He wouldn't follow us; he'd never liked doing the dirty work himself, plus he'd already gotten what he wanted. My teeth clenched.

More guns fired. Something bit into my side, making me fall forward. A vicious sting radiated from the area, and I knew I'd been grazed.

Miles pulled me faster. "There's a black carriage waiting around this block."

"Waiting to take us where?"

"The old warehouse." Our first headquarters when we came to London after Bram died.

If we made it inside, it was the last place Brass or his men would think to look. It *might* be enough to outrun the—

A louder gunshot exploded. Miles cried out and collapsed. We tumbled to the granite setts. I recovered first, rising to my hands and knees. Miles writhed, face creased in pain; he reached for his calf where blood quickly soaked his trousers. My eyes widened, sweat breaking out over my body.

I frenziedly glanced between Miles, the block we needed to clear, and the approaching Lightfoots, knowing I'd never be able to carry him that far. Not as quickly as we needed it. My attention snagged on the manhole next to Miles's bleeding leg. I hefted it up, cursing when my arms trembled. "Plan B."

Adrenaline pumped in my veins, gifting me some of my lost strength but not agility. I dropped down the short ladder, limbs quick but knocking into every piece of metal. I grasped Miles's good leg and pulled. He roared, and I mutely apologized. A few bullets ricocheted off the cobblestones, but the Lightfoots must've been low on ammunition because the fire came more sporadically. A flurry of legs approached in my peripheral.

I pawed his clothes for a better grip and heaved again, maneuvering him into the hole with me. Though I couldn't support his weight—not now—I still tried to soften the single-foot drop to the floor. He roared again anyway.

Lightfoot boots thudded louder, five yards away. Four.

I grabbed the cane and the handle of the manhole and dove down, covering the hole as I did. Then I shoved the cane through the handle, wedging it into metal shafts so it wouldn't dislodge.

Just in time.

Boots slapped the cobblestones and the cover rattled. The

cane held fast. It would buy us two minutes—three, if we were lucky.

Grabbing a long, discarded pipe on the ground, I propped it in Miles's hands to replace the lost cane. "Come on." I struggled to haul him up, but finally hooked an arm around his torso.

Stumbling blindly forward, we twisted down the narrower tunnels to weave a tangled trail—but the truth was, I wasn't strategizing much, all my concentration on putting the next foot forward. We splashed through the black artery flowing down the concave floor, rife with muck, rusty nails, and even bones.

The sour, fecal fog coated my airway, its fumes so thick I struggled to keep my eyes open. Wires strung along the wall, linking carbide lanterns that illuminated cracked arches and chunks of missing bricks. The constant moisture had weakened the structural integrity in large sections. Miles didn't groan in pain anymore, but his breaths came labored and deep, his body still in shock.

"Lovely place," I panted, face puckered. I hefted Miles along, muscles quivering and collapsing, throbbing in protest. My lungs filled too slowly, half-gagging when they did. "Been meaning to visit for the longest time. Really glad we finally made this happen—"

"Shut *up*," Miles breathed. His face was too white.

My breaths puffed, spasms wracking my arms, the signal between my brain and legs flickering and disconnecting. I couldn't carry him much longer. We turned another corner, where the tunnel widened into a cathedral of filth, with walkways on the side and a rushing river more brown than black. I lowered him down near a sluice gate.

Miles's skin was chilled, despite the boiling, humid air. After inspecting his wound, I tore a strip of fabric from my shirt's hem and wound it around his leg. "Lucky dog. It missed the bone."

"Call me lucky when we make it out of this place."

"*If* we make it out." I tied the fabric in a knot. "The Lightfoots have those magic trackers now, and you used your slant in the exchange. Once they get down here, we can't keep running for another five and half hours for our trail to disappear."

"They won't find us," Miles oddly insisted. "Our real problem is finding an exit in this labyrinth."

Which reminded me. "Give me your gun." I stood, a wave of exhaustion making me slump against the wall.

Miles did, then rested his head against the brick, eyes falling closed. I inspected the chamber. One bullet. I exhaled long and steady. My fate had already been sealed, but Miles had thrown his life away for no reason.

"You came back for me," I said quietly.

Miles was silent for a long moment. "I did." It was all that needed to be said, so I was surprised when he wryly added, "It's probably the only thing I've ever done that you didn't plan for."

I sucked in through my teeth, not wanting to break the devastating news to him. "...Actually..."

His eyes snapped open, and he had the miraculous wherewithal to glare at me. "No."

I waved his pistol. "Inside this grip, I left a miniature map of the sewers that might be really useful right about now." I shuffled through the tiny scrolls I'd stashed inside his most prized possession months ago. New train lines, the southwest quadrant—*ah, here it is.*

"You have got to be kidding me." An unbelieving, exasperated scoff burst from between his lips. "How in the ever-loving —? When? Are there other maps you've hidden?"

Ignoring him, I pointed at the paper. "I'm fairly sure we're here. Navigate us out"—I tossed the paper to him—"while I support you again."

"Why didn't you just memorize these sewers as you do everything else?"

"I had every intention to, but in case you haven't noticed, I've been a little *preoccupied* these last few weeks." A clatter rose above the rushing river, pulling me around to scan the offshoots, but the light's amber glow barely touched the corners, betraying nothing. Perhaps it was a rat. Yet my senses remained heightened.

Miles muttered a string of curses, each one louder—I guessed more from the pain than anything, but I couldn't be sure. "You couldn't *possibly* have known this would happen."

"I didn't." I caught movement across the river and raised the pistol. "But I believe the sentence you're looking for is *Thank you for always planning some fail-safes, Ashley.*"

"Yes, *thank you* for being the shifty little"—I fired, blotting out his next word—"you always are."

A Lightfoot agent fell, limp body smacking the concrete. No more bullets. I turned to Miles and tossed the useless pistol back to him. "Time to go then."

"Ash." Miles's grim expression riveted on something beyond my shoulder.

I turned. The outline of Nicholas Hart glowed twenty feet away, one hand gripping the splintered shaft of my cane, the other dripping blood.

A glower darkened Hart's face. He strolled a few steps closer. "I'm glad I missed, up there. *This* is going to be much more satisfy—"

I barreled into him, knowing quick aggression was all I had, plunging us sideways into the river. We hit the bottom and tumbled, limbs striking. Where the bullet grazed me, Hart thrust the cane deep into my side and snapped it off. I arched and cried out, muscles going slack.

He flipped over and pinned me, an arm across my collarbone and his good hand squeezing my throat. Water rushed over my face. My hands gripped his wrists, but they didn't budge. The adrenaline was fading; my stores, draining.

Then I remembered a maneuver Bram had taught me. Lifting my hips, I monkey-pawed his forearms away and tossed him off me, breaking the surface. I gasped in a rancid breath. Swiftly, I sloshed through the grime, hunting for a weapon—any weapon. Because although Hart was injured, I was weak and losing speed.

We both knew who was winning this fight if it dragged on.

"Ashley!"

Miles.

I turned as he threw a knife to me. I caught it and spun—

A rock glanced off my head, disorienting me enough that I dropped the blade. Blood splashed into my eyes. I bent for the knife, hands groping the slimy bottom—and finding the rock.

Hart charged. He was coming too fast. My eyes darted between him and one of the carbide lanterns. I raised my arm and threw the rock at the wall instead—

Glass shattered and the air combusted in a blazing cloud, knocking us in opposite directions. My head smacked the concrete, making me groan. I tried to rise—and slipped. I crawled out of the river, staggered to my feet, and suddenly Miles was there, gray-faced and limping and dragging us forward. I didn't know who was supporting whom anymore.

I didn't look back to assess the carnage, but the explosion had hit Hart harder than it'd hit me. Maybe he'd lost his magic tracker, and if we could turn a few corners...

The pressure in my side built, stinging needles around the protruding wood shards as we hobbled down one tunnel, then another, Miles navigating us through. Everywhere hurt. *I can't do it,* I wanted to say. *I can't take another step.*

But we did.

And we kept on.

After what felt like hours, we came to a set of vertical bars built into an arch that blocked the way forward—a drain gate, and a dead end. Miles hurried to the right and a moment later I saw why: Next to a stack of bricks, a few bars had been bent back, creating a hole just large enough for a man to jam between.

Miles wobbled through first. Once he'd moved on, I followed suit, puffing when my torso twisted and pulled open the flesh of my wound. I ducked farther, sweat intermingling with the blood rolling down my temples. Finally wriggling free of the jagged poles, I rose and—

An arm wrapped around my neck and yanked me against the bars, knocking the wind from my lungs. "You've slipped away," Nicholas hissed in my ear, "for the *last* time."

My hands scrabbled uselessly against his strength. *Miles—* He squeezed harder. This time, no one was coming. Stars stabbed my vision, tilting and whirling and crashing to earth. There was no more air. Down here, in the dark of London's belly, covered in filth and blood and defeat, my luck had finally run out.

Nicholas leaned closer. "And the best part about killing you is...this is just me tying up a loose end." His voice softened to a whisper. "I've already told Dorothy that you're dead."

At the name, an ember, low and deep, flickered and rose, building to a climax and giving every cell *life.* Giving every muscle *rage.* My hand shot to the side, connecting with a loose brick. I rammed it against his head, slackening his chokehold.

I inhaled and pivoted, bringing Hart's arm with me and wrenching it against the bars at an unnatural angle. He cried out. The sound of my teeth grinding reverberated through my head as I seethed at him.

Red burned behind my eyes. "*Don't.*" I slammed the brick into his bloody hand. He howled. "*Speak.*" An inferno raged through every sinew. I brought the brick down again, feeling bones crunch. And again. "*Her.*" Over and over. I saw Hart scream, but didn't hear it. All I knew was fire and loathing and red, red, red. "*Name.*"

The bar gave way. The world trembled and someone jerked me backward. Bricks and bars crashed down where I'd been a moment before, swallowing the arch and Nicholas Hart in a wave of rubble and dust.

61

Nicholas

Pain found me first.

My right hand's fingers were stiff, swollen to the skin's limits and throbbing with slicing agony. I coughed at the dust that had settled in my nostrils. I didn't know how long I'd been unconscious. My mouth set as I attempted to drag myself out of the rubble, every twitch sending a wave of pain that made my eyes roll back. A million spikes skewered the tendons in my wrist, like the bones were pulverized.

With one arm, I crawled, freeing enough debris that I could look down and inspect the damage. My vision tunneled on what I saw.

No hand.

My breaths shortened as I frantically glanced around for the appendage. But it was likely buried deep, and I had neither the time, nor the strength to dig it out. Sweat licked up my back.

Shock blunted the pain enough for me to nestle the open wound against my chest and stagger to my feet. I stumbled back through the tunnels, a trail of blood spatters marking my course. If I could find a Lightfoot agent, I needed to use their SID gun and find a way around the carnage before we lost the Rook's trail. When ten minutes passed, then twenty—with still no sign of another agent—my agitation festered.

I'd stormed down here with half a dozen men. Where were they all?

I turned a corner and found an agent curled into a ball in the middle of a stream of sewage. I tested his pulse and, detecting he was still alive, shook his shoulder. As he slowly roused, I asked, "Where's your SID gun?"

"She," the man mumbled, blinking in confusion, "she took it."

"Who?"

The agent lifted his eyes, which widened when they locked on me. Then he shrieked, clawing at his ears as he threw himself back. I flinched away. His skull cracked against the brick, howling as his fingernails streaked red welts across his neck and cheeks. Madness. It was a sequence I'd witnessed hundreds of times before, and if this agent had it, the others would be in a similar state. That was why they hadn't followed.

The faces of not one, but two people with black hair, swam before my eyes.

I cursed. To the sound of the man's shrill wails, I slowly rose. And cursed again. Louder and louder until I was spinning in a circle and screaming his name down every putrid, shadowy corridor.

Because it wasn't just the agent's SID gun that was missing. It was his memories.

62

Ashley

I remembered slogging. I remembered collapsing somewhere. I remembered hands digging the splintered wood from my side and dressing my wounds. I remembered Miles's voice. I remembered fitful dreams that made me shake and drenched me in sweat.

When I opened my eyes, a scratchy gray linen shirt that smelled of soap pulled against my chest. Miles's brown eyes beheld me from above. Burlap rustled beneath me as I attempted to rise.

"Take it slow," Miles instructed.

I coughed, my tongue like sandpaper. "Yes, Mother."

"Don't get smart."

Though my head wheeled and my muscles buckled from the strain, I forced myself to sit up, begrudgingly accepting Miles's help. I discovered the burlap sacks were strewn over a few pallets to form a makeshift bed. Metal beams crossed the ceiling, one mounted with a winch that dangled halfway to the floor where a smattering of coffee beans had spilled. Our first headquarters was an abandoned warehouse for storing foodstuffs, and the air still carried hints of grain and tea leaves.

From a chair next to the pallets, Miles handed me a cup, his hurt leg propped to the side. The bandage I'd made in the sewers had been swapped for something cleaner, but the dressing was bloody again and needed changing.

After gulping the water down, I said, "I don't need to take it slow—I'm not the one who was *shot*."

Miles frowned. "You took a beating, Ash. And I'm not just talking about yesterday."

I stared blankly at him, wondering how he could know about the torture, when I realized what he was referring to. His boxing enemies that I'd let whip me within an inch of my life in an alleyway. "Ah. That."

"You're an idiot."

I sighed. "When are you going to learn how to say thank you, Miles? It's two little words."

"Maybe when *you* learn to stop punishing yourself. I want the truth. Now. The feathers, the kidnappings, all of it. I need to hear it from your lips."

I tipped my head back. "What do you want me to say? That I'm innocent? Because I'm not. But every time I left a feather, you were there, helping me lift a bracelet, all but the one in the statue. As for the kidnappings, if I'd known it was the Order behind them, maybe I wouldn't have taken the fall so easily, but I did."

"Why?"

"Because it was better that everyone, society, *you*, hate me." I took a massive breath that somehow didn't feel deep enough. "It made the next part easier." Which was a blatant lie.

None of it had been easy.

"Stop—" He held up a frustrated hand, fingers extended. "Stop planning out six moves ahead all the time. Something goes wrong and without fail, you jump on the sacrificial table before anyone has a chance to say anything or fix it. You're not a martyr. You're not a demon. You're not invincible. Why can't you see that you're just a *man*, Ashley?" Anger pulled his expression down, a mask for something that cut far deeper.

I don't need you to shoulder every burden and act like it's all been your fault and then use it as a pitiful excuse to push me away. That was what Dorothy had said. My shoulders slumped.

"A *good* man."

My breath froze, unexpected emotion punching me in the throat.

Miles looked down, and he said quietly, "That night on the sea when Bram was drawing his last breaths...he made me promise that I would never abandon you." His solemn gaze cut up, and we stared at each other for the longest moment, rock and mortar stacking inside crumbled walls. Re-shoring a fortress. "I will never break that promise again."

I blinked quickly, mouth working. Relief melted the tight ball wound at my core. "I'm sorry for it all too. You're all the family I have."

"Well..." He glanced to the side, but when I followed his gaze, found nothing among the crates and rope. He retrieved a scrap of fabric from his pocket and tossed it at me. "Cover your eyes."

I half-chuckled. "What?"

"Only for a minute. Cover your eyes, and if you peek, believe me when I say you will wish you were dead."

He was using that tone—the one he only used when we were in serious trouble. Goosebumps rose on the back of my neck. Someone was here. "Miles—"

"Trust me."

Slowly, I wrapped the fabric over my eyes and tied it at the back of my head. Shuffling sounded to my right, light footsteps that neared the bed. After a moment, a waft of rosewater met my nose, right before a hand placed on my head. Cold sparks of magic rushed through those fingertips and into my brain, swirling through every crevice and making me shudder. It was the better part of a minute before the magic ebbed and the hand lifted.

"You can look now," Miles said.

When I reverently pulled the fabric down, it wasn't Miles's face that swam before me, but one with a pert nose and deep blue eyes. And I remembered it all. More than I knew before.

We used to picnic along the chalky cliffs, all four of us. Afterwards, Marian and I would race through the grass back to the chateau, and I could see the pink globes of sea thrift clutched in her hands—flowers she'd picked for *Mamie*. She always beat me there; back then, her legs were longer than mine. But I'd get my revenge at bedtime by telling spooky stories in the nursery of specters and goblins, then giggling at her screams when I conjured a well-timed illusion.

Most of my childhood. So many of my memories of my parents. Dark men arriving at the chateau and dragging our father away—only this time, Marian's screams were no longer funny. All the experiments, the bloodletting, the pain, the black waves clinging to her tear-stained cheeks as she dove into my memories and stole every one that she'd been a part of. It was as if I'd been living my whole life with a limb missing—not knowing anything different—only for it to materialize, and a world of glittering possibilities opened up.

And then I understood why my magic was mutating.

How I'd gotten two slants in the first place.

"Please don't start screaming," she whispered like a prayer. It was her voice. The woman from my cell.

I studied her face as if through a fog; something so foreign, and yet familiar. My sister. "You're not that ugly," I said, because I didn't know what else to say. But she laughed, eyes glimmering, and she threw her arms around me. Gingerly, I embraced her back.

I had family. Someone who understood the horrors of my past and shared its burden. So much I'd sacrificed to avenge my dead family, when all along, I wasn't the only survivor, and I didn't know whether to be relieved, or livid for the hardships she'd endured. I'd had Bram and Miles; but my sister had been more alone than I ever was.

The memories she'd restored glistened, waiting to be redis-covered, but I couldn't examine them now. There were more important things I needed to know. Gradually, we pulled apart. "You were the object you took from my mind."

She nodded.

"Where were you?"

She sat back on her heels, forming a circle with Miles in his chair. "I disguised myself as one of the agents and pursued you into the sewers, taking the memories of the agents in turn so you could get away. Unfortunately, one of the agents, as well as Mr. Hart, were too quick for me to catch in time. I hope they didn't give you too much trouble."

I lifted my eyebrows and said dryly, "Not at all. You can slant that many people in a row?"

"When I erased memories for the Order, I always had to take great chunks of time while they completed their testing. Usually the two or three days marking the victim's stay. With the agents in the sewers, a single memory is just as effective at driving them insane."

"And where were you all these years?"

She chuckled nervously. "Here." She unwrapped a heel of bread and handed it to me. "You must be famished. Eat, and I'll tell you the story."

I complied, not realizing how hungry I was until I took the first doughy bite.

"Though my slant was never as strong as yours, the Order knew it would be useful, so on that fateful day, while the chateau burned, they unlocked my cell and took me with them. For months, I thought they were keeping us separate. It wasn't until later that they told me about you and Mother."

I looked between my friend and my twin, stuffing the last piece of bread into my mouth. "And how do you two know each other?"

Miles grimaced. "My other promise to Bram."

Something clicked. My eyes thinned to slits. "That feminine thing you kept in your pocket. Those memories you stored away."

His lips screwed to the side apologetically.

Marian continued. "Bram was my godfather too, and knew the Order must be keeping me somewhere. He entrusted the secret to Miles and enlisted him in finding me. Once he did—informing me you were alive—we made a plan for escape. Back then, though under constant surveillance, I still had many freedoms. I could walk about the streets, if an Order member accompanied me.

"I thought my slip-away was clean, but Nicholas saw. He followed me; dragged me back. Moved me underground. I didn't have any leash after that. Through the Mole, Miles contacted me in the Order, and we were able to form a new escape from there—and your rescue too."

It was a lot to digest, but my mind was already racing, plugging in all the relevant information. I frowned. "The Order... With all the bracelets, they're going to start stealing slants soon. Purging the masses." I shook my head. "As grateful as I am, Miles, you should've left me there. The last bracelet was too valuable."

"You mean this one?" Miles opened his fist, a link of sapphires resting in his palm.

I stared at it, dumbfounded. Even from a few yards away, I'd *seen* the bracelet he'd pulled from his coat and tossed to Brass, and it wasn't a cheap reconstruction. It was *exact*. I huffed, amusement pulling at my cheek. "You went to the Artifice. You sly devil." A wave of relief washed over me, and I chuckled.

Miles's lips twitched—the most he ever smiled. "Someone doesn't live with *you* for as long as I have without picking up a few tricks."

"It's about bloody time." Then a different realization dawned, and the amusement snuffed out. "What secret did you give him in exchange?"

Miles's eyes locked with mine, with meaning. But he didn't immediately answer.

Marian glanced between us. "What's wrong?"

"I'm sorry, Ash," Miles muttered, rising and placing his weight on his good leg. "I had to tell him. I had nothing else."

The hair on the back of my neck raised. "If the Artifice knows, you realize who's going to be on our trail. Bloody silt, they live in the same place." I stood, a sense of urgency crackling my nerves. My eyes scoured our surroundings for supplies. Weapons. Anything useful. "We have to keep moving."

Marian stood, blocking me. "What does the Artifice know?"

"That Ashley Gardner is actually the Marquis de Avèjean, back from the dead," a loud voice said.

We jumped in our skin and spun around.

Lark turned a corner and leaned against a stack of crates, sucking on a peppermint stick. "And consequently, the only person alive whose magic is powerful enough to open the second Variance."

A swarm of Talons emerged from the roofs, behind crates and through the windows, ambushing us in seconds. With Miles's leg, Marian's inexperience, and my still-missing magic, none of us stood a chance at getting away. Not this time.

Sauntering forward into a patch of sunlight, Lark pulled the stick out of his mouth which had been sharpened to a point, the summer sun glinting off his white hair and nearly blinding me. A shiny white snake. He stopped in front of our little circle and surveyed us, pointing the peppermint stick at each of us in turn and grinning wide enough to display his candy-red tongue. "Hello, little rooks."

Epilogue
Dorothy

Deep within the *Circle of the Worthy* chamber, in a little dank room, a lone candle burned on the wall. Wax dripped down the scarlet patterned wallpaper, some of the rivulets ancient and cracked, some fresh and flowing like blood. The flame illuminated a sketch of a cowed lion above it, drawn with charcoal or soot. On its head sat a crown, while around its neck wound a heavy chain.

Like the lion, I lowered my head, letting my brown curls hang freely down. Underneath my simple shift, my joints ached from kneeling for so long. This was part of the ritual, Nicholas had informed me; one last test to prove one's worthiness. No sound penetrated the room—nothing but the creak of my bones and the sputter of the candle and my soft, anxious breaths.

A door opened. It didn't scrape. No extra light poured in. I only knew because of the cool draft that whispered over my lap. My clammy hands clenched. It was time.

I raised my head to find five cloaked figures filing into the room. The first four carried sticks of burning incense, leaving trails of smoke that quickly fogged the shadows. It smelled like death. They lined the wall and cast their eyes upward, all but Nicholas on the end, and I got the distinct sense he was breaking protocol.

Scabs slashed his cheekbones and jaw, and lower down, a bandaged stump peeked out from the flowing sleeve of his cloak where his right hand used to be. The price of cutting it too close with a locomotive in the rail yard.

His haunted eyes stayed glued to me, as if afraid of something. Yet, he didn't ask me if I was sure. If I wanted to back out. It was too late for any of that. I was in too deep, and always would be, from this moment on.

The only way out was death.

Or standing upon the organization's ashes.

The last cloaked figure—Sullivan Brass, I realized as he turned to face me—carried the handle of an iron box, oily coal smoke filtering through the holes. A metal rod protruded out of the side.

Without any signal, the cloaked figures began murmuring in unison. "*Ek tēs ischýos anístamentha.*"

Mr. Brass walked down the line, crumbling each stick of incense until gray dust coated his fingers.

"*Kaì axíōs poreuómetha.*"

He approached my kneeling form and said, "Lift your eyes."

The chanting grew louder. "*Ek tēs ischýos anístamentha.*"

I raised my gaze to the ceiling. Up there, a larger, crimson lion loomed, its soulless black eyes staring hungrily down at the other lion. Glyphs wove through its tentacled mane. Its maw stretched wide, black ichor seeming to drip toward me...

"*Kaì axíōs poreuómetha.*"

Using his thumb, Mr. Brass slowly smeared the ash over my forehead in an *A*. For *axios*.

The last chant echoed off the walls and drowned me in its ringing: *"Ek tēs ischýos anístamentha, kaì axíōs poreuómetha."*

Silence descended. Then the room patiently waited. Nicholas's chest rose and fell more quickly.

"From strength we rise, and worthily we walk," I quietly repeated back the translation. My voice didn't sound too afraid.

I was getting better at lying.

Out of the iron box, Mr. Brass withdrew a poker, whose red-hot end formed an *A* like the ashes on my forehead. Like Nicholas's scar.

Like Ashley's—the one on a chest that would never breathe again.

All my blood pooled to my shins, my heart hammering like a stone between my ribs.

Mr. Brass made a gesture, and Nicholas solemnly approached me to pull back the fabric at my collarbone with his good hand. His gaze lightly traced my bare skin before batting away. His throat worked.

The candle guttered, then died, and though none of the other cloaked order members had moved, a chill scuttled up my spine like it had been by design. In the ensuing dark, all I saw was the burning end of the poker and the glint of Mr. Brass's smile. "Welcome to the Order of the Worthy, Miss St. James."

Then the brand seared into my collarbone, and smoke filled my nostrils as I screamed.

TO BE CONTINUED...

Acknowledgments

I wrote the bulk of this book as a newly-minted mom of four who was trying to homeschool two of them, while having recently moved. I was postpartum, exhausted, living in a messy house, and dealing with a debilitating back injury—on top of trying to take care of my neediest baby yet.

I had less time to write than I'd ever had before, and yet... this was my fastest-written book. My baby would only nap for twenty minutes, and instead of taking a much-needed break in those pockets of time, I wrote. I couldn't reread anything, or edit, or agonize over it, I *only* had time to spit words on the page.

Honestly, I'm still amazed I did it.

And honestly, because my process for drafting this book shifted so drastically, I'm still questioning if those words are any good.

But Sally seems to think so. I trust her judgement more than my own, at this point. And while we're on the subject of Sally—your texts are a highlight of my day. Your enthusiasm is infectious. Thank you for teaching me how to love my own story.

I'm so grateful to Tanya and the team at Oliver-Heber for championing this series and seeing its potential.

Thank you to my flipping amazing beta readers who made this story so much stronger with your critiques: Tiffany Thacker, Morgan Matich, Sindy Oroz Ivešić, Kay Ross,

Michelle Hutchins, Lindsay Hiller, Allison Anderson, and Jillian Christensen. You guys gave this story some legs to stand on.

Alayna and Laurie—you guys helped me brainstorm so much of this book, and you can't put a price on ideas. But I will try. It was easily worth $10,000. (I hope you accept IOU notes.)

I'm so thankful to my Heavenly Father for carrying me through the overwhelm, giving me inspiration, and granting me strength when I thought I couldn't do it all. I know I can, with Him.

And lastly, Daniel...guess what? My books are gonna be audiobooks soon. Which means you will have NO MORE EXCUSES for not reading them. You will smile. You will cringe. I am sorry. (I am also kind of not sorry.) I anticipate regretting everything. Oh well.

Also by Jessica Scarlett

Slanted London

Town of Shadows

Smoke in the Mirrors

Wycliffe Family Series

A Lily in Disguise

A Lord of Many Masks

A Lady on the Chase

About the Author

Jessica Scarlett writes amazing books and lame author bios. She hates the pressure of encapsulating everything about herself in a hundred words or less, because she's too divergent, dynamic, and different for that. And simultaneously not that interesting.

She is the author of the Wycliffe Family Series, Slanted London series, and a couple plays. When not writing, she loves composing music, laughing with her four kids, or doing life on a ranch in Utah with her cinnamon-roll husband.

9 7 9 8 9 0 0 4 3 0 8 8 1